TODAY IS NOT FOREVER

ALSO BY RUTHERFORD CASE

Time Springs Eternal Series:
   Time Springs Eternal
   Yesterday's Tomorrow

TODAY IS NOT FOREVER

❧Book 3 of the Time Springs Eternal Series❧

Rutherford Case

TAVA Mountain Publishing

TAVA Mountain Publishing
Melbourne, FL

Paperback: 978-1-953667-04-5
EPUB: 978-1-953667-05-2
First paperback edition November 2025.

Cover art by Becky Fox (innervsion@gmail.com)
Layout by TAVA Mountain Publishing

To Jeanie and Elvira, without whose encouragement I would not have finished this book.

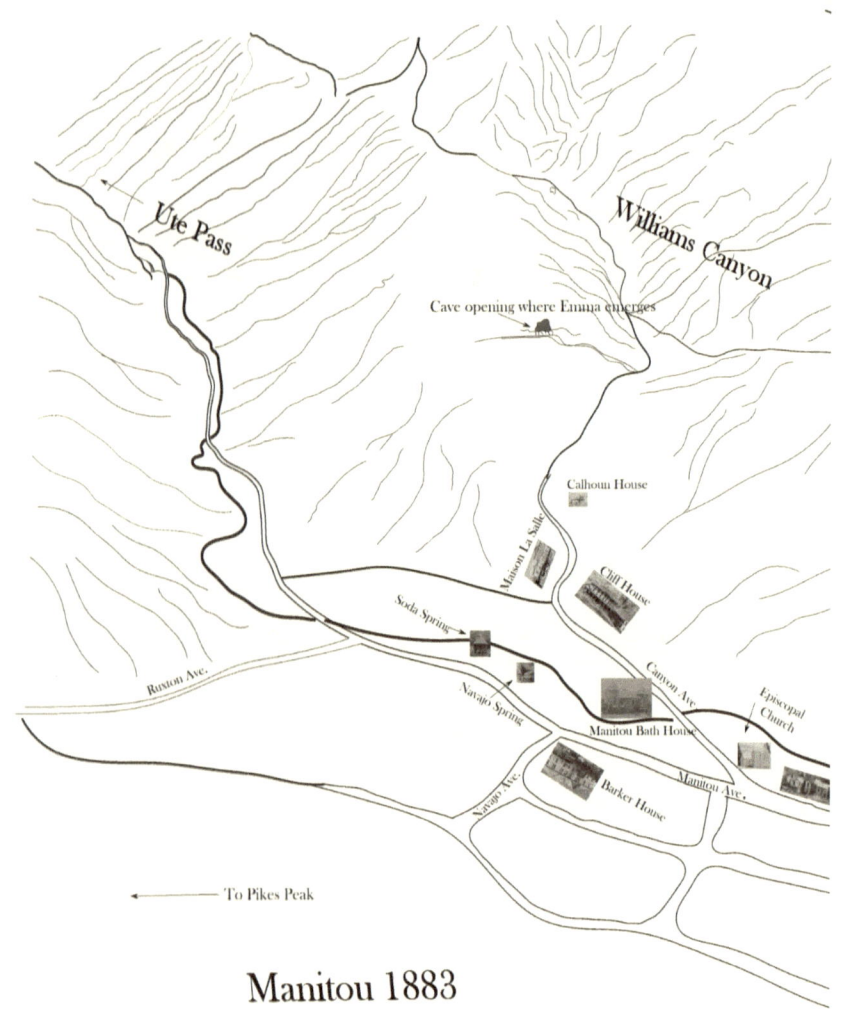

Ute Pass

Williams Canyon

Cave opening where Emma emerges

Calhoun House

Maison La Salle

Cliff House

Soda Spring

Ruxton Ave.

Navajo Spring

Canyon Ave.

Episcopal Church

Manitou Bath House

Navajo Ave.

Barker House

Manitou Ave.

← To Pikes Peak

Manitou 1883

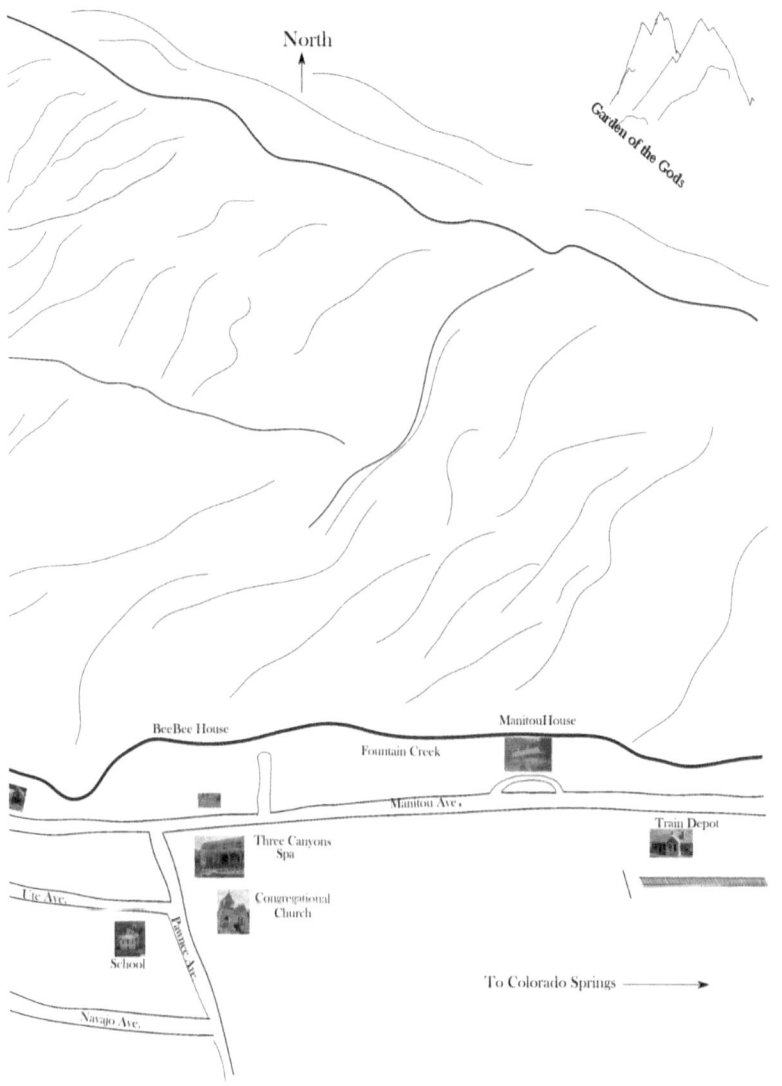

North

Garden of the Gods

BeeBee House

ManitouHouse

Fountain Creek

Manitou Ave.

Three Canyons
Spa

Train Depot

Ute Ave.

Congregational
Church

Penrose Ave.

School

To Colorado Springs ⟶

Navajo Ave.

Acknowledgments

I'm not going to lie—this book was difficult to write. And I might have given up if it weren't for the gentle, undying encouragement of my friends and family. Thank you, Dean C., Dad, Chris, Dean V., Carol, Hector, Deb, Diana, Eva, and Nancey (may she rest in peace).

I especially want to thank two people: Jeanie and Elvira. Jeanie gently prodded and encouraged me, and she read my drafts when they were, frankly, terrible. Her criticism was honest and kind at the same time. Elvira's encouragement came in a different form—firm, scolding, but under that, loving. She is the matriarch of the Rutherford side of my family, and I have the deepest affection and respect for her.

I also want to thank John Posusta for his dedication to running the *Vintage Photos of Manitou Springs* Facebook group. That group has sustained me throughout the *Time Springs Eternal* series—helping me truly feel what it was like in Manitou Springs in Emma's time. And when I felt like maybe I couldn't finish, the group gave me a 'home' to go to where I could regroup and start again.

✂ PROLOGUE ✄

The man opened the front door of the boardinghouse, but he hesitated before stepping into the hallway. The polished floors were spotless, and his feet were dusty from his walk down the town's dirt roads.

Her housekeeping standards hadn't changed.

He wiped his soles carefully on the small rug at the entrance, then stepped inside.

The house was still. The residents were likely at work or out enjoying the warm summer day. He crossed the hallway and entered the parlor, dappled with sunlight filtered through lace curtains. A piano sat against the far wall.

He paused.

She used to play for him, back when things were different —happier.

"Hello?" he called.

No answer.

He approached the piano and lifted the lid. He pressed a few quiet notes from the song she once played—his favorite. The melody sounded thinner now, but familiar.

Maybe it's time to let go, he thought. *Maybe coming here had been a mistake.*

He didn't hear the door open behind him.

He didn't hear the footsteps—soft, deliberate.

But he felt the sudden burst of pain in his back, sharp and searing. Warmth bloomed across his shirt. He gasped, staggered backward, and turned.

A shadow stood before him. He blinked, trying to focus, but the figure blurred. He couldn't make out the face. Just an outline.

Then everything went dark.

He collapsed, facedown, onto the spotless floor.

❦ CHAPTER 1 ❧

JUNE 8, 1883

"**O**uch!"

"Watch your feet," Levi grunted, hoisting the armchair higher as Emma squeezed past. "You shouldn't be lifting anything, you know. Willy would've helped."

"I'm fine," Emma said firmly. "The faster I move in, the faster they can finish the bathrooms. Besides, I'm ready to be out of that tiny room downstairs."

Emma and Levi boarded at Maison La Salle, a two-story clapboard house in Manitou, Colorado. Renovations were underway to add indoor plumbing and gas lighting—luxuries now expected, thanks to the town's rapid growth and the arrival of modern hotels. Claire, Emma's friend and the house's proprietress, had already installed a phone line just weeks earlier. She knew she had to keep up.

"That room is perfect for a bathroom. The entrance is just off the kitchen—easy access for everyone. And Claire still has her private way from her quarters," Levi said, setting the chair down and arching his back.

"Yes, and I'm glad she decided to add one on the second floor too, although you will lose your suite," Emma added.

"I'll move into Josiah's. He'll be leaving soon. It will all be worth it once the work is done."

"Things are falling into place," Emma said with a satisfied sigh as she looked around the room. "Mrs. Whitaker's furniture will fit perfectly—and she practically gave it away."

"She sure was in a hurry to get out of town. It wasn't comfortable for her here after her husband died," Levi reflected.

Emma grimaced. The circumstances of Mr. Whitaker's death had indeed been difficult, and she for one was glad that Mrs. Whitaker was gone.*

"Willy will be home soon," Levi said. "He and I will get the heavier things moved in then, all right?" Levi knew how stubborn Emma could be, but he was sure stronger arms would be needed for the heavy mahogany bed set and divan. Willy Stewart, a fellow tenant who worked at the livery, was as strong as he was kindhearted.

"That'll do for now, then. Thanks for your help, Levi." Emma gave him a quick hug and pat on the back.

She smiled as he left, then turned back to her small parlor. She glanced out the window, catching a glimpse of the mountains beyond. Manitou was beginning to feel like home.

Life had changed in every imaginable way for Emma

---

* Please read book two of the *Time Springs Eternal* series, *Yesterday's Tomorrow,* for the whole story.

Quinn. A freak earthquake in the Cave of the Winds—a tourist attraction just outside of town—had hurled her from 2019 into the year 1882. One moment she was a systems engineer in Washington, D.C., newly engaged to Paul, a man she loved dearly. The next, she was injured, alone, and stranded in the past.

She had once thought every waking moment must be spent searching for a way home. But the answers never came. Acceptance had dawned like morning light—slow, reluctant, but warming. Now she was resolved to build a life here, in this time and place. She had forged friendships—some unexpected, some profound: Alice Guiles, the doctor who had tended her injuries, had introduced her to Claire, who gave her shelter. Levi Warwick, Claire's widowed brother-in-law and the town marshal, had become a friend and occasional ally in sorting out local troubles. Then there was Ancha, a Ute man who lived alone in the cliffs above town, whose quiet wisdom touched something deep in her. And she had made an impression on Mr. Albright, who led the bathhouse build-out and general development of Manitou. Defying convention, he had taken a risk in hiring her as his assistant.

Only these people knew the truth—that Emma was from the future. And every one of them understood how dangerous that truth could be.

Emma went downstairs to the parlor, where she found Claire tidying the room around Levi, who was reading the newspaper in the armchair nearest the window.

"I'll be glad when you are all moved in, Emma," Claire said as she smoothed down her unruly hair. "You keep tracking in dirt!"

Levi laughed at his sister-in-law. "With all the work being done around here, it's going to be pretty dirty for a while. Don't worry so much about it."

Claire scowled at him. "I want the place clean for tonight, or did you forget we are celebrating Alice's grand opening this evening?"

Alice—Dr. Alice Guiles—had been in Manitou for many years. She came as one of the earliest residents to help tuberculosis patients, but the bias against female doctors outweighed her obvious competence, so she found an outlet as the proprietress of the original bathhouse in town. But as the new bathhouse project came into being, she was once again shut out. Not to be deterred, she decided to open her own boutique spa to cater to women, taking advantage of the local mineral springs and her knowledge as a physician. Claire had been one of the biggest investors in the enterprise, and she was hosting a party to celebrate the spa's opening the next day—a full week ahead of the fancy new bathhouse.

"I'll help you get ready for the party," Emma offered.

"I'll leave you ladies to it." Levi put down the paper and reached for his hat on the hat stand in the hall. "I'll see to it your furniture is all moved in before the party, Emma," he said as he left.

"What needs doing?" Emma asked Claire.

"Well, I suppose we should wait to finish cleaning. You can go to the Cliff House and see about the food I ordered while I help Molly in the kitchen. Once Levi and Willy have finished moving in your things, we can clean once and be done with it."

The Cliff House was just across Cañon Avenue from Maison La Salle. It was one of several high-end hotels in town and home to Tommy White, an excellent chef who had recently lost his brother, Carson.* Tommy had been trained at Delmonico's in New York City, and he was always creating new

---

* Carson's story is found in book one of the series *Time Springs Eternal,* of the same title.

and delicious dishes. Emma thought fondly of one night in particular when she and Levi had been invited to a dinner to sample Tommy's latest specialty. The memory made her mouth water.

She found Tommy barking orders in the kitchen, as usual. It was early in the tourist season, but already the hotel was full of guests anxious for lunch. Tommy smiled at her when she caught his eye.

"Miss Quinn! I suppose you are here about Mrs. La Salle's order?" Tommy asked, wiping his hand on a towel before offering it to Emma. Though Tommy was not particularly handsome, his sandy blond hair, congenial blue eyes, and height made him stand out in the bustle of the kitchen.

"Yes, Claire asked me to check that everything was coming together. She is so excited about the party tonight."

"Well, she spared no cost, that's for sure. She wanted a specific type of caviar and insisted on Pol Roger vintage champagne, which was hard to find, I don't mind saying. She's spending a fortune on this party."

Emma nodded but said nothing. She knew Claire was much wealthier than she seemed, though the source of her wealth could not be accounted for solely through the inheritance her parents left her and her late sister, Daphne. Emma was curious but respected Claire's privacy in the matter.

"Will you need any help bringing the food over? Is there anything else you need?" Emma asked.

"No, no. Everything is under control," Tommy said with a wave. "Tell Claire to relax and enjoy her event."

Emma paused at the front veranda of the hotel. The deep cerulean sky, so typical of Colorado, never ceased to bring her joy. The surrounding hills with shades of brown, yellow, and red were spotted with pines and oaks near town, but aspen grew on the higher mountain slopes, their silvery leaves quivering in the breeze. The sight left her no doubt of the existence of a creator and made her feel humble now—just as it had in her own time.

She took in a deep breath and looked at her brooch watch. She had time to check on the status of her own plans for the grand opening of the bathhouse, scheduled for the next Saturday. She felt her stomach tighten with the pressure of making sure the opening went perfectly. Everyone in town, including the town founders, General William Palmer and Dr. William Bell, would be there. Ultimately, her livelihood depended on keeping them happy.

She walked down Cañon Avenue until it merged with Manitou Avenue and continued east to the Manitou House, another fine hotel where she and her boss, Mr. Albright, shared a corner office on the ground floor. She had intended to take the day off to move into her new rooms and prepare for Alice's party, but the stress of the upcoming opening made it impossible to resist checking the status of the preparations.

She found Frederick Albright sitting at his desk, bent over a document he was reading with great attention.

"Good morning," she said.

Albright looked up briefly, then returned to his reading. "Morning, Emma."

She was used to his moodiness and took no offense. Over the last six months, she had come to know and respect her boss, who had taken a chance on her. Never mind that she was successful beyond his wildest dreams at promoting Manitou as a resort destination. It could have been a disaster.

When he finished reading, he said, "I thought you were taking the day off."

"I was, but I couldn't stop thinking about the opening, so I thought I'd come make a few calls to check on things." Emma sat at her desk and pulled out the portfolio where she kept her planning information.

"I'm more worried about after the opening," he said. "Not only will we have the normal steady stream of visitors coming this season, but also, because of your campaign, the Knights Templar will be adding hundreds more on their way to the Triennial Conclave in San Francisco. I hope the town and bathhouse can handle the surges." He handed her the document he had been reading.

"Looks like we will start seeing the special excursions in mid-July with a peak in August. Then some, who will stop here on the return from the Conclave, will be here in September," he summarized.

Emma was familiar with the schedule. She had developed it. Most of the Knights Templar excursions were around 150 people, but at the peak, the excursions overlapped, which meant more than 300 visitors might descend on Manitou at once, on top of the usual number of tourists. Manitou was still small and might be pushed past full capacity in August. The town must not fail to provide all visitors with a good experience. Its future depended on it—so did Emma's.

"I've been in close communication with all the hoteliers in town, and with the Antlers just opening in Colorado Springs. We will have sufficient accommodations," Emma assured Albright. "Also, I have a master schedule for all the hotels where the Templars are staying so that activities and attractions are planned such that no place is overrun." Emma pulled out her schedule mapping hotels to the various attractions in the area.

"As usual, you are several steps ahead of me. I've been so focused on the Antlers opening, I wasn't paying proper attention to how little time is left before the flood," Albright said with a half smile.

"I admit, the bathhouse is potentially an issue," Emma said. "Its proximity to the hotels here in town means people will want to just drop in. We will have to require reservations, I think. I've spoken to Major Wright about extending hours, and he agreed."

It had been Major Wright's brainchild to build the bathhouse in the first place. Emma had had only limited contact with him, though, during the construction. That had been Albright's area.

Although Albright did not offer Emma any more praise, his mood lightened.

Emma looked over the excursion schedule again. The contingent from Boston would arrive on August 11, but it was the one arriving the same day that drew her interest. The Missouri, Texas, and Louisiana contingents were traveling together to the Conclave, with a planned stop in Manitou. Among the chapters from Louisiana was the one from New Orleans.

When Emma found herself in the year 1882, Claire, Alice, and she devised a backstory to explain her sudden appearance in town. She was Claire's distant cousin who had lost her family in a fire in New Orleans, where Claire, Daphne, and Levi had lived before coming to Manitou. On her way to California to begin a new life, Emma contacted Claire, who invited her to stay with her, her only living relative. So far, this story had satisfied the curious. It helped that in the Old West, privacy was respected and people didn't pry. But having people from New Orleans in town made her uneasy.

Just then the clock on the wall chimed the hour, bringing Emma back from her thoughts.

"I just came in to make a few calls," she said as she lifted the earpiece off the cradle. "I need to get back to the boardinghouse to help Claire as soon as possible. You are coming tonight, aren't you, boss?"

"Wouldn't miss it," Albright confirmed.

❧ CHAPTER 2 ❧

"There you are! I was wondering where you'd got to," Claire said when Emma walked into the kitchen.

"Sorry, I didn't expect to be gone so long," Emma said, admiring the cake and other baked goods staged on the large oak table in the middle of the kitchen. She could smell something savory baking in the oven, and her stomach growled. She hadn't eaten since breakfast.

"Where's Molly?" Emma asked, just as the cook came in from the hallway leading to the dining room.

"I'm here doing the work of two!" the flustered woman exclaimed. "Take these candelabras, Emma, and wash them, will you?"

Emma rolled up the sleeves of her shirtwaist and took the heavy objects. She turned to the sink, where some soapy water was waiting, and smiled to herself. It had taken time for Molly to warm to her in the beginning, but now the cook treated her as though she were staff—and Emma didn't mind a bit.

"Levi and Willy finished moving your furniture into your suite," Claire said. "They had a heck of a time with the head- and footboards up those stairs! I've never heard Levi use such words."

Emma reached for a towel to dry the crystal candelabras, realizing that she had not done her share around the boardinghouse that day. It wasn't the first time she had allowed her job to interfere with her domestic responsibilities. She recalled how often Paul had carried the weight of their lives together while she worked long hours. She'd give anything to have that time with him back.

"These are ready," Emma said, picking up the candelabras and turning to Claire.

"Then, if you could go to the dining room and arrange the table, I'll start bringing out the food. Molly, when will the roast be ready?"

Molly opened the oven. "Just a few more minutes. I want it to brown a little more, and then it needs to rest awhile."

Claire looked at the clock. "People will start arriving in an hour. Where is Tommy with the rest of the food?"

"He said he had everything under control," Emma assured her. "I'm sure it will be here shortly."

"You two go get dressed. When the food arrives, I'll see to things," Molly said.

❀

The sun was just ducking behind the mountains when the guests began arriving. Despite the extravagant preparations, Claire had invited only people who had supported Alice's new enterprise, which meant the most powerful members of the community were excluded. The most influential invitee was Claire's banker, Mr. Calhoun, and his family.

"John! So glad y'all could come!" Claire said when she answered the door.

"We wouldn't miss it, Claire. Anything that gives Wright's bathhouse competition is all right in my book."

John Calhoun had led a group of locals in opposition to the building of the new bathhouse, arguing that it violated an agreement that the land it stood on was to be used as a public park and that it threatened the mineral springs upon which Manitou depended as a resort.

Calhoun stepped aside to let his wife and son, John Jr., into the hallway.

Emma greeted them when they entered the parlor. She was sympathetic to Mr. Calhoun's position on the bathhouse, even as she earned her living by promoting it. She searched Calhoun's face for an indication of his feelings toward her, wondering if he resented her role in its existence, but she saw no animosity.

By the time all the guests had arrived, the boardinghouse was overflowing with people. Some were gathered in the parlor, while others surrounded the dining room table, grazing on the excellent food laid out there. Still more lingered on the front porch or in the large hallway. Mr. Albright was the only other person there besides Emma who was affiliated with the controversial bathhouse. Nevertheless, he seemed to be enjoying himself and charming the other guests.

Emma was on her second or third glass of champagne, admiring how expertly Mr. Albright could work a room, when Josiah Turner walked up to her and offered a small dish of chocolate-covered strawberries.

"I hear these go well with champagne," he said.

Emma accepted the dish. "Thank you. I probably need to eat more. I've just been so busy helping Claire play hostess."

"Well, relax. Everyone is having a nice time and can fend for themselves."

Emma smiled and nodded in agreement. "I'm sorry you will be leaving Manitou soon. I'll miss you."

Josiah Turner had been hired by Mr. Albright to design the landscaping for the bathhouse. He had been a tenant at Claire's boardinghouse for the past several months. Now that the project was done, he had decided to move back to his hometown, Chicago.

"The opportunities here are few and far between, I'm afraid. It's been wonderful being here, but it's time to move on." Josiah's voice trailed off.

"When do you leave?" Emma asked.

"The Tuesday after the opening of the bathhouse."

Before Emma could respond, Levi joined them.

"Looks like the party's a success," he said. "I see Alice over there talking up her spa." He gestured with a lift of his chin.

Alice was uncharacteristically animated, describing all the attributes of her spa to a large group of guests. Emma smiled, seeing Alice, ever the stoic, look so happy.

"And what on earth is a Russian vapor bath, Emma? It sounds like torture to me," Levi asked, looking back at her with a little smirk.

Emma and Josiah both laughed. "You'll have to try one and find out for yourself," she replied, replacing her empty glass with a full one as a young man walked by with a tray of drinks. "It's lucky for her that her son Adam is a boilermaker. He has devised the whole system for heating the water at the spa. I understand he will be doing the same for us, and we'll have running hot water once our bathrooms are installed."

"Looks like I am leaving just as Maison La Salle is

becoming a luxurious residence!" Josiah said, amused. "If you'll excuse me, I want to make sure I say goodbye to some folks here. I may not see them again before I leave."

Josiah nodded and walked away.

"I'm really going to miss him," Emma said. "He's always made me feel at ease, and he's a nice balance to Peter." She laughed.

Peter Graham was another tenant at the boardinghouse who was, in general, disagreeable to most people.

Levi stepped closer to Emma so he could whisper. "It looks like Peter is trying to charm that young lady over there."

Emma saw the young woman cornered by Peter. He was making wild gestures with his arms and talking too loudly, while her eyes darted around, looking for an escape route. She also noticed the clean yet musky smell of Levi. She felt his breath caress her cheek. When she turned to speak, he moved away and looked at her with his dark-lashed brown eyes. She forgot her clever comeback and only muttered, "Yes, the poor woman."

"Howdy, folks!" Willy said, walking up to Emma and Levi with a plate of food.

"Willy! I want to thank you for helping me move into my suite today. I know that furniture was heavy." Emma leaned forward and gave the man a kiss on the cheek.

He beamed. "Aw, it was nothin'. Glad to hep." He looked down at his plate and frowned. "Y'all know what this here is? I took it 'cause everyone seemed to be makin' such a fuss, so I thought I'd try it."

"It's caviar, Willy. Eat it with that cracker," Emma answered, gesturing to his plate.

The good-natured man scooped up some caviar with the cracker and put the whole thing in his mouth. The sour expression he made caused Emma and Levi to burst into laughter.

"That may be the worst thang I've ever tried to eat in my life!" Willy said once he'd struggled to swallow. He took a long drink from the glass he had rested on the hallway table.

"Yes, it's an acquired taste," Levi agreed.

"Well, I ain't a gonna acquire it," Willy declared. "I'll leave it to the fancy folks and stick to steak and potatoes." He shook his head in disgust. "I need some punch to get this taste outta my mouth!" With that, he headed back to the dining room.

He walked by Mr. and Mrs. Calhoun on his way, who were huddled with Claire. John Jr., meanwhile, was weaving through the parlor, stopping to shake hands and exchange pleasantries with the more affluent guests. He left people smiling and laughing along the way. Midway to the hallway, he paused to speak to Avery Hutchinson, the owner of the livery where Willy worked. He caught Emma's eye, lifted his drink to her, and smiled.

Levi saw Emma dip her head in return and smile back. When her attention was diverted by a comment another guest made, John Jr.'s eyes lingered on her.

Emma was unsteady on her feet by the time the last of the guests had left the party. One by one, the tenants, in good spirits from the celebration, had gone to bed, leaving only Claire, Emma, and Levi. They retired to Claire's parlor.

"Well, my dear, I'd say your party was a success," Levi said, pouring a nightcap from a decanter in the corner of the room.

"Yes, it was nice to see everyone enjoying themselves— especially Alice," Claire agreed.

"I've never sheen her sho outgoing." Emma slurred. "Hey, Levi, would ya pour me one, too?"

"Maybe that's not such a good idea," Claire said, looking past Emma and shaking her head no to Levi. "You hardly ate, dear, and you've had a lot of champagne."

"Fine." Emma stood petulant but reached for the back of a chair when she began to sway. "I'll just go up to my own place. G'night."

"Levi, would you mind helping Emma up the stairs?" Claire asked. "It's been a long day, and we are all tired. I'll see you both in the morning."

"Of course," Levi said, setting down his glass. "Come on, Emma, let's go."

He reached for Emma's arm and gently guided her out of Claire's parlor. Placing a steadying hand at her waist, he helped her up the steep, narrow steps. She leaned into him for support.

When they reached her door, she turned and leaned against it. Reaching for the lapels of his jacket, she pulled him nearer. She looked into his dark brown eyes. God, they were gorgeous.

"You wanna come in and help me arrange things, since you moved me in?"

Levi gently took her wrists and drew her hands away from his jacket. He kissed each hand before releasing them.

"Some other time, dear. It's very late."

Emma pouted and turned to enter her suite. She peeked through a crack in the door, watching Levi walk down the hallway to his own suite, hoping he might change his mind and come back. She lingered until she heard his door open and softly close.

Levi went directly to his washstand and splashed water on his face. He poured a glass from the pitcher, drank it down in one go, and looked back at the door before setting the glass aside. Emma was drunk, he knew, but her invitation had been tempting. His eyes flicked once more to the door. Then, with a forceful push away from the washstand, he loosened his tie.

❧ CHAPTER 3 ❧

A loud bang woke Emma. She heard footsteps in the hallway. When she lifted her head, it throbbed violently. She set it back on the pillow with a moan and put her hand over her eyes to block out the morning sunlight. Images of the previous day flashed through her mind. It took some time to get them in order and to recall why she had such a horrible hangover. Her eyes sprang open when she remembered Levi walking her to her door. Her already queasy stomach lurched when she recalled how she had clumsily tried to seduce him.

Her mouth was dry, and she wasn't sure she could control her nausea without vomiting. She stumbled to the washstand and poured a glass of water, drinking it down quickly. Food. She needed food.

She leaned against the washstand and looked at her new

accommodations. The suite included two rooms—a sitting area and a bedroom. Through the bedroom door, she saw the parlor furniture that Levi and Willy had moved in the day before.

Fine way to christen your new rooms, she thought grimly. *A seduction attempt and a hangover.*

She was wearing only her chemise and bloomers. She had undressed but had not bothered to put on her nightgown before she fell onto her unmade bed and passed out. Feeling shaky, she put on her calico dress and ran a comb through her hair, but she did not bother to pin it up. She wanted fresh air.

Opening the door a crack, she peeked to make sure no one was in the hallway—especially Levi. Seeing no one, she ran on tiptoe to the staircase and listened for movement below. All was silent. Downstairs, she slipped into the kitchen, which led to the back door and the outhouse.

She opened the door and paused. The morning air was cool and dry. The fog in her head began clearing with each breath she took. Eventually, the wave of nausea passed.

"Good morning."

Emma turned to see Claire standing behind her. She couldn't read her expression, and the tone of her voice seemed even. Still, she felt judged.

"How are you feeling?" Claire asked.

"Fine. Why shouldn't I?"

"You drank a lot of champagne and hardly ate. I generally feel miserable when I do that."

Seeing that Claire was not passing judgment but might, in fact, be sympathetic, Emma released the tension in her shoulders.

"Oh, Claire! I am so ashamed!" Emma hid her face in her hands.

"You had too much to drink and got a little silly, but no real harm was done. Come, sit down and I'll make you some toast. The coffee in the pot is still hot." Claire gently guided Emma by the shoulders to a seat at the kitchen table and poured her a cup of coffee.

"Levi isn't here, is he?" Emma asked.

"No, I saw him briefly this morning before he went out. He said something about going to Colorado Springs."

Claire pulled the toast out of the oven and slathered it with butter. "Here, eat this. It will help," she said, offering Emma a plate with two slices.

Emma nibbled at the toast and sipped her black coffee. The two women sat silently for several moments. Emma knew Claire was waiting for her to share what was bothering her.

"I can never face Levi again," she began. "I've made a fool of myself. I threw myself at him last night, Claire! I asked him into my suite with no doubt of my intentions. Of course, he declined . . . I'm mortified." Emma hung her head.

"Levi is a grown man. He knows you have been working hard, had too little to eat and too much to drink. He'll think nothing of it."

"I hope you're right."

"Maybe there is more to your feelings than just being embarrassed that your inhibitions were lowered with drink," Claire offered tentatively.

"What do you mean?"

"Well . . . again, in my experience . . . sometimes we do things when we've had too much to drink that we've wanted to do, but our self-control prevented it."

"Well, that's not the case this time." Emma frowned and fell silent.

Claire patted Emma's hand. "If you say so." She stood to clear the dishes.

✻

Back in her suite, Emma unpacked a few personal items from the cedar chest she had bought in Colorado Springs shortly after her arrival. At the bottom were the clothes she had worn the day she was thrown back in time. On top sat a small wooden box containing Paul's engagement ring and the necklace Ancha had given her early in their friendship. She took them out, one in each hand.

Once, holding them together had triggered a strange vision—a fleeting sense that Ancha and Paul were somehow connected. Whether real or imagined, the experience had comforted her. But since deciding to accept her life in this time, she had worn them only as keepsakes. She slipped the ring onto her finger.

A hike in the foothills would help clear her head. She dressed in denim dungarees, a plaid shirt, boots, and a rimmed felt hat—the outfit she had once used to pass as a boy when visiting Ancha to avoid drawing attention. Now it was simply practical. Her necklace, she thought with a wry smile, looked better with denim anyway. She slipped it over her head and headed out.

She started on her normal route to Williams Canyon. Summer tourists had gathered at the place called The Narrows, posing for photographers, so she climbed the rocks on the steep canyon walls to avoid being seen on her way to Ancha's cave.

Ancha had stayed behind when the Ute people were relocated to a Utah reservation in 1881. Soon after Emma arrived in the past, he saved her from a bear attack, and they became close. As a medicine man, he knew things she was eager to learn—especially dreamwork. Through lucid dreams she had reached Paul, but she had also come to understand that looking back was no way forward.

When she reached the narrow opening in the rock that led

to Ancha's cave, she looked around to make sure no one could see her pass through. The small, flat area in front of the cave had a fire pit, but it was clear no fire had been there recently. Emma called out for Ancha. No answer. She whistled the special call she used when looking for him. If he didn't hear it, surely his faithful dog, Kwiyaghat, would.

She sat cross-legged near the fire pit and waited. With her eyes closed, she focused on the feeling of the soft breeze against her face and the warmth of the sun. Dry, dusty air filled her nostrils. The whoosh, whoosh of air through a bird's wings entered her awareness and grounded her.

She heard slow, steady footsteps and quicker, lighter steps approaching, and she opened her eyes. Kwiyaghat came bounding toward her, his tongue hanging loosely from his grinning mouth. She crouched on her haunches and opened her arms to welcome him.

"How are you, you sweet thing?" she greeted the animal, rubbing his sides and dodging his rapidly wagging tail. The dog barked enthusiastically in reply.

"Kwiyaghat," Ancha said firmly. The dog stopped barking and came to his master's side. A woven basket hung from Ancha's shoulder.

"What have you been gathering today?" Emma asked.

"I don't know the English words for them," he answered, setting the basket next to her.

She looked at the contents. "Looks like raspberries and dandelions."

Ancha sat beside her. "If you say so."

Ancha spoke excellent English, and could write too, thanks to the education he had received in his youth from the Mormons. But he was a man of few words. Emma knew very little about his past or how he had ended up living alone in the foothills of Pikes Peak—or Tava, as he called the great mountain. All she knew was that he had refused to leave when the rest of the Utes were relocated, and he had been left alone by the authorities—so far.

"You don't look well," he observed.

"I had too much to drink at Alice's party last night. I've felt better."

Ancha nodded but said nothing more.

Emma watched her friend gently stroke his dog—his only companion.

"How do you live like this, Ancha? Don't you get lonely?"

"Like you, I miss what I cannot have," he replied.

"But I'm trying to have a life—friends, a home. Don't you think you deserve the same?"

Ancha huffed cynically. "What I deserve and what is possible are different things."

"Well, I think this isolation is bad for you. I would miss you terribly, but I hope you will consider rejoining your family."

"At the reservation? No."

"Please think about it. I don't see how you can go on like this, all on your own. We all need someone."

Ancha merely looked down and scratched his dog behind the ears. The conversation, such as it was, was over.

He disappeared into the cave and returned with a clay jar and a small metal pot. Without a word, he built a fire in the pit, set the pot on a grate, and poured in water from the jar. Then he ducked back inside and emerged with a small tin and a single clay cup.

When the water boiled, he added a pinch of dried herbs from the tin. The scent rose gently—earthy, warm, and slightly sweet.

"What's in this?" Emma asked, accepting the cup when he handed it to her. She took a sip and added, "It tastes like licorice."

"I don't know the English name," he said. "But it helps."

He held out the tin. Emma sniffed, dipped a damp finger in the powder, and tasted it. "Definitely licorice . . . or maybe anise?"

Ancha shrugged. "It's good for your stomach. I thought you might need it."

Emma smiled at him over the rim of the cup. "I did. And thank you."

He said nothing, but she saw the corner of his mouth twitch—not quite a smile, but something close.

✳

Claire stopped dusting the occasional table in her parlor when she heard a knock at her door. She opened it to find Levi standing in the boardinghouse hallway.

She stepped aside to let him in. "I was just tidying."

Levi stepped inside and just stood.

"What's wrong?" she asked.

Levi looked at Claire but didn't answer.

"What's happened, Levi? You're scaring me."

"Oh, it's nothing that serious. I just don't know where to begin."

"Well, sit down. I'm afraid the coffee is cold, but I can warm it up on the stove if you'd like."

"No, I'm fine."

Claire sat opposite Levi and set her dusting cloth on the table. "Well, let's have it, then."

Levi sighed, apparently struggling to find his words.

Claire waited a moment, and when he remained silent, she said softly, "Is this about Emma?"

Levi relaxed and gave Claire a sheepish grin. "Did she tell

you?"

"She mentioned something to me this morning, yes. She's quite embarrassed. But I told her you would understand—that she'd just had a bit too much to drink and to think nothing of it."

"Yes, yes, that's true."

"Well, then, what's the problem?"

After another moment, Levi blurted, "Claire, you have no idea how much I wanted to accept Emma's invitation! I very nearly did," he said, rubbing his temples. "And I wanted to. God help me, I did."

He hung his head and put his hand over his eyes, shielding himself from Claire's gaze.

"It's been nearly two years since Daphne died," she began. "I know you miss her as much as I do—and in a way only a husband could—but you must live your life, Levi. It's obvious you are fond of Emma. Why not court her properly?"

"I'm not sure she's ready. She seems to be trying to accept being here, in our time, but I sense she hasn't completely given up on finding a way back—or maybe she simply still loves Paul. I don't want to add to her confusion."

"Her inhibitions may have been compromised by the champagne, but I think she needs to get on with her life as much as you do, and what she did last night shows it. Let her decide for herself what she is and isn't ready for. You worry about what's right for you. If you're interested in her, let her know." Claire patted Levi's knee and smiled.

❧ CHAPTER 4 ❧

Emma returned to the boardinghouse, mostly recovered from her hangover and grateful for Ancha. Time with him always steadied her, no matter her mood. She unlocked her door and stepped into her new home. A few strokes of luck had made it possible—her job with Mr. Albright paid well, and bonuses for the bathhouse campaign would soon start her nest egg. Then Claire decided to add indoor plumbing, and Emma's small room by the kitchen was needed for the one downstairs. A portion of Levi's suite would become the upstairs bath, making him her neighbor across the hall once Josiah moved out. The thought brought a flush of memory—her behavior the night before—and a quick surge of shame.

No time for that. I've got to get to Alice's.

She hadn't meant to stay so long with Ancha and was

running behind. She washed up, changed, and made a quick attempt at her hair. Resigned, if not satisfied, with the results, she reached for her key on the side table and opened the door —

Levi stood there, his hand raised to knock.

Her heart skipped at the surprise, then she felt a flush in her face.

"Oh! Levi. I was just heading to Alice's spa opening. I'm running late." She hoped he would accept her reason for urgency and simply let her pass.

"Well, how lucky for me. I stopped by to ask if you wanted to join me at the opening. It's only one o'clock; I don't think we're very late." He stood uncertainly, hat in hand, like a man who wasn't sure if he was coming or going.

Emma paused only a second. She would have to deal with him eventually. Better to get it over with. "All right, yes. That would be nice." She smiled stiffly and followed him down the hall.

It was a short walk to Alice's new business, the Three Canyons Spa, named for the three canyons that converged at Manitou: Engelmann Canyon, Williams Canyon, and Ute Pass. Emma had helped Alice choose the name. They agreed it reflected both the spirit of the town and the quality of the spa Alice envisioned. Emma thought it would capture customers' imaginations better than simply naming it after Dr. Guiles.

They stepped onto Cañon Avenue and turned toward Manitou. The bathhouse's power plant loomed ahead, its smokestack rising above the rooftops, but the twin towers of the main building were visible beyond it—clean, proud, and ready for the grand opening.

"It's a beautiful day," Levi offered—the safest line he could find.

"Mm-hm."

He glanced at her, hoping for more. Nothing came. They walked on in silence.

"Listen, Levi, about last night . . ."

"No, no," he cut in. "You don't need to say anything. You've been working hard, eating little, and the champagne just went to your head. Think nothing of it." He smiled, a little too quickly.

They paused to look at the bathhouse. Its freshly painted clapboard gleamed in the afternoon light—gables and scrollwork everywhere—a proud example of Victorian ambition. The garden beds out front were newly turned, with Josiah's plantings just beginning to settle in.

"It's a fine-looking place," Levi said, searching for a safer topic. "I haven't seen the inside yet. I reckon you have?"

"I have," Emma said. "It's just as gorgeous. But I won't spoil it for you. Josiah's landscaping turned out better than I had imagined."

"It's beautiful." He paused, gathering courage. "I'm looking forward to the gala next Saturday. I know it's been a big effort on your part."

"Yes," she said. "I'll be glad when it's over. The real test will be managing the influx of visitors afterward. That's where the work truly begins."

"Still," Levi said, "I hope you'll take a moment to enjoy the day. You've earned it."

He was about to ask if she'd let him accompany her when she added, "Mr. Albright and I will be fully engaged—welcoming guests, escorting the bigwigs through the facilities. It'll be nonstop."

Levi hesitated, then let the moment pass. It wasn't the right time to ask.

They continued on in companionable silence, the warmth of the afternoon sun softening the awkwardness. Familiar townsfolk tipped their hats or offered a polite nod; tourists drifted past in small groups, admiring the shops and scenery.

Outside the Mansions Hotel—known locally as the BeeBee House—a cluster of visitors was gathered for a photograph. A few sat awkwardly atop rented burros, trying to look adventurous while the photographer adjusted his equipment.

"It's a bit late in the day for Pikes Peak," Levi remarked, shading his eyes.

Emma grinned. "They're probably just posing for the picture. Who knows if they'll even try the climb. Sometimes the story's more important than the real experience."

They both chuckled, the moment easing the tension between them.

Just across Manitou Avenue, at the corner of Pawnee, stood Alice Guiles's new spa. Its location had been well chosen—nestled among the finest hotels and only a stone's throw from the train depot. Visitors coming into town would pass it before seeing anything else. Judging by the steady trickle of people through its doors, it was already making an impression.

Unlike most of the town's wooden and stone buildings, the Three Canyons Spa stood out—a three-story Spanish-style stucco structure with iron-railed balconies and flower boxes beneath the windows. Its soft adobe tones blended with the landscape. The sage and desert blooms in the front garden gave off a faint, earthy fragrance.

"I take it you've seen the inside?" Levi asked, holding one of the double doors open for her.

"No, I haven't. Alice kept the finishing touches under wraps—even Claire had to wait until last week to see it."

Inside, Claire stood in the reception room beside a long table dressed with refreshments and bouquets of summer blooms. She looked up and beamed.

"There you are! I was beginning to wonder. Here—take a

brochure and help yourselves to something to eat. Alice or one of her children will take the next tour group in just a minute."

Emma reached for the pamphlet, her gaze drifting toward a small cluster of people waiting nearby. Among them, John Calhoun Jr. caught her eye and smiled. She smiled back.

Levi ladled punch into two glasses and handed one to Emma. "Would you like a cookie?" he asked.

"No, thanks. Come, let's join the others for the next tour," Emma said.

Levi followed her gaze to the group and saw John Jr.

"If we miss this group, we can catch the next," he noted, turning back to the refreshments. "The food looks delicious. Are those stuffed mushrooms?" When he turned again, Emma was already walking toward the group. He let out a frustrated sigh and joined her.

"Good afternoon, Emma, Levi!" John Jr. said cheerfully when they approached, though his eyes were fixed only on Emma. "So happy to have you in our little group. I think either Sarah or Adam will be our guide. Dr. Guiles had the group just before ours."

"It's nice that the whole family is involved in Alice's enterprise," Emma said. "You know, Adam built the boiler that heats all the water. Her other son Leonard plumbed the place. Sarah will act as a receptionist, I understand."

As the group murmured their agreement, Adam walked up to greet them.

"Welcome, everyone. My name is Adam Guiles. I am the son of the proprietress of the Three Canyons Spa, Dr. Alice Guiles. I recognize some of you—John, Emma, Levi." He nodded to each of them. "I offer those of you from out of town my warmest welcome to Manitou and to our establishment. Come, follow me and I'll show you our facility and describe our services." He swept his hand forward to usher the group ahead of him.

John Jr. took Emma by the elbow. She glanced back at Levi just as John Jr. bent down and whispered, "I didn't know Adam could be so refined."

"He does clean up well," Emma replied with a soft laugh—teasing, but not unkind.

John Jr. guided Emma inside, leaving Levi to follow behind.

Adam took the guests upstairs to the guest rooms before proceeding to the therapeutic areas at the back of the ground floor. These featured a Russian vapor bath, which Emma thought looked like nothing more than a wooden steam sauna; an electric bath; and a treatment room that resembled a massage parlor. A recovery lounge in a glassed sunroom led to a back garden.

"I had no idea this place was so luxurious," Levi marveled, looking up at the glass dome of the sunroom.

"Yes, thanks to your sister-in-law," John Jr. said.

"Why, this place must have cost well over ten thousand!" one of the out-of-town guests exclaimed.

John Jr. smiled but did not directly respond to the estimate. Emma knew he would not go into the details of Claire's investment in the spa. He had once mentioned to Emma that she was the bank's biggest depositor, but beyond that, he would not share. Claire herself never spoke of money directly, but it never seemed to be an issue for her. She had backed Alice's venture without hesitation.

When they returned to the reception area, Alice was standing next to Claire, collecting brochures in preparation for the next group. She smiled broadly when she saw Emma, Levi, and John Jr.

"Well? What do you think of the place?" she asked.

"It's simply beautiful, Alice," Emma said, reaching for

Alice's hand to give it a squeeze.

"And you were so right to emphasize catering to women, Emma," Alice said, squeezing back. "Why, my appointment book is filled for all services for the next ten days! Let the big bathhouse chase after the men. I'm happy to serve the rest."

Emma had tried to persuade Major Wright to reconsider the bathhouse's schedule, arguing that too many hours were reserved for men. But he wouldn't budge. Frustrated by the imbalance and her limited influence, she took comfort in having tried. In the end, she advised Alice to focus her services on women, where the real opportunity lay.

Levi, Emma, and John Jr. said goodbye to Claire and left together. On the street, John Jr. stopped Emma.

"Emma, I was wondering whether you had an escort to the grand opening of the bathhouse. If not, I'd be pleased to escort you."

Emma's pause was almost undetectable. "Oh, that's kind of you. Mr. Albright and I will be busy with the guests, but if you don't mind being neglected, I'd like it very much."

John Jr. chuckled. "Happy to bask in your neglect."

He turned to Levi and extended a hand. "Levi—good seeing you."

Levi shook it with a nod. "Likewise."

John Jr. gave Emma one last smile before strolling off, visibly pleased.

⊷ CHAPTER 5 ⊷

Emma let out a long sigh as she stepped into her suite. *Alone at last.* She dropped her key on the table by the door and glanced around the room—hers now, a private sanctuary. Since the earthquake had dumped her in 1882, she'd rarely had a moment to herself. And as an only child, solitude wasn't just a preference—it was a necessity.

The furniture was heavier and darker than Emma liked, but it was functional. She eyed the secretary desk by the front wall. It would be better by the southwest window, with a view of the foothills. She began nudging it slowly, trying not to scratch the floor. *I need something to help me push this. Rags from the kitchen should work.*

When she opened her door, she found Claire's calico cat, Lulu, looking up at her. The cat released a plaintive meow.

"I suppose you want in?" Emma opened the door wider. The cat sauntered past her and jumped onto the divan.

"By all means, make yourself at home." Emma shook her head and smiled at the feline's audacity.

In the kitchen, she found Molly finishing up dinner preparations.

"Back from Dr. Guiles's opening?" Molly asked.

"Yes. It was lovely," Emma replied, accepting the stack of rags she'd requested to help move the desk. "Elegant without being fussy. I think she's off to a great start."

"I pray it's a big success. Dr. Guiles is a fine woman and deserves it."

"I couldn't agree more."

Molly turned back to the stove and opened the oven door. A waft of deliciousness hit Emma's nose, and her mouth watered. She realized how little she had eaten again that day.

"Can you take this out in half an hour?" Molly asked. "I was late getting dinner started, and I really need to head home."

"Yes, of course. I'll take care of it."

When she returned to the second floor, she found Levi and Willy carrying a divan from Levi's suite down the hall. They set it in front of the stairs to the attic.

"Levi!" she called, sharper than intended. He froze.

"What?"

"What are you doing?"

"Just putting some things in the attic," he said, confused. "While renovations are happening."

Emma glanced at Willy. "Could I speak to you—privately?"

Willy stepped back obligingly. Levi shrugged at him and followed Emma to her suite.

As soon as the door shut, Emma hissed, "You know my

Grenet cell is up there, charging my phone! What if someone saw it?"

Levi exhaled and rubbed the back of his neck. "Right. I forgot."

She scowled at him. "Levi, you can't forget. If anyone finds that phone—"

"I understand," he said quietly. "I'll wait. In the meantime, can you hide your phone down here for now?"

"Yes, I will." She hesitated, then continued, "You know, there will be Templars from New Orleans coming. What if someone from there knows you or Claire and becomes curious about me? We must be careful."

He nodded and left. Emma waited until she heard the thump of the divan being returned to his suite before opening her door.

Of all the things she worried about, this—her secret—was the most dangerous. If someone discovered she was from the future, she'd be branded a charlatan at best. At worst, she'd be hunted for information she could never ethically give. *No. Thank. You.*

Once the coast was clear, she slipped into the attic and retrieved her phone. The Grenet cell charger she had built was bulky and slow, but it worked. It would have to stay in the attic. She cradled the phone in her palm. Photos. Music. Paul's voice. Her old life, compressed into pixels and memory. Dangerous in the wrong hands, yes—but to her, it was a lifeline.

❀

Levi poured himself a whiskey and drank it in a single swallow. Nothing had gone right that day. His talk with Claire had stirred a flicker of hope—maybe it *was* time to move forward, and maybe Emma could be part of that. But everything since had left him feeling like a fool.

He'd missed his chance to escort her to the bathhouse opening. Worse, she was angry with him—and rightly so. He should have remembered her phone was in the attic. She trusted him to protect her secret, and he'd let her down.

And she may have more reason to worry about the New Orleans contingent than she realized—much more.

He rubbed a hand over his face. He had to do better.

One thing was painfully clear: if Emma had decided to build a life here, he wouldn't be the only man hoping to be part of it.

❧ CHAPTER 6 ❧

JUNE 16, 1883

The day had finally come. The grand opening of the Manitou Bath House would bring hundreds of people from Colorado Springs, Denver, and Manitou itself. Emma had spent months preparing for this day. When she woke, she looked out her window and was pleased that, at least for now, the weather was cooperating.

She jumped out of bed. She had a lot to do before the event, and not much time. She went to her wardrobe and pulled out the outfit she had had made for the occasion. It was a lacy summer dress—not Emma's usual style, but so light and cool that she was willing to abandon her preference for practicality. The accompanying hat featured silk flowers of cream and pink, which set off her dark hair and deep blue eyes. Though it had cost a small fortune, Emma didn't mind. The seamstress, Miss Lillian Price, had done masterful work, and working with a local woman who could customize to Emma's exact measurements and produce such fine clothes made the cost worth it.

"My, my, my, ain't you a purty sight!" Willy said, standing from his place at the table when Emma entered for breakfast.

"Thank you, Willy! I am pleased with my new outfit, too."

Levi turned to look at Emma. While the outfit was lovely, it was the gleam of her blue eyes and the glow of her face that he was sure Willy noticed. He stood and reached out to take her hand.

"Willy is right. You are a vision of loveliness. May I escort you to your seat, Miss Quinn?" Levi said with a good-natured bow.

Emma giggled and, taking Levi's hand, said, "Why yes, Mr. Warwick, you may."

Josiah shifted aside so Levi could pass and seat her.

The whole household was at the table. Claire sat at the head near the sideboard, with Emma, Josiah, and Peter to her left, and Willy and Christine to her right. Levi took his usual place at the far end. As always, Claire asked everyone to join hands for grace. The routine was comforting.

As they were clearing the breakfast dishes, a knock came at the front door, followed by the sound of footsteps entering the hall.

"Hello?" a man's voice called.

Emma stepped into the parlor and found John Calhoun Jr. in the hallway, bowler hat in hand, dressed smartly for the occasion.

"Oh! Hello, John!"

He started slightly when he saw her. "Emma, you look

beautiful."

She beamed. "Thank you. You look dashing yourself."

"I hope I'm not too early. I thought you'd want to be at the bathhouse well before people started arriving."

"Your timing is perfect. Let me just go up and grab my reticule. I'll be right down," Emma said as she began climbing the stairs.

From the dining room, Levi had heard the brief interchange. Before he had time to take his dishes to the kitchen and return to greet John, Emma was descending the stairs.

"I brought my buggy," he heard John Jr. tell Emma. "I thought we should avoid walking on the dusty roads."

"That was thoughtful," Emma said approvingly, and the two walked out of the boardinghouse, arm in arm.

❀

There was no place to leave the buggy at the bathhouse, so John Jr. helped Emma down and went to have it kept at the livery. He returned to the bathhouse with a spring in his step. Today promised to be a good day.

Emma stepped into the octagonal reception area and spotted Mr. Albright with the principal investors, the bathhouse architect, Mr. W. F. Ellis Jr., and Miss Diffendarfer, the ladies' attendant.

"Gentlemen, Miss Diffendarfer—you all know Miss Quinn," Albright said. The group nodded in greeting.

"She is largely responsible for the success of our campaign to promote the bathhouse and Manitou," he continued. "Because of her work, many of the Knights Templar traveling to San Francisco for the conclave are stopping in Manitou along the way."

Her boss's willingness to share credit was rare—in this time or hers.

"Ah, and here comes Josiah Turner, the landscape architect," Mr. Albright said as Josiah entered.

The group chatted briefly, praising the building and landscaping before reviewing assignments.

"And you will stay here, Miss Quinn, at the reception desk. You can greet everyone and organize them in groups for the tour," Mr. Albright concluded.

She knew that would be her role, and it was fitting given her position as promoter. But she couldn't help being amused. In her own time, she had often supported industry conferences as a "booth babe." In some ways, things never changed.

"Mr. Jackson will be here to take photographs," she reminded Albright. "I'll help him with that, too."

"Hello, John," Josiah said, glancing over Emma's shoulder.

John Jr. joined them, greeting the men with ease. When Emma mentioned her assignment, he eagerly offered to help at the desk.

And this was where they were, laughing congenially at some private joke, when Levi and Claire arrived some forty-five minutes later.

After exchanging greetings, Emma said, "Claire, please go to the left—Miss Diffendarfer will show you the ladies' dressing area and baths. Levi, if you head right, Dr. Fuller will take you through the men's areas. You'll both end up at the plunge pool, where Mr. Ellis will explain the rest."

Levi and Claire stepped aside to let the next visitors approach.

"Emma did a fine job on the brochure," Claire said, admiring the engravings. When Levi didn't respond, she looked up. He was still watching Emma interact with guests.

"Levi?"

"Hm? Sorry—what did you say?"

"I said Emma did a good job."

He looked down at the rolled booklet in his hand. "Oh. Yes, I'm sure she did."

"I'll see you at the plunge pool. Try not to fall in," she said, rolling her eyes as she walked away.

Emma glanced up to see a large group entering from the newly arrived train. *It's going to be a long day,* she thought.

Just before one o'clock, she began gathering the special guests for the luncheon at the Barker House. The event had been tricky to arrange—every hotel had lobbied to host it. Emma had preferred the Cliff House, but the Barker's larger banquet hall and superior menu had won out. Its location, directly across Manitou Avenue, also made logistics easier.

She left John Jr. at the desk and started making her rounds to notify the guests.

By the time Emma had confirmed all the dignitaries were en route to the luncheon, it was nearly two o'clock. She found Joseph Jackson, the men's attendant, and asked him to watch the reception desk while she was away. He happily agreed.

"Come on, John!" she called to her escort, still behind the counter. "We're going to be late."

John Jr. grabbed his hat and followed her out.

Though the Barker House sat just across the street, the walk in the afternoon heat left Emma perspiring. She silently thanked Miss Price for the cool fabric of her dress.

Inside, a waiter seated them beside Mr. Albright at the banquet table.

"Sorry we're late," Emma said, catching her breath. "I had to make sure everyone found their way."

Mr. Albright glanced down the table. "They did. So far, so good."

Emma exhaled as a waiter placed a napkin in her lap.

"This menu is outrageous," John Jr. said, scanning the offerings. "Salmon, mutton, beef, duck, chicken, buffalo, and ham—I don't know where to begin."

Mr. Barker, the hotel's proprietor, had taken pride in assembling the lavish spread. Emma knew he'd likely taken a loss for the sake of prestige.

"Just wait until dessert," she teased.

Nearly everyone of note was present: the bathhouse investors, town councilmen, Dr. Solly, and Mrs. Dunbar. Solly had recently published a book on the town's mineral waters, featuring a prizewinning essay by Mrs. Dunbar on the other attributes of the area—an idea Emma had pitched. She gave the woman a nod and exchanged a wave with Mr. Benjamin Steele, editor of the *Colorado Springs Gazette,* seated nearby.

When the champagne glasses were filled, Mr. Albright stood to give a toast. Emma tapped the side of her glass to call for attention.

"We've worked a long time for this day," Albright began, raising his glass. "It took all of us to make the bathhouse a reality. I hope we'll continue to act as a community for our mutual benefit. May Manitou prosper!"

"Hear, hear!" came the chorus, followed by sips all around.

Midway through the main course, Major Wright, seated opposite Albright, leaned forward. "Frederick, I must say—this is more successful than even I imagined."

It had been a year ago that Major Wright had convinced Dr. Bell and General Palmer to finance a world-class bathhouse in town. Mr. Albright had overseen the project and worked with Wright to realize the vision.

"I couldn't have done it without Miss Quinn," Albright began.

"Yes, yes, every man needs a competent secretary," Wright cut in, already turning to Dr. Solly. "Tell me, Doctor, how do you determine the composition of the spring waters?"

Albright and Emma exchanged a rueful glance.

Wright's rudeness was easy enough to forgive—this day marked the fruition of his idea. Still, Emma found him hard to read. Beyond his fixation on turning Manitou into a resort destination, she knew little. He was a Union veteran, likely connected to General Palmer from the war. And war connections were a strong bond. Lean and long-necked, he had a hawkish profile: sharp eyes, narrow lips, and a pointed goatee. Whatever else he was, she hadn't figured it out yet.

Emma would have welcomed an afternoon nap after the heavy meal, but the festivities at the bathhouse would continue until nine o'clock that night.

About an hour after their return, William Henry Jackson —the famed photographer of the West—arrived to set up the official photograph. Emma hesitated to leave John Jr. at the reception desk, but he seemed in his element, happily greeting and directing visitors.

He's pleasant company. And fun, Emma thought, smiling as she followed Mr. Jackson across the little footbridge over Fountain Creek. He wanted to capture the whole building in frame.

Once positioned, he gave Emma instructions: fill the ground-level veranda, place a few people casually in front of the building, ensure the second-floor band faced his camera, and—oddly—fill the open right tower with the best-dressed ladies.

Emma headed upstairs to fulfill Jackson's orders and found Levi and Claire in the reading room, enjoying the band on the balcony.

"Oh, Emma! Everything is spectacular!" Claire called,

waving her over.

"Have you seen everything? Did you tour the power plant?"

"That was the most interesting," Levi said. "All the power for heat and lighting generated onsite."

"I liked the plunge pool," Claire added. "Imagine—thirty-three thousand gallons!"

"I thought it would use mineral water," Levi said. "But we were told it comes from Fountain Creek."

Emma laughed, a little ruefully. "We let Mr. Calhoun think it was a compromise. Truth is, it was just easier to engineer. Spring water would've been more complicated."

She still felt uneasy about the deception. Her work often conflicted with her reverence for Manitou's natural beauty.

But there was no time for reflection. She asked Claire to gather the women for the tower shot and continued on to instruct the band.

❀

"Well, I guess that's that," Emma said when, thirteen hours after she and John Jr. had arrived, she shut the doors behind the last of the visitors. She was tired, and her feet hurt. "I can't imagine this was much fun for you, John. I appreciate you staying with me the entire time."

"I thoroughly enjoyed my day with you," he said, smiling broadly. "And I saw so many of the townspeople, which can only help my standing. A banker needs to know his customers."

"I never saw your father come through. Did he decide to stay away on principle?"

"Yes, I'm afraid so. Please don't take it personally."

"Oh, no, I understand. And honestly, I'm more than a little

sympathetic to his feelings about it."

"I'm not," John Jr. said abruptly. "I really don't understand why he is taking his position. He's a businessman, after all."

"Even a man of business might take issue with progress ruining the place he calls home," Emma pointed out.

Just then, someone knocked on the heavy front door.

"Who on earth could that be?" Emma asked as she went to answer it.

It was Willy, bringing John Jr.'s buggy from the livery. Emma was glad they wouldn't have to walk, even if it was just around the corner. The buggy carried only two people comfortably, and Emma detected relief in John Jr.'s face when Willy declined his invitation to ride back to the boardinghouse with them.

When they arrived, John Jr. helped Emma down and walked her to the door.

"Thank you, Emma, for a wonderful, memorable day. You should feel proud. The opening was a complete success."

"Thank you. And thank you for all your help today."

"I know it's late, and perhaps not the best moment to ask, but would you like to go to Garden of the Gods for a picnic next Sunday?"

Emma hesitated a moment before answering. "Sure—yes, I would like that."

"Very good! I can pick you up after church, say, eleven o'clock?"

She nodded in agreement. He bent down and gave her a kiss on the cheek, then jumped back in his buggy and continued up the hill to his house before she could reply further.

❧ CHAPTER 7 ❧

"There's no illustration?" Emma exclaimed. "I ought to speak to Mr. Steele. Did you read what it says? I quote: 'We have several times published in the *Gazette* a cut of the Manitou Bath House and therefore do not print it with the article on the opening. A new cut is being engraved, which we will publish later.'" She threw the newspaper onto Claire's side table.

"Yes, I found that rather odd," Claire agreed. "But my dear, the article is otherwise very thorough, don't you think?" She poured more coffee into Emma's cup. "And he somehow got it out in today's edition. Heavens! He had only a few hours after the opening before going to press."

Emma frowned and took a sip of her coffee.

"I suppose you're right," she admitted, though not without reluctance. "Still, I'm amazed how often people who depend on

Manitou's success miss chances to promote it."

Claire didn't think the article—a full half page—was an example of that, but she knew better than to argue the point with Emma.

"Did you enjoy your time with John Jr.?" she asked, changing the subject.

Emma brightened. "Yes, I did! More so than I expected."

"Oh?"

"Yes, I was sure he would get tired of standing around, watching me work, but he seemed to genuinely enjoy himself, and he was very pleasant company. He has a good sense of humor, you know."

"No, I didn't know."

"Well, he does. We're going to Garden of the Gods next Sunday after church."

"You are?"

"Yes." Emma looked at her brooch watch. "Speaking of church, we'd better go or we'll be late."

❋

After church, Alice stopped Emma, Claire, and Levi to invite them to the Three Canyons Spa for coffee. She and her family lived there in a small wing on the ground floor. Emma accepted, but just as Levi looked as if he, too, would accept, Claire interrupted.

"I'm sorry, Alice. I have something to see to at the boardinghouse, and Levi said he'd help me."

"Did I?" Levi asked.

"Yes, you silly goose," Claire said, tugging his arm.

"Maybe next Sunday, Alice?" She pulled a little harder.

Levi shrugged at Emma and Alice and followed his sister-in-law's pull.

"That's odd," Alice said. "Claire never turns down a post-church visit."

"She didn't mention any chores this morning," Emma added.

The two women turned to walk to Alice's place, which was practically next door to the church.

"What chore is so urgent that we couldn't have stopped at Alice's, Claire?" Levi asked when they were out of earshot.

"I wanted a word with you alone."

"All right. I'm all ears."

"Have you given any thought to the conversation we had a few days ago . . . about Emma?"

"I have, yes. I do feel it might be time to try to build a new life."

"And do you think you'd like Emma to be a part of that?"

"I am open to the possibility," Levi said casually, then paused. "I was going to ask to escort her to the bathhouse opening, but John Calhoun Jr. beat me to it."

"And that might have been a more serious tactical error than you realize." Claire's tone was tight.

"What do you mean?"

Claire stopped and turned to face him.

"She thoroughly enjoyed her time with John Jr.," she began in a singsong voice. "And they have plans to see each other next Sunday. She mentioned Garden of the Gods. She says he is 'pleasant company' and 'has a good sense of humor.' These are very appealing and relatively rare qualities in a man. If he also proves to be a good listener, you may have missed your chance."

"Well, what am I supposed to do about it, Claire? She's a grown woman."

Claire rolled her eyes. Men could be so obtuse.

"I hope you see that he would be a good catch for practical

reasons alone. He will inherit the bank from his father, no doubt. And did you see how he was at the open house? Congenial and charming—making everyone he interacted with feel important and special. Why, he may even have a future in politics! He will be a successful and influential man, I tell you."

"Ah, you know Emma doesn't care about all that." Levi waved his hand dismissively.

"I'm not so sure. She's been exposed to many influential men in the short time she's been here. She certainly doesn't shy away from it. But no matter, because it appears he has all the other attributes necessary to sweep a woman off her feet, as well."

She paused, waiting for Levi to speak. Finally, she said quietly, "I've never known you to be a coward, Levi. If you want a chance with Emma, step up."

❧ CHAPTER 8 ❧

With the bathhouse opening behind her, Emma turned her attention to coordinating with hotels and attractions to manage the coming flood of tourists. Her scheme to link guests to different activities based on their lodging was well received —once she explained it. Hotels would offer special prices and transportation to the activity featured for them on a given day, thereby avoiding too many guests attempting to do the same thing at once. The main activities were Cave of the Winds, Williams Canyon, Garden of the Gods, and burro rides to Pikes Peak. She was glad there weren't more attractions to juggle— no Cog Railway, no Cliff Dwellings, no Incline—at least not yet. She looked forward to seeing if her plan would hold under July's pressure. At least she'd have time to adjust before August's surge.

Ironically, her biggest challenge was the bathhouse itself. Major Wright—who had both conceived the project and now managed it—had very definite ideas about how it should run. Emma's prior attempts to persuade him to consider alternatives had failed. She walked into the bathhouse and took a deep breath, preparing to try once more.

"Good day, Miss Quinn," Joseph Jackson, the gentlemen's attendant, greeted her from the reception desk. She had arrived during men-only hours—but that was hard to avoid. Only two hours a day were set aside for women.

"Hello, Mr. Jackson. I'm here to see Major Wright. Is he in?"

"Yes, I believe he's in the reading room. If you'll wait, I'll let him know you're here."

Emma waited until Joseph was safely up the grand staircase before peeking at the register. The bathhouse could accommodate many more clients than were listed, and a quick glance confirmed it had been underbooked since the opening. The ladies-only hours, however, were full.

She heard Major Wright's booming voice and Joseph's quieter one approaching and quickly returned the register to its original spot.

"Miss Quinn," Wright called. "Did Albright send you? What can I do for you today?"

"No, Major Wright. I came hoping to talk to you about the master schedule. Is there somewhere we can speak? I also have some ideas for—"

"No need, Miss Quinn. I'll remain open to the public all season. I won't favor one hotel over another. Thank you for coming by. I'm quite busy, so if you'll excuse me." He dipped his head curtly and turned to go.

"What about the discounts?" she pressed. "I've run the numbers—I'm confident volume pricing would increase profits.

For example—"

"As I've said, the rates will remain unchanged. Discounting would make us look desperate. Now, if you'll excuse me." He turned and climbed the stairs.

Emma looked at Joseph, who had returned to the desk and was pointedly avoiding eye contact. Whether it was to spare her pride or dodge involvement, she couldn't tell.

Wright refused to take her seriously, dismissing her as Albright's errand girl. If Albright had brought the same suggestions, Wright would have invited him upstairs for a Havana cigar—and maybe a whiskey to go with it. He would never have left him standing in the lobby like a fool.

Her reception was better at the BeeBee House, Barker House, and Manitou Vista hotels. The proprietors' main concern was whether they had any latitude on the attraction discounts. But the goal was to manage crowds, not favor hotels, so standard rates had been set weeks earlier. To enforce it, Emma had official tickets printed with the hotel name, date, and discount clearly stated. Of course, a hotel could offer deeper discounts by cutting into its own profits—but word would get out. Manitou was a small town.

She stopped by the boardinghouse for lunch. The house was quiet. Even Molly was nowhere to be found. Emma surveyed the kitchen table for what was available as the midday meal: cold cuts from yesterday's roast, sliced cheese, bread, and pears. She briefly missed Sweetgreen, the trendy salad restaurant in Tysons Corner, Virginia, where she routinely ate lunch in her day. She sighed and fixed herself a plate.

Her mouth was full of too-dry roast beef when Peter Graham walked into the kitchen.

"Good day, Emma," Peter said, reaching for a plate from the cupboard.

Emma reached for her glass of lemonade and took a big

swallow to wash down the meat. "Hello, Peter."

"It looks like we are the only ones here—a bit unusual," he said.

"I was thinking the same thing. I wonder where Molly is."

"Mind if I join you?" Peter asked after fixing his plate.

"Not at all."

Emma did not remember ever being alone with Peter at the boardinghouse. She looked at the man, struggling to chew his roast beef. He surrendered and took a deep drink, as she had.

"A bit dry, isn't it?" she offered sympathetically.

Peter laughed a little. "A bit, yes."

He was her least favorite fellow tenant. It seemed easy for him to find an offensive thing to say in nearly all circumstances. Sitting here next to him, though, she wondered if she had rushed to judgment.

"I'm realizing I know nothing about you, Peter," she began. "I don't even know where you're from or how long you've been here."

"I'm from Virginia," he said. Emma almost blurted out *Me too,* but he went on: "That's the thing about the West—people can leave their past behind."

"Did you leave something behind?" Emma asked softly.

He looked steadily at her. "I fought in the War Between the States. I couldn't cope with its aftermath there, in Virginia. I thought it best to come somewhere without such a painful history. We do our best to move on, don't we, and hope the past doesn't catch up with us."

His words hung in the air like smoke. Emma realized she was on thin ice if Peter reciprocated her curiosity. She straightened and said more brightly, "I'm surprised you're here in the middle of the day . . ."

"I have business in Colorado Springs this afternoon."

Peter stood and walked to the sink, pumping the handle to draw water and rinse his plate and utensils. He looked over his shoulder at Emma. "Are you finished? I'll wash your dishes."

"Oh, thank you." Emma handed them to him.

When he was finished, he wiped his hands on a towel and said, "Well, I'm off. I expect I'll see you at dinner?"

"Yes. See you then."

He walked briskly out of the kitchen. It was the first exchange with him that had not left Emma angry. Yet she felt unsettled.

Emma went to her suite to freshen up. The hot, dry, windy day had left her feeling grimy. She washed her face and fixed her hair, wishing she had a clean chemise and shirtwaist. Christine Sully, her fellow tenant and laundress at the Manitou House, had taken her laundry that morning. Why people wore so many clothes regardless of heat or labor was beyond her. After fiddling with her hair for several minutes, she threw down her brush and scowled at her reflection.

One step outside told her the effort was wasted. Dirt blew down the streets with every gust from the canyons. By the time she reached the Manitou House, she looked worse than before.

She heard the voices before she opened the office door. She pushed it a crack and peeked through to make sure she was seen before entering. Mr. Albright sat at his desk, with Major Wright opposite, legs crossed and cigar casually balanced between his thumb and index finger. They paused their conversation when they heard the door and saw Emma.

"I'm not interrupting, am I?" Emma asked before entering further.

"Not at all. Come in," Albright said matter-of-factly.

Neither man stood when Emma walked in and sat at her desk. Wright's eyes swept over her unruly hair.

He looked at his pocket watch and the wall clock. "You're a liberal employer, Frederick, letting Emma come and go as it suits her." He didn't look back at Emma.

"Yes, well, I believe we are done. I will let you know if anything changes." Albright ignored the barely veiled insult and stood to shake Wright's hand.

Wright shoved his cigar between his teeth and unwrapped his long legs to stand, apparently surprised at the sudden ending to their meeting.

"Very well," he said, removing the cigar from his mouth and shaking Albright's hand. "I'm looking forward to it," he added.

He gave Emma barely a glance as he walked past her desk to leave.

"Thanks a lot!" Emma scolded her boss as soon as Wright was out of earshot.

"What do you mean?" Albright asked, genuinely clueless.

"I appreciate the way you give me credit for the work I do. Why didn't you do it just then with that jerk?"

"Jerk?" Albright's brow furrowed deeper. He truly had no idea what she was talking about.

"A scoundrel. An obnoxious, pompous, rude man."

"Oh! That's a very good word. I'll have to remember it."

A fleeting fear that *jerk* might cause some weird butterfly effect crossed her mind—but her annoyance won.

"That is not the point!" Her voice rose slightly. "He insulted and belittled me, and you said nothing."

"I rather took it as an insult to me. And as you said, he is a 'jerk.' I try not to react to what jerks say."

Emma sighed. "Be careful with that word. I don't think it's been used that way yet."

"Pity. It's a good word."

❀

Emma stopped in the hallway, arrested by a divine blend of aromas. She set her reticule on the hall table and joined the other tenants in the parlor.

A tray of hors d'oeuvres sat on the occasional table beside a large bouquet of flowers. Levi, Willy, Peter, and Josiah were at the card table, playing poker. Christine was huddled by the kerosene lamp on the end table of the sofa, crocheting. Claire was in the process of seating herself at the piano. Through the threshold to the dining room, Emma saw that the table was set with dishes and crystal she had never seen before.

"Come sing for us, Emma!" Claire ordered. She began playing 'Reuben and Rachel,' a house favorite.

This was Josiah's last night at the boardinghouse. Tomorrow he would be leaving for Chicago. It was the second time in as many weeks that Claire had arranged for the Cliff House to cater a special meal. No wonder Molly hadn't been around earlier.

Emma walked over to the piano and began singing. The tenants had told her she had a lovely voice, and she had been invited to sing at some of the hops in town. She didn't take her talent seriously, but she enjoyed the smiles on people's faces when she sang. She saw such a smile on Josiah's face as he clapped along to the melody, and her eyes began to water. She would miss him. She sang another song and then stopped to let the men continue their card game before dinner.

"It's the last time I'll be supplementing your income, Peter," Josiah said good-naturedly. "I fold, and I'm hungry." He put his cards on the table and pulled out his wallet, laughing as he handed Peter his winnings.

All the men laughed along.

"I may have to get a second job to cover the shortfall,"

Peter said, and they redoubled their chuckles.

They drifted to the table, settling into their usual seats. Claire said the same grace she always did at dinner. The only difference between this meal and countless others Emma had shared with her fellow tenants was that they were served Tommy White's gourmet food by Cliff House staff—and there was wine.

"When will the bathrooms be ready?" Josiah asked.

"The one downstairs should be done by the end of the week," Claire said. "Once Levi moves into your suite, the upstairs one can begin. That one should take another couple of weeks."

"I'll miss you, Josiah, but I am really looking forward to that bathroom!" Emma said, and they all laughed.

Claire opened the bottle of wine and went around the table, pouring some for everyone. When she returned to her seat, she raised the glass.

"I'd like to make a toast to our friend Josiah Turner. Josiah, you have made a real contribution to our little town, and I have enjoyed having you live here in my boardinghouse. We know you must move on. You have a bright future ahead of you. But we will miss you."

"Hear, hear," everyone said in unison. Emma saw Christine wipe away a little tear with her napkin.

After dinner, they resumed the party in the parlor. As the night drew to a close, Claire played 'For He's a Jolly Good Fellow,' and they all sang.

❀

The mood was somber the next morning. The tenants gathered around the wagon in front of the boardinghouse to say goodbye to Josiah. Willy sat at the reins, ready to take him to the train depot.

"Good luck to you, good man," Peter said, shaking Josiah's hand. "I'll miss our card games most, I think."

"I'm sure you will!" Josiah laughed. "You made a small fortune off me."

"Godspeed, Josiah," Levi said, slapping him on the back. "I know you'll show Chicago how it's done."

"Thank you, Levi." Josiah turned to Emma. "I'll miss you. You've brought so much life and joy to this house. Never a dull moment since you arrived."

"I'll miss you, too—very much." Emma felt tears welling. "You were kind when I first came, and I consider you a dear friend. I hope we can write. Next time I'm in Chicago, maybe we can have dinner."

"I'd like that. I'll write as soon as I arrive so you'll know where to reach me."

She threw her arms around him.

"Hate to break up this here tender moment," Willy called out, "but we've got to get to the depot. The train ain't gonna wait."

Josiah gently pulled away.

"Thank you all for your friendship," he said, sweeping the group with his gaze. "My time at this little boardinghouse will always warm my heart."

He put on his hat, climbed into the wagon, and said, "Let's go, Willy."

He didn't look back.

The others watched the wagon disappear around the bend. No one spoke as they turned and walked quietly back into the house.

❧ CHAPTER 9 ❧

Sadness washed over Emma. She had been so preoccupied the last several weeks that she had not prepared herself for Josiah's departure, and now he was gone. She pulled a handkerchief from her sleeve and dabbed at her eyes. The other tenants dispersed to their rooms, the kitchen, or, in Levi's case, out the front door. Claire stood in the parlor, staring out the window. Emma sniffed and said, "I need to make a call." She went to the hallway and lifted the receiver.

When she returned to the parlor, Claire was still staring, but now she was sitting on the sofa.

"I didn't expect to feel this sad," Claire said wistfully. "I knew from the start he would be here only a short time. A lot of people are here only a short time. Why am I so sad?" She looked at Emma, asking sincerely.

"He was a sweet man," Emma said. "I feel sad, too. But I have something that might cheer up both of us."

"Oh? What's that?"

"An afternoon at Alice's spa—my treat."

Claire brightened. Her eyes flicked upward, as if weighing whether she could break away.

"Yes! That would be fun, Emma! What time?"

"One o'clock."

"I'll be ready!" Claire stood and pressed her hands together. "Thank you."

Emma laughed at herself as she returned to her suite. She used to hold mild contempt for women who soothed themselves with manicures, pedicures, or massages—proof, she thought, of a superficial mind. Even today, she questioned her own motives. Could pampering really lift their spirits? And if so, did it cheapen their sadness? Or maybe she should just lighten up and let pleasure be a balm. Yes. That's what she'd do.

One of the best parts of her job was the freedom. Mr. Albright cared about results, not hours. She valued that even more than the pay. Today, she could take the afternoon—and she would.

With several hours before her spa date with Claire, Emma donned her hiking clothes and set out to find Ancha—time with him always lifted her spirits.

She found him by chance on her way to his cave. As usual, Kwiyaghat revealed them with his exuberant greeting before Emma actually saw Ancha.

"We are happy to see you," Ancha said. "It has been a long time."

"I know. I'm sorry." Emma patted the dog. "I've been so busy the last couple of weeks, and I'll be busy again soon. But I have a break today, and I wanted to spend some time with you.

Where are you off to?"

"To find food." His deadpan tone carried the silent question: *Where else would I be going?*

"Sounds good. I'll help you."

They walked up the canyon and through a little pass to the next canyon west. Emma knew this area as Waldo Canyon, a place she had once loved to hike but that had been devastated by wildfire in 2012. She had not been able to hike there since. Awed by the views of Pikes Peak, she paused to take them in.

"I cannot eat the view," Ancha said.

"Sorry. It just takes my breath away." She did not want to tell him how scarred the land was in her time. It still hurt her heart to think of it.

They came upon a lush, green meadow—a stark contrast to the rugged, rocky Williams Canyon. Ancha paused and surveyed the meadow, deciding where to begin.

"There." He pointed to a large clump of dandelion. "You can gather the leaves. Leave more leaves than you take. If you find a large plant, dig out the root, but do not take more than three or four."

Emma nodded her understanding. He left her and went to the edge of the meadow, where a stand of ponderosa pines stood. With no basket of her own, she shuttled dandelion leaves to Ancha's, making trip after trip across the meadow. She noticed the variety of plants expand as Ancha filled the basket with leaves, flowers, roots, and mushrooms. She had no idea so many edible plants existed, much less in one meadow. She finished harvesting the dandelion and joined Ancha.

"What are you picking?" Emma asked.

"Onions."

Emma watched for a few minutes, then looked around for more to harvest. She spotted a cluster a few yards away and went to gather some. When she returned to put it in the basket,

Ancha yelled, "No!"

Emma froze. Ancha never yelled—except that time at the bear.

"What?" she asked.

"That's poisonous," he answered more calmly.

She looked at the plant in her hand and at the plants Ancha had just put in the basket and saw no difference. "How can you tell? They look the same to me."

"Sit down. I will show you."

Emma squatted next to her friend. He took the plant from her hand and one from the basket and laid them side by side on the ground.

"This one is an onion." He pointed to the plant on the left. "I do not know the name of the other one, but it will make you very sick. First, see the color? The onion is a bluer color."

Emma saw the difference and nodded.

"Also, if you turn the leaf like this, it has a U shape and is smooth." Ancha showed her a cross section of the long, narrow leaf. "The poisonous one has a V shape and is rough, like grass." He picked up the onion and put it under Emma's nose. "The onion smells like an onion." He exchanged it for the other plant. "This one does not."

He put it back on the ground. Emma could see the differences Ancha described.

"Now, go see if you can find onions," Ancha said encouragingly.

Emma walked around the area and, when she saw a plant that resembled the onion, she inspected it more closely. It met the criteria he had taught her, so she dug it up and brought it to her teacher.

"Very good, Emma," he said, smiling. He placed it in his basket.

When the basket was filled with dandelions, onions,

mushrooms, ponderosa pine needles, and a variety of leaves that neither Ancha nor Emma knew the English names for, they started back.

"Will you come to my cave?" Ancha asked. "I am making soup."

Emma imagined a soup made with their harvest would be flavorful, but she explained that she had a spa date with Claire. They parted where they had met, and Emma continued to the boardinghouse alone.

Along the way, she thought about Ancha. She knew he spent much of his time during the late spring and summer foraging, but in the winter the days were short and the nights cold. She had worried about him frequently the past winter, but he did not seem perturbed by the harsh weather. He must hunt —his winter pemmican made that clear—but she had never seen what or how. She didn't know whether Ancha felt lonely, only that she would in his place.

❧ Chapter 10 ❧

"**T**hat was heavenly," Claire cooed. "Thank you, Emma." They were wrapped in robes and lounging in the sunroom, gazing at the garden and foothills while sipping lemonade. The heavily upholstered chaises beneath them felt like clouds.

"I was surprised you had not tried the vapor bath before," Emma said lazily.

"To be honest, it sounded unpleasant to me. I never imagined it would be so relaxing."

"I don't know what was in that massage cream, but it melted every ounce of tension from my body," Emma added.

"It's not the cream, my dear. It's the expert technique of the masseuse," Alice said good-humoredly as she pulled up an armchair and joined them.

"I'll buy that," Emma replied. "I've had my share of massages, Alice, but none better than this one. Is it something they taught in medical school?"

Alice described it as *medical gymnastics*. To Emma, it sounded like a mix of chiropractic care, physical therapy, and massage.

"You are definitely onto something special in your approach to women's medicine. Trust me," Emma said.

Alice and Claire exchanged a glance. They knew not to press Emma on why she was so certain. They would, indeed, just trust her.

"Your body was very tense, Emma," Alice said. "You must be more mindful of how much stress you are allowing in your life. Don't forget, even God needed one day of rest a week."

"That's why I decided to take today off. I will have plenty of time to relax once the season is over."

"Recuperation isn't a seasonal thing. It's like eating. Just keep it in mind," Alice pressed.

"Yes, doctor," Emma said in a slightly mocking tone.

"I'd love to spend the afternoon chatting, but I am fully booked." Alice rose and returned the chair to its original spot. "See you at church Sunday?" She looked specifically at Emma, whose attendance was sporadic.

Emma sighed. "See you Sunday."

"You know she's right," Claire said to Emma when they were alone.

Emma laughed. "Right about my stress or my church truancy?"

"Both, but I'm referring to the stress."

"I am taking something like a vacation now, before the crunch that comes in July and August. And I have the outing with John Jr. Sunday after church," Emma countered.

"It's not just how you spend your time; it's what occupies

your thoughts and how effectively you relax," Claire persisted.

"All right, all right! For heaven's sake, I didn't expect to be ganged up on by you and Alice. This was meant to be relaxing, but I'm feeling anxious now." Emma sat up and slid her bare feet into the slippers Alice had provided. "I'm getting dressed."

Claire sighed. She hadn't meant to bully Emma, but she did worry about her friend—so driven, often skipping meals or working long hours. She noticed her own anxiety rise, realizing it was triggered by Emma's speech. Emma often used expressions unfamiliar in the 1880s. *Ganged up on* was one such phrase. Claire only hoped no one else noticed—and started asking questions Emma couldn't answer.

❋

Reverend Jones's sermon that Sunday was on the importance of the Sabbath. Emma wondered if Alice had suggested it for her benefit. Just how much tension had Alice felt in her muscles to warrant so much concern?

Still mulling it over, she barely noticed Claire and Levi's compliments to the reverend as they stepped outside. She didn't register her name being called until she reached the corner.

"Emma! Emma!"

She turned and saw John Jr. running toward her. She stopped and waited.

"I'm sorry. I was lost in thought and didn't hear you at first," she said when he reached her.

"I just wanted to remind you that I'll pick you up at eleven for Garden of the Gods," he said, breathing heavily.

"Yes! I'm looking forward to it," she said.

"See you then!" He rushed off to join Mr. and Mrs.

Calhoun, waiting in their wagon.

"It's awfully hot today," Claire observed as they continued home. She glanced sideways at Levi. "I hope it won't be uncomfortable on your outing."

"Quite hot," Levi agreed, not sure what the glance meant.

"It's hot whether I'm at Garden of the Gods or sitting on our front veranda," Emma replied.

"There are cooler places on a day like this. Seven Falls, for instance. Don't you agree, Levi?"

"Yes, of course," he said, still not following.

"I'm sure the road to it is good. It should be, if they're charging ten cents to use it," Claire continued, now glaring at Levi.

Finally, Levi caught the hint.

"I'm sure it's a beautiful ride," he said brightly. "Would you like to see it, Emma?"

Seven Falls had only just opened, and Emma hadn't yet visited. She'd hiked it often in her own time, but figured she ought to see it now—if only for work.

"I would like that, yes. Maybe sometime this week?" she answered.

By the time they reached the boardinghouse, they had agreed on Wednesday.

Levi climbed the stairs with wings on his shoes. With Claire's clever help, he finally had an opportunity to start courting Emma.

❋

"That's the funniest story I believe I've ever heard!" Emma said, laughing until her sides hurt.

"You should have been there!" John Jr. said. "I don't think I've ever seen a man run so fast." He laughed boisterously.

Emma took another sip of wine and looked at Pikes Peak from the high vantage point they had chosen for their picnic. She drew a deep breath of the warm, dry air.

"John, this is so lovely. Thank you for the invitation. And please send my compliments to whomever prepared the meal. It's delicious."

"I'll pass that along to our cook."

They paused to eat the roast beef sandwiches the Calhouns' cook had packed.

John swallowed and asked, "So, how are you adjusting to life here?"

"Life here?" Emma's heart skipped a beat. Was he referring to her being back in time? How did he know?

"Yes. I imagine it's been hard after losing your family, and Manitou is much different from New Orleans."

"Oh, yes, of course," she said, relieved. "It has been difficult. I miss my family terribly, but things have been happening so quickly since I arrived—it helps keep my mind off my loss."

"It's my good fortune that Claire invited you to stay with her," John Jr. said, smiling. "How are you related again?"

"We are cousins."

John nodded. "And your family owned a bookstore in New Orleans? That's where the fire happened?"

Emma disliked the direction of the conversation. The less specific her invented history, the better, and she did not want to encourage his curiosity.

"Let's not dwell on the past. It's painful. I prefer to look forward."

"Of course. I didn't mean to pry. I'm just interested in getting to know you," he said gently.

"You've made your mark already in Manitou," he added, brightening. "Albright is telling everyone it's because of you that the Knights Templar are making our town a highlight on their way to the conclave. You've earned his respect, and that carries weight."

"I have to admit, things have gone better than I could have hoped, though I think timing had as much to do with it as anything."

"Don't underestimate yourself, Emma. Sure, it helped that so many are traveling west for the conclave, but it was your efforts and competence that made them stop here." He raised his wine glass to her.

"Thanks," she said, raising her own.

"And when you're ready, I'd love to be your banker!" he added, laughing.

The shadows cast by the rock formations grew long. John Jr. had told one funny story after another, and she was sure her sides would be sore from laughing. After a particularly hilarious tale, he sighed. "I suppose we should head back." He gestured toward the sun hovering over Pikes Peak. "It is getting late."

She glanced at the sky. "Yes, I suppose we should."

John Jr. stood and offered Emma his hand to help her up. They passed Balanced Rock on their way back and saw a group of tourists posing in front of it for a photographer.

"They should stand on the other side," Emma said. "The sun is behind them."

"You've got an eye for detail. Anyone ever tell you that?"

Emma thought a moment. "No, I can't say anyone has," she concluded.

At the boardinghouse, John Jr. helped her out of the carriage and walked her to the door.

"I hope we can do this again," he said, holding both her hands. He looked into Emma's eyes.

"I had a very nice time, John. Thank you." She thought he

was about to bend and kiss her cheek when the door flew open, nearly hitting her in the back.

"Oh!" she yelped, startled.

"Sorry, Emma," Claire said, a broom in her hands. "I didn't realize you were there."

"Yes, well, good evening, Emma. I'll see you soon, I hope." John Jr.'s disappointment showed in his voice.

"Yes, thank you again, John." Emma smiled and walked through the open door.

She thought she should be annoyed with Claire, but she couldn't quite muster the enthusiasm for it.

❧ CHAPTER 11 ❧

Emma's hopes for a quieter week quickly evaporated. Shortly after she made plans with Levi to visit Seven Falls, she realized she had left the new attraction off her hotel itineraries. It was impossible to fit all the activities into a two-day schedule—the length of most Knights Templar visits. But other tourists stayed several days, sometimes weeks. She began working on extended itineraries, wishing she had access to a good spreadsheet program. Sorting out the logistics on paper was difficult and time-consuming.

"It's well past six o'clock, Emma. Do you plan to go home tonight?" Albright asked.

"You're still here," she said, looking up from her chart.

"I live here. It's just as easy to read my newspapers and magazines here as in my suite."

"Mm-hm. Well, it's just as easy for me to develop matrices here as in my suite."

"But you'll miss dinner. Again. Would you like to join me in the restaurant? There's something I've been wanting to discuss with you anyway, and now seems a good time."

It was unnerving whenever a boss wanted "to discuss" something. Emma knew she wouldn't be able to concentrate on her work with that worry looming over her.

"Yes, all right." She stacked her papers neatly.

"Are you ready?" Albright asked as she reached for her reticule on the coat rack.

"I am."

They had finished their meal at Albright's usual table in the Manitou House restaurant and were enjoying coffee when Emma asked, "So what did you want to talk to me about?"

Albright looked down at his cup. The longer he remained quiet, the faster Emma's heart raced. What on earth did he need to tell her?

"What is it, boss?" she demanded when she could stand the silence no longer.

"You know I'm fond of you, Emma. You're like a daughter to me." He looked up at her. "I value your loyalty and discretion. I particularly value how accepting you are of my predilection. You have earned my absolute trust."

Last winter, during their trip to New York City, Emma had learned of Albright's preferences for romantic company. To prove his secret was safe with her, she had confided to him that she was from the future. Neither had mentioned it since—until now.

"Do you have a lover?" Emma whispered.

Albright laughed. "No, no. I've learned my lesson. It's not safe having one here, in such a small town. That is part of the reason I've made a decision . . . I'll be leaving Manitou and

Colorado Springs soon."

Emma's heart dropped. She had been extraordinarily lucky to have Albright as her advocate and employer. He treated her as an equal in a way no boss ever had—in any time.

"No!" she exclaimed. "Where will you go?"

"General Palmer wants me to focus on his railroad business. I haven't decided where I'll call home yet. I'll be traveling between New York, Chicago, Denver, and San Francisco, so maybe I won't have a home, per se, for a while."

Emma sat back in her chair, taking it in. She could see why Albright would want to leave the area he had helped develop, but she would miss him. Without him, she'd be exposed—to what degree, she couldn't yet say.

"I've recommended to the board that you replace me here," he continued. "The role will be a little different, with most of the development done. The emphasis will be on what you've already been doing: promotion. There will be more development, of course, but not at the same pace."

Emma was honored. "Thank you, boss. Do you think the board will accept your recommendation?"

Albright looked down at his cup again. "I'm not sure, to be honest. Major Wright is positioning for more power, and he has different ideas."

Emma thought back to the day she had walked in on his meeting with Wright. It was clear the major would be no friend to her.

"I have a lot of pull with General Palmer and, to a degree, Dr. Bell. But Wright has the fact that he's a war veteran on his side, and he's spent a great deal of energy winning over the other board members. I'm telling you this now, Emma, so you can do what you can to gain their favor—if that's what you want —before I leave."

"When are you leaving?"

"After the season is over—September, probably. But I'll be spending more of my time on my new job before then."

They fell silent. Emma was no good at politics. She had begun to appreciate how important a skill it was in her own time, and now it threatened her again.

"Thank you for telling me, boss," she said at last.

Albright nodded. He caught the waiter's eye and motioned for the bill. When it arrived, he signed it to his tab, and they left without saying anything further.

❀

Emma wasn't in the mood for an outing the morning she and Levi set out for Seven Falls. Since her conversation with Albright, she had been preoccupied, trying to sort out what she should do to secure her future. She grappled with her aversion to lobbying for position and her desire to continue doing her job, which she felt she had done well so far.

"Emma?"

"I'm sorry, what?" She wasn't sure how long Levi had been talking or what he had said.

"I was saying what a beautiful day it is, but it's clear something is on your mind. What is it?"

She had hardly seen Levi since her dinner with Albright, so he knew nothing of her boss's plans. When she had finished telling him, he said, "I understand why you're concerned. This town is run by just a few men, and most are not progressive."

Emma wanted reassurance that everything would work out in her favor, but she knew Levi was right.

"I'm not trying to make light of it, but maybe the best thing for now would be to enjoy today as best we can," he continued.

Emma smiled and put her hand on his knee. "You're right. Let's enjoy our outing."

The ten-mile ride to Seven Falls was slow but scenic. They followed the roads from Manitou to the base of Cheyenne Canyon, then paid the toll for the rugged, narrow road up to the falls. Emma found herself once again comparing how things appeared that day to her memories from her own time. Except for the absence of houses near the base of the canyon—which in her time were old and quaint—there was surprisingly little difference. The steep, rocky canyon had resisted development in 2019 just as it did in 1883.

Seven Falls itself was another matter. Instead of an air-conditioned visitor center, elevator, and metal stairs with guardrails, there were only rickety wooden stairs clinging to the side of the high, cascading falls. Emma preferred it this way.

"There," Levi said, pointing. "There's a good place to lay out our picnic." He pulled the carriage up to a small grassy spot beside the stream below the falls. From there, they could see the full height of the cascade and feel the occasional mist, which offered cool relief on the rapidly warming day.

They set out the food Molly had packed and began eating.

"I have hardly seen you these last few weeks, Levi. I've been so busy. What have you been up to?" Emma asked.

"What?" Levi cupped his ear. "I can't hear you over the falls."

Emma moved closer and repeated her question.

"I'm happy to say being marshal of Manitou is perhaps the least eventful occupation in Colorado," he said with a laugh. "I spend my days walking around town, visiting the shopkeepers, saloons, and hotels, just making sure all is well. It's a sociable way to make a living, but a bit dull. So far this season, I've only had to keep someone overnight in the jail four times—all for public drunkenness."

"You've been fishing a lot, haven't you?" Emma realized she really didn't know how Levi spent much of his free time.

"Oh yes. I've caught most of the fish we've eaten at the boardinghouse lately. And of course, I spend some time at the billiards hall . . . we should play again soon. We haven't played since last year."

The memory of Levi teaching her billiards—and her winning her first game—brought a smile to her face. "Are you sure you're ready to be beaten again?"

He shook his head and grinned. "You're a saucy one, my dear." The wink he gave her showed off his long lashes.

The breeze shifted, and Emma caught his musky scent. It was the same one she had noticed the night of Alice's party. Her heart thumped, and all at once, she felt hot.

He held her gaze. She thought of Paul, hoping the memory would quell the heat building in her. But the months apart were wearing down her resolve. Her sense of fidelity—misguided though it was—still held just enough weight to keep her in check. Besides, she was not about to embarrass herself with Levi again.

She pulled away and changed the subject. "I know I've been too busy lately; I've not been paying attention to much else besides work. Claire and Alice scolded me about being too stressed the other day."

Levi dropped his head briefly, then raised it again. "You bit off a lot, and you're still adjusting to being in this time. I think you're coping extraordinarily well. You're a strong, capable woman. You have responsibilities and big challenges ahead. Yes, it's stressful, but you can manage it. And you're not alone."

She hadn't realized how badly she needed to hear that until he said it. For the first time in days, she exhaled fully.

❧ CHAPTER 12 ❧

Emma was back in the office the next day, working hard to catch up after taking so much time off earlier in the week. After a productive day, she stopped by the post office on her way home, hoping for a letter from Josiah confirming his safe arrival in Chicago and telling her where to send her replies.

"Good evening, Mr. Williams," Emma said to the postmaster. "Any letters for me today?"

"Why yes, Miss Quinn—and there's one for Mrs. La Salle too, if you'd like to take it to her." He turned to the bank of cubbyholes behind him and retrieved two letters. "Here you are," he said, handing them to Emma.

She smiled and thanked the postmaster before glancing at the envelopes. Her eyes caught on the one addressed to Claire —from a Mr. Mouton in New Orleans. A jolt struck her chest.

New Orleans. She reminded herself there was no reason to panic. It was a large city; plenty of people might know Claire, even know her well, without necessarily knowing Emma. In the backstory she and Claire had established, they were distant cousins who had scarcely been acquainted in New Orleans. Even so, a faint tightening crept into her throat as she slid Claire's letter beneath her own.

The envelope addressed to her wasn't from Josiah as she'd hoped, but from Queen Palmer. Disappointment gave way to a smile as she recognized her friend's elegant handwriting. Queen Palmer, the wife of General Palmer, was living in New York City with their daughters. She and Emma had become friends when they traveled east together a few months earlier. The thin Colorado air was hard on Queen's health, so she and her children had relocated permanently to New York.

When Emma reached the boardinghouse, everyone was gathering for dinner. She slid Claire's letter under her door and carried her own upstairs, deciding to read it later. After a quick wash, she joined the others at the table.

They were well into the meal when Emma remembered. "Oh, Claire, I nearly forgot—you received a letter today. I stopped at the post office and Mr. Williams gave it to me." She paused to decide how much to say, then simply added, "I slipped it under your door."

"Thank you, Emma. Did you notice from whom?"

Emma was torn between wanting to evade the question to avoid risk and curiosity about who this Mr. Mouton was. Curiosity won.

"A Mr. Mouton, from New Orleans."

Claire froze, her fork suspended halfway to her mouth. She glanced at Levi, who appeared to have frozen as well, then murmured a meek, "Oh . . . thank you."

The reaction was lost on no one at the table. Peter Graham

shifted in his seat and looked from Levi to Claire as if hoping for an explanation, but neither provided anything more.

"I hear the hop at the BeeBee house for the fourth of July will be quite the production," Christine said to break the silence.

"And you and I are gonna show 'em how it's done!" Willy said to her, winking.

Christine smiled and lifted her shoulders girlishly.

Emma, of course, knew about the hop. She planned to attend in her official capacity to see how visitors were enjoying their time in Manitou, but she hadn't considered needing an escort.

"Levi, would you be willing to escort me to the dance?" she asked abruptly.

Levi's head jerked back, eyebrows climbing. Once again, the table fell silent, forks and knives stilled.

"W . . . w . . . well, yes, of course. I . . . I'd be delighted," he stammered once he had recovered.

After another pause, the quiet clink of silverware resumed.

❋

Emma was relieved to retreat to her suite. Dinner had been awkward enough after she mentioned Mr. Mouton. Who was he, and why had his name provoked such a reaction from Claire and Levi? And was it her imagination, or had Peter's expression shifted, too?

Then she had only made things worse with her clumsy request that Levi escort her to the hop. She knew she had put him on the spot. In truth, she had only just realized she would need an escort and had acted on impulse—embarrassing everyone in the process.

Worse still, she had revealed an alarming lack of awareness of the social conventions of the time. And that kind of mistake, if repeated, could eventually expose her.

To settle her nerves, she poured a glass of brandy and sat down to read Queen's letter.

June 18, 1883

My dear Emma,

I have received a telegram from William informing me that the grand opening of the bath house was a most notable success. Allow me to offer my heartfelt congratulations. I am certain the credit is yours, and William is of the same opinion.

I confess I miss you greatly. New York City is filled with culture and endless amusements, and the girls keep me well occupied. Yet I long for the comfort of a true friend. The social circles here are most difficult to enter. Unless one enjoys the favor of Mrs. Astor, one is scarcely regarded as of consequence. In truth, the Palmer fortune is a modest one when set beside the vast wealth of the Astors, Vanderbilts, and Morgans.

It may matter little, for soon the girls and I shall depart for England, where I hope the climate will restore my strength. I shall grieve the separation from William, but we must be content with visits. For all the allure of the city, I find my heart drawn back to the mountains and to Glen Eyrie. Life seldom unfolds in the manner we design, does it?

I hope you may contrive to visit me before we sail for England. You shall ever be welcome there as well.

Your devoted friend,
Queen

Emma drained her glass in one long swallow. The letter she had hoped would lift her spirits had done the opposite, despite Queen's generous praise for the bathhouse opening. Instead of feeling buoyed, Emma felt a heaviness settle over her. Queen's words revealed a loneliness in New York that made Emma ache for her friend, and now she was moving even farther away. The distance pressed against Emma's chest. She would wait until her thoughts were steadier before attempting a reply.

❋

"So, he's found us, after all this time," Levi said, swirling the amber liquid in his glass. "I wonder how."

Claire sat back, her sherry untouched, eyes fixed on the envelope on the table. "I don't know. . . . Oh Levi, this could be my ruin—yours too."

"Well, before you doom yourself, perhaps you should read the letter."

Her fingers tightened around the stem of her glass. "I'd rather burn it," she said through clenched teeth. She drew a long breath, then set the glass aside. "But you're right. I can't afford not to know what he wrote."

❧ CHAPTER 13 ❧

"**F**or heaven's sake, Molly, you've got flour everywhere. Can't you bake without making such a mess?"

Emma heard Claire's sharp voice as she reached the kitchen doorway. She stopped short. Molly stood by the counter, confusion and hurt on her face.

"I'm sorry," the cook said, glancing around, trying to locate the mess Claire was referring to. "I'll clean it up right away."

Emma scanned the room. It looked no different than it ever did during meal preparation. Nothing out of place. Claire swept past, holding a platter of scrambled eggs.

"And the eggs are cold," she snapped, brushing past Emma. "It's about time you came down. Grab the bacon."

Emma gave Molly a questioning look. Molly shrugged

helplessly. Neither of them had ever seen Claire like this.

At the breakfast table, the mood stayed brittle. Claire and Levi barely spoke, their thoughts clearly elsewhere. The other tenants filled the silence with talk of the day's plans, but no one could ignore the tension.

"Don't forget—room and board are due today," Claire announced abruptly as she stood to clear the table.

Emma gathered the remaining dishes and followed her into the kitchen.

"Claire, what's wrong?"

Claire glanced toward Molly, who was scrubbing pans at the sink. "Nothing. Why do you ask?" Her voice was clipped, distant.

It was clear: whatever troubled her, she wouldn't say in front of Molly.

"You just seem . . . tense," Emma said hesitantly.

"Don't be silly. I'm fine." Claire grabbed a towel and began drying dishes with brisk, unnecessary energy.

Emma gave a slight nod and returned to the dining room, hoping to catch Levi, but his seat was already empty.

Later, at the office, she found herself unable to settle. Mr. Albright was away in Denver, and there was nothing urgent on her desk. She paced the room, glancing out the window again and again. The day felt heavy with unspoken things.

I can't stand it here. I'm going to find Levi.

She grabbed her hat and reticule and left.

Manitou's tiny jail was her first stop—one cell, a narrow office. Empty.

It was early for ten pins or billiards, but she tried the hall next. She didn't find Levi, but Frank Bowman, the lanky proprietor, was behind the bar restocking shelves. His salt-and-pepper hair and bushy mustache gave him a genial look, and his wide mouth broke into a grin.

"Howdy, Miss Emma! What brings you to my establishment so early?"

"Good morning, Frank. I'm looking for Levi. Have you seen him?"

"As a matter of fact, he came in not long ago—picked up a couple bottles of beer. Had his rod with him. Said he was goin' fishin'."

"Did he say where?"

"No, but I think he likes Ruxton Creek. He says it's cleaner, being upstream of town."

Ruxton Creek began several miles up the canyon. It would be fruitless to try to find him.

Emma sighed. "Thank you. If you see him, will you let him know I'm looking for him?"

"Surely, Miss Emma."

As she stepped out of the establishment, a man walked directly into her.

"Pardon me, miss—the sun was in my eyes and I didn't see you."

They recognized each other at the same time—Major Wright.

"Oh, Miss Quinn," he said, a sneer curling his lip. "Taking advantage of your liberal employer again, I see. Though even I'm surprised to find you *here* at this hour."

Emma froze, unprepared to defend herself.

"I say—surely you haven't been drinking." His voice carried mock concern, the implication sharp as a blade.

"Of course not!" she snapped, finding her voice. "I'm looking for my cousin, Marshal Warwick." She emphasized the title, hoping Levi's authority—and her association—would put Wright in his place.

"I see. I trust you aren't in need of him in his official capacity." He tipped his hat. "Good day to you."

He stepped past her into the hall, unconcerned with his own hypocrisy.

Emma walked briskly back to the office, her frustration mounting. Claire remained on her mind, but Wright's contempt now dominated her thoughts. If he gained more power—as Albright feared—she would be an early casualty.

She considered going to Alice for advice, but didn't dare risk being spotted out of the office again. Not today. Not with Wright on the prowl.

Instead, she sat at her desk, drew a sheet of writing paper toward her, and lifted her pen.

June 29, 1883

Dear Queen,

Thank you for your letter. It brightened my day to receive it. Yet after reading it, I could not help but feel concerned for you. Frankly, my friend, you sound lonely. Are you truly well? Is there anything I can do? You should know that I miss you, too. I am fortunate to have good friends here, but just now there seems to be no one in whom I can confide.

It is heartening to know I have General Palmer's confidence as well as yours. Mr. Albright will soon leave Manitou to assume broader responsibilities for the railroad. I wish him well as he has been a true friend to me. He tells me he has recommended that I continue overseeing tourism promotion for Manitou and Colorado Springs. Yet some on the board of directors prefer Major Wright now that the bath house is completed. I have had several encounters with Major Wright, and I know he does not approve of me. I cannot tell whether it is because of his own ambitions, because I am a woman, or because he has genuine doubts about my abilities. Perhaps it does not matter, if he succeeds in persuading the board to choose him. The outcome seems to depend on the relative influence of Albright and Wright, and I confess I am anxious.

I hope you will remain in New York City for several more months before moving to England. I would dearly love to visit before you leave, though I cannot get away until late autumn. Is there any chance you might come here first?

I once believed life could be planned. I thought that if one had a plan and followed it, events would unfold accordingly. I no longer think so. We may do our best, yet life sets unexpected turns in our path. All we can do is meet them as honorably as we are able. You and General Palmer have shown me what that looks like, and you have my undying admiration.

Please write soon. Your words lift me.

Your devoted friend,
Emma

Emma spent the rest of the day on mindless work: filing, answering routine letters, and sorting Albright's inbox to prioritize the most pressing matters. Yet her thoughts kept drifting back to Claire. She could not recall ever seeing her friend so rattled.

What was troubling her?

Emma retraced the day's events, then thought back to the night before. Claire had seemed perfectly fine at dinner until Emma mentioned the letter. That was when things had shifted. Claire had gone quiet. Levi, too. They had both reacted to the news with the same wariness. Who had sent that letter from New Orleans? A French-sounding name. What was it— Mouton?

Her concern deepened when Claire was unexpectedly absent at dinner that evening. That had never happened before.

The room was subdued; no one asked about her, though everyone clearly noticed. They were taking their cues from Levi, who carried on as if nothing were amiss.

After dinner, Emma knocked softly on Claire's door.

"Emma, I am sorry, but I don't feel like company tonight," Claire said, closing the door she had only opened a crack.

Emma pushed her way through. "You may not feel like company, but I believe you need it all the same." She met Claire's eyes. "You have been there for me on every difficult day since I arrived." She paused, softening. "Let me be there for you now. Please—tell me what's wrong."

Claire released a deep breath. "Sit down." She walked to the accent table and poured them both some brandy before joining Emma on the sofa. When she remained silent, Emma asked, "Who is Mr. Mouton?"

Claire let out a dry laugh. "He was always charming when it suited him. Clever, persuasive, even generous when it served a purpose. But underneath it all, he is someone who looks out only for himself. He leaves wreckage behind, sometimes without even noticing, but always without caring."

"He doesn't sound like someone you would associate with. How do you know him?"

"He was an associate of my husband's." Claire took a long drink from her glass. "I had so hoped I had seen the last of him the day Levi ran him out of town."

Emma waited patiently. Claire had never spoken of her past before. It was clearly painful for her.

"I was fifteen when the War Between the States began. Tensions had been mounting for years, but New Orleans was different. It was the largest city in the South and the fourth-largest port in the world. Our population was a blend of French, English, free people of color, and enslaved people. Foreigners from the West Indies, Cuba, and beyond frequented the city, and some made it their home.

"It made for a unique and complex society—beautiful, colorful, and alive. Despite its seedier side, I loved it.

"By the summer of 1862, New Orleans was under Union control," Claire continued. "The port was blockaded, and most exports ended up aiding the Union cause. Southern producers starved, their slaves starving beside them.

"My husband and Phillip Mouton were partners in the export business. I will give them their due—they adapted. They smuggled cotton through Texas to Brownsville, then over the border to Matamoros, Mexico. From there, blockade runners sailed to Havana, and the cotton reached world markets."

She paused, then added bitterly, "They made a fortune. That is where my wealth came from, Emma. One could rationalize that it was necessary to smuggle Southern goods under the circumstances. But it did not end there."

She stared into her brandy. "Their profits were over three hundred percent while the producers starved. Worse still, they began selling information—to anyone who would pay. They picked up intelligence from smugglers, traders, and even soldiers on both sides, then sold it to the highest bidder. Sometimes, that meant the Union. Sometimes, it meant the Confederacy. They didn't care which."

Emma sat quietly, absorbing the weight of it.

"I was young. I knew slavery was wrong—knew it should end. But I believed, foolishly, that there were gentler ways. That the war was madness. Most Southerners did not even own slaves, but the ones who did would rather burn the world down than change.

"I married Gaston La Salle when I was nineteen, just after the war. My father had warehouses in New Orleans and had stored cotton for Gaston. That's how we met. Papa knew about the smuggling, but I doubt he knew the rest. Gaston was twenty years older than me, but I was smitten. He was kind, affectionate . . . I loved him."

Emma reached out and touched her friend's hand.

"He died believing he had protected me," Claire went on. "It was not until after he passed that Mouton told me everything. Told me where the money really came from. He seemed almost smug about it."

She looked up at Emma. "He expected something from me after that. Something I was not willing to give."

Claire stopped and took a drink. Emma absorbed all Claire had said, searching for how to respond. She reached out and put a comforting hand on Claire's arm.

"None of this is your fault, Claire. Surely you know that."

"Oh yes, I know. But it is still blood money. I believe that Gaston and Phillip's actions prolonged the war and resulted in more suffering for so many. When I learned the truth about my wealth, I vowed to God I would do only good with the money, as a form of repentance. I can't believe he has found me." Claire wrung her hands in her lap.

"What do you mean? He didn't know you were here, in Manitou?"

"Oh, Emma, it is such a sordid mess. I don't even know all the details, and I don't want to. Mouton was out of the country when the war ended. I don't know where he was or what he was doing, but he must have made a great many enemies, because he didn't return until just after Gaston died in 1873. He showed up one day and claimed that as Gaston's partner, he had a right to my inheritance. That was when he shared all the details of how Gaston became so wealthy. I went to my father, who retained one of the best lawyers in New Orleans. Gaston was not perfect, I know, but he did structure his affairs with my best interests in mind. In the end, Mouton could not touch any of my inheritance. He left New Orleans shortly after—largely because of Levi's threat to expose him. His good standing would have been destroyed if people knew all he had done.

"Mama and Papa died of yellow fever in 1875. Daphne and I had some inheritance from Papa. A few years later, Daphne became ill, and she, Levi, and I came here. I never dreamed Mouton would ever find me."

Emma had never seen Claire so distressed. "He sounds like a truly dangerous man, but what harm can he do to you now? Did he threaten you in his letter?"

"Not in so many words." Claire stood and walked into her reading room. Emma heard the squeak of a drawer open and close. Claire returned with an envelope and handed it to Emma.

Emma removed the letter and unfolded the pages.

June 14, 1883

My dear Claire,

Imagine my surprise when I learned you were living in Manitou, Colorado! It was quite by chance that I discovered it when one of my fellow Knights Templar brought a Colorado Springs and Manitou city directory to a planning meeting for our excursion there. I see Mr. Warwick is with you, too, and is the town marshal. I trust your sister is well.

I imagine you are part of high society in town, given your wealth. Do they know how you came by it? And what might the townspeople think of their marshal if they knew how willing he is to bend truth?

I arrive on the special train August 11. I look forward to seeing you and getting caught up.

Yours truly,
Phillip Mouton

Emma put the letter back in the envelope and handed it to

Claire. "Does Levi know what he wrote?"

Claire nodded. "Yes."

"What are his thoughts?"

Claire hesitated. "He tried to put a bright face on it at first. But when he read the letter, he saw it was serious. He said that Mouton always did have a talent for finding people's weak spots and exploiting them."

Emma's stomach twisted. "So he thinks it is a threat?"

Claire met her eyes. "He does. He did not say it directly, but I could tell. He said we would have to be careful—that Phillip isn't the kind of man who shows up just to reminisce."

Emma's voice dropped. "What can we do?"

Claire's composure faltered. "I don't know. We can't prove Mouton has ill intent. He hasn't done anything—yet. But Levi said he will be watching for him. He will be ready if it comes to anything."

Emma reached for her friend's hand. "Then so will we."

❧ CHAPTER 14 ❧

Claire was more herself when they left for church that Sunday morning. During the summer months, Pastor Byrne, the Catholic pastor from Colorado Springs, held Mass in Manitou every other Sunday, so Claire, being Catholic, attended Mass. Levi and Emma went as usual to the Congregational church. Emma had a complicated relationship with organized religion in her own time, but here in the past, she had grown to appreciate its role in community life. Rev. Jones's messages of kindness, tolerance, and compassion felt not only relevant but radical compared to the dogma she remembered.

"Your sermon was just what I needed today, Reverend. Thank you!" Emma said, smiling.

Rev. Jones took her hand in greeting as they left the

church. "I'm glad. Does this mean you will be joining our congregation formally?" he said—half-teasing, half-serious.

"Perhaps."

"And you, Levi? I've noticed you have been more regular in your attendance as well."

"We'll see, Reverend. There may be hope for me yet." Levi laughed and shook the reverend's hand.

Alice was waiting for them at the bottom of the church steps, a determined look on her face.

"Please join me for coffee," she said before they could greet her. "There's something I need to speak to you both about. It's important."

Whatever it was, her tone was serious. Emma and Levi glanced at each other before Levi said, "Of course, Alice."

"What in the world is wrong with Claire?" Alice said without preamble when they sat in the sunroom for coffee and cake.

Emma wasn't sure how much Alice already knew or how much Claire wanted her to know. She dipped her head and looked at her coffee cup, waiting for Levi to speak first.

"She received an unwelcome letter from someone in her past—someone who will be coming through Manitou on his way to San Francisco," Levi said, truthfully.

"Claire's always been private about her past. What little she's shared were stories about her parents and Daphne. She's barely mentioned her husband. Was it an unhappy marriage?"

"No." Levi paused and considered what else, if anything, he should say. Finally, he added, "But he did give her reason to be ashamed, and this man knows why. Beyond that, I'm not at liberty to say. If you want to know more, you'll have to ask Claire."

Alice opened her mouth to say something, but some of her guests walked into the sunroom and sat at the table beside them, so she said nothing and sipped her coffee.

Emma stirred her cup, unsure if Claire would want Alice to know more or if the time for secrets was coming to an end.

❁

"I'm sure Alice had more to say. I wish we hadn't been interrupted," Emma said to Levi as they walked home.

"I'm just as glad we were. I feel that I said more than I should have as it is." He furrowed his brows.

"I thought you handled it perfectly. She knows in general why Claire is troubled, but nothing specific."

He gave her a rueful smile. "I know it sounds unkind, especially after the sermon Rev. Jones gave us today, but I really had hoped Mouton was dead. Frankly, I'm surprised he isn't. He is trouble incarnate."

"You knew him well?"

"I knew his character well enough to stay away from him."

"Claire showed me the letter. He seemed to be threatening you as well." Emma glanced sideways at Levi, hoping to read something in his face that he might not share in words.

"Mouton can't hurt me. It's Claire I'm worried about."

Emma waited, hoping Levi might share more. When he didn't, she lifted her voice a little and said, "I want to apologize for putting you on the spot the other night at dinner, when I asked if you'd escort me to the Fourth of July dance." She tried to be casual about it. "I understand if you'd rather not."

Levi stopped and turned toward Emma. He gently put his hands on her shoulders. He looked into her eyes—those lovely blue eyes—and said, "Nothing would make me happier than to take you to that dance, or any dance for that matter. I'm only sorry I didn't ask you first." He brushed her cheek with the side of his finger, his smile gentle, almost reverent.

Emma went straight to her suite when they got home. Her body was still tingling from its response to Levi's intimate brush of her cheek, but her brain would have none of it. Levi was a trusted friend, that was all. Besides, she had enough to manage without being distracted with romance.

An image of Paul flashed in her mind, then disappeared. She went into her bedroom and knelt in front of her cedar chest. She wore the key for it on a long, fine chain around her neck. She took off the chain and unlocked the chest. On top lay an old rag, containing her cell phone. She unwrapped the phone and began playing her favorite playlist on low volume while she scrolled through her photos. The years went back to 2010 at her high school graduation. Her first smartphone had been a graduation gift from her mother, and she had gone crazy taking pictures before and after the ceremony. She smiled as she saw the selfies she had taken of herself and her friends, so excited for the future. She panned through the years and saw pictures of when she and Paul first met and fell in love. She saw her grandfather, who had later died, and her eyes began stinging. She saw the last picture of her and her friends before they went on the tour of Cave of the Winds that ended in the earthquake and her being cast back in time. "Places I Remember" by the Beatles began playing. *In my life, I've loved them all,* she sang along softly. A tear struck her hand. She wiped it on her skirt and turned off the phone.

❀

Emma admired herself in the mirror before meeting Levi in the boarding room parlor for the Fourth of July hop. She wore a simple gown of light-blue cotton, with a fitted bodice, ruffles at the shoulders, and a white chemise. She thought it successfully struck the balance between elegant and professional. More importantly, it was cool and relatively light-weight. She had no jewelry that was appropriate for the occasion, so her neckline was bare. But at least her hair was finally getting long enough to pin up without it falling out of place with the slightest provocation. Overall, she was satisfied with how she looked. Now, if she could just get over her jitters.

Since their walk home together on Sunday, Emma had not been able to forget how she had felt when Levi touched her face and smiled at her. She could not deny any longer that there was chemistry between them, but acting on it posed a lot of risk. She needed him as a friend far more than she needed him as a lover, and she had never been able to straddle the fence between the two. To further complicate matters, she had no idea how to behave in this time. She had seen other women flirt with Levi—most notably Mrs. Whittaker after her husband's untimely death—but the art of flirtation eluded Emma. It still bothered her how favorably Levi had responded to Mrs. Whittaker. *Just how far had things gone?* She pushed aside the unpleasant thought and headed downstairs.

Levi was alone when Emma entered the parlor. He was standing at the table nearest the brandy decanter, sipping his drink when she walked into the room. He smiled broadly at her.

"I hope I didn't keep you waiting too long," Emma said, glancing behind her at the clock in the hallway.

"No. Willy and Christine just left. They said they'd see us there," Levi replied.

"We aren't riding with them, then?"

"No. I've rented a little carriage for us. It's waiting outside." Levi set his glass down and folded his arms across his broad chest. "You are simply lovely tonight, my dear." He quickly raised an arm, his index pointing to the ceiling. "Ah, I have something for you." He turned behind him and picked a corsage off the table.

"Oh! It's lovely!" Emma beamed.

"Well, step closer and I'll pin it on you," he said, laughing.

She walked over and stood in front of him, trying to control her shallow breathing. He gently worked the pin through the flowers and secured it to her bodice.

"It's just a little token," Levi began. "Of my fondness for you, Emma, and in celebration of all you have accomplished since you arrived."

"There." Levi rested his hands on her shoulders. He bent forward and gave her a kiss on the cheek, barely touching her with his lips.

"It's just beautiful, Levi." She smiled up at him. "Thank you!"

The same band that had played on the balcony of the bathhouse on opening day was playing at the hop in Saratoga Hall at the BeeBee House. The opening dance had already happened, and a large crowd was on the floor, doing their best to navigate a waltz without stepping on toes, when Levi and Emma arrived.

"What a fine turnout!" Emma exclaimed. "Was it this crowded this time last year?" She asked Levi.

"I honestly can't say. I didn't attend any hops last summer."

She winced. Of course Levi hadn't come last year—he was still in mourning.

"Good evening, Emma, Levi!" They both turned to see who was speaking and saw John Calhoun Jr. standing there.

John Jr. took both of Emma's hands and looked her up and down. "My, you are beautiful . . . care to dance?"

"I, uh . . ." Emma, still not sure how social protocol worked in this case, was she supposed to wait for Levi's permission? She looked at Levi for help.

"You don't mind, do you, Levi?" John Jr. persisted with a smile.

"Not at all. Just bring her back. The next dance is mine." Levi tipped his head slightly at John Jr. and glared at his back as he led Emma to the floor.

"It's quite crowded, isn't it?" Emma murmured. She could feel John Jr.'s legs pressing against her skirts on one side, and the back of a stranger's legs on the other. There was no more than six inches between her and John Jr.'s body.

"It has its advantages, though, don't you think?" John Jr. grinned and pulled her ever so slightly closer.

They began waltzing, and as they spun awkwardly to avoid others, Emma looked for Levi. He was no longer standing where she had left him.

"I was hoping you'd be here tonight," John Jr. continued. "Claire interrupted us before I could ask to see you again, and I haven't seen you since."

Emma caught sight of Levi. He was dancing with Alice's daughter, Sarah, who was no more than sixteen. She relaxed.

"Emma?"

She looked back at John Jr. "I'm sorry. It's just so close here on the dance floor; I feel a bit distracted. I've been very busy since our outing—hardly time to think." She smiled and hoped it didn't look as wooden as it felt.

"Well, the next big event is Colorado Day, on August 1st. I think the hop that night is here again. I'd be honored to be your escort." John Jr. gave her a spin in an unexpected opening on the floor just as the song ended. They broke to applaud the band, and before Emma had a chance to respond, Levi appeared.

"My turn, my dear." He took her hand in his and placed

his other on her back, giving John Jr. a friendly nod of dismissal.

Despite the congestion of people, Levi sailed effortlessly across the floor, gliding as if on air, never bumping into anyone. She had danced with Levi several times before. In fact, he had helped teach her the dances of the day before her first hop at this very hall the previous Thanksgiving. She always had the feeling that she was an extension of his body, not knowing beforehand what his next move would be, but following it without thought. She caught herself wondering if he led as well in other ways, and she blushed.

"Are you warm, Emma? Your face is red." Levi looked at her, concerned.

"No, no, I'm fine."

"It is crowded here tonight. If this is any indication of the numbers of tourists we will have this season, it will be record-breaking, I think."

Levi's comment reminded her that one of her tasks that night was to get some sense of how the tourists were enjoying their stay in Manitou. She had lost interest in that task, however.

As the night unfolded, Emma danced with Mr. Albright, who also was surprisingly light on his feet, and Willy, who was not. A man visiting from Buffalo, New York, cut in during her third dance with Levi, and even though he was a bit of a klutz, it did give her an opportunity to find out how well he was enjoying his stay.

By the time the crowd had thinned out, Emma, who had not stopped dancing all night, was tired. She and Levi had just finished a galop when she saw John Jr. heading her way from the far side of the hall.

"I'm ready to leave, Levi." She turned away from John Jr., pretending she had not seen him.

"All right." He didn't question her abruptness or argue with her. He simply walked with her out of the hall and to the main entrance.

Levi offered to get the carriage.

"It's not far, but I'd be happy to bring it to you."

"No, I'd like the walk in the cool night air." Emma rested her hand in the crook of his bent arm.

Emma looked up at the sky. There was no moon or clouds, and the stars were out in force. She could see the Milky Way clearly.

"Oh, Levi, look at how beautiful the stars are! This is one of my favorite things about being in this time."

"What do you mean?"

Emma made it a point not to say much about the future. Levi didn't want to shut her down if she was willing to talk about it.

"We can scarcely see the stars for all the city lights. Even in remote areas, the stars are often drowned out by what we call 'light pollution.'"

"There are that many arc lights in your day?" Levi was aware that arc lighting was used in New York City and even New Orleans to light city streets.

"No, not arc lights. Forget I said anything, but can we ride to Rainbow Falls on our way home and just look at them awhile?"

Rather than taking the fork in the road to Cañon Avenue, Levi stayed on Manitou Avenue and followed it to Rainbow Falls. Because of the new moon, it was, indeed, very dark. They let the horse take her time. When they arrived, they stopped near the falls, but not so near they couldn't gaze at the sky above them.

Emma sat close to Levi and looked up.

"Never take this for granted, Levi," she said, then she

shivered and wrapped her arms around herself.

"Come here." He opened his jacket so he could wrap it around her and pulled her close with his arm to keep her against his warm body.

Emma stopped shivering. Her nostrils filled with Levi's musky scent, intoxicating her. Her eyes filled with stars. In that moment, she was truly, completely content.

❧ CHAPTER 15 ❧

The morning sun lit the office, but Emma barely noticed the golden beams filtering through the window.

"Emma?" Albright repeated, more loudly this time.

Emma was gazing out the window behind him. She started when she heard him call her name.

"I'm sorry, what did you say?"

"You've been staring off into space all morning. Are you all right?"

Emma smiled slowly. "Oh, yes, I'm very well."

"Well, if you don't mind, can we get back to work? I need to dictate some letters."

Emma opened her desk drawer and reached for her notepad. She moved to the chair on the other side of her boss's desk and opened the pad.

"I'm ready, boss."

Albright made a little scowl at her casual remark. Emma could be quite informal. He didn't mind when it was just the two of them, but he worried that if she were not more aware of it, it would be off-putting to others, particularly those who had a say in her future.

"Emma, you know I'm fond of you, but we are in a place of business. You'd do well to act accordingly."

"Hm?" Emma looked up at her boss, obviously not taking in what he'd just said.

"Oh, never mind." He sighed. "Now, for the dictation. . . ."

"I'm leaving for the board meeting now," Albright said when he was finished. "I don't know if I'll be back today, but I'll let you know how it went when I see you again."

Emma stopped scrolling paper into her typewriter and looked at her boss. Albright was the only advocate she had with the board, and time was running out to convince them to give her the position as director of tourism.

"I'm sorry I've been distracted this morning. I had a very interesting evening last night, and I'm still mulling it over."

"Whatever it is, this is not the time to lose your focus," Albright said. The message was firm, but his tone was gentle.

Emma nodded her understanding and watched him leave. He was right, of course, but she could not get her evening with Levi the night before out of her mind—or more accurately, her heart. She had never felt that way before, even with Paul, and she did not know what to make of it.

When they had returned to the boardinghouse, they walked upstairs together. It was awkward because, since Levi lived directly across the hall from her, normal parting rituals were impossible. So there they stood, searching for a way to say goodnight, when all they had to do was turn and walk into their respective suites.

"I had a wonderful evening, Emma," Levi said. He took her hands in his and looked into her eyes.

"So did I." She held his gaze, hoping for something, but not sure what.

He bent down and gave her a kiss on the cheek, but he lingered a moment, resting his cheek against hers. Then he gently kissed her forehead. She wanted to pull him closer and hold him tight. She wanted the kisses to continue. She wanted to feel the warmth of his body against hers. She wanted . . .

"Good night," he whispered and released her hands. She took a step back and looked at him again before turning and entering her suite. She wandered around her sitting room in a swoon and could not seem to wipe the smile from her face.

Who are you? she thought. *You're acting like a teenager.* But she stayed in this state while she readied for bed. Her last thought as she drifted to sleep was: . . . *except I have never felt this way before, even as a teenager* . . .

The phone rang loudly, startling Emma back to her desk in the office.

"Hello, Mr. Albright's office," she answered.

"Hello, Miss Quinn?" the urgent voice at the other end said. "This is Major Wright. May I please speak to Mr. Albright?"

"I'm sorry, Major Wright, Mr. Albright is not in the office. May I take a message?"

"Hang it all. . . . Do you know, is he on his way to the board meeting?"

Emma hesitated. She did not normally disclose information about her boss's whereabouts, but since he seemed to already know about Albright's meeting, she said, "Yes, he left only a couple of minutes ago. I believe he went by carriage."

"Thank you, Miss Quinn." She heard the click of the

receiver ending the call.

✿

That evening, back in her suite, Emma sat at her secretary's desk with her journal. She looked out the window at the last light of day, which was turning the hillsides dark shades of blue and gray. What had started as a dreamy, beautiful day had ended in nagging anxiety. At least Emma was familiar with that sensation. Journaling often helped her settle down.

July 5, 1883

I'm a mess. I hardly know where to start, so I'll just dive in. Levi took me to the Fourth of July hop last night after I put him on the spot and asked him to, right in front of everyone at dinner the other night. But he was wonderful. He gave me the sweetest corsage. He told me it was to recognize my accomplishments in promoting Manitou and planning a successful grand opening of the bathhouse, but could it have meant more? Anyway, we had a great time at the dance—he does dance wonderfully. I find it strange the way it is socially acceptable for men to cut in on a dance, though. John Jr. probably thought I was there with Levi as my cousin, and I know he thinks he's courting me, so I suppose his behavior was to be expected, but that fellow from Buffalo didn't know me at all!

It was what happened after the dance that has been on my mind today. Levi and I went stargazing, and I felt so warm and safe with him. Then, when we said goodnight, I realized I wanted him—badly. And I'm having feelings I've never had before. I don't trust them. I've been away from Paul for eight months. Maybe it's just loneliness, or biology. But it feels like it could be more.

And then there's Claire. She has been better the last few days, but that letter from Phillip Mouton really shook her. I hope nothing comes of his visit here.

My biggest fear is the future of my career. I have worked so hard the last few months, and it's starting to bear fruit. But Mr. Albright is moving on, and I may not have a job much longer if Major Wright gets his way. What will I do then? I was extraordinarily lucky to get my current position. Will I have to leave Manitou to find work? I have only just started to feel like I belong here. And to think I once imagined life was simpler in the past!

She closed her journal. It had helped to write down her thoughts. What lingered, however, was how she had felt when she and Levi parted the night before. Was it just biological, or was there something more? She had loved Paul, hadn't she? Why had she never felt with Paul what she felt last night with Levi? Perhaps there was a way to get some insight. . . .

❀

"Did you enjoy your evening with Emma?" Claire asked Levi in her parlor after dinner.

Levi grinned boyishly. "I did."

Claire waited, and when Levi said nothing more and merely sipped his coffee, she hit him playfully on the knee.

"Come on, tell me about it!"

"We danced, we went to Rainbow Falls and admired the stars, and we said goodnight."

"Are you being difficult on purpose, or does it come naturally to you? What are your feelings about her? Do you have a sense of her feelings for you? What's next?"

Levi's face became more serious. "Claire, I'm afraid I'm smitten. She is so lovely, so smart . . . so challenging. I admit, I'm terrified."

"But this is wonderful, Levi! It means you have rejoined the living. Don't be afraid."

"The more I feel for her, the more I feel I can't afford to fail."

"Think that all the way through. If you let fear determine your actions, you are guaranteed to fail. It might be risky, but the only viable option is to pursue her."

"Darn it, Claire, I know that. I didn't say I was giving up. I am just saying I'm scared."

Claire's heart swelled for her brother-in-law. He deserved happiness. He deserved a family.

"But enough about that," he continued. "You seem to have recovered from the shock of hearing from Mouton. You haven't said anything about it recently."

Claire gave a small, practiced smile. "Alice and I talked, and—as usual—she hammered some sense into my silly brain. She reminded me there's nothing I can do about the past. And really, nothing about his visit either. So, I've decided to carry on as if he doesn't exist."

Levi frowned, uncertain whether Claire's strategy of dismissal was strength, denial, or both.

"Well, I'm here. Don't forget that. We're in this together. And I am the marshal in this town, after all."

Claire's smile softened. "Thank you, Levi. You always make me feel safe."

❧ CHAPTER 16 ❧

E mma arrived at the office before sunrise. The chunk of bread and apple she had grabbed on her way out that morning lay untouched in her satchel. She told herself she came in early to get ahead of the flood of tasks looming over her: the board meeting fallout, Major Wright's mysterious and urgent call yesterday, and the logistics for the first surge of summer tourists. But that wasn't why she had fled the house in the half-light.

She couldn't face Levi.

Not yet.

She had barely slept. Her mind kept looping through the moments at Rainbow Falls—his jacket around her shoulders, the scent of him, the way his voice softened when he said her name. The way her body had leaned into his without thought.

She was no stranger to desire, but this was different. Deeper.

When Albright walked in, his expression brightened in surprise. "Well, good morning, Emma! I didn't expect to see you this early."

"I figured I'd make up for yesterday's woolgathering," she said, forcing a smile. "There's a lot to juggle this week."

Albright gave a thoughtful nod. "You're usually sharp as a tack. Everyone's entitled to an off day every now and then."

She appreciated the grace in his tone and hoped he meant it.

"I have some news for you," He began, refocusing on work. "The board has formally begun the process of deciding who they will want as the Director of Tourism. I was successful in getting agreement on the criteria for selection, which I believe will help your chances." Albright paused and walked over to the safe against the wall opposite Emma's desk. He began turning the dial to open it.

Emma wanted to express her appreciation, but he seemed preoccupied. The timing was off. Instead, she asked, "Did Major Wright find you before the meeting? He called shortly after you left. It seemed urgent."

"He did. I'm afraid he is rather upset with me. He felt there was no reason to have a formal selection process. In his mind, he is the clear choice. He wanted my support." Albright laughed under his breath. "He simply can't understand why I so strongly advocate for you, which is ironic, given what happened during the rest of the meeting."

He returned to his desk with a ledger and a small metal strongbox. Opening the ledger, he continued, "We reviewed the financial results from June that you compiled from the reports submitted by the consortium of hotels and businesses. The board was impressed with the numbers with one curious exception that I'll get to later. If I've done my math correctly—

and I'm happy to have you confirm it—you earned a bonus of $220.00."

Albright opened the strongbox and counted out the amount. "And with your weekly salary of $20.00, that's $240.00 total." He counted out the rest of the money and made a log in the ledger.

When Emma had first started her job with Albright, she negotiated an incentive plan based on how successfully she promoted Manitou. She never dreamed she would achieve results like this. Her jaw dropped when Albright set the money on her desk. She looked up at him, speechless.

He laughed again. "You should be pleased with yourself, Emma. You've done very well. Very well."

"Thank you, boss," she said, still in dismay. Then she remembered Wright. "But you mentioned something about what happened during the rest of the meeting. What did you mean?"

Albright sat back in his chair and folded his hands on his desk. "We reviewed these numbers." He gestured to the ledger. "They were satisfied that they included occupancy and capacity rates. All the hotels and tourist operations were up significantly from last year. Of course, the bathhouse and Dr. Guiles's spa were not in operation last year, so there was nothing to compare them with directly. But the bathhouse underperformed expectations given the occupancy rates of the hotels and boardinghouses. Alice's spa, on the other hand, overperformed. It was embarrassing to Wright, of course."

"Yes, I can imagine," Emma responded, frowning.

"The good news is that he realized the timing was bad to suggest they hand the job to him without further consideration. The bad news is that he's even more annoyed about having to compete with you."

Emma had seen this before, in her own time—too often.

People, often women, who worked hard and focused on results were passed over in favor of those who knew how to play the power game. She had always focused on the work itself and never mastered politics. She had admired Paul because he managed to work less hard yet receive greater rewards, simply because he knew how to "work people." Now she found herself in the same situation again, just as clueless about how to navigate it as she had been in 2019.

Albright pulled a folded piece of paper from the inside pocket of his jacket. "Here is the set of criteria I proposed and the board accepted for selecting the director of tourism." He handed it to her. "I suggest you focus on these things if you want the job, but never forget: at the end of the day, it's all about connections."

❀

Emma was once again alone in the office. Albright caught the late-morning train to spend a few days in Denver. Time was running out for Emma to secure her place.

The criteria Albright had shown her were fair and clear. If they really based their decision strictly on her performance, she would feel more confident. But she knew how things could be twisted so that another decision might be taken. She looked at the money Albright had put on her desk. How much longer would the money be coming in? With resolve, she picked up the earpiece on the phone.

"Good morning, how may I connect your call?" the operator answered.

"2377, please," Emma said.

She heard the operator establish the connection.

"Good morning, Rocky Mountain National Bank, how may I help you?" the voice on the other end asked.

"Good morning, this is Miss Emma Quinn. May I speak to John Calhoun Jr. please?"

"One moment."

"Emma? What a pleasant surprise!" John Jr.'s voice came across a moment later. "What can I do for you?"

"Hello, John. I was wondering if I could come in this afternoon and talk to you about some financial matters." Emma got straight to the point.

"Of course, of course. Please, come in anytime."

They settled on a time and said goodbye.

Emma put her money in an envelope, sealed it, folded it, and placed it in her reticule. It made her nervous to have so much cash on her person, but it would not be for long.

She caught the first train to Colorado Springs after lunch. She always sat on the left side so she could look out upon Garden of the Gods and the mesa between Manitou and Colorado Springs. No houses dotted the edge of the mesa as they did in her time. She admired the unadulterated landscape with a kind of backward nostalgia, knowing that within a hundred years the area would look much different, and arguably not in a good way. She knew the world would take its course, and while she worried about inadvertently influencing the future, she did not really believe she could significantly change it. It was better for her to do what she could to mitigate the negative impacts while benefitting as much as possible from her foresight. A small voice inside her suggested there was something wrong—something opportunistic—about this, but she tamped it down, reasoning that she should be able to capitalize on her situation. Indeed, she would be a fool not to.

With that internal argument resolved for the time being, her mind turned back to Levi and Paul. Why couldn't she be as practical about that conflict? She had wanted to go see Ancha that afternoon and discuss her experience—or lack thereof—

the night before. She had tried using her ring and necklace to induce a lucid dream of Paul, as she had in the past. Nothing had happened. She hoped Ancha could explain why, but the urgency of addressing her financial situation necessitated that she wait to visit him.

"Sit down, sit down, make yourself comfortable," John Jr. said when she entered his office.

Bank offices were much the same as in the year 2019, Emma thought. The wall of his office facing the lobby was glass, although wainscoting protected chairs from making direct contact with the glass. This was a real risk because the office was quite small. Emma squeezed into the leather chair and waited for John Jr. to take his seat on the other side of the desk.

"Now, what can I do for you?" He smiled warmly.

"Before I start, I ask that you keep everything I'm about to share confidential," Emma said.

"Absolutely, Emma, I commit fully to keep what you tell me in confidence."

Emma had seen firsthand how careful he was not to disclose anything about Claire's affairs, and she believed he would be equally discreet in her case. She nodded and began.

"I've been working for Mr. Albright and, by extension, the Colorado Springs Company. I negotiated a performance bonus tied to the revenue growth of the consortium participants of hotels and businesses. Today, I received my first bonus. I'd like to invest it."

"Invest it? In what, may I ask?"

"I was hoping you could advise me. I've heard Standard Oil might be a sound investment." She caught herself before saying *in the future.*

"Well," he said slowly, "buying Standard Oil stock would require contacting a broker in New York. We'd wire him the funds and he'd purchase the certificates. Then, he would forward the dividends when they're issued."

"What are the fees?" she asked.

He hesitated. "Are you sure this is worth the trouble? It's quite a process, especially for a modest amount."

Emma placed the envelope on the desk. "$240. To start."

John Jr.'s eyebrows rose. "That's a considerable sum." He grew more serious. "But if you buy stock certificates, your money won't be easily accessible. You'd have to hold the certificates until dividends are issued—and there's no guarantee of capital gain if you sell later."

"What are your bank's interest rates?"

"Not favorable. Negative inflation at the moment, you know. You'd be better off keeping your money here for safekeeping—or, better yet, looking for local businesses to invest in. Like your cousin Claire has."

Emma nodded, kicking herself for not thinking of that first. "That's a good suggestion. I'll speak with her."

"In the meantime, I suggest you either deposit the money in your account or rent a safety deposit box. You don't want that kind of money lying around."

Emma agreed. She had opened an account shortly after her first payday. It already had a healthy balance from several months of savings, but this would more than double it. While she was in the process of filling out a deposit slip, a question occurred to her.

"John, what financial rights do married women have?"

John Jr. looked up at her abruptly. "Why? You aren't getting married, are you?"

Emma laughed. "No, of course not. I just want to know."

"Well, in Colorado, married women can maintain and control their own money, so long as it is kept separate from their husband's. They can buy and sell property that is not jointly owned. In some ways, married women have more financial rights than men."

Emma doubted that, but she was pleased to learn married women had more rights than she thought.

"You said, 'in Colorado.' Are these rights determined by state law?"

"For the most part, yes. Colorado is one of the most progressive states where women's rights are concerned."

"I see. Thank you for the education." Emma stopped to complete the deposit slip, scratching her signature on the bottom and dating it.

"Very good," John Jr. said. "Now, if you will allow me, I'll take your money and deposit it."

She handed him the envelope. He left her in the office a few minutes before returning with a receipt.

"Here you are. $240.00 deposited in your account. You can get some or all of it any time you need to." He sat back down at his desk.

"Is there something more we need to do?" Emma asked, wondering why he wasn't concluding their meeting.

"No, but I was hoping you would allow me to escort you to the hop on Colorado Day? I tried asking you the other night, but Levi interrupted before you had a chance to answer."

Emma paused so briefly she was sure he hadn't noticed. "I'm sorry, John, but I've already said I'd go with Levi."

"Oh . . . I see . . . well, I'm sure I'll see you there, then. Please leave an opening for me on your dance card." He attempted a smile.

"Absolutely," Emma said to get past the awkwardness of the moment.

❧ CHAPTER 17 ❧

"What am I going to do?" Emma threw her arms up into the air.

"Well, it's not that bad, is it?" Claire asked, laughing.

"Yes! Didn't you hear me? I told John that I couldn't go to the Colorado Day hop with him because I'd already said I'd go with Levi . . . but Levi hasn't asked me, and after what I did at dinner the other night—asking him in front of everyone and embarrassing us all—I certainly cannot ask him again, even in private."

She didn't mention the deeper reason: the storm of feelings Levi stirred in her, or how much more vulnerable it made her feel.

Claire laughed again. "Yes, I am very clear on the situation. Relax, Emma. I am sure it will work out."

"How can you be so sure?"

Claire sighed. How could two people so sharp in other respects be so thoroughly blind about their own feelings? "Call it intuition," she said gently.

Emma scowled at Claire, but before she could say anything, Claire changed the subject. "Now, you said there were 'some things' you needed to talk to me about. What else is on your mind?"

Emma settled. "I received my first bonus today. It was sizable, and I wanted to talk to John about how best to invest it. I'm embarrassed to admit it didn't even occur to me to come to you first. That would've made far more sense. But I panicked. With Mr. Albright leaving and Major Wright waiting in the wings, I felt like I had to act quickly and get what money I have working for me."

Claire nodded, letting Emma gather herself.

"But I didn't consider how much banking and investing has changed from my time. It was only as we were talking that it became clear there were far fewer options for me now. I had to speak very carefully to avoid saying something wrong." Emma stopped and sighed.

"So, what I wanted to talk to you about is: how should I invest my money?" Emma looked expectantly at Claire.

"I see. Well, I don't know how much help I will be. My reasons for what I invest in have more to do with making amends than making a profit. But I'll tell you what I can."

"Have you made a profit, though? Even though that wasn't your objective."

"Yes, more than I could ever have hoped."

"Then whatever you are doing works, so tell me how it's done."

When Claire was done with her explanation, Emma did not feel much better. It seemed to her that providence brought

Claire opportunities to invest as if by magic. How were such opportunities to come to her?

"It seems luck had a lot to do with your success," she said.

"Perhaps, but intent did as well. I was always open and looking for worthy causes."

Emma nodded. This was consistent with things Ancha had taught her about setting intention.

❀

Emma woke at dawn's first light. She washed and dressed quietly in her suite, not wanting to wake the others by running water in the newly finished upstairs bathroom. A cool breeze filtered through her open window, and the cheerful chirps of birds lifted her spirits. She draped her necklace around her neck and slipped her ring onto her finger. It was essential to have them with her today.

In the kitchen, she tripped over Lulu while gathering a small meal: an apple, some biscuits, and leftover fried chicken from the night before. She let Lulu outside, then collected four eggs from the hens in the backyard coop, leaving the rest for the other tenants.

As soon as the light was strong enough to guide her steps, she set out toward Ancha's cave.

Kwiyaghat barked before she even reached the fire pit. At first the sound was defensive, but when he recognized her, the barks turned playful. By the time she reached the clearing, the dog was hopping with joy, his tail wagging furiously.

"Shhh, Kwiyaghat." Emma knelt to greet him. "You'll wake Ancha."

"Too late."

Emma looked up to find Ancha standing at the cave's

entrance. He looked as though he'd been awake for some time. She thought she saw the faintest smile tug at his lips.

"Good morning, Ancha. Isn't it beautiful?" She gestured toward the eastern sky, where the first light bounced off scattered clouds in vivid hues of gold, crimson, and orange.

"I brought food," she said, handing him the bundle.

"Thank you. Come." He motioned for her to follow.

She hesitated. She'd never been inside the cave before. It felt like stepping into his private world—almost like entering a bedroom. Still, declining would be rude.

Inside, it took a moment for her eyes to adjust. Beyond the sunlight filtering in from the entrance, there was no light. Gradually, shapes emerged: a neat pile of blankets and animal skins along one wall, bundles of drying herbs strung overhead, clay pots and woven baskets nestled in rock crevices. The space was small—no larger than the boardinghouse parlor—and appeared to have just one chamber.

In the center, near the back, a flat stone lay on the ground beside a smooth, rounded one. On the flat stone were crushed plant remnants.

"Sit," Ancha said, folding a woven blanket into a cushion.

Emma lowered herself cross-legged to the ground. Ancha resumed grinding.

"I'm almost done. Then we talk."

She watched him work. He moved his whole body with the rhythm, not unlike the ab-wheel exercise from her gym days—an odd, fleeting memory.

When he finished, he scraped the ground herb into a small clay pot and sealed it with a lid, placing it against the wall.

"What is that?" she asked.

"This name I know. Mormon tea."

"What do you use it for?"

Ancha chuckled. "Mostly for drinking. Good for the

chest."

Emma's eyes scanned the cave. "Are all these jars filled with herbs?"

"Most. Some are empty. Some hold winter food."

She nodded. "Ancha, I need to talk to you. I hardly know where to begin." She paused. Ancha waited.

"The other night, I tried to use my necklace and ring to connect with Paul in a dream. In the past, even without vivid dreams, I could feel something—a current, an energy. But this time, nothing. Nothing at all."

"I thought you decided not to seek Paul in your dreams anymore."

"I had. But . . ."

"But something made you try. What?"

Emma hesitated, then blurted, "I think I'm developing feelings for Levi. But it feels like a betrayal of Paul. I just . . . wanted clarity."

Ancha's small smile returned, and he shook his head slowly.

"What?" she asked. "Why are you shaking your head?"

"You live in your head. Always trying to understand with your mind. But not everything can be understood this way."

"Okay, then how?"

"How do you feel when you walk in these hills? When you see the sunrise or the hawk fly?"

Emma sat quietly. She knew the answer. It wasn't a thought—it was a feeling: a bone-deep joy, a sense of rightness. A connection beyond explanation—no words could contain it.

"Yes," Ancha said softly, as if he could see her thoughts. "You begin to see. The most important truths cannot be spoken or understood in the mind."

"Then why didn't I feel the energy?"

"Because your heart did not want to. Your heart already

knows what it needs to know."

❧ CHAPTER 18 ❧

She remained unsettled after her visit with Ancha. More than anything, she longed for space—mental and emotional—to understand better how she experienced the world. Ancha's quiet wisdom had changed her more than she expected in the short time they'd known each other. He was right: she lived too much in her head.

But how could she stop?

How did a person stay connected to the heart when life demanded constant focus and performance? She couldn't afford to drift inward now. The first wave of summer tourists would arrive by week's end, and with them, her chance—or her failure—to prove herself to the Colorado Springs Company board.

"Emma," Claire whispered, gently nudging her elbow.

"Stand up. It's time to sing the doxology."

Startled, Emma rose with the congregation, realizing she hadn't heard a word of the sermon.

Outside the church, Claire gave her a teasing glance. "Are you sure your brain didn't find its way back to your time and leave your body behind? You hardly seemed present at all."

Emma smiled faintly. "I'm sorry. I know I've been distracted. But I'm very aware of where—and when—I am."

"Well," Claire said, her tone softening, "unless there's something pressing that you need to handle today, try to let that busy mind of yours rest. That might be the best preparation for what's ahead."

Emma nodded, though she wasn't sure how to quiet her mind. Easier said than done, she thought. Maybe another visit to Ancha would help.

❀

"Use the same way I taught you for dreamwork," Ancha said matter-of-factly. "It moves your mind out of the way."

"I feel like I should have known that," Emma said, lying down on the blanket he had unfolded for her.

"Now you know. No more talk. Practice."

She closed her eyes and focused on her breath—slow inhale, hold for five, slow exhale. In . . . hold . . . out . . . in . . . hold . . . out . . .

Suddenly, she became aware and opened her eyes. The light had shifted. She sat up quickly.

"What happened?" she asked.

Ancha was seated nearby, calmly smoking his pipe while Kwiyaghat dozed at his side.

"You fell asleep."

Emma propped herself up on her elbows. "How long?"

"I don't know. The sun has moved to late afternoon."

She sat up fully, cross-legged. "Why didn't you wake me?"

"Why would I wake you?"

"Ugh. You are exasperating, Ancha. I was trying to learn how to get out of my head, remember? I need to be able to do that and stay awake."

"Who says?"

"What?"

"Who says that you have to be able to do that and stay awake?"

"Well, what good does it do me to fall asleep every time? We are all out of our heads when we sleep."

"You fell asleep this time. You will not fall asleep every time. Practice."

"Yes, all right, I will practice." She knew she would get no more pearls of wisdom from him that day.

After a quiet stretch, she asked, "Have you thought any more about what I said . . . about you living here alone?"

"I live as I choose." He scratched Kwiyaghat gently behind the ears as the dog stirred and stretched.

"Would you at least consider coming to town for dinner at the boardinghouse?"

Ancha turned to her, meeting her gaze with unflinching clarity. "No."

His answer was simple, but it struck deep. She held his gaze for a moment, then nodded. There was nothing more to say.

They sat in silence until her legs grew stiff. She stood and stretched, feeling the power of their wordless bond.

"Thank you, Ancha. I'll see you soon," she said softly as she turned to go.

On her way back to the boardinghouse, she concentrated

on each step along the steep canyon trail. The loose rock on hard-packed dirt could be treacherous, even when dry. With her attention narrowed to the rhythm of her movements, her mind finally quieted. She became acutely aware of every detail: the crunch of gravel beneath her feet, the wind slipping past her ears, the dry pull of air through her nose, the heat of the sun pressing against her clothes.

But more than anything, she felt the subtle ache blooming in her chest—a quiet, formless longing she could neither name nor explain. It didn't rise from fear, or lack, or even loneliness. It was just there. A presence. A knowing.

And for once, she let it be.

❀

Emma spent the first part of the week visiting hotels throughout Manitou and Colorado Springs, soliciting feedback on their projected occupancy rates and suggestions for improvement. At every stop, she made a point of sharing that she was being considered for the director of tourism position and asked each proprietor for their support.

The responses were largely positive. Occupancy projections were higher than they had ever been, and most credited Emma's campaigns in the eastern cities for the surge. Several even noted that the upcoming influx of Knights Templar was largely thanks to her efforts.

Still, a note of caution emerged: would this spike in visitors become a dependable pattern, or was it a one-time swell?

Emma took it seriously. She promised to return after the first wave of tourists departed to gather more detailed feedback.

By late Wednesday, she was back at her desk. She had

been poring over her notes for hours.

"Emma, it's time to go home," Albright finally said, standing at the doorway with his hat in hand. "You've been at this all evening, and I, for one, am hungry."

Emma blinked at the wall clock. It was nearly 7:00 p.m.

"You're right," she said, rubbing her eyes. "I lost track of time."

She declined his offer to join him for dinner. "I'll find something at home," she said, gathering her notes into a folio.

As they left the office together, Albright watched her with a mixture of admiration and concern. He had seen few people work as hard—or with as much heart. But he wondered if she realized the toll it was taking.

Emma found bread and cheese in the boardinghouse kitchen and a pear that was more bruised than ripe. *This will have to do,* she thought.

Back in her suite, she sat at her desk with her simple supper and reopened her folio. She noted which hotel owners had been enthusiastic and which had responded more coolly. She marked those she needed to win over. Every voice counted.

She worked long into the night, her lamplight flickering as shadows climbed the walls. By the time she turned down the wick, it was nearly midnight.

Her body ached from tension, her mind from exhaustion. But her purpose was steadfast.

❧ CHAPTER 19 ❧

Emma tightened her corset as far as it would go. She had never been able to do that before. She frowned at her reflection. Her striped suit, once her favorite, hung a bit too easily on her frame. Another skipped meal. Another long day chasing perfection. She missed the simplicity of her own time —of grabbing takeout on the way home, of stocked pantries and soft clothes.

At least today she was ready with plenty of time to sit down with her fellow tenants and have a proper breakfast. She could smell the food wafting down the hall the moment she opened the door of her suite, and her stomach growled loudly in response.

She was the last one to breakfast. Everyone else was already seated and eating when she entered the dining room.

"Ah! Emma!" Levi said when she came in. "So glad you are joining us."

His tone denoted no sarcasm, but she felt defensive just the same.

"What do you mean? I eat with you all the time," she responded.

Forks paused. Eyebrows rose. No one said anything.

"Yes, of course you do," Claire said quietly. "Come, eat while everything is still hot."

After finishing her eggs and toast, Emma spotted a letter on the hall table addressed to her. With no time to read it, she slipped it into her folio just as Peter Graham descended the stairs.

"Do you mind if I walk with you?" he asked as they left the boardinghouse.

"No, not at all," Emma replied.

They walked in silence for half a block before Peter finally spoke.

"You've been scarce these last few weeks."

"I know. I've been working long hours this summer. I'm hoping I can breathe a little easier come fall. Most of the first surge of tourists left this week—I'm eager to see what the numbers look like."

Peter nodded but didn't reply. His silence dragged.

"How is business at the bookshop?" she asked.

"Good. Very good. I'll need to order more local maps before the Templars arrive."

"They'll be here before we know it," Emma said.

Peter didn't answer right away. He glanced toward the mountains.

"Manitou's never seen so many strangers—from so many places—at once," he said at last.

"If I've done my job right, this won't be the last."

"I just hope there won't be any clashes," Peter murmured.

"Why would there be clashes?"

They had reached his storefront. He pulled his key out of his pocket, but before turning to unlock the door, he looked directly into Emma's eyes and said, "You're too young, I suppose. But the wounds from the war have scarcely scarred over." He dipped his head and added, "I'll see you at home, Emma."

Emma stood there for a second longer, watching the door close behind him. That was the second time he had made a vague reference to the war and its aftermath. She was well aware how deep a scar the Civil War had left. Only a couple of years before she was sent back in time, white supremacists had marched in Charlottesville, Virginia, and afterwards, partly in response, there had been a big movement to remove Confederate statues in many locations. Yes, there were still hard feelings, even in 2019.

❋

When she arrived at the office, she sorted through the mail the desk clerk handed her, finding nothing that required immediate attention. She took her papers from her folio and found the letter she had quickly tucked away there on her way out that morning. She turned over the envelope and saw it was from Josiah. Her heart lifted as she opened it.

July 8, 1883

My dear Emma,

I apologize for taking so long to write to you. It took me longer than I expected to find a permanent residence. I suppose I was trying to find a place like Claire's boarding house, and there is no such place here in Chicago. In many ways I am glad to be back in a city. Certainly, there is more opportunity for me here. But I can't deny that I miss the quiet and the beauty of Manitou. I hope I will have occasion to return from time to time.

And it's not just the scenery that I miss. I miss the people. Most especially you. Oh, I know we were never more than friends, but you are different in a way I can't put my finger on, and it's delightful!

I do hope you will let me know when you are coming through on your next trip back east. I will take you to dinner at my favorite restaurant (which I haven't yet found) and show you how the locals entertain themselves.

In the meantime, letters will have to do. Please write soon and let me know how everyone is doing and how this tourist season is unfolding.

My address is 107 ½ Dearborn Ave., Chicago, Illinois.

A Mrs. Eliza Colburn is the landlady. She seems a fine person, but she's no Claire La Salle, and she has some rather strict rules. The location is very good, though.

Your good friend,
Josiah

Emma wrote a short letter in response before gently folding and returning Josiah's letter back in its envelope. She missed him. She wistfully looked out the window just as the passengers arriving on the morning train were emerging from the depot. It was a large crowd. She watched as they made their way west on Manitou Avenue toward the attractions and hotels.

The sight of all the tourists brought Emma back to her main task of the day: to complete the analysis of the first surge of tourists that had arrived the previous week.

Hours later, Emma stood to stretch her stiff back and to light the gas lights in the office. The late afternoon sun no longer provided enough ambient light. She glanced at the wall clock. If she left now, she would be home in time for dinner. If she sat back down to pore over the financial reports, she knew she would not stop until she was done. But there was one trend that concerned her, and she wanted to understand it fully before considering the best way forward. It would bother her all night if she left it now. She took a deep breath and sat back down to the stack of papers filled with numbers.

Hours later, satisfied that she had come to the right conclusions, she closed the folder containing the bathhouse report. It was only mid-month, but once again it underperformed the other businesses. If the capacity rates were at the same levels as the rest, its profits would be well within expectations—but they weren't. She did not have information in sufficient detail to confirm that the volume of visitors was higher during the women-only hours, but she suspected it was. She would have to pay Major Wright a visit soon to try to get him to see reason. For now, she was too tired to put much more thought into it.

When she walked into the boardinghouse, the other tenants were gathered in the parlor. Emma was too tired to stop and socialize, so she gave them a quick greeting and said she was making an early night of it.

A hot bath was what she needed. In her suite, she neatly hung up her clothes and put on her robe. With everyone else still downstairs, she walked to the new bathroom unseen. It really was a luxury having access to running hot water and an inside toilet. She slowly dipped into the deep clawfoot tub. *Ahhh*, she thought as she lay down as far as she could, letting the hot water reach just under her chin.

The water had cooled considerably and her fingers were wrinkled when she decided it was time to get out of the bath.

She got out and dried off before putting on her robe and rinsing the tub. She felt a passing irritation when she heard voices from the staircase, getting louder. She would have preferred getting back to her room without being seen, but such was life in a boardinghouse. She waited a moment, hoping for a clear passage to her suite, but the male voices seemed in conversation that did not sound likely to end soon. She opened the door to see Levi and Peter in the hall.

Resigned to having to walk by them, she slowly opened the door. They stopped talking when they saw her walking toward them.

"Did you have a nice bath?" Levi asked, smiling.

"Oh, yes, it was very . . ." Emma began to feel woozy and couldn't finish her thought.

"Emma! Emma! Wake up!" Emma opened her eyes and saw Levi leaning over her, gently patting her cheeks. She felt drunk and confused.

"What happened?" she mumbled.

"You fainted. I sent Peter to let Claire know and to fetch Alice."

Emma started to lift herself, but the queasiness overcame her again, and she lay back down. Just then, Claire came running up the stairs with a glass of water.

"Oh, my heavens! Is she all right?" Claire exclaimed. "Help her sit up, Levi, and I'll give her some water."

Levi gently lifted Emma, propping her against his chest. Claire put the glass to Emma's lips.

"Here, dear, drink some water. Slowly now," Claire said encouragingly.

Emma sipped the water. Then, realizing how thirsty she was, took the glass herself and drank it down. Within a short time, she felt more clear-headed.

"I think I can stand now," she said. Levi and Claire helped her to her feet. Levi supported her and helped her walk while Claire went ahead and opened the door to Emma's suite. Levi guided Emma to her divan and helped her recline.

"I would like more water, please," Emma said.

"Of course," Claire responded, walking to the pitcher at the wash basin. It was empty.

"I'll go refill this," she said as she walked out of the room.

"Are you feeling better, Emma?" Levi asked, his brow furrowed with concern.

"Yes, much, thank you."

Emma closed her eyes and took a deep breath. She still looked pale, and Levi noticed her skin was clammy when he felt her forehead to see if she seemed warm. His stomach tightened as a sudden, unwelcome memory flashed of hours spent by Daphne's side as she slowly and painfully succumbed to tuberculosis. A panic flooded over him that Emma might be seriously ill.

Claire returned with a full pitcher of water and refilled Emma's glass. Levi took it from her.

"Emma, my dear, here's more water for you," he said tenderly.

Emma opened her eyes and took the glass, but her hands were unsteady.

"Here, I'll help you hold it," Levi said. He put his hands over hers and steadied the glass while she drank, then set the empty glass on the table. He looked at Claire, who was wringing her hands and frowning, and wondered if she, too, had thought of Daphne.

"Come, have a seat while we wait for Alice," he said to Claire. Emma seemed to be sleeping, so they waited in anxious silence for Alice to arrive.

❀

"Your blood sugar fell too low, and you are dehydrated," Alice said flatly, pulling the stethoscope out of her ears.

"Oh, good, I'm glad it's nothing more," Emma said.

"When was the last time you ate?" Alice asked.

"I had breakfast with everyone here this morning."

"And what exactly did you eat?"

"Let's see . . . toast, eggs, coffee. I think that's it."

"And before that?"

"Oh, for goodness' sake, I don't remember, Alice!"

Alice sat in the armchair and leaned in. Her face was serious, but not stern, and it frightened Emma.

"Listen to me carefully," Alice began. "You are not taking care of yourself, and it has begun to take its toll on your health. This self-neglect must stop immediately. Why, you wouldn't treat an animal the way you have been treating yourself. Overworking, skipping meals, little real recuperation . . ."

"Yes, but . . ."

"Don't interrupt me!" Alice scolded. "I am dead serious, Emma. I can see your ribs and collarbones sticking out. You're malnourished, which is simply inexcusable. You have ready access to good meals every day. Why are you mistreating yourself so?"

Emma stopped to consider the question. She hadn't intended to be neglectful. She was just singularly focused on being successful at her job. What would happen to her if she lost her position? Especially with Albright leaving. She was afraid not to put all her energy into her work. She simply had to keep her job. Her very survival depended on it. But she didn't know how to explain it all to Alice. Truly, she was only now realizing just how deep her fear ran. She looked over to Alice, dumbstruck.

"Well, give it some thought," Alice said. "But in the meantime, you must eat regularly, and by that, I mean three times a day—and enough. You must drink more water. You must get at least eight hours of restful sleep each night. And, whether you come to church or not, you must take at least one day off a week for true recreation, meaning you don't think about or do any work. This is not a suggestion. It is a prescription. Do you understand me, Emma?"

"Yes, I understand," Emma answered. She could see Alice was serious. And whether or not she agreed, it would be foolish to argue with the doctor.

"Good. Now, I'll help you get into your nightclothes."

After getting Emma to bed, Alice stopped at Claire's quarters, where she found both Claire and Levi eagerly awaiting her diagnosis.

"Please do what you can to help Emma follow my instructions," Alice said after explaining Emma's condition. "I know she's a grown woman and should be able to take care of herself, but we all need help from friends and family from time to time. She is troubled and seems driven for reasons not entirely clear to me—or maybe even herself."

"Yes, of course we will help her," Claire said. "Thank you for coming so quickly to attend to her."

"It's nice to be able to be a real doctor every once in a while. Emma's condition is temporary and completely reversible, if she will only take better care of herself."

Once Alice had gone, Levi sat heavily on the divan, his face in his hands.

Claire joined him, resting a hand on his shoulder. "She's going to be okay."

"I know. But when I saw her lying there . . . I thought of Daphne. I can't lose Emma too. Not when we've only just—"

He broke off. Claire said nothing, just gave his shoulder a reassuring squeeze.

After a moment, she said, "Then don't lose her. If you care about her, stop waiting. Be clear. Be brave."

Levi looked up, meeting Claire's eyes.

"She told John Jr. she was going to the Colorado Day hop with you," Claire lightly added. "Even though you haven't asked her."

Levi blinked, then gave a quiet laugh.

"Well," he said, standing, "that's something I *can* fix."

❧ CHAPTER 20 ❧

To avoid all the grief she would get from Claire, Alice, and Levi if she blatantly ignored Alice's instructions, Emma agreed to rest the day after her fainting episode. She stayed in bed that morning, hoping for some quiet time to come to terms with the fear that was driving her to work so hard. What did she think was the worst that could happen? She would lose her job and have to find another one—so what? She had found this one. Why did a part of her feel that her very survival depended on being successful at this job?

These were the thoughts bouncing around in her head when she heard the door to her suite slowly open.

"Emma?" Claire called in a whisper. "Are you awake?"

"Yes, yes, please, come on in," Emma called out from her bedroom.

"I have a tray of breakfast for you, dear. Would you like it out here or in bed?"

"Oh, thank you. I'll get up and eat it in my sitting room." Emma threw her covers off and put on her robe. On her occasional table, Claire had set down a tray with a generous helping of eggs, bacon, potatoes, toast with jam, coffee, and a glass of water. It looked like enough food for three people to Emma, and she did not eat bacon, but she had the good manners to say, "It looks delicious, Claire. Thank you for bringing it to me."

Claire sat in the armchair and crossed her feet. "You are welcome. Now, sit down and eat."

Emma smiled, ignoring her sense of being intruded upon and mothered. Claire was just trying to help her take better care of herself, she knew. And if she were being honest, her track record taking care of herself *was* suspect. She sat on the divan and began eating.

"It's a lovely day," Claire observed as she looked out Emma's window. "Mind if I open the window?"

"Not at all," Emma mumbled through her toast.

A gentle, cool breeze filled the room with fresh air. Claire returned to the armchair. It was apparent to Emma that her friend did not plan on leaving until she had finished eating.

"I'm glad you agreed to take a day off. Should I ring Mr. Albright and let him know you won't be in today?" Claire asked.

"No. He's still in Denver as far as I know. He is in the office infrequently now and until he leaves permanently." Emma sipped her coffee. She already missed her boss.

Claire, realizing she was losing Emma to her anxious thoughts, replied brightly, "Good! Then you are free to enjoy your day." She went on to suggest various pleasant ways she and Emma might spend it, ending with, "Or, we could go into

Colorado Springs for some shop browsing and lunch? Maybe the bookshop for a new book to read?"

"All of those are nice ideas, but no, I think I'll go hiking in the hills—maybe see Ancha."

If Claire was disappointed, she didn't show it as she nodded her approval. "Sounds like a fine idea . . . well, looks like you're done with your breakfast!" Claire dipped her head toward Emma's empty plate. "I'll take your tray downstairs. Say good-bye before you leave. I'll have some lunch ready for you to take with you."

Emma felt surprisingly rejuvenated after her substantial meal—more energetic than she had in days. She walked over to the window to gauge how to dress for her hike. It looked to be late morning, maybe close to noon. She looked around for her brooch watch, but when she found it on her nightstand, it had wound down to a stop. *No matter*, she thought, and began dressing for her outing.

She found Molly and Claire in the kitchen.

"I'm leaving now," she said. "I'll be back in time for dinner." When she saw the skepticism on Molly's face, she added, "I promise."

"Here you are, dear," Claire said as she handed Emma a satchel. "There's some lunch in there for you when you get hungry."

Emma gave Claire a peck on the cheek. "Thank you. You really don't need to make such a fuss over me. I've gotten the message, and I will take better care of myself. I appreciate your effort, though."

Emma left through the kitchen door and headed up to Williams Canyon. Her walk took her past some of the larger homes in town, including the one belonging to the Calhoun family. She was glad to see no signs of activity there. She preferred her treks to see Ancha go unnoticed—mostly for his sake.

✻

"The doctor is right," Ancha said as they walked along a steep slope near the spot where Emma had emerged from Cave of the Winds the day she was sent back in time. "You must take better care of yourself."

They were heading toward a patch of plants Ancha had spotted a couple of days ago—he believed they'd now be ready for gathering. The small meadow lay just south of the Williams Canyon opening. Emma had never been so close to town with Ancha before, and it made her a little uneasy. She was surprised he'd venture so near to the encroachment of white men.

But when they reached the spot, she understood the temptation. The little field was filled with ripe, juicy blackberries. She began helping him pick them, gently placing each into his gathering basket—but she couldn't resist popping a few into her mouth. They were sweeter than any she could remember.

"Do not pick them all. And please, put some in the basket," Ancha said with gentle reproach.

Emma smiled at the reminder. He had taught her many times not to overharvest—every plant, every fruit, was to be shared with other creatures. She loved the way he lived in harmony with nature and all its inhabitants. She paused and looked toward town. If only her own kind lived the same way.

Back at the cave, Emma took out the lunch Claire and Molly had packed and shared it with Ancha and Kwiyaghat.

"What will you do with all the berries? Won't they spoil before you can eat them all?" she asked, handing him a water jug.

"I will eat some, but most I will dry and add to my—" He hesitated. "I don't know the word for it . . . my winter food."

"I believe it's called pemmican," Emma said. "Will you teach me how to make it?"

She was thinking it might be a good emergency food—something she could keep on hand for the days she forgot to stop and eat.

Ancha nodded. "When I have the other ingredients, I will show you."

They spent the rest of the afternoon sitting outside the cave. Emma opened up about her fears—about her job, her future. There was something about the way Ancha listened without interruption or correction that helped her speak freely. It made her feel safe.

"How complicated the white man's world is," he said when she finally fell silent. "You are feeling the same way you would if a bear or mountain lion chased you. But you cannot feel this way every day. It will kill you. That feeling is for running for your life, not living it."

Emma laughed, startled by the clarity of his wisdom. "You are absolutely right, Ancha."

"Pay attention," he said. "Always ask: What do I see? What do I hear? What do I smell? What do I feel? When you are hungry, eat. When you are tired, sleep. When you are cold, cover yourself. When you must work, work. When you hear an animal coming, run. It is not hard."

He shook his head slowly, as if bewildered by the unnecessary complexity humans created for themselves.

Emma took his advice to heart on her walk back to town. The last time she'd truly paid attention, as he put it, had been her previous visit to him. She realized she hadn't practiced any of his teachings since. That would have to change.

As she passed the Calhoun house, she caught a flicker of

movement at an upstairs window—just enough to spot a hand slip back from the curtain. She froze for a moment. Could that have been John Jr.? Had he seen her coming down from the hills? From Ancha's?

She adjusted the strap of her satchel and kept moving, but the thought lingered.

Just as promised, Emma returned in time for dinner. And afterward, instead of heading straight to her room to work, she joined the other tenants in the parlor. She asked the men if they would teach her to play poker—though she already knew how and simply couldn't admit it without inviting questions.

They agreed, a bit reluctantly. Claire played piano while Christine stitched quietly in a corner.

"Well, you sur picked that up quick!" Willy exclaimed after Emma won her third straight hand. "You sur you haven't played before?"

"Oh, I've seen it played, I suppose," she said, feigning modesty. "But no, not really."

"Then here ya go," Willy said, digging coins from his pockets.

"Oh, I don't want your money! It was just beginner's luck."

"Nope. Far is far," he said, stacking four quarters on the table.

"Take it, Emma. We can't have you wrecking the house rules," Peter said, grinning. "Otherwise I'll be washing dishes to pay my rent."

"You mean like I'mma gonna have to do?" Willy shot back, and the room erupted in laughter.

Later, everyone made their way upstairs. At the landing, Levi and Emma paused outside their suites.

"It was nice having you join us tonight—for just a normal evening," Levi said.

"I really did enjoy it. I hope to do it more often."

After a brief silence, Levi added, "I'm going fishing tomorrow morning. It's probably not anything you'd be interested in, but I'd love to have you join me."

His tone was so tentative, it gave him a boyish vulnerability that surprised Emma.

She almost declined—out of habit more than anything—but caught herself.

"Yes. I'd love to go."

Levi's face lit up. "Wonderful. I know just the place."

They agreed on a time and said goodnight.

❧ CHAPTER 21 ❧

"Here," Levi stopped and set down his fishing gear and messenger bag containing their lunch on the bank of Ruxton Creek. "I've had good luck at this spot lately."

Ruxton Creek ran from the northeast of town, following Englemann Canyon. The creek flowed into Fountain Creek near Soda Spring, which in turn flowed through the center of Manitou. They had walked the steady incline of Ruxton Avenue, well past the Manitou Vista hotel. She remembered that Frank Bowman, the proprietor of the ten pins and billiards hall, had said that Levi preferred to fish upstream of town. The spot was perfect: quiet, but not too far from town, and the water was no doubt cleaner.

It promised to be another perfect Colorado day, but it was early morning, just after sunrise, and the light breeze was cool.

Emma turned to see the vivid oranges and yellows of the sunrise between the foothills and took a deep breath.

When she turned back to the river, Levi was looking at her, grinning.

"What?" she asked.

"Nothing." He shook his head dismissively. "I just find you disturbingly cute, dressed like a boy."

Emma blushed. As usual, she had chosen practical outdoor clothes, but only after some deliberation. Since she wasn't sure whether this outing was a proper date or simply Levi helping her follow Alice's prescription for rest, she'd decided to treat it as the latter. Still, she was glad he found her boyish attire appealing.

"Come, sit here next to me and I'll bait your hook." Levi sat on the embankment and patted the dirt next to him.

"Oh, yes, well, about that . . . I'm happy to be outside and to spend time with you as you fish, but I'd rather not myself."

Then she told him the story of the time she had joined her grandfather to go fishing. She went just to spend time with him; they had so little time alone together. She had never been fishing before, and when they got to the creek, her grandfather baited her hook, helped her cast her line into the creek, then walked a short distance upstream to do the same. Emma had not expected to catch anything and, in fact, had no intention of doing so. She was there to be with her grandfather. But when she got a bite, she did not know what to do. She screamed and screamed for her grandfather, who did not hear her for some time over the sound of the water flowing. When he finally came and helped her bring in the fish, she told him she wanted to throw it back, unharmed. Unfortunately, in the time it took for her grandfather to help her, the poor fish had swallowed the hook. Her grandfather explained that the kindest thing would be to keep the fish. Not realizing how sensitive she was about the creature, he hit it over the head with a large wrench and tossed it into the cooler. At the end of the day, it turned out to be the largest catch. Her grandfather was so proud! When they got home, he traced the fish on a piece of cardboard and cut it out as a trophy, dating it on the back. That night at dinner, he honored her by serving her the fish. She had never gotten over the trauma of it all.

Levi listened intently to her story. When she was finished, he said, "Then just sit here with me."

She settled next to Levi. Just being outside was enough for her, and she could not deny that she had looked forward to spending time alone with him. She watched the water rapidly wash over the rocks and small boulders in the creek. It wasn't particularly deep, and Emma wondered how big the fish could get in such shallow water.

"What kind of fish do you catch here?" she asked.

"Cutthroat trout."

"I can't imagine they are very big."

"Most are about eight inches long. I don't keep them if they aren't at least seven."

Emma admired that. Certainly, there were no regulations to force him to release the smaller fish. His respect for nature reminded her of Ancha.

Levi reached into his bag and took out a small leather pouch, a simple wooden case, and a silver matchbox. She watched him fill his pipe, strike the match against a rock, and light the tobacco with a quiet reverence that made the entire ritual seem sacred. The smell was rich but not cloying—earthy, with a note of sweetness. She looked at the profile of his calm face. *My God, those eyelashes.*

They sat in comfortable silence for several minutes. She sat there beside Levi, smelling his tobacco smoke, listening to the water babble, and feeling the gentle breeze, which had already begun to warm.

"You know, Colorado Day is coming up," Levi said casually.

"Yes, it is," Emma responded, suddenly reminded that she had told John Jr. that she was going to the Colorado Day hop with Levi, even though Levi had not asked her. She had forgotten all about it. Her languid state of mind abruptly shattered.

"I was hoping I could escort you," Levi said, glancing sideways at her.

"Oh! Yes! I'd like that very much!" Her relief was obvious, she knew, and she hoped he didn't find her overeager.

"Good. I'm looking forward to it," he said with a little nod, then returned his attention to the line.

Emma sat a while longer, but the quiet tension in her body wouldn't release. Her legs were getting stiff, and she felt restless. Just then, Levi caught a fish, and she had to stand and move aside to allow Levi room to reel it in.

"That's a nice one!" He smiled.

"It sure is!" Emma replied, though she couldn't ignore the sympathy she felt as the fish flopped on the dirt.

"I think I'll go plant-gathering," she said. "Ancha has been teaching me about the plants here and their uses, but it's difficult because neither of us knows many of the English names." She smiled. "I thought I'd start a book of pressings so I can record their uses and what they look like. Doesn't really matter what they're called, I guess. 'A rose by any other name,' right?"

Levi looked up. It struck him that she had no interest in fishing—none at all. She'd come just to be with him. The realization sent a quiet thrill through him.

❀

They returned with enough fish for supper. While Levi cleaned the catch, Emma slipped away to her suite with a bundle of plants she'd gathered along the creek. She pressed the leaves between the pages of a thick book, stacking others on top to weigh them down. Over time, she'd developed a knack for sensing which plants held promise and which were merely weeds—though their exact uses still eluded her. She planned to bring the pressings to Ancha so he could tell her their uses and begin her catalog. The idea had come to her unexpectedly, while she and Levi sat in companionable silence on the creek bank. Now, with her purpose blooming, she was eager to begin.

After a quick bath and a change into her favorite summer dress, Emma ventured downstairs to the parlor to see how the other tenants might be occupying themselves. She found Christine in her usual place at the end of the divan, close to the light of the window, crocheting.

"Hello, Emma," the young woman greeted her cheerfully.

"Hello." Emma smiled fondly at Christine and sat next to her. "May I see what you are making?"

Christine handed Emma her project, which appeared to be the beginning of a very small bootie, crocheted in fine thread. Emma looked up at Christine, wide-eyed. Christine laughed heartily.

"Of course they aren't for me, silly goose! Though I hope one day I will need baby booties. No, these are for a maid at the Manitou House who is expecting."

Emma, embarrassed that her reaction was so transparent, let out a self-deprecating chuckle. "Well, it's lovely. I'd like to learn how to crochet, if you would be willing to teach me. You're quite good at it."

"Thank you. I should be. I've been doing it since I was

nine, when my granny taught me."

Emma handed the work back to Christine and watched as she resumed looping the thread around the hook and pulling through, loop after loop.

"How are things going with you and Willy?" Emma tentatively asked.

"Fine. I'm very happy with him, and he seems to be with me as well . . ."

"I hear a 'but' coming," Emma encouraged.

Christine set down her work in her lap and looked up at the ceiling, releasing a sigh. "But I'm not sure what his intentions are."

"How long have you been courting?"

"I'm not sure exactly when it started," Christine said thoughtfully, "but at least four months, I'd say."

Emma wasn't entirely certain what passed for proper timing in a courtship in 1883—but surely, in any era, four months was long enough for a woman to know where she stood.

"Have you asked him?"

Christine's head snapped around. "Heavens, no!"

Realizing she'd tripped over some unspoken rule of Victorian etiquette, Emma raised her hands in mock surrender. "Sorry—of course you haven't."

Fortunately, Willy chose that moment to stride into the parlor, saving Emma from further embarrassment and drawing a quick flush to Christine's cheeks.

Oblivious, he grinned and asked, "What're you gals chattin' about?"

"Nothing," Emma said quickly. "I was just asking Christine if she'd teach me how to crochet," she added, hoping her tone sounded more innocent than it felt.

"Well, ya couldn't find a better teacher, that's fur sur," he said, beaming at Christine.

"I see Levi's brought home supper," he added.

"Yes, and I suppose I should check if Claire needs a hand in the kitchen," Emma said, rising and smoothing her skirt.

"I'll come with you," Christine said, setting her needlework on the end table.

Willy watched them go, a slight frown tugging at his brow. He wasn't sure what he'd walked in on, but he had the vague feeling he'd missed something.

✻

The next morning, with her book of pressings tucked beneath her arm and a growing sense of purpose in her step, Emma made her way to Ancha's cave. The sun was still low, casting long golden beams between the foothills. The scents of dust, sage, and pine filled the crisp morning air like a fading dream.

Kwiyaghat met her well before she reached the small clearing at the cave's entrance, where she found Ancha sitting by a spent fire, whittling a piece of wood.

He looked at her and said, "You brought something."

"I have." She knelt beside him and opened the book. "I found these along the creek bank. They aren't fully pressed yet, but I was hoping you could teach me about them. What are they used for?"

Ancha took the pressings in his weathered hands and studied them with the reverence of a priest unfolding a relic. He picked up a lacy sprig first—pale and delicate, but sturdy beneath the weight of its tiny, clustered blooms.

"This one," he said, "closes wounds quicker than needle and thread. Stops bleeding. Also brings down fever—when used well. But too much, and it will stir the blood instead."

Emma raised her brows. "It didn't occur to me that a plant

could be both helpful and harmful."

He nodded. "As most things can."

Next, he lifted a large, thick, velvet-like leaf.

"This," he said, "eases the chest. Good for coughs, when the lungs rattle like a snake. Put in hot water, breathe the steam . . . also good to clean after you . . . I don't know the word . . . after you eat and the food goes through you. . . ." He made a small, apologetic gesture with his hand, miming something coming out of his backside.

It took Emma a moment, then she laughed. "Oh, I see— after you poop! Yes, it would be good for that." Far better than the old newspapers and catalogs she used, she thought.

"This one," he said more quietly, "cleans from the inside. When water doesn't flow right. Or burns."

Emma blushed slightly but nodded.

"Bears eat the fruit. I use it in my winter food."

He gently placed the pressings back in her book, then looked at her squarely. "You have a good eye. Keep gathering. And next time, bring stories with the plants. Where you found them. Were they blooming? What direction did they grow?"

Emma smiled and nodded, proud that her teacher saw promise in her.

❧ CHAPTER 22 ❧

Emma adjusted the cuffs of her blouse and straightened the small leather folio under her arm. The early morning sun filtered through a haze of dust as she walked down Manitou Avenue, the scent of fresh bread wafting from the bakery mingling with the metallic tang of horse tack from the livery. The town was already stirring with activity—just the way she liked it.

She had a plan.

Today was about visibility, persistence, and polite persuasion. The board of directors had notified her that they would conduct interviews for the director of tourism the first full week in August, after the July business results were reported. She was determined to make her case with the town's proprietors. And while Emma had gained a healthier perspective about the consequences if she failed, she still wanted this job with her whole being.

And she was running out of time.

Her first stop was the BeeBee House, where she had arranged to meet with Mrs. BeeBee—the only female hotelier in town now that Mrs. Whitaker was gone. Emma hoped she might find some sympathy and support from the lady. She entered the lobby, dim and cool after the bright street, and was grateful for the momentary relief from the heat. Mrs. BeeBee greeted her with a warm smile and a nod.

"Miss Quinn! Always a pleasure."

"Likewise, Mrs. BeeBee. I won't take much of your time."

The proprietress waved her toward a chair and asked the desk clerk to fetch tea. "Always have time for you, Miss Quinn. I'm told the board will be interviewing soon to replace Mr. Albright."

"Yes, early August, I understand."

"And you're putting your hat in the ring?"

"I am," she said plainly. "I believe I've already been doing the work. I'd like the chance to do it with the town's backing."

Mrs. BeeBee studied her for a moment. "You've been effective, I'll grant you that. I've never had so much business."

Emma inclined her head. "Thank you. This season is only the beginning. Now that we're better known in the major eastern cities, I have a plan to build on that and expand."

After tea and a few well-placed questions about guest satisfaction and seasonal trends—along with some subtle hints about her future plans—Emma moved on, winding her way from hotel to merchant to restaurant owner. By afternoon, she had spoken with nearly a dozen business owners, all of whom confirmed what she suspected: the town recognized the increase in business this season over past years. And more than one admitted—sometimes grudgingly—that she had had a lot to do with it.

It was when she reached the bathhouse that her mood took a turn. She had put off visiting because she dreaded the conversation she needed to have with Major Wright. But she could delay no longer. The bathhouse was underperforming, and though it might help her cause to see Wright fail, it was her responsibility to help him understand how he could improve. She took a deep breath and steeled herself.

"Late as usual," Major Wright said as she extended her hand.

She glanced at the clock: a minute past the hour. Hardly late by anyone's standards. She knew apologizing would signal weakness, so she ignored his comment.

"This won't take more than fifteen minutes," she replied, hoping the line struck the right balance between courtesy and firmness.

"Well, then, have a seat," Wright said, gesturing to an armchair in the bathhouse's reading room. He took the one opposite.

Emma pulled the relevant papers from her folio and spread them on the table.

"This data is non-attributed, as participants agreed, but it is by category," she began. "It shows that, compared with other establishments—including the attractions—the bathhouse capacity rates are significantly below average. That suggests fewer people are choosing to come here with their limited time in Manitou."

She pointed to the column of numbers supporting her claim.

"There must be an error in the analysis," Wright said dismissively.

"I assure you there isn't. I reviewed them several times. Mr. Albright also looked them over."

"You did the analysis?"

"Yes, based on the reports participants submitted."

"Well, how do we know their information is correct?"

"Are you suggesting the participants would misreport? Why would they do that? The point of the consortium is mutual benefit. If anyone falsifies data, it hurts us all. It would also violate the agreement they signed."

Wright scowled. Had her dispassionate logic flustered him?

"Well . . . well . . . even if their reports are correct, how do I know your analysis isn't flawed?"

"I'd be happy to review my methodology with you, if that would help clarify."

That seemed to agitate him even more.

"No, blast it! I don't need some little lady explaining mathematics to me. I'll take it up with Albright when he returns. When is that, by the way?"

"I haven't heard from Mr. Albright in several days. I don't know."

She tried again. "Major, I do have some thoughts about why the bathhouse isn't faring as well. I believe with a few minor adjustments—"

"I'm not interested in your thoughts, Miss Quinn. I'll speak with Albright when he returns."

He looked at his pocket watch. "I see your fifteen minutes were more like twenty. No wonder you're always late."

Emma stepped into the afternoon sun, blinking against its glare. She walked a few paces along the boardwalk and stopped to take a breath. Her pulse was quick, her cheeks hot—not from the heat, but from the way he'd spoken to her. As if she were a child fumbling with sums. As if her efforts, her intellect, her results meant nothing.

I have a degree in engineering, for Pete's sake.

She gripped the folio tighter. She hadn't risen to his bait. That was something. And she hadn't let him see how deeply he'd rattled her.

But he had rattled her.

Still, facts were facts. The numbers didn't lie, and neither did the business owners who'd quietly backed her that day. She took another breath, steadying herself.

She had a week before the end of the month. Let Wright stew in his arrogance. She would win the position not with bluster, but with results—and the town was already beginning to see it.

Emma lifted her chin and kept walking.

❧ CHAPTER 23 ❧

L evi rinsed his straight razor in the basin and dabbed his
face dry with a towel. He needed an early start. The recent
swell of visitors crashing down on Manitou had brought more
business, yes—but also more drunkenness, more scuffles. So
far, nothing serious had erupted, but managing it all alone as
the town's only lawman was wearing thin.

And now the Knights Templar were coming.

He felt a dull pang in his gut at the thought. It was bad
enough that hundreds of them would be flooding into town at
once. But if Phillip Mouton was among them . . . well, all hell
could break loose—and not just for Manitou.

Still, he had one thing to look forward to that week: the
Colorado Day hop. He and Emma hadn't had a moment alone
since their fishing trip over a week ago. She seemed better—

eating regularly, sleeping more. Her face had filled out a little, and if anything, she looked even more beautiful. But when it came to recreation, well . . . no one in town had much time for that now.

Levi dressed quickly and headed downstairs. A glance at the hall clock told him it wasn't yet six. He would be the one missing breakfast that day.

With a sigh, he grabbed his hat from the rack and stepped out into the new morning.

❃

Emma sat at her office desk. The temperature was high, and her back stuck slightly to the chair, but she hardly noticed. Her focus was on the growing stack of papers in front of her—July business reports trickling in from members of the tourism consortium.

She had already grouped the data by category—lodging, dining, attractions, and shops—and had begun calculating average occupancy rates and comparative year-over-year growth. The metrics were favorable, even more so when compared to the board's official selection criteria for the director of tourism: seasonal growth, profits, visitor satisfaction, and business engagement.

One report stood out again: the bathhouse. It continued to underperform the others in its category of attractions.

She tapped the end of her pencil against her chin. Wright had stonewalled her during their last meeting and made it clear he neither welcomed her feedback nor believed her data. He was combative, insecure, and increasingly dismissive.

She knew better than to provoke him further. No, she was done trying to help him. She considered taking the matter to the board, but it might not appreciate a direct attack, and even if she could prove his mismanagement, it could come across as vindictive. She needed to let the numbers speak. But she also needed a strategy to prevent his bluster from muddying her message.

Emma leaned forward and began organizing her thoughts. This wasn't about her—or about Major Wright. It was about the town. The people who ran the boardinghouses, the men and women opening shops, building restaurants, offering excursions. It was about helping Manitou grow with intention, preserving its charm while positioning it as a destination that could sustain itself long after the rail lines moved on. Her strategy, then, was simple: keep the focus on results, not personalities. Let the numbers speak plainly—businesses across town were thriving, visitor satisfaction was high, and cooperation among consortium members had led to real, measurable gains. If the bathhouse continued to underperform, that was a data point, not a personal slight. Emma would highlight what was working, uplift what could be improved, and keep her message centered on the town's potential. Wright could bluster all he liked, but she wouldn't engage in drama. She would speak of vision, community, and shared prosperity. Let him try to argue with that.

Just then, Emma heard the gas hiss, and the room became brighter. She looked up to see Albright lighting the sconces.

"There, is that better?" he asked.

"Much, thanks, boss."

"You've been working terribly hard at preparing for this interview, Emma. Don't fall into your old pattern of self-neglect. You'll need to be sharp in front of the board."

Emma set down her pencil. "I won't. I have to admit, I am feeling much better since following Alice's directions." She let out a little laugh. "Amazing what a difference eating and sleeping can do." Although I'm still falling short on the recreation part.

"Yes, isn't it, though," Albright responded dryly. He sat back at his desk and said, "I have a few more documents to review before I leave, but why don't you call it a day?"

Satisfied that she was at a good stopping point, Emma stacked her papers neatly and said, "I think I will."

Before she left, she turned and looked at her mentor—her friend. "I'm gonna miss you, boss."

Albright looked up at her. "You aren't rushing me out, are you?" He smiled, then looked back at his papers before adding, "I'll be here until September."

But to Emma, that was too soon, and she already felt his absence.

Emma closed the office door behind her, the soft click of the latch punctuating the end of a long day. As she stepped onto the Manitou House veranda, her eyes burned from the golden wash of late-afternoon light. The town buzzed with quiet industry. Two boys on ladders hung crimson and gold bunting from the balcony railings of the hotel. Along Manitou Avenue, a woman in a wide-brimmed hat adjusted a patriotic ribbon bow on the bakery's porch column. Even the livery had put up a canvas banner, painted brightly.

Colorado Day was the next day, and the town was dressing itself with pride.

Emma decided to stop at the BeeBee House and see how preparations were going at Saratoga Hall, where a few workers were sweeping the floor and testing lanterns strung along the ceiling. In her mind's eye, she could already see the room filled with movement—fiddles playing, couples swirling, laughter rising over the music.

Later that night, gathered in the parlor with the other tenants, talk turned to music and dancing and who might be giving commemorative speeches before the festivities at Soda

Spring. Willy bragged about wearing his best boots, freshly polished, to the hop and that Christine had promised him every third dance. Even Peter, grumbling as usual about crowds and noise, admitted he might at least watch the fireworks display.

As laughter echoed through the house and the last sliver of dusk faded behind Pikes Peak, Emma felt something shift—something light and hopeful. The town was coming alive around her, and for once, she didn't feel like an outsider

❀

The first firework arced into the sky just as the sun slipped behind the mountains. It burst into a spray of gold and green, casting long shadows across the gathered crowd. Emma stood with her fellow tenants, Alice, and Alice's family along the edge of Soda Spring, her eyes reflecting the light of each explosion above.

Children clapped and squealed. Couples leaned into one another. Even Alice, ever composed, allowed herself a soft gasp as a brilliant blue sphere shimmered against the darkening sky. Beside her, Peter Graham remained silent, arms crossed, jaw set. He had made no attempt to hide his disdain for the holiday or the crowd. Claire, in her childlike glee, clapped happily and exclaimed, "Ooooooh!"

Emma glanced at Levi, who stood just behind her shoulder. He had one hand in his coat pocket and in the other, he held his hat. She could feel the warmth of his presence and the tension in his stillness.

"Beautiful, isn't it?" she said, her voice low.

"It is," he replied. She turned to find he was looking at her, not the sky.

She smiled and quickly faced forward again, the next burst of red and silver drawing a collective cheer from the crowd.

When the final volley echoed off the canyon walls and the last trails of smoke curled upward, the crowd began to disperse. Emma and her friends gathered together, brushing dust from coats and skirts.

"Well," Claire said briskly, "Saratoga Hall awaits."

Willy offered Christine his arm with a flourish that made her laugh. Peter grunted that he would come along, "if only to keep an eye on the rabble."

"Good!" Claire said. "I need an escort. Come, Peter!"

The poor man looked panic-struck when Claire took him by the arm.

"You ready?" Levi asked softly, offering his arm.

She nodded and took it. "I am."

The walk to the BeeBee House was a short one, lantern-lit and lined with streamers that fluttered in the light breeze. Saratoga Hall glowed from within, warm and bustling. A fiddler tuned his strings onstage as guests removed gloves and hats and found their places along the edges of the polished floor. The event had drawn a full house—Emma estimated well over a hundred tourists among the mix of locals, more than she had ever seen in one place in Manitou. Visitors from near and far crowded the hall, their eager faces alight with the novelty of a mountain celebration. It was the most festive Emma had seen Manitou, and she allowed herself a quiet moment of pride for having helped make it so.

Willy and Christine were among the first on the dance floor when the band began the opening galop, Christine laughing with delight. Claire stood near the refreshment table, speaking with a well-dressed out-of-towner.

But not everyone was caught up in the merriment.

Peter lingered near the punch bowl, his arms folded as he watched the dancers spin across the floor. The music grated more than it delighted. A burst of applause sent a spike down his spine. He needed air. He needed space. He slipped out the side door of Saratoga Hall just as the next tune began. The music faded behind him as he strode down the road, boots crunching on the gravel-strewn walk.

He wasn't in the mood for waltzes and ribbons. The flood of tourists this season set his teeth on edge, and the looming arrival of the Templar excursions from Boston and Missouri, among them those from New Orleans, stirred a deeper unease. Bringing the North and the South together in such close proximity could be a tinderbox, and Phillip Mouton could be the match. Yes—he knew the man. He was as surprised as anyone that night at dinner when Emma said his name. How did Claire know such a dangerous man?

Peter stepped into the smoky, shadowy interior of the Ten Pins and Billiard Hall, where the din of clinking glasses, loud voices, and the clack of billiard balls filled the room. Tourists and locals mingled with the buzz of holiday energy, but Peter Graham wasn't there to socialize. He just wanted a drink. He sat at the only empty stool at the bar and signaled for Frank Bowman's attention.

"What'll it be, Peter?"

"Double Scotch, neat."

"Thought you'd be at the hop," Frank said as he set the drink on the bar.

"Not my cup of tea."

Frank knew Peter—not well, but well enough to know the man was often sour. Still, Peter's mood seemed even darker than usual.

"Somethin' on yer mind?" Frank looked at Peter and leaned on the bar, indicating he expected a sincere answer.

Peter took a long draw from his drink.

"Just a feeling. The town is all aflutter with the booming season we are having, but I have a feeling trouble is on its way."

He swallowed the rest of his drink and ordered another.

"What trouble?" Frank said, placing the refill in front of Peter.

"The Knights Templar coming to town—all at once."

"I think the town can handle the crowd, don't you?"

"It's not the number of them," Peter said. "It's who they are. Boston men. Missouri men. New Orleans. All in one place —at the same time."

"Just a minute," Frank said as he went to attend to another customer.

Peter stared at his drink. Many people out west happily left their past behind, but some wounds weren't easily forgotten.

"What does where they're from have to do with anything?" Frank said when he rejoined Peter.

"Men from the North and the South here, in numbers, at the same time—it's a powder keg just waiting for a spark." Peter took another drink.

"Come on, Peter! They're good men, all part of the same society, here to enjoy the scenery on their way to the conclave. They're not looking for a fight."

"Where are you from, Frank?" Peter looked the bartender squarely in the eye.

"Iowa. What of it?"

"Not from the South. You don't understand how deep the resentment is still—and for a long time to come, I'd wager—in the South over the War Between the States. Mark my words, the situation is ripe for trouble."

❀

Back at the hop, Emma and Levi joined the other dancers on

the floor. The evening swept them up in its rhythm. Waltzes, reels, and polkas spun them across the floor. Emma danced with Willy once, and Levi with Christine. Claire danced with a visiting judge.

After their third dance ended, Levi stepped away to get refreshments. Emma fanned herself, her cheeks flushed with exertion and the warmth of the room.

The scotch had done little to settle the feeling in Peter's gut. He returned to Saratoga Hall just as a burst of laughter rose from the dancers. The room was warmer now, fuller, the air thick with perfume and exertion. He paused at the threshold, debating whether to go in.

The fiddler launched into another reel. Couples twirled past in a blur of bright fabrics and flushed cheeks. Peter's eyes skimmed the floor, noting familiar faces with practiced disinterest.

Near the center, John Calhoun Jr. gave a short bow and extended a hand to Emma Quinn. Peter barely registered the gesture before turning toward the refreshment table. He had no stake in their little ritual.

John Jr., oblivious to Peter's return, offered his hand. "May I have this one, Miss Quinn?"

A flush of guilt swept over Emma, remembering the lie she had told him at the bank.

"Yes, of course."

As they spun into a moderately paced quadrille, he leaned in just enough for her to hear.

"I haven't seen you since that day at the bank."

"I know. I've been so busy since then."

"I've missed your company."

Not knowing how to strike the right balance in her response, Emma remained silent.

John Jr. seemed to abandon that line of conversation and

went on.

"You've made quite the impression this season," he said. "You're becoming indispensable to the town."

"I hope to be. That's the idea," she replied with a small smile.

He hesitated, then added, "I don't mean to overstep, but I feel as your friend I should share some of the murmurings I've heard from people who may be involved in your future."

It wasn't like John Jr. to be indiscreet or to betray a trust. Whatever he had to share must be important.

"What murmurings?" Emma asked.

John Jr. took a deep breath before continuing.

"I'm sure he's a fine fellow," John said quickly, "but Ancha . . . he's not exactly the sort those of influence in town consider a proper association."

Emma's eyes narrowed slightly. "Proper association?"

"Well, appearances matter, Emma. Especially now, with the interviews so close."

Emma kept her steps even, but her shoulders stiffened. "You're suggesting I distance myself from someone I value because he's a Ute man?"

"Please, understand me. I have nothing against the man. He's lived peacefully here for years. But you need every advantage, and some may see your friendship with him as . . . well . . . imprudent. I only mean to spare you a setback."

The words struck like a slap. She had always liked John Jr.—trusted him. Yet beneath the polish of his concern lurked an unsettling bargain: that ambition required compromise, that principle must bend to respectability.

"I'll take your advice under consideration," she said coolly, breaking from the set before it ended and leaving him to trail after her.

Levi was waiting with her punch. John Jr. gave him a short

nod.

Levi returned it but said nothing. He handed Emma the glass, watching as John Jr. disappeared into the crowd.

"Is everything all right?" he asked.

"Yes." Her voice was clipped, her expression strained.

Levi waited, but she offered nothing more. When the next tune began, he set her empty glass aside, then simply reached for her hand and led her back to the floor.

With him, the tension eased. They moved together fluidly, with the unspoken trust of close companions—and something more, something just beginning to bloom.

Later, as they walked home, the streets still hummed with revelers. Laughter spilled from open windows and doorways, echoing against the mountains. But the boardinghouse stood quiet beneath the stars.

At the second-floor landing, they paused outside their suites. The hallway was dim and hushed. Emma reached for her doorknob, then hesitated. Levi stood just behind her, his hat in his hands.

"Thank you," she said, turning back toward him.

"For what?"

"For tonight. For being exactly the person I needed."

He stepped just a little closer, and for a moment she thought he might change his mind. But then he leaned in, brushed his lips lightly to her cheek—then, seeing no resistance, to her lips. It was brief and uncertain, but electric.

When he pulled back, Emma's heart was fluttering.

"Good night, Emma."

"Good night, Levi."

She stepped inside, closed the door gently behind her, and leaned against it, her smile wide and private in the dark.

❧ CHAPTER 24 ❧

Emma woke to birdsong carried by the mild morning breeze through her open window, gentle as the brush of a feather across her face. For a moment she lay still, waiting for her dreaming mind to return to reality.

Her first conscious thought was of the kiss.

Her heart skipped a beat, and she smiled. *What a kiss. More of that, please.* She and Levi had kissed before, not long after she arrived in the past. It had been in the heat of a dance lesson to music from her own time—admittedly, a bit steamy. She had been embarrassed and regretted it—well, maybe not as much as she should have, if she were being honest. Last night's kiss was different. It was deliberate and tender, every bit as erotic as the first, but for all the right reasons. It felt like a real beginning, not a mistake.

She thought about Levi's face after the kiss, as he slowly opened his eyes. His gentle, loving eyes. And those eyelashes. She had the urge to jump out of bed and go find him, but then anxiety clenched her chest.

Be careful. People behave differently now than in your time; you'll have to follow his lead.

Another memory interrupted her thoughts, making her even more unsettled but for entirely different reasons: John Jr.'s voice, low and polished, urging caution. Urging compromise. As though friendship with Ancha might tarnish her somehow.

Respectability requires compromise.

That was the implication. He hadn't said it outright, but it was there, a coarse thread pulled tight through the fabric of his words, impossible to ignore. She had trusted him. Admired him, even. But now . . . ?

Emma sat up, pushing the blanket aside. The air had become still, and it was already growing warm. She swung her legs over the edge of the bed and reached for her robe.

John Jr. had meant well—she believed that—but well-meaning didn't mean right.

Let the numbers speak, she reminded herself, echoing her own mantra from the day before. But numbers wouldn't speak to character. They wouldn't prove that friendship was not a liability, that integrity was not a hindrance to leadership.

But as for Levi . . . she smiled again at the memory.

❋

Levi adjusted his hat as he stepped off the boardinghouse porch, his boots striking the dirt with steady rhythm. The air was warm and clear, edged with wood smoke and the promise of another hot day. He reached Manitou Avenue, nodding to early risers tending shopfronts and sweeping walkways.

He had taken this route a hundred times, but today the familiar stretch felt different, like the air after a storm. Last night's kiss hadn't been planned, nor had it been impulsive. It had felt natural but full of energy. And now it lingered in his mind like persistent stirring, deep and slow.

He replayed it—the moment outside their doors, the way Emma had looked at him, the quiet between them brimming with anticipation. She hadn't pulled away. She hadn't seemed surprised. That, more than anything, stayed with him.

Levi stopped to speak briefly with the grocer about an incident the night before—a drunken argument near the stables that hadn't amounted to much. He made a note in his pocket ledger, then continued on, his mind returning to Emma.

He paused outside the BeeBee House, glancing up at the now-quiet windows. He wanted more time with her. Real time. Not just dances and brief exchanges in crowded rooms. *Be careful. She needs different things than most women. Follow her lead.*

As he passed Saratoga Hall—now quiet, the bunting limp in the morning stillness—he thought of the hop the night before, of John Calhoun Jr., of the tension palpable when Emma returned from that dance with him. She hadn't said much, but her voice had been tight, her shoulders rigid. Whatever had passed between them had bothered her. Was John Jr. persisting in his courtship against Emma's wishes?

The thought made Levi's jaw clench.

He tipped his hat lower against the sun and resumed his walk. He'd finish his rounds, then maybe see about a way to speak with her privately. No pressure. No expectations.

Whatever came next needed to start with that.

❀

Emma stepped into the inviting, light-filled reception room of Alice's spa, the air thick with the scent of juniper and mineral salts. A woman's high-pitched laugh cut through the low murmur of voices from the rooms beyond the reception area. Alice's daughter, Sarah, was at the desk.

"Good morning, Sarah! Is Alice available?" Emma asked the fresh-faced girl.

"I'll see, Miss Quinn. Please, have a seat." Sarah motioned to an overstuffed armchair. "There's lemon water in the pitcher, if you'd like."

Emma poured herself a glass and sat down.

"Emma!" Alice exclaimed as she came through the doorway to the back rooms. "I'm surprised to see you here. I thought you'd be recovering from Colorado Day. I heard the music from the hop well after midnight."

Emma smiled sheepishly. "It was quite a party, but I've been up since just after dawn."

"Are you here for your checkup?"

Alice had told Emma to see her again a few weeks after Emma's fainting spell.

"Yes. Things will be too busy soon, so I thought today was a good day. Besides, I wanted to talk to you about something."

"All right, then, come this way." Alice led Emma to a comfortable treatment room.

"What do you do in here?" Emma asked when Alice returned with her stethoscope, thinking the room too homey to be useful for any type of therapy.

"Facials."

Emma hadn't known Alice's services included facials, but she didn't pursue it. She sat as Alice took her pulse, listened to her heart, and plucked at the backs of her hands.

"Well, you're obviously taking better care of yourself," Alice said when she had finished. "Your face is fuller; your pulse is strong and regular. You are a little dehydrated, so keep an eye on that. How are you feeling?"

"Physically, I feel well—better than I have in some time," Emma admitted reluctantly.

"But otherwise?" Alice probed, detecting Emma's not-so-subtle hint.

"Oh, Alice," Emma sighed. "As they say, 'the world is too much with us.'"

"It was not 'they'; it was Wordsworth. But I'm glad his work is still known in your time. Be that as it may, can you be more specific?"

After Emma gave Alice a stream-of-consciousness summary of all that was weighing on her mind, she ended with, "And then last night after the dance, Levi and I kissed."

"Well, it's about time," Alice quipped.

Emma turned quickly to her friend. "What do you mean?"

"Oh, for heaven's sake. Anyone could see there were sparks between the two of you—have been from the start. Took you two long enough to figure it out."

Alice's matter-of-fact reaction eased some of the tension in Emma's shoulders. "It's all right, then—Levi and me?" *And what of it if it isn't?* Emma hadn't been aware that part of the burden she was carrying was concern about the appearance of that relationship.

"Well, of course it is. Levi has been a widower for a long time, and you are a suitable partner for him. Honestly, Emma, you do create a lot of your own drama." Alice put her hands on her hips.

"What about the advice John Jr. gave me?"

"That is a real dilemma," Alice admitted. "I'm afraid you

will have to decide if you're willing to take the risk to your job and your place in society if you persist in your relationship with Ancha. Look at it objectively. Not only are you nurturing the friendship, which I believe is innocent, if unconventional, you are also spending considerable time alone with him, which, my dear, is simply not proper. You've gotten away with it so far, but your luck will run out eventually."

Emma took in her friend's brutal advice. Alice was right, as usual. There was no easy answer for her. She would have to make a tough choice.

❀

The long oak table was already set when the household began to gather. The air was thick with the comforting scent of rosemary potatoes and stewed tomatoes. Molly moved efficiently between the kitchen and dining room, her apron dusted with flour and her cheeks flushed from the heat.

"Y'all sit before it gets cold," she said, setting a platter of roasted chicken on the table with a practiced thump. "I've been cooking for hours—don't make me come fetch you."

Claire stopped playing the piano and chuckled. "Yes, ma'am, Molly."

They took their places around the table and said grace. They murmured thanks and praise over the food as steaming bowls were passed. Claire noticed Levi and Emma glancing at each other when the other wasn't looking—more than once.

Willy dug in first, predictably. "That farworks display was somethin' else," he said, his mouth half-full. "Heard someone say they shipped in extra powder from Denver just for the finale."

Christine swatted his arm. "Don't talk with your mouth full."

"It was grand," Claire agreed, spooning creamed corn onto her plate. "And I haven't danced so much in years."

"I saw you spin that poor visiting judge until his spectacles fogged," Levi said with a grin.

Laughter circled the table.

Only Peter remained still, his plate untouched. He sat near the end of the table, arms resting on either side of his chair, his gaze unfixed. Claire noticed.

"You didn't dance, Peter," she said gently.

"No," he replied. "Not much for crowds."

"You came, though," Christine said with some surprise. "That's something."

Peter gave a brief nod but offered nothing more.

Emma, who had stayed quiet until now, reached for her water glass. "I had a conversation with John Jr. last night." She wasn't sure how wise it was to mention it.

Claire raised an eyebrow. "Oh?"

Levi sat straighter in his chair.

Emma set down her glass. "He warned me that some people might view my friendships as . . . impractical—said appearances matter if I want the Board's support for the tourism position."

A hush fell over the table. Even Willy paused mid-chew.

Levi's voice was low. "He said something about Ancha, didn't he?"

Emma nodded. "Without saying it outright. But it was clear."

Peter stirred, not looking up. "Accepting social norms maintains order," he said.

Emma looked at him, wondering exactly what he meant.

Claire, breaking the tension, said, "Well, anyone who knows you would take you as you are. The results you've achieved are irrefutable."

Emma smiled faintly. "Thanks. But I'm learning not everyone's ready for someone like me."

"Don't back down, Miss Emma. You're the brightest star 'round here," Willy said.

"That's right!" Christine echoed.

Conversation drifted on. Molly returned with pie—blackberry, still warm—and the mood lightened with coffee and the soft clatter of forks on china.

But Peter stayed quiet, his pie untouched. And Claire, for all her good cheer, watched him closely, as if sensing a tide turning that the rest of them hadn't yet seen.

❀

After dinner, the residents all went their separate ways. Emma, hoping for some quiet time on the porch, found Levi already there, quietly rocking and puffing his pipe. She paused in the doorway, her heart lifting at the sight of him.

She reminded herself: follow his lead. No assumptions. No pushing. Just the comfort of his company.

"Mind if I join you?" she asked.

Levi turned, surprised but clearly pleased. "Not at all. I'd welcome it."

He shifted slightly as she took the rocker beside him. He'd told himself the same thing only moments ago: let her set the pace. Don't push, don't hope. Just be grateful she's here.

They watched the light soften over the foothills, letting the rhythm of the rockers fill the silence between them. The air carried a faint scent of tobacco mingled with pine and earth. Somewhere down the avenue, someone was playing a fiddle.

Emma finally spoke. "Did you notice Peter at supper?"

Levi nodded once. "Yes. Withdrawn and curt, even for him."

"He hardly touched his food."

They sat in silence again, then Emma added, "He seems worried about all the tourists, particularly about the Templars from the North and the South being here at the same time."

"He has a point, I'm afraid," Levi said quietly.

The rockers rolled out a slow, steady rumble beneath them, like thunder from a distant storm.

❧ CHAPTER 25 ❧

"**H**urry, Miss Emma! You'll miss the train!" Emma heard Willy call from the bottom of the stairs. She was giving her hair a final inspection in the upstairs bathroom mirror. The solution of gum arabic and rose water that Christine had shared to keep her hair in place seemed to be doing its job. *Please behave yourself just this once,* Emma begged her unruly locks. She quickly pinned her hat to her hair.

"I'm coming!" she called back.

She grabbed her folio containing several copies of her carefully prepared report to the Board of Directors of the Colorado Springs Company. Today was her interview for director of tourism, and she was taking the first morning train to Colorado Springs, where the company was headquartered.

Willy had thoughtfully readied a wagon to take her to the train so she wouldn't get dust on her best outfit.

"Come along, come along!" Claire waved Emma urgently toward the door. "You look lovely, my dear. Now hurry!" Claire gave Emma a quick peck on the cheek followed by an encouraging pat.

Willy helped Emma onto the wagon, jumped in quickly beside her, and gave the horse the signal to move with some speed.

"Ya look mighty fine, Miss Emma," Willy said as the wagon lurched into motion.

They hit a hole in the road. "Oh!" Emma squealed, reaching up to steady her hat.

"Sorry 'bout that," Willy said, tightening the reins.

They reached the train depot just as the last of the passengers were boarding. Emma spotted Levi standing on the platform, hands in his pockets, eyes scanning the crowd— waiting for her.

She approached him. "Are you heading to Colorado Springs?" she asked, catching the rail of the nearest car.

"No, but I wasn't going to let the train leave without you." He smiled. "Good luck, my dear. I know you'll do brilliantly."

Her heart swelled. He was always there for her. She leaned over and gave him a kiss on the cheek.

"Thanks, Levi."

The train lurched. Emma turned and climbed aboard, her footsteps light but purposeful. She waved to Levi through the window as the platform began to slide away.

She took a deep breath. She'd cut that entirely too close. Normally, she enjoyed staring out the window at the scenery between Manitou and Colorado Springs, letting her mind wander. But today she used the time to review her talking points and report, rehearsing one last time before the interview.

Still, her thoughts drifted briefly to Levi. Since the kiss, they'd had precious little time together, but their intentions were clear now, and they had moved forward with comfortable ease. Having to wait until the Templars were here and gone before they could resume their courtship only sweetened the anticipation.

The train's arrival in Colorado Springs brought her back from her pleasant reverie. When she exited the station, she began looking for a hack to hire. The walk to East Huerfano Street wasn't far—nothing was very far in 1883 Colorado Springs—but she did want to avoid the street dirt.

"Miss Quinn?" a young man approached her.

"Yes?"

"I'm here to take you to the board meeting. Follow me, please. My rig is right here."

Emma was surprised. Someone—she suspected Albright—had made arrangements for her. The formality both impressed and weighed on her.

The driver helped her down and led her up the stairs of the office building to the second floor. He opened the door and announced her to the reception clerk, a man of about thirty.

"Follow me, Miss Quinn," the clerk said, leading her to the boardroom. He opened the door and, after confirming the board was ready for her, stepped aside and allowed her through.

Inside, she saw the board members. General Palmer was both the president of the company and the chair of the board. She was well acquainted with him and nodded back when he acknowledged her entrance. Dr. Bell, the vice chair, was less well known to her, but he smiled a greeting. George H. Parsons had been the secretary and treasurer since the company's inception in 1871. He was occupied writing in his notepad.

There were two other members: Mr. Nichols, proprietor of the Cliff House, and James E. Ellis Jr., who had designed the bathhouse. The last man in the room was Mr. Albright, whose role on the board Emma suddenly realized she didn't know.

Mr. Albright stood and reached out a hand. "Miss Quinn. Good to see you."

"Thank you for having me," Emma said. She followed his formal lead and shook the hand he offered, then inclined her head politely to the other gentlemen.

General Palmer gestured to a chair at the end of the long table. "Please, Miss Quinn, join us. We've looked forward to hearing your vision for the position of director of tourism and how you would fulfill it if selected."

Emma took her seat, carefully placing her folio on the table. "Thank you, General. I look forward to sharing that vision."

After General Palmer made the formal introductions, Emma began. "I've prepared an updated analysis of the season's tourism results, along with a brief summary." She opened her folio and passed copies of her report down the table.

"This appears quite thorough," General Palmer said, flipping through his copy. He looked up. "Please walk us through your findings."

Emma began with a clear and concise comparison of last season with the current one, showing an average increase of 20 percent in hotel and boardinghouse occupancy rates—the only comparative data available.

"And now for the analysis based on the performance goals the board outlined," Emma continued. "Tourism in Manitou and Colorado Springs has steadily increased from June to July, with notable gains in hotel and boardinghouse occupancy, as well as shop sales and attraction revenue. Visitor spending across the participating establishments rose by approximately 12 percent in July compared to June." She paused again before adding what she thought was her clearest victory. "And with the arrival of the Knights Templar, I expect a 20 percent surge based on advance bookings."

"That's a significant increase," Mr. Parsons acknowledged. "But is there an error, Miss Quinn? The bathhouse results appear flat."

"No, I have confirmed the numbers more than once. The results are as reported."

"Interesting," Mr. Nichols said, flipping through the document. "I believe we all expected the new bathhouse to be a primary draw to the area. Wasn't it a centerpiece in your publicity campaign earlier this year?"

Mr. Ellis frowned. "Do you believe the facility is to blame?" he asked before she could respond to Mr. Nichols.

"Not at all," Emma answered Mr. Ellis first. "The bathhouse is beautifully designed and constructed, and the landscaping adds elegance to the town." She paused for effect before continuing. "The analysis suggests it lacks consistent promotion. Attendance is flat and far below capacity. Hours are comparatively limited. I've included guest commentaries in the back section of the report. As you will see, there is also a perception that it's too expensive for some visitors, especially those staying in modest accommodations."

Dr. Bell leaned forward. "And how would you address this?"

"I've proposed a promotional bundle—discounted bathhouse entries combined with lodging and attractions, such as The Narrows, burro rides to Pikes Peak, or excursions to Garden of the Gods or Seven Falls. It's a way to integrate services and encourage longer stays. Additionally, I recommend clearer signs, perhaps colorful banners, and a revised rate structure during off-peak hours. Extending the women-only hours would also help, I believe."

There was a pause as the board absorbed her suggestions.

The members seemed genuinely concerned about the bathhouse results. Emma resisted the temptation to say more. *Don't talk past the close,* she remembered Albright had once said to her.

General Palmer exchanged a look with Dr. Bell, then addressed Emma again. "Miss Quinn, some members of the board are concerned about your association with individuals who may be seen as unconventional or even controversial. Do you believe your personal relationships impact your ability to represent the town's best interests?"

Emma's jaw tensed, but she met his gaze squarely. "General, I believe that character is best judged by action and results. My relationships are guided by respect, fairness, and the values this town was founded on—your and Dr. Bell's values—values I believe we all share. I let the numbers speak for themselves, and I stand by my record."

A silence followed. Not hostile—thoughtful.

Albright's mouth twitched, just slightly.

General Palmer gave a small nod. "Thank you, Miss Quinn. That will be all for now. We'll notify you of our decision soon."

Emma rose and offered a composed smile to each board member. "Thank you for your time."

She stepped into the hallway, her heart thudding harder than it had all morning.

❧ CHAPTER 26 ❧

"**F**or all that is holy, Emma, stop bouncing," Mr. Albright ordered.

Emma stood beside her boss at the train depot, bobbing on her toes and craning to see farther down the railway.

"I can't help it, I'm so nervous," she said.

Not only was she eager for the arrival of the first wave of Templars from Boston, she was also still rattled by the news Albright had shared that morning in the office.

"Well, Wright's gone and shown his true colors," he had said, hooking his hat on the wall rack with more force than necessary.

"What do you mean?" Emma asked. She guessed he was referring to Wright's interview, which had taken place the previous day.

"That bastard showed them false numbers for the bathhouse, then had the gall to suggest your analysis was flawed in general—cast doubt on everything you claimed during your interview."

"What?" Emma had leapt from her chair, stunned.

Albright slammed his folio on his desk and raked his hand through his hair.

"I'm sorry, Emma." He turned to her and shook his head slowly. "I should have anticipated he'd do something like this. It's just like him."

Emma stood there, dumbstruck, trying to keep her balance as the floor of her dreams cratered into an abyss.

Albright took a breath and, in a softer tone, added, "All's not lost. The men on the board tolerate Wright—he's had good ideas now and then, and there's some old army loyalty between him, Palmer, and Bell. But they know him. I've spoken to them. You've still got a shot. I'm just angry—at him, and at myself—for not anticipating he'd lie."

Emma tried to let his words act as a balm, but angry tears pooled in her eyes and fell down her cheeks when she blinked.

He gently took her hands. "Steady now. The board won't finalize anything until their next regular meeting later this month. I'll keep talking to them. For now, let's focus. The Templars start arriving today—and all your work is about to be put to the test."

So here they were, waiting for the Boston contingent. The next few days would determine the success of Emma's months of planning. She'd known it would be high stakes work. But now—thanks to Wright—they were higher still.

❋

"Well, all the Templars from both the Boston and Missouri contingents have arrived and checked in at their hotels," Emma reported to Albright later that day. "There was a minor hitch here at the Manitou House, but we got it sorted quickly, and everyone seemed satisfied."

Albright swiveled in his chair and looked out the window. "It's bustling, all right. Looks like a lot of fellas are heading to the billiards hall."

A steady parade of Templars was moving toward the establishment next door to the Manitou House hotel.

"I hope Frank is all stocked up." Emma grinned as she leaned over her boss's shoulder to see the crowd.

"Maybe I'll head over there myself." Albright stood and grabbed his hat. Before leaving, he turned and added, "So far, so good, Emma."

She looked back at him. "Yes, so far, so good." Then she turned to the window again. *Good thing there aren't any fire codes. That hall's packed to the rafters.* A steady stream of men still poured in.

She watched Albright stroll toward the entrance of the establishment and disappear inside. Just as she was about to turn away, she spotted Levi approaching from the train depot. He paused briefly to hold the door open for a small group of men, then stepped inside behind them.

The Ten Pins and Billiards Hall thrummed with masculine energy—boots scuffed the floorboards, low-pitched laughter rumbled beneath the haze of cigar smoke, and the sharp crack of billiard balls competed with the thud of falling pins. The Boston men, just returned from a leisurely wagon tour of the Garden of the Gods, had claimed the corner tables near the windows and were taking turns at billiards. Clad in jacquard vests and neatly tied cravats, they were overdressed for Manitou but seemed perfectly at ease in their formality. Two men stood slightly away from the rest, awaiting their turns.

"Remarkable formations," said the stocky one, swirling a small glass of brandy. "That great red boulder—what did the driver call it? 'Balanced Rock'? Defies sense, sitting up there like that."

The tall man gave a quiet sniff of agreement. "Yes. Though I favored the 'Kissing Camels.' The whole place feels like a cathedral built by nature. I understand why the Utes consider it sacred."

"Quite so." The stocky man nodded.

The rest of their conversation was lost in the growing din. From across the room came the louder, earthier voices of the Missouri contingent—heels striking the boards, cue sticks tapping, and laughter rolling like thunder.

The mood in the hall, though outwardly genial, carried the unmistakable weight of division. The Boston men clustered near the windows, speaking in measured tones and sipping from short glasses with practiced grace. Every gesture, from the tilt of a head to the flick of an ash, was precise. Across the room, the men from Missouri, Texas, and Louisiana had gathered closer to the bar—boots stretched out, vests unbuttoned, voices booming. Where the Bostonians gave off the air of a gentlemen's club, the Missouri contingent carried themselves like men who measured worth in grit, not pedigree.

At one of the long tables, the most polished, swarthiest of the group—a silver-templed man with a neatly trimmed beard —leaned back in his chair, a faint smile playing at his lips. He was better dressed than most of his companions—his shirt clean, his boots shined—and he carried himself with quiet authority.

He lifted his glass and nodded toward the Boston contingent. "Looks like nothing's changed," he said in a smooth drawl, just loud enough for his table. "Those Yankees still think they're better than the rest."

Some of the men around him chuckled; others tightened their stare at their northern brothers. One of the latter added in a sinister tone, "They think the war is over; that's where they're wrong."

Levi walked with purpose toward the Missouri group. "I figured I'd find you here, Phillip," he said flatly.

"Well, if it isn't Levi Warwick." Phillip set down his glass without breaking eye contact. "Been a long while."

"Could I have a word?" Levi said—all business.

"No 'hello'? No 'it's good to see you'? I must say, Levi, seems like you've forgotten your manners."

Levi's eyes swept the hall before he said, "I haven't forgotten anything." He looked back at Phillip Mouton. "Can I have a word?" he repeated.

Phillip Mouton gave the men around him an apologetic glance and stood.

"Lead the way." He gestured for Levi to walk ahead of him toward the bar.

"Can I buy you a drink?" Phllip offered.

"I'm not here to socialize with you, Phillip." Levi kept his eyes steady on the other man's. "I'm here to warn you. I don't know why you came . . ."

"Well, the Templars decided to make this a stop on the excursion," Phillip interrupted. "But when I learned Claire—and you, of course—were here . . . well, that was just icing on the cake." He licked his lips and grinned slowly.

"Well, you've wasted your time. I'm here to tell you: stay away from Claire. You've done her enough harm. Leave her alone."

"Or what?" Phillip stared back at Levi.

"I've protected her from you before; I'll do it again. Don't test me."

Levi turned and walked out of the hall, leaving Phillip standing alone at the bar.

Neither man noticed Peter Graham behind the column, watching.

❧ CHAPTER 27 ❧

AUGUST 13, 1883

Monday morning dawned bright and clear, the kind of August day that made Manitou Springs look like a picture postcard—sunlight slanting through cottonwoods, glittering off Fountain Creek. Shopkeepers unlocked their doors. Hotel clerks readied their guest registers. A milk wagon clattered along Manitou Avenue.

The Boston men lingered over breakfast at the Manitou House, trading travel stories and commenting on the previous day's excursion. Meanwhile, the Missouri contingent—who had rooms at the BeeBee House and the Barker House—gathered out front of the livery stable, where a guide waited to lead them up Pikes Peak. A slow wagon ride through the Garden of the Gods had been deemed far too tame for their tastes.

"Brother Larson, I believe we're too heavy for these burros," said Brother Strope, eyeing the animals with dismay.

Larson laughed. "I, for one, would bring the poor beast to its knees! No, no—we're not riding them. They're here to carry our supplies—food, water, gear."

Brother Strope, ever the soft-hearted man, let out a sigh of relief.

Larson scanned the group and counted heads. "Well, it looks like everyone's here."

Strope frowned, looking around. "Isn't Brother Mouton joining us?"

"I told him to sign up at the front desk if he wanted to," Larson replied. "I got the feeling he had something else to do today."

"He's a mystery, that one," Strope muttered. "Hardly said a word the whole way from St. Louis."

"He did become markedly reserved once we joined the Texas and Missouri chapters."

Strope nodded, then gestured toward a man approaching with a tripod and camera case. "Looks like the photographer's here."

Back at the BeeBee House, Phillip Mouton sat at a window table in the dining room, savoring a quiet breakfast and scanning that morning's edition of the *Colorado Springs Gazette*.

"Mind if I join you?"

Phillip looked up at the man standing before him, recognition slowly dawning. He folded the paper with deliberate precision and laid it aside.

"Well, well, well," he said, with the faintest trace of a smirk. "Didn't expect to see an old customer. Yes, by all means —have a seat."

❀

The tenants of Maison La Salle left the boardinghouse early. Levi, aware of rising tensions in town, had begun his rounds before sunrise. Willy worked nearly around the clock at the livery, lured by generous tips from out-of-towners. Christine was bracing for laundry day at the Manitou House, thankful extra help had been hired for the laundress. Emma had already settled into her desk, eager to dive into last week's tourist reports. Peter opened the bookstore an hour ahead of schedule, hoping to sell more newspapers.

And Claire—Claire was grateful for the quiet.

With the house to herself, she gave Molly the day off. There would be no meals served to tenants today. She thought about visiting Alice later. She hadn't seen much of her since the spa opened. She missed her friend—though she was proud of her success and glad to have invested in it. Humming a familiar tune, Claire carried the basket of laundry to hang on the line in the backyard.

She continued humming as she pinned a damp sheet to the clothesline. A breeze flapped the fabric against her arm as she reached for the next clothespin. She worked in rhythm—shake, pin, repeat—as the sheets billowed like sails in the breeze.

Claire heard the wall clock from the hallway faintly chime half past ten. Her arms ached pleasantly from the work, and her dress smelled faintly of soap and sunshine.

She set the empty basket on the kitchen table and shut the back door. A faint breeze brushed her cheek—where was it coming from?

She stepped into the hallway. The front door was open.

"Hello?"

No answer.

She crossed the floor and shut the door, then turned toward the parlor.

She gasped.

There, lying facedown on the floor, was a man—a dagger jutting from his back.

She ran to him and knelt. Was he still alive?

Then she saw his face.

Phillip Mouton.

A strangled cry escaped her throat as she stood and stumbled back, one hand pressed to her mouth.

The front door opened. Claire heard the voices, but she couldn't move.

Emma froze in the threshold, Levi just behind her.

"Claire?" Her voice faltered as she took in the scene—the body on the floor, Claire's trembling hands.

"Oh my God . . ."

❧ Chapter 28 ❧

"I have to find the mayor. Latch the door behind me—the back one too—then take Claire to her quarters. Pour her a brandy," Levi said calmly, though his eyes darted as he spoke.

Emma nodded, understanding but frozen in place.

"Quickly!" he urged.

That snapped her into motion. After he left, she turned to Claire and approached slowly, as if nearing a wild creature she didn't want to startle. Claire was still staring at Mouton's body, her hand pressed over her mouth.

"Come, my dear," Emma whispered. "Let's go to your rooms."

Claire let Emma take her trembling hand and followed without a word, like a child.

In Claire's parlor, Emma took Claire to the bathroom and washed her face. She checked Claire's hands and clothes for bloodstains but found none. She guided Claire back to her sitting room and poured a tall glass of brandy for her.

"Drink this."

Claire blinked. "It's too early," she said, her voice distant and confused.

"Yes, it's early, but it's to calm you. Drink it, my dear."

Levi returned with Mayor Nichols sooner than Emma expected—the same Nichols who ran the Cliff House across the street and the same one she'd interviewed with as a board member just days earlier. She let them both in when she heard the urgent knock at the door. Nichols gave her a quick nod of greeting but said nothing as he followed Levi to the body on the floor. Emma returned to tend to Claire.

Moments later, Levi stood beside the body, arms folded, jaw set. The room smelled of lemon and wood polish. Behind him, Mayor Nichols paced nervously.

He stopped beside the body and exhaled sharply through his nose.

"Well," he said at last. "God help us."

He crouched beside the body but didn't touch it. He only looked, taking in the angle of the shoulders, the blade's handle, the pooling stain on the dead man's coat.

"Looks like a letter opener," he observed.

"Yes, I recognize the handle. It's usually on the hall table," Levi offered.

After a moment, Nichols straightened. "He's an out-of-towner. Any idea who he is?" he asked, still looking at the victim.

Levi nodded. "Yes."

Nichols's head snapped from the body to Levi. "Who is he?" the mayor demanded.

"His name is Phillip Mouton. He's from New Orleans."

Nichols smoothed back his thinning hair, then pinched the bridge of his nose. "A murder in a respectable boardinghouse during high season—and on top of that, a Knights Templar. How the devil do you know him?"

"We were acquainted—years ago back in New Orleans."

"Is that why he's here, at your residence?"

"I don't know why he's here. I wasn't expecting him." Levi considered the words—not quite a lie, but more hopeful than true.

"And Claire? She knew him, too?"

"Yes."

The mayor looked out the window, toward the main street he could picture lined with carriages and promenading guests.

"This could be a disaster, Levi, for the area, our reputation."

He paused, then added, "And you know as well as I do—you can't be in charge of this."

Levi bristled. "I'm the most qualified."

"You also know the victim. And the woman you found standing over the body is your sister-in-law." Nichols sighed. "Dammit, Levi, the situation is bad enough. This is a mess, and I need you clear of it so I can manage the fallout. I'll call Sheriff Dana and the coroner. Once I do, this will be all over town."

They stood for a moment in silence, the weight of it all pressing down.

Nichols put his hat back on. "For what it's worth, I trust you'll help. Quietly. Not officially."

Levi gave a single nod, eyes still on the body. "Understood."

Nichols left to make his calls, the weight of the scandal already shifting to his shoulders. Levi lingered a moment, then turned and quietly joined Emma and Claire.

Claire sat curled in her armchair, brandy untouched on the side table. Her hands were folded tightly in her lap, white-knuckled, as if releasing them might break loose her controlled emotions.

Emma was sitting on the sofa. She looked up expectantly when Levi entered.

He closed the door gently behind him.

"Did the mayor leave?" she asked.

Levi nodded and moved to stand near Claire. He looked at her calmly, then answered Emma.

"He's seen the body. We've spoken."

Claire remained silent. Her gaze dropped to her hands.

Emma stood. "What did he say?"

"That I can't be involved in the investigation," Levi said quietly. "Because I knew Phillip." He paused and looked at Claire. "And so did you."

Claire blinked. "But—" Her voice cracked. "But you're the best one to handle this."

"It will be all right," Levi said, and something in his voice cracked too—barely.

Emma stepped closer. "Who, then, if not you?"

"Nichols will ask the sheriff to send someone—someone impartial."

There was a long silence.

Claire looked up at him, pale and dazed. "I didn't kill him, Levi."

He met her eyes. "I know."

Emma moved to stand beside Claire, resting a hand gently on her shoulder.

"But officially," Levi continued, "I can't be part of the case. Unofficially . . ." He gave Emma a glance that said more than his words did. It wouldn't be the first time they had pursued the truth without authority—but the stakes had never been this high.

Claire closed her eyes. A tear slipped free, but she said nothing.

❦ CHAPTER 29 ❧

Levi sat bolt upright in the hallway chair outside the El Paso County sheriff's office, shoulders tight. It was the morning after Phillip Mouton's body had been discovered. Mayor Nichols had summoned him. Levi clung to a sliver of hope that the mayor and others in authority had reconsidered excluding him from the formal investigation—but that hope waned with each tick of the wall clock. If not for that, why had they called him?

The office door creaked open. Sheriff Dana stepped into the hallway, his expression unreadable.

"Levi," he said. "Come on in."

He and the sheriff were on good terms, which made his stiff formality all the more unsettling.

In the office, Levi found the mayor and a man he knew,

though not well, as Edward Clark. Both men stood when he entered.

"Thank you for coming, Levi," Mayor Nichols said. His voice carried an edge of discomfort. The gratitude was perfunctory; Levi hadn't been given much of a choice. He dipped his head in silent acknowledgment.

"Levi," the mayor continued, "this is Mr. Edward Clark, from Denver. He will be the special prosecutor handling the Mouton case. I requested his appointment, with the sheriff's backing. He has an excellent reputation with General Palmer."

Clark, dressed in a dark, crisply pressed suit, stepped forward and extended his hand. His gaze was sharp beneath heavy brows.

"We've met," Clark said to the mayor, then turned to Levi. "Good to see you again, Mr. Warwick."

Edward Clark had defended Josiah Turner the previous fall in an equally serious case. Levi knew him to be shrewd and highly competent. He was a good choice as far as the leaders and businessmen of the community were concerned, though maybe at the expense of the accused. Naming him special prosecutor meant they were serious about holding someone accountable and restoring the area's reputation.

Levi took Clark's offered hand. "Mr. Clark."

Clark gave a courteous nod. "Mr. Warwick. I understand the circumstances are delicate. My aim is to proceed thoroughly—and without unnecessary disruption to your town or its people."

The men each took a seat around the sheriff's desk. Sheriff Dana opened a cedar cigar box and offered it around. All three declined politely.

Once settled, Mayor Nichols cleared his throat.

"I reckon you're wondering why you're here," he said, looking to Levi.

Levi nodded, his tone guarded. "Yes. My understanding was that I'd been taken off the case. Has that changed?"

"No, no, I'm afraid not," the mayor answered. "We simply thought you should know where things stand—who's in charge. Ground rules, that sort of thing."

"This has to be handled strictly by the book," the sheriff added. "No mistakes."

Levi took no offense. In a small town with only a marshal, practicality often meant bending rules and the letter of the law. Everyone understood that and normally agreed to it. But this situation called for a more disciplined approach.

He nodded again and began answering the men's questions.

"Thank you, Levi," Clark said when they had finished. "Can I trust that you will see to it Miss Quinn and Mrs. La Salle join you at the inquest this afternoon?"

"Yes. We'll be there," Levi promised.

✺

Alice gently touched the sleeve of Claire's dress. "Try to eat something, my dear. You haven't had a bite since yesterday, if then."

It was the morning after the terrible shock Claire had suffered—finding Mouton, the man she had hoped she would never see again, dead on her floor.

Alice had arrived at Claire's door just moments after Sheriff Dana and Mr. Perkins, the coroner. The men were examining and preparing to remove Mouton's stiffening body from the boardinghouse. They had stood in her path, not allowing her to get close to the scene, but she did see the handle of the weapon protruding from the dead man's back. In the past, they had occasionally, and reluctantly, solicited her medical opinion on deaths. But this time she was as compromised as Levi and Claire, and she would not get an opportunity to examine this victim, even as a professional courtesy.

She found Claire in her quarters, Emma gently coaxing her to drink a brandy.

"Oh, Alice!" Emma ran to the doctor and hugged her. "I'm so glad you're here. I think Claire is in shock."

"Well, of course she's in shock. Anyone would be." Alice walked over to Claire and wrapped her arms around the silent, staring woman.

"How did you hear about it?" Emma asked.

"When the mayor called the sheriff, the operator was listening. It was all over town before the call was finished." Alice's disapproval was plain on her face, as if she'd smelled something rotten.

She turned back to Claire. "My dear, Emma is right. Take a sip of the brandy, won't you?"

Claire stirred at the sound of Alice's voice. "Alice . . . what are you doing here?" she asked weakly.

"Where else would I be? Now, do as I say and take a sip."

Claire looked down at the glass in her hands as if noticing it for the first time. She raised it to her lips. After a few sips, Alice gently took the glass and set it on the table. She checked Claire's pulse and touched her forehead.

"Yes, yes . . ." she cooed, as if to a baby. "You've had a terrible shock, my dear. I'll stay with you. You'll be fine." She turned back to Emma. "Where's Levi?"

"I'm not sure," Emma said, seemingly surprised he wasn't there. "He went with the mayor to meet the sheriff. That's the last I've seen of him."

"I'll stay with her," Alice said, leaving no room for debate. "She's in no physical danger, but it may take some time for her nerves to recover."

"Thank you. I'm at loose ends. I only came back this morning because I forgot my brooch watch." Emma glanced at the clock. A wave of panic crossed her face. "Oh no—I was supposed to meet Albright two hours ago to go over the financials." She looked back at Claire, torn.

"I can handle this," Alice said, reading her thoughts. "I'll take her to my place."

Emma hesitated.

"It's all right. Now go," Alice repeated gently.

After Emma left, Alice telephoned the spa and asked Sarah to come help her pack Claire's things: she would be staying with them awhile.

❀

Levi jumped off the train before it came to a full stop and strode quickly from the depot. He needed to get Claire and Emma to the inquest, and there wasn't much time. They needed to take the early afternoon train back to Colorado Springs.

During the short walk, he reflected on everything that had happened since he and Emma had found Claire standing over Mouton's lifeless form. After he had escorted the sheriff and the coroner to the scene, he discreetly left, taking advantage of the fact they didn't want him there anyway. He went to the BeeBee House, where he knew many of the Missouri contingent were lodging. After confirming that Mouton had been staying there, he made sure the man's room was secured and left undisturbed. There might be vital evidence there. That done, he went by the billiards hall, where the news of the murder had already stirred the customers into a loud and anxious buzz. In a back corner, he had pulled Frank aside for a quiet word. Their brief exchange confirmed what he already suspected: the tension between the northern and southern Templar delegations had been simmering from the moment they arrived. How this case would ever be resolved was beyond him.

For the first time, he almost felt relieved it wasn't his responsibility anymore.

Emma, who had been anxious since arriving at the office, was looking out the window when Levi came out of depot. Seeing the determination in his step, she grabbed her hat, gloves, and shawl, and headed out the door.

"Where are you going?" Albright asked.

"I see Levi. He's back from his meeting with the sheriff. I must go—sorry."

Emma rushed out the door, closing it loudly behind her.

Albright remained at his desk, staring at the door. The weight of what had happened hadn't escaped him. Mouton's murder wasn't just a tragedy—it was a crack in the foundation of everything they were trying to build. And Emma—Emma was in the thick of it now.

He exhaled strongly through his nose and looked back at his papers, which suddenly felt irrelevant.

"I saw you from my window. Is everything all right?" Emma said, short of breath, as she approached Levi.

"The inquest is this afternoon. We all need to be there." Levi said.

"Claire is probably at Alice's by now. She's unwell, Levi. I'm worried about her."

They walked quickly to Alice's spa.

"Sarah, I'm looking for Claire," Levi said without preamble when they entered the spa's reception area.

"She's in our living quarters with mother." She told them, the concern showing on her young face. "Go on through."

They found Claire sitting in an armchair nearest the back

window of Alice's sitting room, staring blankly.

"Claire, my dear," Levi murmured, leaning close.

She blinked but didn't otherwise respond.

"Claire, I'm here to take you to the inquest. It's this afternoon," he continued gently.

"No, you're not," came a voice behind him.

Levi turned to find Alice standing there, hands planted on her hips.

"Alice, we have no choice," he said.

"Maybe you don't. But I won't let a patient of mine in this condition testify. Frankly, I'm not sure she's even legally competent to."

Levi looked back at Claire and tended to agree. But it wasn't that simple.

"See here, Alice—the coroner, the sheriff, the mayor—every man on the jury, most likely—knows how close you are to Claire. Many know she's the financial backer for this spa. If you're seen interfering in her testimony, you may do more harm than good."

Alice pursed her lips, her brow creased in thought.

"Well, then I'm coming too. Let me fetch a shawl for Claire."

Emma stood helplessly. Things were happening so fast, and her instincts told her this wasn't good for any of them.

❋

Levi steadied Claire as she stepped down from the train, his hand firm beneath her elbow, Alice close behind. Claire's expression was still distant, but she walked without prompting. Emma followed them off the train, her gloves clutched tightly in one hand.

"How are you feeling, dear?" Emma asked Claire.

Claire blinked, her gaze not quite landing. "I'm cold," she said simply.

Alice wrapped the shawl more tightly around her shoulders. "She'll be able to speak, I think. But don't expect clarity or insight."

Levi nodded and glanced toward the courthouse up the street. "We'd best not be late."

By three o'clock, the small courtroom was crowded and close. A few townspeople had come out of morbid curiosity, but most of the seats were filled with familiar faces—Mayor Nichols, Sheriff Dana, and the men of the coroner's jury, summoned that morning. The Templars who might have been interested were unable to attend. They were already leaving for San Francisco.

Claire sat beside Alice on a bench near the front, her hands folded in her lap. Levi sat next to Alice, while Emma sat stiffly on the other side of Claire, acutely aware of every glance cast in their direction.

Mr. Perkins, the county coroner, opened the proceedings in a flat voice.

"This inquest is convened to determine the cause and manner of death of one Phillip Mouton, found deceased in the Maison La Salle boardinghouse on Cañon Avenue yesterday morning. As the jury has already examined the body and reviewed the preliminary findings of Dr. Wiley, we will now proceed with witness testimony."

A murmur rippled through the gallery.

Levi kept his expression unreadable, but he could feel the tension rising in his body.

The courtroom fell into an uneasy hush as Mr. Perkins cleared his throat and shuffled his notes.

"I'll begin by calling our first witness," he announced, looking toward the seating area where Claire sat pale and motionless.

Before he could say her name, Alice rose from her seat.

"Mr. Perkins," she said clearly, her voice measured but firm, "as Mrs. La Salle's physician, I must object to her testifying at this time. She is in a state of psychological shock, and in my professional opinion, testifying now could cause lasting harm. Furthermore, I question whether she is currently capable of giving reliable testimony."

A murmur rippled through the room. Perkins blinked, thrown off balance. He looked to Clark.

The special prosecutor stood, smoothing his vest. "We all recognize Mrs. La Salle's importance in this matter. But we also have an obligation to ensure the integrity of her testimony—and of these proceedings. The medical objection is noted and will be entered into the record."

He turned toward the jurors. "In the interest of proceeding without delay, I recommend we begin with Miss Quinn, who was also present at the scene shortly after the body was discovered."

Emma straightened slightly in her seat. She hadn't expected to go first, but the weight of it settled quickly. She looked at Levi, who gave her a small nod of encouragement.

Clark gestured to the witness chair. "Miss Quinn, if you please."

Emma crossed the room and took her seat at the front of the chamber, smoothing her skirt before folding her hands tightly in her lap. Her pulse beat fast, but steady, beneath her collar.

"Miss Quinn," Clark said, standing before her. "Please state your full name for the record."

"Emma Lella Quinn."

"And your current residence?"

"The Maison La Salle boardinghouse in Manitou."

"Your occupation?"

"Assistant to the director of economic development for the Colorado Springs Company. I also assist with town promotion and tourism reporting."

Clark gave a single nod, glancing briefly at the paper in front of him. "Now, Miss Quinn, tell us what happened on the morning of August 13. Start from when you arrived at the boardinghouse."

Emma hesitated—just a flicker—before answering.

"I ran into Marshal Warwick on Manitou Avenue, not far from the boardinghouse. We exchanged a few words and realized we were both headed there, where we both reside. We walked together. When we arrived, we found Claire—Mrs. La Salle—standing over a man who later turned out to be Mr. Mouton."

Clark's brow furrowed slightly. "So, you did not know the man?"

"No, we'd never met."

"What happened next?"

Emma steadied herself before continuing. "He was lying face down on the parlor floor. There was a blade still in his back."

Clark's voice was quiet. "Did either of you touch the body?"

"I did not. Marshal Warwick checked for signs of life, but it was clear Mr. Mouton was already dead."

Clark nodded solemnly. "And Mrs. La Salle?"

"She was in shock," Emma said softly. "Frozen. She wasn't saying anything. When Marshal Warwick left to summon the authorities, I helped Mrs. La Salle to her living quarters."

"And Mrs. La Salle? Did she know Mr. Mouton?"

"She said she knew him in the past. That was all."

"Indeed?" Clark responded. "She said this after you took

her to her living quarters?"

Emma realized the inquiry was heading toward a dangerous place and hesitated a second. "No, before that."

"When, exactly?" Clark's tone denoted his growing frustration.

"Several weeks ago." Emma held her tone even.

"Please, Miss Quinn, be forthcoming. How did the subject of Mr. Mouton arise before August 13?"

Emma paused. She wanted to be truthful, but she had to be careful. "She had received a letter from him a few weeks ago. She merely said she had known him when she lived in New Orleans."

"I see." Clark made a note on his papers. "Did she say anything after you escorted her to her living quarters?"

Emma hesitated again. "She said . . . she said he hadn't changed."

There was a pause. Clark's eyes lingered on hers for a moment, then he gave a slight nod.

"No further questions," he said.

"You may step down, Miss Quinn."

Emma rose, her knees shaking beneath her skirt, and returned to her seat. She did not glance at Claire, and she avoided Levi's eyes entirely.

Levi was called next.

He stepped forward, his boots echoing with finality in the chamber. He nodded to Clark, then took his seat at the front of the room. He kept his hat in his lap, hands folded over it, gaze steady. By all appearances he was calm, but his gut was as tight as a drum.

"Please state your full name for the record," Clark began.

"Levi Martin Warwick."

"Your position?"

"Town marshal, Manitou."

"Mr. Warwick, tell us how you came to discover Mr. Mouton's body."

Levi's jaw flexed once. "I'd left the boardinghouse earlier that morning to tend to town business. Shortly after ten o'clock, I happened to see Miss Quinn on Manitou Avenue. We exchanged a few words and discovered we were both headed back to the boardinghouse."

"Was there a reason you were returning at that particular time?"

A pause. Levi looked past Clark to the windows high on the wall, then back. The truth was, he'd returned only to steal a few more minutes with Emma—but that was none of Clark's business.

"I was getting hungry and hoped to find something in the kitchen for lunch."

Clark waited a moment before continuing. "What did you encounter upon arrival?"

"Miss Quinn and I were engaged in casual conversation as we entered the boardinghouse. We immediately saw Mrs. La Salle in the parlor, standing over Mr. Mouton's body."

"And the condition of the body?"

"Prone. Face down. A blade was visible, lodged in his back. He showed no signs of life, though he was still warm." He took a breath. "And there was a clear bloodstain around the handle of the blade, blooming on his jacket."

Clark gave a slow nod, glancing briefly at his notes. "Did Mrs. La Salle say anything to you?"

"No, she appeared to be in shock."

"Did you speak with anyone else before contacting the authorities?"

"No. I left Miss Quinn to care for Mrs. La Salle and went straight to get the mayor."

There was a small but noticeable pause before Clark spoke

again.

"You and Mrs. La Salle are related, are you not?"

"Yes, Mrs. La Salle is my sister-in-law."

"And you both lived in New Orleans before coming to Manitou?"

"That's right."

"Did you know Mr. Mouton?"

"I did."

"Do you know why anyone would want to kill him?"

"Frankly, I'm surprised someone hadn't killed him long ago."

The room let out a collective gasp.

"Did you want to kill him, Marshal?"

"Once, in New Orleans. But that was a long time ago."

Clark stopped for a moment, considering whether to pursue the matter. Deciding it was not the purpose of that day's proceeding, he said, "Thank you, Marshal. No further questions."

Levi rose and returned to his seat, his jaw set. He could feel Emma's eyes on him but didn't look her way. Whatever she thought—whatever she might suspect about why he'd come back to the boardinghouse with her—would have to wait.

Clark stood and approached the seating area, where Claire sat, still wrapped in a shawl even though the room was hot. Alice had her hand on Claire's knee to offer comfort.

He spoke softly but clearly, his voice carrying enough weight for the jury and officials to hear.

"Mrs. La Salle. I know this is difficult. But as the first person to find Mr. Mouton's body, your account is vital to this proceeding."

Claire didn't move.

Clark turned slightly toward Alice. "Dr. Guiles, I understand you have reservations. I give you my word—should you determine at any point that the questioning must stop, I will honor that without delay or debate."

Alice gave the slightest nod.

Clark returned his attention to the witness. "Mrs. La Salle, may I ask you to step forward?"

Alice touched Claire's arm gently. "You aren't alone. I'm right here."

Claire stirred at that, and with visible effort, rose from her seat. She stood to be sworn in, guided more by Alice's strength than her own awareness.

Once seated, she looked up—just once—and then away again.

Clark spoke with careful modulation. "Mrs. La Salle, for the record, please state your full name and occupation."

"Claire Michelle La Salle," she said in a barely audible voice.

"And occupation?" Clark repeated.

"I own and run the Maison La Salle boardinghouse." Her voice trailed.

"Please, speak more loudly, Mrs. La Salle, so the jury can hear you properly."

Claire nodded.

"Thank you. Now, can you tell us what happened yesterday morning?"

Claire blinked slowly, her eyes unfocused at first. Then her hands tightened slightly around the handkerchief in her lap.

"I had been out hanging laundry. It was Monday." She swallowed.

"Take your time, Mrs. La Salle," Clark said.

"I heard the clock strike half past ten. When I finished with the laundry, I came in through the back door. I felt a draft in the house and looked to see where it was coming from. I saw that the front door was open." She stopped.

"Did you close the door?" Clark prompted.

"Yes."

"And then?"

"I turned and saw . . . and saw . . ." Claire's face pinched.

"That's enough!" Alice stood and shouted.

"You saw the body?" Clark continued.

"I said, that's enough!" Alice repeated.

Clark raised a hand in surrender. Claire was nodding frantically and wringing the handkerchief in her hands. Alice was at her side in an instant, guiding her gently but firmly from the chair.

Clark cleared his throat. "Let the record show that Mrs. La Salle testified under visible distress, and that Dr. Guiles acted appropriately in intervening."

He turned to Mr. Perkins. "Unless there are objections, I move to recess for a brief adjournment before continuing."

When no objections came, Mr. Perkins gaveled the session to recess.

The courtroom emptied onto the front lawn in a slow trickle, voices hushed and speculative. Levi stood alone under the shade of a cottonwood near the courthouse steps, arms crossed, eyes distant. Emma had wandered a few paces off with Alice and Claire, who sat on a bench, dabbing her temples with a handkerchief.

Inside the courthouse vestibule, Clark removed his spectacles and polished them with a square of linen. Mayor Nichols appeared beside him, uncharacteristically quiet.

Clark didn't look up. "You heard all that?"

Nichols nodded slowly.

Clark's voice lowered. "I think this is the tip of the iceberg."

"You can't believe Claire La Salle actually killed the man?"

"I believe," Clark said carefully, "that I will begin my investigation with her."

Nichols crossed his arms. "And Warwick?"

Clark shrugged. "He's lying about something. I don't know what he's hiding . . . yet."

Nichols gave a small nod, then turned toward the door as the gavel sounded from within.

By the time everyone had filed back in, the room had cooled slightly. Claire resumed her seat beside Alice, wrapped in silence. Emma and Levi sat behind the women without exchanging a glance.

The jury had already assembled and settled into their chairs. Mr. Perkins cleared his throat and began.

"The testimony has been recorded," he said, glancing at his notes. "A man, Phillip Mouton, was found deceased on the morning of August 13, 1883, in the parlor of the Maison La Salle boardinghouse. Cause of death was a deep stab wound to the upper back, penetrating the heart. The instrument— believed to be a letter opener—was embedded in the wound and removed during examination."

He looked to the six men seated as jurors. "Gentlemen, you've heard the testimony. You may now deliver your conclusion."

The foreman, a sturdy man with callused hands and sun-reddened cheeks, stood. "We find that Phillip Mouton died from a puncture wound to the heart, inflicted by person or persons unknown. We rule the death a homicide."

The room did not react. The jury's finding was expected. Perkins gave a single nod and tapped the gavel once. "Let the record reflect the finding. This inquest is adjourned."

The scrape of chairs, the rustle of fabric, and the shifting murmurs filled the room like a tide beginning to rise.

Clark stood beside the prosecutor's table, one hand

resting lightly on his notes. His eyes settled briefly on Claire, then shifted to Levi—and lingered a moment longer.

The hunt, it seemed, was beginning.

❁

Sarah walked in quietly and set the tea tray on the parlor table.

"Thanks, hon." Alice gave her daughter an affectionate smile as she left the room.

Emma sat curled on a cushioned bench in the corner, turning her gloves over and over in her hands. She hadn't said much since they'd arrived. Across from her, Levi leaned against the fireplace mantel, his hat tucked under his arm. Alice poured tea with deliberate care, her brow furrowed in thought.

Claire had been coaxed into a treatment room, where Alice had given her a light sedative. She would be asleep for hours.

"I think I made it worse," Emma said at last.

Levi looked up. "You had no choice. You were asked, and you were under oath."

"But it put Claire in the worst possible light."

Levi crossed the room and lowered himself into the chair by the hearth. "Clark is thorough and competent. He'd have found out eventually."

"I hope you're right about him." Alice spoke over the rim of her cup, then set it down with a faint clink. "Hope he's smart, too."

"What do you mean?" Emma put her feet on the floor and straightened.

Alice gave a mirthless huff. "Think about it. The murder weapon was a letter opener—hardly reliable—and she had a kitchen full of knives to choose from. Do you know how much strength and precision it would take to kill a man Mouton's size with a single stab?"

Levi's expression sharpened. "You're right. I don't see how Claire could have done it physically. Alice, what would it take to deliver such a wound?"

"I'm making assumptions, of course," Alice said, "since I haven't been able to examine the body properly. But no signs of a struggle or defensive wounds were mentioned at the inquest, so I'll assume there were none. That means Mouton was most likely mortally wounded with the first—and only—stab. A stab through his clothes, between the ribs, at just the right angle to pierce the heart." She let out a skeptical laugh. "So Claire was either extraordinarily lucky and graced with strength beyond any woman I know, or . . ."

"Or what?" Emma prompted.

"Or someone else killed Mouton—obviously."

❧ CHAPTER 30 ❧

Mayor Nichols closed the door to his office and gestured toward the leather-backed chair across from his desk. "Have a seat, Steele."

The editor of the *Colorado Springs Gazette* obliged, removing his hat as he sat. He looked every bit the newspaperman: jacket gently worn but neatly buttoned, a faint smudge of ink on his cuff.

Nichols remained standing, hands clasped behind his back as he looked out the window toward Pikes Peak. "I saw you at the inquest."

Steele gave a short nod. "It's the biggest story in town. Where else would I be?"

Nichols turned to face him but said nothing.

"Why am I here, Nichols?" the newsman asked bluntly.

"I need you to be a good steward, Steele."

Steele raised an eyebrow.

Nichols began to pace a short line behind his desk before blurting, "We have an image to protect. The future of Colorado Springs and Manitou depends on people coming here to spend their time and money."

Steele leaned back, tapping the brim of his hat with one finger. "You want me to sugarcoat the truth so it doesn't send the tourists running for—pardon the pun—the hills?"

Nichols finally sat, exhaling. "Of course not. I want the truth—just framed with context. No headlines about 'bloody violence' or 'danger to guests.' Emphasize that it's being handled swiftly, professionally. That it appears to stem from an old personal dispute—not some random act. And for God's sake, remind readers the springs are flowing and the hotels are open."

"You believe you know who killed Mouton?"

"That's not the point. The point is to contain the damage. Reassure them now, and they'll move on."

He leaned forward, elbows on his desk. "Just downplay it as much as possible. Can we agree?"

Steele stood and answered slowly. "I understand."

He was a man of integrity, but he knew as well as Nichols that his future was tied to the region's reputation. He'd find a way to report the truth without ruining the town. Still, something in Nichols's tone—or maybe the way he avoided the question—gave him pause.

Steele nearly bumped into Edward Clark in his haste to leave.

"You seem in a hurry, Mr. Steele," the special prosecutor said good-naturedly.

"Pardon me, Mr. Clark," Steele replied, not meeting his eyes. "I have a paper to get out."

Clark entered Nichols's office and closed the door. "What was that about, Mayor? The fellow seemed flustered."

"Oh, nothing. I just wanted to make sure he understood how delicate this Mouton situation is. Please, have a seat." Nichols gestured to the chair Steele had just vacated.

Clark wiped his brow with a handkerchief. "It's blessed hot today."

"My apologies for not offering. Would you like tea or lemonade? I can summon the kitchen to bring whatever you'd like." Nichols's office was at the Cliff House, the hotel he owned and operated.

"A lemonade would be welcome, thank you."

Once the men were refreshed, Nichols asked, "So, where do things stand?"

"I telegraphed the circuit judge—he's in Pueblo—and notified him of the inquest verdict. He agreed to impanel a grand jury as soon as possible. He understands the sensitivity. He can't be here until the end of next week, but we'll need that time to prepare."

"Well done, Clark. The sooner we put this matter to rest, the better."

"Yes, yes, but . . ."

"But what?"

"It's rushed, Ed. I can't promise I'll have a case ready that soon."

"Just do your best and let the grand jury decide. The point is to move fast."

❀

"We can't just sit by and do nothing," Emma said, pacing tight circles in her sitting room.

"I'm doing no such thing," Levi tamped down a swelling

irritation. He knew its source wasn't Emma, but her pacing didn't help. "Please sit, and I'll tell you what I *have* been doing."

Since finding Claire standing over Mouton's lifeless body, Emma had thought of little else. She'd overseen cleaning the parlor—was it really only two days ago? Willy had done most of the work, bless him, though even Peter had pitched in, oddly helpful. She'd spent her energy calming Christine—who wasn't sure she could ever set foot in the parlor again—and filling in for Claire at the boardinghouse. Meanwhile, Claire was still under Alice's care at the spa. And Levi—Levi had been off meeting with the sheriff and doing who knew what.

Emma dropped into a chair with a frustrated sigh. "I'm listening."

Levi ignored the sharpness in her tone. "I had Mouton's room at the BeeBee House secured in case there's evidence. I've asked every hotel and boardinghouse to preserve their registration ledgers. I told managers to question staff about anything unusual that morning—especially if anyone saw Mouton. I asked them to report to Mr. Clark."

He paused. "I can facilitate, but if I start collecting evidence or questioning witnesses myself, I risk tainting the case. That's why we have to trust Clark to do his job."

Emma's shoulders stiffened. "But I don't trust him, Levi!"

"He seemed a good sort when he defended Josiah," Levi said evenly.

"Oh, I'm sure he's capable. But his real client was the Colorado Springs Company then, just as now. I trust him to protect their interests—not Claire's."

She tapped her fingers against the arm of her chair. "Why is everyone ignoring the obvious problem?"

Levi swallowed his frustration. He didn't expect gratitude,

but her refusal to acknowledge his efforts stung. "And what's that?"

Emma looked up at him. "Even as we speak, the Templars are leaving town."

It was true. The Boston contingent had boarded the first train out that morning—over one hundred and fifty men. One hundred and fifty possible murderers. And that afternoon, the Missouri contingent, equally numerous, were departing.

"I think we can use that to our advantage," Levi said.

Emma perked up. "How?"

"It's plausible it could have been any of them—or anyone in town that day. We just need to plant that idea in enough people's heads, and it will make its way into the minds of the grand jury."

"Well, if that's true, won't they just move the grand jury to Denver or somewhere more neutral?"

"You think that's simple?" Levi shook his head. "We're not back east, where every city has its own judge. Our judge rides the circuit, and Denver is another district altogether. Besides, we both know the real priority here isn't finding the killer—it's preserving the town's reputation. And time is of the essence."

Emma nodded, but without conviction. "So how will we ever find out who did it?"

Levi smiled gently. "My dear," he said softly, "you think in terms of logic. But this isn't an equation—it's politics. Our mission is to clear Claire's name, not uncover the truth. And here, that gets done with influence, not proof."

❋

"Then we're agreed. I'll talk to Mrs. BeeBee and Mr. Albright. You'll go to the billiards hall and talk to Frank, then Avery Hutchinson at the livery. There is not time to write a letter to

Queen Palmer, but I will send a telegram. It's a direct line to General Palmer. I confess I am not as well acquainted with Dr. Bell . . ." Emma stopped to take a breath.

"Yes, and when I make my rounds, I'll work it into casual conversation. We can't be too obvious or people will sense we are manipulating them," Levi cautioned.

"But that's exactly what we're doing." Emma looked up, brows knitting. "Isn't it?"

Levi shook his head. Could he trust Emma to do her part without alerting everyone to their true agenda? He changed tack. "We will get Alice to help. She sees many of the town's women, and they can plant the seeds of doubt in their husbands. But please, Emma, try to be more discreet with your intentions."

"What about Steele?" she persisted, as if not hearing him.

"Yes, he poses his own challenge. I think you have the better relationship with him. Do you think you can talk to him?"

"Of course. I speak with him all the time; we're on friendly terms."

Levi was uneasy but agreed that she was the better one to speak to the newspaperman. Seeing his troubled face, she added, "I've heard you, Levi. Trust me."

❀

Over the next two days, Emma and Levi quietly set their plan in motion. Emma made her rounds with practiced poise, slipping in a seed of doubt here and there as she gathered feedback and reports from members of the tourist consortium. She was more explicit with Mr. Albright, who didn't doubt Claire's innocence but was acutely aware of the politics and had to tread carefully. She managed a cautious, coded conversation with Mr. Steele at the Gazette. Each exchange required diplomacy, a skill Emma found more draining than any engineering puzzle.

Levi took a different approach, weaving casual observations into his daily rounds. A comment here, a raised brow there—just enough to nudge townsfolk toward what many already suspected: that the killer could have come from outside. Alice proved especially helpful. She didn't gossip, not exactly, but after a long soak or massage, many of the town's wives left her spa wondering aloud whether it had all been a little too convenient—with so many strangers, now gone.

Still, the weight didn't lift. Claire remained at the spa, hidden away. The grand jury loomed. And Emma had begun to sense that goodwill—once abundant—was beginning to fray.

Especially after her conversation with Mrs. BeeBee.

Emma found her behind the front desk, pencil in hand, reviewing a guest ledger. "Miss Quinn," the hotelier greeted her quietly, her usual warmth muted. She glanced around the lobby, then lowered her voice. "Could I have a word with you? In my office?"

Inside, Mrs. BeeBee closed the door behind them. "I debated whether to tell you this . . ." She hesitated, her fingers folding the corner of a blotter. "But I'm fond of Claire—and of you—and I thought you should have the chance to prepare."

Her seriousness sent a chill through Emma. Mrs. BeeBee, usually sunny and quick to charm, looked as solemn as a widow at a graveside.

"What is it?" Emma asked. "Please—tell me."

"Well, you know Marshal Warwick came by after Mr. Mouton's death and asked us to secure his room in case anything useful turned up. The next day, one of the maids accompanied the deputy—Mr. Clark's man—while he cleared the room. She found a letter in the nightstand drawer. It had been opened, clearly read, maybe several times. It was addressed to Phillip Mouton." Mrs. BeeBee paused. "Emma . . . it was from Claire."

Emma stared at her.

"The maid didn't read it, of course—she handed it straight to the deputy. But it's solid evidence. Whatever it says, I can't imagine it will help Claire's cause. I thought you should know."

❧ CHAPTER 31 ❧

A lice poured three cups of tea, though only hers had been touched. Emma sat on the divan, staring out the window. Across from her sat Levi, rubbing his temples with one hand. The tension among the friends was palpable.

"We have to know what she wrote in that letter," he said through clenched teeth. His frustration leaked through despite himself.

Emma had told Levi what she'd learned immediately after leaving Mrs. BeeBee, and they had gone directly to Alice's to confront Claire.

"I can't believe she never told us she had replied," Emma said, frowning. "You didn't know either, Alice?"

"No. Though it may be my fault she didn't tell us."

"Why is that?" Levi said stiffly.

"She came to me when she got his letter. I told her to focus on what she could control and let the rest go. At the time, she seemed relieved . . ." Her voice trailed off.

"How much do you know about her history with Mouton?" Levi asked.

"Not much. Only what she shared that day. I gathered he had been a business partner of her husband's and that not all of their business was legitimate during the war. When he returned after Gaston died, he made romantic overtures toward her. When she didn't return his interest, he threatened to take half her inheritance."

Emma blinked. Claire had not been clear with her that Mouton had tried courting her. So that's what she meant by *He expected something from me after that. Something I was not willing to give.*

"Then she left out the worst of it," Levi muttered. He stood and paced from the fireplace to his chair.

"Oh, my heavens. That explains so much," Alice sighed after Levi had filled them in on Mouton's treachery during the war—and his aggressive romantic overtures toward Claire. "Oh, what have I done?"

"You couldn't have known how evil the man was," Emma tried to reassure her.

"I should have seen the seriousness of the situation. I'd never seen her so shaken," Alice said, her voice low. "Instead, I fell back on my usual advice to toughen up."

"Well, what's done is done," Levi said, though part of him agreed: Alice had misread the moment.

"What is Claire's condition now, Doctor?"

Emma didn't like his tone.

"Levi, stop," Emma snapped. "Alice didn't fail her. Claire made a choice not to tell the whole story. Don't blame Alice."

After a pause, Levi looked at Alice and said, "Emma's

right. I apologize. I'm distraught about Claire. Is she going to be all right?"

"She's still not herself. She startles easily. She's not sleeping through the night, often waking from nightmares. She stiffens if I mention her going home. She won't talk about that day—or about him. She shows no feeling, not even for things that used to interest her. And she gets irritable if I press her at all. In short, she's suffering from nervous exhaustion."

Emma was no expert, but it sounded like Alice was describing a trauma response—which would be no surprise. "When will she be better?" Emma asked.

"I don't know. It could take some time. What I mistook for shock is something deeper. Seeing him dead didn't give her peace—it ripped the past wide open."

Emma finally sipped her tea. "She needs someone—not us —who can represent her now and, God forbid, in court if it comes to that."

"Yes." Alice nodded. "And not someone who sees her as overwrought or fragile. She needs someone who will believe her." She looked directly at Levi. "Do you know anyone like that?"

Levi met her eyes. "Yes. I just might."

❀

Gabriel King was a man who had weathered life with dignity, though not without pain. His suit was modest and well kept, if a bit worn at the edges, and his mustache lent him a certain gravity that matched the quiet steadiness in his voice. His pale blue eyes reflected a timeless sorrow—something old and unspoken—but it hadn't hardened him. Rather, it had smoothed his sharp edges, like river stone shaped by years of current. He spoke little, listened well, and carried himself with the air of someone comfortable in his own skin. He had nothing to prove.

"Hello, Levi," King said, extending his hand.

"Gabe, good to see you." Levi shook the lawyer's hand. "Thank you for coming. It's difficult for Claire to get out just now." He turned to Alice and Emma and made the introductions.

King had agreed to come that evening when Levi telephoned earlier that day.

"Please, make yourself comfortable," Alice said, motioning for him to sit.

After they had briefed him on the general details of the situation, including a stern warning from Alice about Claire's condition, King stood. "I understand. And now I'd like to speak to my client alone."

"He seems like just the right sort for Claire," Emma said to Levi after King had left the room. "How do you know him? I don't recall your mentioning him before."

Levi poured himself a whiskey and took a sip. "I met him fishing some time ago. Turned out we had a lot in common." He set down his glass quietly.

About an hour later, King returned to the sitting room. They all looked at him with anxious anticipation, waiting for him to speak.

"Thank you for asking me to represent Claire, Levi. I'd be honored to take the case." He shook Levi's hand, bowed his head to Alice and Emma, and quietly left.

The friends looked at one another. No one knew what to say. Relief mingled with worry—they had a lawyer now, but the road ahead was still uncertain.

A moment later, Claire entered the room.

"Would you like a refreshment, my dear?" Alice asked.

"Some tea would be nice."

Alice left the room to see to it, leaving Levi, Claire, and Emma together.

"Thank you, Levi, for securing a lawyer for me," Claire said softly. Her head still hung low, and she fidgeted with her hankie, but the vacant stare was gone.

"You're comfortable with Gabe, then?" Levi asked, guiding Claire to a chair.

"Oh yes. Surprisingly so." Her voice was still subdued, but the dull flatness that had haunted it since the murder was gone. She looked directly at Levi as she answered.

Levi and Emma exchanged a glance. Claire seemed noticeably better—if not yet herself. Whatever Gabe King had said or done, it had helped.

"Did you know his wife also died of tuberculosis?" Claire asked Levi.

"Yes, I did," he said. "He and I have spoken of our losses at length."

Emma searched Levi's face but could not read anything in his calm expression.

Alice returned with the tea tray and began serving. When she handed Claire her cup, and Claire responded with an almost cheerful "Thank you," Alice blinked in surprise. She looked from Levi to Emma, who both gave nearly imperceptible shrugs. They were as mystified as she by Claire's sudden change.

✎ CHAPTER 32 ✎

"**I**s the situation as dire as that?" Emma asked, reading the sour twist of Albright's mouth as he stepped into the office the next morning.

He dropped into his chair and rubbed his temples. "Coffee. Please tell me there's coffee."

Emma went to the sideboard without a word, pouring him a cup and stirring in two sugar cubes.

"Too much to drink?" she asked, raising a brow. She'd never known her boss to overindulge; he had too much riding on his good judgment.

"No, although it might have helped if I had," he said, reaching for the cup she offered. "No, the meeting just ran long, and there were a lot of opinions."

"So . . . what happened?"

The Colorado Springs Company had called an emergency meeting the day before to discuss damage control after Mouton's murder. Emma had not expected to be included, but she couldn't help feeling slighted. She was the one who liaised with the papers, placed the ads, courted the correspondents. She understood the media landscape better than any of them and could have offered ideas—had they asked.

"The consensus was to launch a campaign promoting our virtues—natural beauty, clean air, health benefits, wholesomeness."

"That sounds like a sensible approach," she admitted. "Why are you so harried?"

Albright took a sip of his coffee and let out a deep breath. "Because the obvious course of action would have been to have you coordinate such a campaign. I said as much . . ."

He paused, searching for words. Emma waited, tension knotting in her gut. When she could stand it no longer, she said, "But?"

He looked at her apologetically. "But they are aware of your relationship to Claire, who we both know is the only suspect in Mouton's murder."

Emma sank into the chair across from Albright. Her knees suddenly felt weak. She had been so focused on Claire's well-being since the murder that she had given no thought to her own vulnerabilities. She felt she had handled the concern about her association with Ancha well during her interview, but another questionable connection might be too much for the board to overlook.

"I see," Emma murmured, absorbing the blow. But something inside her urged her to fight back. She lifted her chin. "No one needs to know it's me arranging the campaign. How would anyone outside our area know of my connection to Claire anyway? The board can't ignore the results of my work so far."

"You are absolutely right about that. In fact, they approved your July bonus, which means they've accepted the financial reports from the consortium members." Albright pulled out his check ledger. "We don't have enough cash in the safe to cover your bonus," he said as he scratched out a check.

Emma's jaw dropped when she saw the amount; It far exceeded her wildest expectations.

"I'll talk to the board again, off the record. Perhaps I can still salvage this," Albright said.

❋

Emma finished her work as quickly as possible. She wanted to visit Claire before returning to the boardinghouse to relieve Molly. She and Christine were doing their best to fill in for Claire. The men were trying, too, but the women agreed it was easier to manage without them. They required too much guidance. Still, their willingness was endearing.

Emma found Claire in the sunroom, crocheting. Seeing her friend engaged in a perfectly ordinary activity again lifted her spirits.

"What are you making?" Emma asked as she pulled a chair closer.

"An antimacassar. I think Alice needs a lot of them around here." Claire looked up and laughed when she saw the puzzled look on Emma's face. "It's a cloth placed over the back of a chair to protect the upholstery."

Emma nodded. "The bathhouse could use them too, I'd imagine." She pictured the men with grease in their hair, sitting in the reading room smoking their cigars.

Claire set down her work. "Well, I'm sorry, dear, but you'll have to go somewhere else for those."

Emma let out a soft laugh. She was thankful to find her friend more herself. "You seem to be feeling better," she ventured.

"Yes. Among the living again, at least." Claire smiled. "Alice is being very protective, of course—shielding me from any responsibility or annoyance. I needed that at first, but I'm starting to feel that I can handle daily life again."

"I'll be the judge of that," Alice said crisply as she joined them.

"Alice, you don't need to make such a fuss over me. I'm all right."

In truth, Claire's improvement since meeting Gabe King bordered on miraculous.

"You are better, I admit, but there is no need to rush." Alice patted her friend gently on the shoulder.

"Alice is right. Christine, Molly, and I are managing at the boardinghouse. Take your time." Emma paused, looking at Alice for some cue. At Alice's small nod, she asked, "Have you spoken to Mr. King since your first meeting?"

"Yes. He stopped by today. The grand jury is going forward, and he says there is nothing much we can do until they reach a decision. In the meantime, he is beginning a strategy for a defense, if it comes to that."

"You seem comfortable with him."

"Oh yes! It's remarkable, really. He is so easy to talk to." Claire's brow furrowed slightly. "I can't explain it. . . ."

Alice walked Emma out after her short visit.

"I'm happily surprised at how well Claire is doing," Emma said.

"Yes. I don't know whether to trust it or not—it was so sudden," Alice admitted.

"Do you know anything about Mr. King? Did Claire know him previously? I never heard Levi or her mention him before."

Emma paused at the front door.

"Not really. I know of him. He came with many others in hopes of a cure for his wife, much like Levi and Claire. I'm not sure how Levi came to be acquainted with him, or how well he is. He has a good reputation professionally, though I have no idea what his experience is in cases like Claire's. I suggest you speak to Levi."

"I will."

❀

"Oh! Emma, I'm sorry!"

Molly nearly collided with her on the front steps of the boardinghouse.

"I told my husband I'd be home by six, and now it's half-past! Dinner is still in the oven. Take it out in fifteen minutes. Gotta dash!" She didn't wait for a reply and rushed down the street.

Inside, Emma found Levi setting the table—or trying to.

"You see it every day," he muttered. "Why can't you remember?"

She hid a smile as he scolded himself under his breath.

"Do you need help?" she asked.

Levi looked up, clearly relieved. "If the table's to be set properly—yes."

She smiled and took the utensils from him.

"I am paying attention for future reference," he said, sitting down to watch.

Emma explained—probably for the third time—where everything went. This time, he seemed to be following. He even nodded at the logic behind the arrangement. Her heart softened at his earnestness, then grew into longing. They hadn't had a quiet moment since Mouton's death. Since then, they had both been preoccupied. She wondered how much of a setback they had suffered.

But then her thoughts turned to Claire.

"Do you know Mr. King well?" she asked, catching Levi off guard.

"I don't know how to answer that." He collected himself. "How can we ever know another? I know he lost his wife, as did I. I know he grieved, may still grieve, deeply. I've observed him to be an honest man with integrity. And . . . " A faint smile touched his lips. "He's an excellent fisherman. Knows all the best spots."

What Levi didn't say was how easy it was to open up to the man—how Gabe King drew truths from him that no one else had. It was that gift—his quiet, patient listening, the way he encouraged without pressing—that Levi had hoped would reach Claire.

Later, Emma soaked in the tub, grateful for the solitude. The day's weight pressed in around her, but her mind drifted—first to Claire, then Albright, then finally to Levi.

"How can we ever know another?" he'd said.

It was a perennial question. But Emma didn't want to merely wonder. She wanted to know him—really know him—as much as anyone could ever know another—if he'd let her.

✑ CHAPTER 33 ✎

The next few days were oddly calm—uncomfortably so for Emma. There was no way of knowing how the Mouton case was progressing. She was used to working outside formal authority, but never had both she and Levi been intentionally frozen out of an investigation before. Except for Mrs. BeeBee, the townspeople seemed unwilling to discuss the matter with them at all. All she knew was that the grand jury was meeting in the next few days. Surely they couldn't indict Claire on the flimsy evidence the special prosecutor had.

But then there was that letter Claire had written. Alice had advised her and Levi not to question Claire about it. Despite her improvement, Alice thought distressing her might set her back. All they could do was make Gabe aware of its existence. Maybe he could get Claire to tell him what she had written.

Emma couldn't even take comfort in how smoothly the tourist season was going since Mouton's death. While the extraordinary peak caused by the Templars had come and gone, the number of visitors had remained high compared with the previous year. Her rotation scheme that sent hotel guests to different attractions had proven resilient and was still in place.

So Emma found herself pacing in her suite with nothing pressing to do but much on her mind. She decided to work off her nervous energy by visiting the hoteliers.

Meanwhile, Levi was also pacing in his suite. A man of action, he was helpless to do anything for his sister-in-law. His restlessness became unbearable, and he grabbed his hat.

They opened their doors at the same time.

"Oh, Levi! I didn't realize you were home," Emma said.

"Yes. I was just heading out to do the rounds. I'm surprised you aren't at your office."

"I'm caught up with administration, and Albright is gone again. I was also heading out to visit the hotels—see how things are going."

"Well, perhaps . . ."

"Would you mind . . ."

They saw the opportunity to spend some time together simultaneously.

"Please, you first," Emma said.

"Would you mind if I joined you?" he asked hopefully.

"I'd be delighted." She smiled and reached for his arm.

The day was overcast, and the dark clouds over the mountains promised rain. Emma could smell it in the air.

"It hasn't been this stormy all summer. I hope we don't get a flash flood," she said, inspecting Fountain Creek as they walked across the bridge. It didn't seem higher than normal, but then it wouldn't—until it was too late.

"A 'flash flood'? I haven't heard that term."

"Really? Well, I'm sure you've had them, with three canyons feeding the creek right in town." Emma knew very well how sudden and damaging flash floods could be to the area.

"Oh, I gather what you're saying. I've just not heard the term. I've heard them called sudden floods, or torrents."

Just then, a few large, cold drops of rain fell on them, and the wind picked up sharply.

"Perhaps we should find shelter. The BeeBee House is closest." Levi took Emma's elbow and helped her scurry to the hotel as the rain began to fall in earnest.

Before they reached the door, pea-sized hail pelted them painfully. Levi threw his arm around Emma, shielding her as best he could.

"This reminds me of the sudden flood we had last summer," he said, brushing the water off his jacket on the patio before opening the door for her.

Inside, they looked out the window as strong winds blew the hail sideways down Manitou Avenue. A few people outside were still running for cover.

"How often do we get sudden floods?" Emma asked. She realized she had never thought about it, even though she knew the area was susceptible. She became anxious for the tourists at The Narrows and the group of people riding burros to Pikes Peak. Had a group gone to Seven Falls that day?

"Only once since I've been here," Levi said absently, his eyes still scanning the sky.

"Emma! Levi!" a voice behind them called.

They turned to see Mrs. BeeBee bustling over, eyes wide.

"You look a fright! Please, go to the restaurant. I'll have tea brought to your table."

They didn't argue. In the restaurant they found a table near a window. The wind still howled, but the hail had given way to heavy rain. By the time the tea arrived, the worst of the storm had passed.

"Ahh, the tea is perfect," Emma said with a sigh, cupping it with both hands.

"Yes, just the thing for a rainy day." Levi smiled as he lowered his cup. His gaze drifted to her hair, still damp. Gently, he reached out with his napkin and dabbed at the lingering drops.

Emma felt the heat rise to her cheeks. She looked down at her cup, suddenly shy.

"We've had no time together, have we?" Levi said softly.

"No. None."

"Well—when this is all over . . ."

"You look better," Mrs. BeeBee said with a warm smile as she wheeled over a cart filled with pastries and cookies. "Would you like something? On the house, of course."

They each chose a treat, thanking her as she bustled away.

"And now look!" Levi said, nodding toward the window. "The sun is shining."

When they were done with their tea, they decided their routes differed too much and they would have to separate.

"I'll see you at dinner?" Levi asked as he put on his hat at the hotel steps.

"Yes, see you then." Emma watched him walk away, then turned back into the BeeBee House.

"Have you heard anything you can share—about the Mouton case?" Emma asked Mrs. BeeBee at the end of their short business meeting in the hotelier's office.

Mrs. BeeBee fidgeted in her chair. "Nothing definitive . . . but I'm more curious about what *hasn't* happened. No one has been by since they cleared out Mr. Mouton's room. It's as if there's no investigation happening at all."

Emma left with a renewed resolve. She had to know what Claire had written in that letter. Based on Mrs. BeeBee's observation, that letter might well be the only real evidence the prosecutor had to make his case against Claire—and apparently, they were not looking for any that might exonerate her. She walked directly to the Three Canyons Spa to confront Claire.

"I'll be gentle, Alice, but I must try to find out just what we're up against—just how incriminating the letter is," Emma said when she settled into Alice's sitting room.

"Isn't that Gabe King's job?"

"Yes, but the more we know, the better we can help her, don't you think?"

Alice sat in thought for a long moment, then let out a sigh. "If she will confide in us, it might afford us a chance to strengthen her defense." She conceded. "I'll fetch her."

"Alice . . . if you wouldn't mind, I'd like to talk to her alone. You are acting as her doctor now, and it might make her more restrained."

Alice opened her mouth to argue, but before she could, Emma continued. "You can speak to her alone, too, and we can compare notes. We might learn more separately than together."

Alice nodded and left to get Claire.

Claire entered the sitting room alone. Her hair was neatly pinned up, and she wore a simple calico dress. She looked fresher and more alert than the last time Emma had seen her. Claire was stronger than anyone gave her credit for, Emma thought.

"Good afternoon, Emma," Claire said, almost cheerfully.

"It's good to see you, Claire. We miss you at the boardinghouse."

"I keep telling Alice I'm well enough to go home, but she's

being a mother hen." Claire smiled and sat opposite Emma. "Did you see that awful storm that blew through?"

"I did, yes. But I'm not here to talk about the weather—or to simply pay a friendly call," Emma said softly.

Claire's smile faded. "Has something happened?"

"No. Nothing—and that's the problem."

Claire frowned, puzzled.

"Listen, Claire. It's very difficult for Levi or me to know what Mr. Clark and his team are actually doing—what evidence they may have—but Mrs. BeeBee mentioned that no one seems to be investigating at all. What we do know is that they have the letter you wrote to Mouton. In fact, that may be *all* they have. Have you shared the details of it with Mr. King?"

For an instant, Claire's face went blank, and Emma feared she had triggered a relapse. But just as quickly, Claire's features crumpled, and tears spilled down her cheeks.

Emma moved without hesitation, wrapping her arms around her friend's shoulders.

"It's all right, my dear. You're safe," she whispered. She poured a small glass of brandy and offered it to Claire.

"Please, tell me what you wrote in the letter," Emma said gently after Claire had taken a sip.

"I can't believe he can still humiliate and shame me so— even from the grave," Claire began, her voice rough with emotion.

Emma waited patiently.

"It's bad enough that the community may learn the truth about the source of my wealth—that it's blood money, no matter which side of the war you were on. But I can't bear to think about, much less speak of, the personal violation that horrid man perpetrated on me."

She took a long drink of the brandy. Her eyes brimmed with heavy tears, and suddenly, the picture came into focus for

Emma. Levi had called Mouton's actions *aggressive romantic overtures*. Claire had said Mouton wanted something from her she was unwilling to give. People in that day did not always speak directly, especially about taboo topics. Could they mean something more sinister than she had realized?

"Oh, Claire," Emma said slowly. "Did he . . . did he *rape* you?"

All Claire could do was nod—first slowly, then rapidly—before collapsing into sobs. Emma gently took the glass from her hands and sank to her knees, enfolding her in a tender embrace.

Claire wept for a long time, her sobs wrenching and wild until they faded into soft, hiccupping breaths—those broken gasps that come only after a soul has been emptied of everything it can hold.

When at last she stilled, Emma guided her to the chaise longue near the window and helped her recline.

"Should I fetch Alice?" Emma asked softly.

"No, no. She'd only want to know what's wrong, and I don't want to talk about it." Claire closed her eyes briefly. "Some water would be welcome, though."

Emma poured a glass from the carafe and returned to her friend's side. When it seemed Claire had calmed enough to continue, Emma risked the question.

"Can you speak about the letter—what you wrote?"

❋

Back at the boardinghouse, Emma pulled Levi into Claire's parlor and locked the door behind them.

"I'd have killed the bastard myself if I'd had the chance." She let out a muted scream, then turned away, pacing once before facing him again.

"So, she told you all of it, then?" His tone carried both apprehension and relief.

"Yes. I can't believe I didn't understand it sooner."

"And did she tell you what happened afterward?" Levi kept his head down, glancing at her from under his brow.

"She said you confronted Mouton and told him that if he didn't leave town—if he didn't leave Claire alone forever—you'd expose him for smuggling and spying. It would have ruined his standing in society. You convinced him you had the proof, though you'd have had to fabricate it if he'd called your bluff. I think he got off easy. How did you not kill him then?"

"Believe me, I wanted to. But Claire just wanted it all to go away."

Emma let out a cynical huff. "Well, she wouldn't be the first woman to want that."

"So how did you leave things with her?"

"She didn't share the contents of the letter she wrote, though she admitted it's incriminating. She did agree to tell Mr. King about its contents. She would prefer not to discuss the sexual violation with him, but she agreed to either you or me telling him."

"Really?" Levi said, surprised. He paused, weighing the ramifications. "Perhaps I should be the one. It's a delicate subject, and more straightforward man-to-man. Besides, I saw the aftermath. I know how damaging it was."

Emma nodded her agreement.

Levi took her face gently between his hands and kissed her forehead.

"It's going to be all right. You'll see," he whispered.

❧ CHAPTER 34 ❧

Levi sat in his sitting room nursing a whiskey. It had been a long day. It had been a trying day. It had been a delightful day. He gazed out his window at the clear sky—a drastic difference from the hailstorm that had caught Emma and him by surprise earlier. That storm—and their tea—had been the highlight of his day. Certainly, it had been the best moment since that scoundrel Mouton showed up dead in their boardinghouse. Levi hadn't spared one moment of pity for the man; he deserved no better. But more and more, it looked like he was going to inflict one more blow on someone Levi loved before he spent eternity in hell. And if there was a God above, he *would* spend eternity in hell."

A soft knock came at the door. Levi's heart leapt, hoping Emma was on the other side. It crashed just as quickly when he opened it and found Peter Graham standing before him.

"Peter?"

"I'm sorry to intrude, Levi, but do you have a moment? There's something I'd like to discuss."

Peter's direct manner was nothing new, but Levi didn't remember the man ever knocking on his door before.

"Of course. Come in." Levi opened the door wider to allow the man through. "Can I offer you a drink?"

"Yes, that would be most welcome." Peter stood awkwardly in the center of the room.

"Please, have a seat—make yourself comfortable." Levi handed the drink to Peter and added, "What can I do for you?"

"Funny, isn't it?" Peter said, swirling the whiskey slowly, his voice low and almost wistful. "We've lived in the same boardinghouse nearly three years, yet know almost nothing about one another." His tone was speculative, his look too direct. Was he hinting at something, or merely stating a fact? "But that's one of the appeals of the West, isn't it?" He set the glass on the table and smiled—a sad smile, or was it a threatening one? He looked back at Levi. "Leaving our past behind. Starting a new life."

"Peter, I'm happy you've decided to broach a friendship after all this time, but I admit I'm curious—why now?" Levi didn't know what Peter was playing at, and he certainly wasn't going to show his hand first.

"Yes, our social interaction has mainly been cards in the parlor. Well, perhaps tonight will change that."

"Please, how can I help?" Levi's unease only increased with each oblique statement Peter made, and his patience was wearing thin.

"It's I who can help you, I think." Peter took a long, slow drink of his whiskey.

Levi waited until he thought the man would say no more. Finally, Peter broke the silence.

"I feel it only fair to tell you that I've been to Mr. Clark, the special prosecutor for the Mouton murder."

"Oh?" Levi's body felt the jolt. "You know something?"

"I know—or knew—*someone*. Mouton."

And then Peter Graham shared the story of his life as a young man in the Confederacy.

"I was stationed in Havana in '63. Officially, I was there with a Confederate procurement detail—logistics, black-market arrangements, keeping the blockade runners supplied and the brass happy."

He paused to take another sip of whiskey.

"That's where I met Mouton. He came ashore one day with a polished smile and a case of documents he guarded as if they were gold. He met with Colonel Bryce—my commanding officer at the time. I assumed it was just another delivery of forged bills or port ledgers."

Levi narrowed his eyes. "It wasn't?"

Peter shook his head. "No. It was information—specific troop movements, supply lines, Union ship manifests. And he sold it as if he were auctioning off fine art. He even carried similar intelligence about the Confederacy, offering Bryce the chance to buy it before he sold it to the Yankees."

"So you knew Mouton was a profiteer."

"Exactly," Peter said grimly. "He was a merchant of war. Played both sides. I heard he sold similar documents in Nassau later that month. Always one step ahead."

"And Colonel Bryce just accepted it?"

"He wasn't the only one," Peter muttered. "Some in command thought men like Mouton were a necessary evil. I didn't. I think men like Mouton prolonged the war, costing people their livelihoods and lives."

Peter looked away then, out toward the dark street beyond Levi's window. "But when I saw him here in Manitou—smiling, well dressed, passing himself off as a gentleman—I couldn't stomach it. That's why I went to Clark. I told him what I'd seen, what I knew."

"And?"

"Clark listened. Nodded. Said the grand jury would decide. Told me my story was interesting but unprovable, and not useful."

"Not useful," Levi echoed, disgust in his voice.

"No. He just wants a ruling on Claire—one way or the other."

"Even if he gets the wrong one."

"Even then," Peter said. "That's why I'm here. I've said my piece to him. Now I'm saying it to you."

※

"This is wonderful news!" Emma exclaimed when Levi told her about his conversation with Peter. "Surely this will cast enough doubt to protect Claire from prosecution."

"It may be enough to prevent a jury from finding her guilty in a trial, but it's unlikely to influence the grand jury's determination." Levi hated to burst Emma's bubble, but it was true. Clark would present the evidence he had against Claire, independent of any other possibilities. Gabe wouldn't have an opportunity to offer evidence casting doubt on her guilt until trial. And a trial itself was what they all feared. In a trial, it would come out how Claire knew Mouton. It would come out where Claire's wealth came from. It would come out what Levi had done to protect her all those years ago—and why. And perhaps most dangerous in the long run, it could expose the lie they had told to protect Emma. In the end, a jury might very well find Claire guilty despite the doubt Peter's story offered. Their priority had to be avoiding a trial at all costs.

Emma sat down heavily on her divan. She knew Levi was right. "So what now?" she asked.

"We stay the course. I will arrange for Peter to tell Gabe what he told me. I'll share with Gabe the horrid story of how Mouton violated Claire. But all of that will only be useful if Claire is brought to trial. Perhaps Gabe can appeal to Clark with Peter's information and convince him to drop the charges against Claire, though we must accept this is a long shot."

"I feel so useless, Levi." Emma slumped deeper into the divan.

"Yes, I do as well."

Just then they heard a commotion downstairs and opened the door. A chorus of joyous voices emanated from the parlor. Levi and Emma looked at each other quizzically. Levi followed Emma downstairs, where they found Claire being welcomed home by Willy, Christine, and Peter.

"Claire!" Emma cried, joining the others in welcoming her home with a big hug.

"I have escaped Alice's suffocating care!" Claire said, laughing. "She surely would have coddled me forever if I'd let her, but I told her the best thing for me was to get back to my responsibilities here. I'm not sure she agreed, but she didn't argue with me either."

"You've wasted away to nothing!" Christine said. "I'll go to the kitchen and fix you a plate. Molly made her excellent fried chicken for dinner, and I believe there's still some apple pie left, if no one has sneaked into the kitchen and helped themselves to it. Would you like it in your rooms or here in the dining room?"

"Thank you, Christine, but I'm not hungry. Come, let's gather in the parlor, and y'all can tell me what's been going on while I was at Alice's."

"Oh, please play the piano for us," Christine begged. "It's been so morbidly quiet here."

Peter looked at his shoes while Levi softly cleared his throat. Christine's enthusiastic but ill-chosen words squelched the mood, and an awkward silence fell over the group.

"On second thought, I am feeling a bit tired. I think I'll just go to my rooms and rest," Claire said, smiling weakly at Christine. She turned and slowly walked to her quarters, quietly shutting the door behind her.

"Oh, I'm such a fool!" Christine said in frustration.

"You meant well, honey," Willy murmured, wrapping his arm around her shoulders and giving her a gentle squeeze.

Emma gave Levi a discreet tip of her head toward Claire's door. He followed as she crossed the hall, tapped lightly, and—without waiting—eased it open.

Claire sat on her flamboyant purple velvet sofa, Lulu curled in her lap, the cat's tail twitching lazily.

"She missed you," Emma said with a smile. "When she wasn't trying to trip us all, she made herself at home in my suite."

Claire's lips curved faintly, her gaze never leaving the cat.

Emma settled beside her, while Levi poured a brandy and set it next to Claire.

"Are you sure you're ready to be back?" Emma asked.

"I'm not sure," Claire admitted, stroking Lulu as the purr grew louder. "But I couldn't stay at Alice's another day—she meant well, but she was smothering me. I'll be fine once I adjust." She took a sip.

"Well, I'm glad you're home," Levi said. "Emma, Christine, and Molly have kept the place going, but no one runs it as smoothly as you. And I'll be hanged if I can remember how to set a table."

That earned a small smile from all three.

"I have some hopeful news," Levi went on. He pulled an armchair closer, leaning toward Claire to take her hand.

Her brows lifted. "I could use good news. What is it?"

He told her about his conversation with Peter.

"This is good for you, Claire," Emma said. "If Mr. King plays it well, maybe you won't have to reveal your source of wealth or . . . the other matter."

"Perhaps," Levi said, "but let's not chance it." He met Claire's eyes. "We should get Gabe here. Time to lay all the cards on the table and plan our strategy."

Claire nodded, her fingers tightening briefly around his.

❧ CHAPTER 35 ❧

"Is that all?" Gabe King asked after Levi paused. Levi had met him at his Colorado Springs office first thing that morning, as arranged by telephone the night before. He had just shared Peter Graham's account and the truth about Mouton's violation of Claire. Gabe had listened without a flicker of expression, even at the most disturbing parts.

"No, there's more—but Claire will have to tell you." Levi then went on to explain about the letter. "She has agreed to tell you what she wrote. Can you come back with me to Manitou? I think she would be more comfortable talking in her own surroundings."

Without a word, Gabe stood, reached for his hat, and gestured to Levi to lead the way.

They walked in companionable silence past the gleaming

new Antlers Hotel to the station. During the short train ride, they exchanged barely a dozen words, yet Levi felt no awkwardness. Perhaps it was Gabe's calm acceptance of whatever circumstances life presented him—a lesson hard learned after the loss of his wife. Or perhaps it was his quiet confidence. Whatever the reason, Levi felt more at ease with Gabe than with any other man.

They nearly walked right into Mayor Nichols as they exited the Manitou train depot.

"Levi. Mr. King." Nichols nodded to each man in greeting. "Funny I should bump into you. I was just on my way to Colorado Springs. The grand jury on the Mouton matter convened yesterday, as I suppose you know."

Levi bit back irritation; even off the case, Nichols might have kept him better informed. Gabe was less restrained.

"No, I did not know," the lawyer said angrily. "This is highly irregular and patently unfair to my client. I expect to be kept informed about developments that concern Mrs. La Salle."

Nichols sputtered before replying, "I—I—I apologize, Mr. King. I had assumed Mr. Clark's office would have informed you."

"And what business do you have at the grand jury?" Gabe pressed. "Last I checked, grand juries were held in secret. You aren't a juror, are you?"

Nichols seemed to recover and replied stiffly, "You know I couldn't tell you that, even if I were."

"Then why are you on your way there now?" Gabe demanded.

Nichols hesitated. "That's not what I meant. I have other business in Colorado Springs. I was only passing along the information. Now, if you'll excuse me—I have a train to catch."

He stepped around them and strode toward the platform.

The two men shared a knowing look and got back on the train to Colorado Springs.

✻

Emma saw none of this from her office window; she was too busy poring over the mid-month financial reports from the consortium members. The numbers were staggeringly positive. She smiled, imagining the board trying to ignore results like these when deciding her future. If only Albright were here to gloat—but he had all but moved on to his new position and was in Denver now.

She worked through the afternoon, compiling the data into her summary for the board and making a quick calculation of what her bonus might be. By day's end, the report was tied with string, stamped with the board's seal, and ready for the courier. She carried it to the front desk, feeling the warm satisfaction of work well done.

Bursting to share her good news, she turned her steps toward Three Canyons Spa. Alice would want to hear this.

In the reception room, Alice was seeing out Mrs. Calhoun.

"Oh, hello, Mrs. Calhoun!" Emma greeted her. "I haven't seen you in an age. I hope you are well?"

After reviewing her various aches—and praising Alice for curing them—Mrs. Calhoun added, "I will be relieved when this whole Mouton business is behind us. How is Claire?"

Emma glanced toward Alice before saying, "She's bearing up well, thank you."

"Well, anyone who knows her at all knows how ridiculous it is to think she had anything to do with the man's death."

Just then, John Jr. arrived to collect his mother.

Normally, he beamed at Emma, but today his greeting was stiff.

"Miss Quinn. Dr. Guiles." He greeted them with a nod. "Are you ready, Mother? I must get back to Colorado Springs as soon as possible." He gave Emma a quick glance before ushering his mother out the door.

When they had gone, Alice said quietly, "Well, that was awkward."

"Yes . . ." Emma wondered at his coolness, but she had good news to share and brightened her voice. "Do you have time for tea? I've something to tell you."

Over tea and cake, Emma laid out the figures.

"Well," Alice said, "the board would be foolish not to give you the post."

Emma smiled with pride.

"I'm sorry to change the subject, but I'm glad you're here. I've news from around town I don't want Claire to hear. It's not good for her." Alice hesitated, then recounted the talk among the ladies. Mrs. Calhoun was in the minority; most believed Claire guilty.

"Where do they get such ideas?" Emma asked, exasperated.

"From their husbands, no doubt."

"Then they're all fools."

"No argument—but it doesn't matter, does it? It seems to be the prevailing view."

Alice set down her empty teacup. "More tea, dear?" she asked, lifting the pot toward Emma's cup.

"No thanks, Alice. I need to get home. This is the first day I've been at work since Claire returned, and I want to help with dinner, if I'm needed."

"Tell her I'll be by in the morning to check on her." Alice hugged her at the door. "And Emma—you deserve the job."

❀

The second-floor meeting room was warm that afternoon, the air close despite both windows being propped open to catch what little breeze there was. Outside, the rumble of carts and men's voices drifted up from the street, mingling with the faint smell of dust and horses.

The jurors—all men—sat around a scarred oak table, their coats draped over chair backs and hats piled in the corner.

"We've heard all we're going to hear," said Ezra Bell, the foreman, resting his broad hands on the table. "Mr. Clark's made his case plain enough."

John Calhoun Jr. leaned back, folding his arms. "Plain, maybe. But one-sided. We didn't hear from everyone who might've had more to say about Mr. Mouton's death. And what about all the out-of-towners? Any of them might be the culprit."

"It's not our job to run the investigation," muttered another juror. "We just decide if there's enough to send it on."

"And if there isn't?" Calhoun pressed.

Ezra's jaw tightened. "Then we say 'no true bill' and be done with it. But I'd caution you—refusing to indict sends a message in this town, and it won't be taken kindly by some."

Calhoun let his gaze travel the room. A few men murmured agreement; others glanced uneasily at their neighbors. His own eyes dropped to the tabletop, his thumb tracing a deep scratch in the wood.

"Let's take the first vote," Ezra said, passing around slips of blank paper. "Make your choice, fold it, and pass it back."

Chairs creaked, pencils scratched. Outside, a wagon rattled past, its wheels crunching over dry gravel. Inside, the weight of the decision seemed to thicken the air.

❋

The coffee in Claire's cup had long gone cold. She sat with Alice and Emma in her sitting room that evening, the three of them staring blankly out the window.

"They've been in there since midday," Alice said, her voice brisk but her hands betraying her as she tapped the teaspoon against the saucer in a quick, nervous rhythm. "We should be hearing some word soon, I should think."

Claire's head turned slowly. "Unless the jury can't decide."

Alice set the spoon down, folding her hands tightly in her lap. "Yes, I suppose it would take longer in that case."

Emma felt her stomach tighten. The fact that it was taking so long could only mean there were men on both sides of the decision. That would have a lasting impact on the community, no matter what.

Claire said nothing, only resting the cup in its saucer and staring at the dark surface of the coffee, as though the answer might be reflected there.

The minutes stretched, filled only by the faint sounds of the boardinghouse and the muffled voices of people outside, going about their perfectly normal days.

Then—boots in the hall. Two pairs. Heavy, deliberate.

Emma's pulse quickened. She looked at Claire, then at Alice, whose eyes had gone wide.

The footsteps stopped at the door, followed by a firm knock.

Emma's breath caught. Claire rose slowly, smoothed her skirt, and opened the door.

Levi and Gabe stood there, dust clinging to their coats, the sharp scent of horse and sweat drifting into the room. Levi's hat was in his hand; Gabe's expression was unreadable.

Claire stepped aside to let them in. Emma could feel the heat they brought with them as they entered. Levi closed the door softly behind them.

Gabe remained standing. "I'm sorry, Claire."

Emma and Alice both gasped. Claire stood tall and straight, though her eyelids fluttered ever so slightly.

"The grand jury has indicted you," he said, his voice measured. "The sheriff has agreed to let you come in on your own. You need to be in Colorado Springs tonight."

Alice reached for Claire's hand. Emma's own hands clenched into fists before she realized it.

"This is absurd," Emma said sharply. "Those cowards are just looking for the easy way out, where they can look like they've done something—right or wrong."

"Emma." Claire's voice was quiet but firm. "Please."

That one word stopped her cold. Claire drew in a slow breath. "I'll change and be ready shortly."

"Come on, Gabe, let's give the women some privacy." Levi motioned to the lawyer, who followed him to the boardinghouse parlor.

As the men stepped into the hall, Emma turned to Claire. "We'll be with you every step of the way," she said, her voice low but fierce.

❋

The courthouse foyer smelled faintly of varnish and old paper. Gabe knocked confidently on the sheriff's office door. Sheriff Dana opened it quickly, as though he had been waiting for the knock.

"Mrs. La Salle," he said, bowing slightly. "Thank you for coming as agreed."

Gabe answered for her. "We're here to surrender voluntarily, Sheriff. The bond is arranged." He held up a folded document already bearing the judge's signature.

The sheriff nodded, glancing toward the doorway across the hall, where his wife, Mrs. Dana, had appeared, wiping her hands on a towel. "My wife will see to you and your companions while we handle the paperwork," he told Claire. "You'll be more comfortable in the waiting room."

The windowless room was small and simply furnished with wooden chairs lining the walls. A small table stood in the corner, holding a pitcher of lemonade and a plate of cookies Mrs. Dana had presumably provided. Without asking, she poured lemonade and pressed the dish of ginger cookies on the women, her manner brisk but not unkind. All declined the cookies. Claire accepted a glass but did not drink; Emma did, if only to have something to do with her hands. Alice drank thirstily.

Beyond the doorway, they could hear the muted voices of men—Gabe at the clerk's desk, Levi somewhere nearby.

Fifteen minutes later, Gabe came to the waiting room with the sheriff. "Bond's posted, recognizance signed," Gabe said. "You're free to go."

Claire rose, smoothing her skirt. "Thank you, Mrs. Dana," she said.

The sheriff's wife nodded but said nothing.

In the hall, the sheriff added, "You'll be notified when the arraignment is set. Until then, ma'am, you're at liberty—so long as you remain in the county."

They stepped back into the night. It was over for now, but the cloud of what lay ahead followed them out the courthouse door.

The return trip was a subdued affair. The horses plodded along the dirt road between Colorado Springs and Manitou, their harnesses jingling in a slow, steady rhythm. The August heat had quickly given way to the cool night air, and the smell of leather, dust, and faint traces of horsehair filled the wagon.

Claire sat between Alice and Emma on the back bench, her gloved hands folded neatly in her lap. She gazed straight ahead, her expression composed, though Emma could see the tension in the set of her shoulders. Alice kept her arm lightly against Claire's, as if offering silent support.

On the forward bench, Gabe held the reins while Levi sat beside him, one boot braced against the floorboard. The two men spoke little, their low exchanges lost under the creak of the rig and the sound of hooves over the loose gravel.

As they neared Manitou, the mountains loomed closer, the dark silhouettes of Red Mountain and Iron Mountain stood like sentries. A cool breeze trickled down from the canyon, carrying with it the scent of pine.

The rig rolled over the bridge and onto Cañon Avenue, drawing a few curious glances from people milling about. Gabe reined in at the boardinghouse, and the group climbed down without a word.

Inside, Christine looked up from her needlework, her eyes moving quickly from one face to another. She didn't ask what had happened—their faces said it all.

Back in Claire's sitting room, Alice went straight to the brandy decanter while Claire removed her hat and gloves with slow precision. Emma lingered by the window, watching the dark shadows on the street.

"At least there was no cell," Claire said finally, her voice calm but low. "For now."

Emma turned toward her. "You're not facing this alone. Not for a moment."

Claire met her gaze, the faintest hint of a smile touching her lips. "I know. That's the only reason I can face it at all."

Outside, the sound of wagon wheels faded into the hum of the town going about its business. The quiet settled around them for a moment—until Gabe's voice cut through it.

"All right," he said, his tone steady but edged with resolve. "It's time to plan our defense."

❧ CHAPTER 36 ❧

"All the evidence is circumstantial," Emma concluded when, an hour later, the group had reviewed all the facts.

"That gives us an opportunity to plant doubt in the jurors' minds. For a start, the town was full of tourists. Many of the Templars with the Missouri contingent could have known Mouton, and if Peter testifies as to his past, any number of them might have had reason to kill him."

"Yes, all that is true," Levi agreed. "But the window of opportunity is very narrow, and Joseph at the burro rides told me that many of the Southerners were on the trail to Pikes Peak that day. The rest, he said, had gone to the Garden of the Gods."

Emma let out a sigh.

"Perhaps the special prosecutor doesn't know that," Alice offered.

But they all knew not to count on it.

"We must proceed with the knowledge that most cases are decided based on circumstantial evidence," Gabe said. He put his hand gently on Claire's shoulder. "Don't fret, Claire. It's my job to build a defense that will persuade the jury, and I will move heaven and earth to see it done."

Emma and Levi exchanged a glance. It was unlike Gabe King to be so expressive.

"The trial starts in just over a week," the lawyer continued. "I'll meet with Mr. Clark first thing Monday morning. He cannot spring your letter upon us; he must show it if he intends to use it."

Claire nodded her understanding. "It's just so humiliating."

"Don't give it a second thought," he reassured her. "Anyone in your position would have done the same."

"Perhaps, but I forbid you to disclose why I wrote it," Claire said firmly. "I will not have it known what that vile man did to me. Not under any circumstances."

"Even if it saves you from a guilty verdict?" Emma asked, surprised.

"Even then."

Just then they heard a soft knock on the door.

"My heavens," Alice said. "Who can that be so late in the evening?"

Levi answered it and found Peter Graham standing there. "Peter?"

"I know it's late," Peter interrupted. "I hope you will forgive the intrusion."

Levi looked back at Claire for a cue.

"Not at all, Peter. Please, come in," Claire said. "What

brings you to my quarters this evening?"

"It's an abomination, Claire!" He nearly shouted. "Anyone who knows you at all knows you couldn't possibly have killed that wretched man, Mouton." He looked at Levi and asked, "Have you shared what I told you the other night?"

"Yes, everyone here knows."

"I'm here to let you know I that am at your full disposal, Claire. I will testify to everything I know about the scoundrel—whatever I can do to help you, I'm at your service."

He gave a bitter laugh. "No one had more reason to hate that man than I, and but for my cursed alibi, I'd be as likely a suspect as you—more so, in fact."

Peter, of course, had no idea about Claire's past with Mouton, but his resolve was beyond doubt.

Claire's eyes welled. "Thank you, Peter. Your support means more than I can say."

Levi offered Peter a drink, but the man declined.

"No, no. I know you all have work to do, preparing for Claire's trial. I only wanted to convey my full commitment to doing what I can to help."

He turned and quietly let himself out.

"Well, well, well," Emma murmured. "Who would have imagined Peter could be so honorable?"

"There's more to us all than meets the eye," Levi said.

"Mr. Graham is right. It's late," Gabe said. "It's been a long day. Let's get some rest and take a break tomorrow—it is the Sabbath, after all." He went to Claire and took her hand in his. "Try to take your mind off all this for a while. I'll be in touch Monday." He gently patted her hand before releasing it.

Emma, Levi, and Alice followed Gabe out after saying their good evenings.

Emma and Levi stood in front of their respective doors upstairs. Gabe was right; it had been a long day and both were tired. But Emma gave Levi a quick kiss on his cheek before saying, "Good night."

In her own suite, Emma admitted one thing to herself: they could not trust the judicial process to arrive at the right conclusion where Claire was concerned.

❋

After the congregation sang "Immortal Love, Forever Full," the next morning in church, Reverend Jones said, "Turn now to Matthew 7:1," and, in a clear, steady voice, he began: "'Judge not, that ye be not judged. For with what judgment ye judge, ye shall be judged; and with what measure ye mete, it shall be measured to you again.'"

He paused, letting the words settle over the pews. "My brethren, the Master bids us temper our zeal for judgment with humility. Too often we see the speck in our neighbor's eye while ignoring the beam in our own. We are quick to condemn on appearances, forgetting that beneath every life lies a story unseen by us but known to God. Let us not mistake suspicion for truth, nor gossip for fact, lest we burden an innocent soul with the weight of our own failings."

It was hard to miss the kind reverend's point—or how it applied to Claire, who was listening with her gaze resting on the Bible in her lap. Ironically, the church was unusually packed. Emma, sitting next to her, suspected—cynically, perhaps—that many were there to gawk at Claire. All the more reason to be grateful for Reverend Jones; his words landed like a rebuke to the scandal-seekers who needed setting straight.

After the service, Alice, as she often did, invited them all to join her for coffee and cake, but Emma needed something church never seemed to provide her: grounding and centering. She felt the weight of the coming week pressing in, and only

Ancha's calm wisdom ever steadied her nerves. She declined the invitation and waved as Claire and Levi walked with Alice to Three Canyons Spa.

She donned her hiking garb and went in search of her mentor. But instead of skulking toward Williams Canyon, worried about who might see her, she walked with purpose right up Cañon Avenue. She wandered for some time, whistling for Ancha and Kwiyaghat before the loyal dog came bounding toward her, barking happily. But Ancha was nowhere in sight.

"Where's your papa, Kwiyaghat?" Emma asked the squirming dog. She bent to ruffle his ears, and he wriggled away, intent on his task.

The dog barked, ran a few yards in a direction opposite Ancha's cave, and turned to look at Emma.

"All right, I'm coming," she said, laughing.

Emma followed Kwiyaghat through a tangle of brush until the dog led her into a dry, rocky clearing. The sun sent long shafts of amber light across the ground. She caught the scent long before she saw the scene—rich, metallic, heavy on the air.

Ancha was crouched near a low fire. A blackened pot rested on the embers, where pale chunks of fat sputtered, releasing a greasy smoke that clung to her throat. He lifted a strip of meat, long and thin as a ribbon, and draped it over a makeshift rack of willow branches. Dozens more hung already, the edges darkening and stiffening in the dry mountain air.

The clearing carried the smells of every stage of the task—iron and blood, the acrid sting of smoke, the cloying weight of tallow. Beneath it all lay the clean, resinous breath of the nearby pines, a reminder of the wider forest that seemed oddly distant from this harsh, intimate work of survival.

Kwiyaghat flopped down in the dirt, panting, ears swiveling at every sound. Emma felt reassured by his presence —no bear or cougar could come close without the dog raising alarm.

She stood for a long moment, both fascinated and appalled. Back in her own time, she had been a vegetarian for ethical reasons; now, she ate meat sparingly, but this—this was more graphic than she had ever imagined.

"Looks like you are busy," Emma said, choking down the bile threatening to rise.

Ancha glanced up, his dark eyes weary but calm. "Hello, Emma. Yes, but it must be done. Kwiyaghat and I will need food for winter. By morning, the meat will be drying well, and the fat will be pure. It must be done while the day is still warm."

She nodded, though her stomach knotted. More than the gore, what struck her was how alone he looked, shoulders bent under work that should have been shared with his family— maybe even a wife. Compassion pressed at her chest, outweighing her queasiness.

"Let me help," she said. "Even if I'm no good at it."

His mouth curved with the faintest trace of amusement. "Thank you."

And though the smell turned her stomach, Emma stepped closer, determined to share in her friend's burden.

She hesitated before reaching for the strip of flesh he handed her. It was slick and warm, and she fought down a shudder as she stretched it over the drying rack.

"There," Ancha said, watching her hands. "Not so hard."

"Not so pleasant either," she admitted, looking for something to wipe her hands on. "But I understand why it has to be done."

He nodded, returning to the pot of tallow with slow, practiced movements. The fire popped and hissed as he stirred. It merged with the sound of Kwiyaghat's steady panting and the whisper of aspen leaves.

Emma's chest tightened. This wasn't why she had come—

not really. She cleared her throat.

"Ancha," she said softly, "I didn't only come to help with this."

He didn't look up, but his hands stilled on the stirring stick. "Why did you come?"

She took a breath. "I need your wisdom. I feel like I'm drowning." She went on to tell him about Claire.

He listened intently, without interruption, gently stirring the pot all the while. At last he met her eyes. In his gaze was the same stillness she had come to rely on—the gravity of someone who lived close to the earth, whose strength came from an ancient understanding of things.

He gestured to the rocky ground beside him. "Sit."

Emma lowered herself onto the earth.

Ancha set aside the stirring stick and gazed toward the aspen stand, their pale trunks catching the waxing sun. "Among my people," he began, "we say the deer gives itself twice—once when the arrow strikes, and again when we honor what it has given. If we waste it, or forget to give thanks, the spirit of the deer will not return. The hunters will find no game, and the people will starve."

Emma didn't see the relevance, but she knew to be patient. Ancha always had a reason for what he shared.

He paused, letting the words sink in. "So we use it all—the meat, the hide, the fat. Even the bones. Each piece has its place. Each piece has value."

"Even the stuff in the intestines?" Emma asked—a weak attempt at humor.

Ancha gave her a blank look but continued.

"Even that. I left it where I cleaned the deer, as an offering to bear and cougar. We must value it all and treat it all with respect. Only then is there balance. Only then can the cycle complete. As it is with the deer, so it is with us. You feel unsteady because you try to keep some things and cast aside others. But strength comes when you take all of it—the grief, the anger, the duty, the love—and give thanks for what each teaches. Nothing wasted."

Emma sat very still, understanding more than she could put into words. The fire cracked, the fat in the pot popped, and in the quiet clearing she felt, for the first time in days, her own breath moving evenly in her chest.

"Yes," she murmured at last. "I've been trying to hold on to some things and reject others, as though I could shape the world to my liking. Claire's ordeal, my own . . . ambitions." She almost laughed at the smallness of that word against the weight of everything else. "But maybe you're right—maybe I need to accept it all, even the things I would rather cast off."

Ancha's lips curved in the faintest smile. "It is the only way."

She looked at him, suddenly struck by the completeness of his solitude—no wife to tend the hide, no brother to share the labor, no child to learn the work at his side. Yet he had made his own life, with Kwiyaghat, with this fire, with the earth and sky.

As she rose to help him turn the strips of meat, Emma felt steadier than she had since Mouton's death. Claire would need her strength. Levi would, too. As for herself, she could stop trying to separate the pieces of her life into what she thought was useful and what was waste.

Nothing is wasted. For the first time since Mouton's death, she felt her balance return—and she silently gave thanks to Ancha, who always seemed to know how to restore it.

❀

Emma's route home took her past the large Victorian house

where John Calhoun Jr. lived with his parents. Usually, she avoided walking by the house after a visit with Ancha because she wanted to keep a very low profile where her friendship with him was concerned.

But those days were over. She knew exactly where she stood regarding her friendships, and she would no longer be ashamed.

As she reached the gate, John Jr. stepped out onto the front porch. He saw her at once. A thin smile, not his usual gregarious one, lifted and fell as he raised a hand. She returned the greeting and kept on down Cañon Avenue, hoping to escape any conversation. She still smarted from his coolness at Three Canyons Spa, where he had all but ignored her. But if his friendship was the only thing she lost in all this, she could bear it.

"Emma! . . . Miss Quinn!" he called, and hurried down the path.

She stopped.

Up close, he gave her a quick look—worn hat, plaid shirt, denim trousers, boots. On another day he might have asked her about her unconventional attire. Today he had other business.

"Miss Quinn—Emma—I'm glad to see you . . ." he began. "I owe you an apology, and I just didn't know how to go about it."

"An apology? . . . For what?" She really wasn't interested in a prolonged interaction. The sun was behind Pikes Peak, and she was already late for dinner.

"I was rude to you the other day at Dr. Guiles's spa. Granted, I was required in Colorado Springs and was in a hurry, but that was not the reason for my poor manners."

A wagonload of tourists returning from Williams Canyon rattled by, and they stepped aside to let it pass.

"It's all right, John. I understand. Think nothing of it."

He stepped into her path to block her way. Not aggressively, but to steal another moment of her time.

"No—I'm afraid you don't. I probably shouldn't tell you this, but I can't let you think me a cad. The reason I was rude was . . . I . . . I was a juror on Claire's grand jury, and I had to get back for the vote."

"Oh . . . I see." She realized she hadn't considered who the jurors were. "Well, in a town this size, it was bound to happen that someone we knew would be on it. I really must—"

"That isn't all," he said. "I want you to know I did not vote to indict Claire. They needed nine votes. They had nine. Mine was not among them. I do not believe she did it."

Emma felt the tension in her body release. She was relieved to know that John Jr., whom she thought she knew well and liked, had not betrayed Claire, even in the face of what she imagined was significant pressure from the other jurors. She knew how much his reputation and standing in the community meant to him. It was a sign of both his integrity and his trust that he was sharing this information.

"Thank you, John. It means something to me that you voted your conscience, knowing which way the room was likely to go."

"I am her friend. Yours, too. And I am sorry for my manners."

Emma smiled. "I accept your apology."

They walked a little way toward town together. At the boardinghouse Emma wished him good evening and went in feeling, if only slightly, less burdened.

❧ CHAPTER 37 ❧

"Come in, please, Mr. King," Edward Clark said. "Thank you for seeing me this morning, Mr. Clark. With my client's trial starting next Monday, there are some important matters I'd like to discuss with you." Gabe King got right to the point.

"Of course. Can I offer you something to drink—tea or coffee?"

"No, thank you. I will make this brief. Your time is valuable, as is mine."

"Very well. Please, be seated."

The two men took seats on opposite sides of Clark's desk.

"I am aware of a letter allegedly written by my client that may be in your possession," King said. "If this is true, and you plan on introducing the letter as evidence, I would like to see it."

"Of course, that is only proper. But we will have to walk over to the sheriff's office, where it is secured," Clark said evenly.

King studied Clark's impenetrable face. He knew and respected the man: a very competent lawyer, who did everything by the book and was completely committed to his duty. In this case, his duty was to present the most compelling case against Claire La Salle as possible. After a long moment, reading nothing in Clark's expression, King stood.

"Shall we go and see the sheriff?"

The men walked the short distance to the sheriff's office. The sheriff was out, but the clerk showed them to the room where the letter was stored. He unlocked the cabinet, handed the letter to King, and then stood quietly in the corner. "I'm afraid it's quite damning, Mr. King," Clark said. King thought he detected some regret in the special prosecutor's tone.

King examined the envelope. It was posted from Manitou and addressed to Phillip Mouton in New Orleans. He carefully removed the letter and read it. Clark was right—it was damning.

"You understand that you'll have to establish its authenticity without Mrs. La Salle. You cannot compel her to testify against herself," King said flatly, returning the letter to its envelope and handing it back to the clerk.

"This is not my first prosecution, Mr. King."

"No, of course it isn't."

Back in Manitou, Emma was in the office, trying to focus on work. It was early afternoon. By now, Gabe King would have met with Mr. Clark and seen Claire's letter. Emma wondered just how bad it was.

She rose from her desk and looked out the window. The

train from Colorado Springs was just arriving. Maybe King was on it. If she hurried, she might intercept him and learn something. She scanned the stream of passengers leaving the depot across the street, though she doubted she could pick him out in the crowd.

Behind her, the door opened and Albright walked in. "Boss!" Emma said, surprised. "I wasn't expecting you today."

"Good afternoon, Emma," Albright said without enthusiasm.

"I didn't see you get off the train."

"No, I came in yesterday. There was an emergency board meeting this morning." His expression softened. "I'm sorry about Mrs. La Salle. I know how much she means to you."

"Thank you. It is a difficult time." Emma accepted his sympathy, but her thoughts leapt to the meeting. "What was the meeting about?"

Albright poured himself a glass of water and sat heavily at his desk. His shoulders sagged with travel weariness. "I'm afraid the board's decision about my replacement has been postponed. The scandal over Mrs. La Salle and the murder of—what was his name again?"

"Phillip Mouton."

"Yes, Phillip Mouton. Anyway, they want to wait until her trial is settled."

Relief rushed through her. She wanted to be there for Claire—of course she did—but her future had been looming just as large. Now she could give herself wholly to Claire without feeling she had abandoned her own prospects. And with August's numbers still climbing, the delay might even help her cause.

"That seems wise," she said.

"Oh, I agree. I never understood their rush in the first place." He drank, then exhaled heavily. "All this travel—Denver last week, Chicago the week before—trying to balance everything. It's wearing thin."

Emma offered a rueful smile. Balancing loyalties and responsibilities seemed to be what life was all about.

Albright shook his head as if to clear it. "Have you eaten? I'm famished."

"No . . . I've been too anxious. But yes, I could use something."

"Then let's go forget all this for an hour or so." He took up his hat and gestured her toward the door.

Emma followed, but her thoughts lingered across the street at the depot, where she imagined Gabe King stepping from the train with Claire's fate in his hands.

Gabe King had, in fact, been on the afternoon train. He had telephoned Claire after his meeting with Mr. Clark and arranged to see her as soon as possible. Now, in Claire's sitting room, the gravity of her situation weighed heavily in the air.

Claire sat rigidly in her armchair, the cup and saucer in her hand rattling almost imperceptibly. Gabe King closed the folder in his lap, the rustle of paper loud in the hush of the room.

"As I said, the letter is damaging—very damaging," he said quietly. His pale blue eyes fixed on hers, steady but grave. "In it, you clearly threaten Mr. Mouton. Mr. Clark will seize upon that and say it is proof you meant to kill him. He will argue premeditation—and with it, the gallows."

Claire's breath caught. She pressed a trembling hand to her mouth. "Is there no hope?"

"Of course there's hope." Gabe leaned forward, softening his tone. "A jury may hear Clark's words, but they must weigh them against reason. A phrase written in fear is not the same as a plan to murder. I will remind them of that."

Her eyes brimmed with tears. "And if they don't accept

your argument?"

"Then the law provides degrees," he continued. "First degree is deliberate, willful murder. That would bring a sentence of death by hanging." He paused, letting the weight of it settle, then continued more gently. "Second degree is less immediately grave. The punishment then would be life at hard labor in Cañon City. It spares you the rope, but the conditions there might kill you."

Claire's voice broke. "Is there no better outcome if I'm found guilty?"

"Manslaughter," Gabe said, almost reluctantly. "Killing in sudden fear or passion. That could mean years in prison, but not for the whole of your life. Still, the evidence does not fit it well. Clark will tell them as much. I will counter his argument by stressing that you are innocent, period. But I will be honest —manslaughter is an unlikely outcome should the jury find you guilty."

Claire rose and stood at the mantel, where a photograph of her husband depicted a happier time. For a long moment neither spoke. At last, Gabe rose and crossed to her side. He did not touch her, but stood near.

"Claire." His voice softened, losing the courtroom steel. "I will fight for you with all that is within me."

She looked at him then, truly seeing the lines of care on his face—the strength in his eyes. Her lips parted as if to speak, but no sound came. Instead, she whispered, "You are very good to me, Mr. King."

He gave a faint, kind smile, and for an instant the gravity lifted. "Not good, merely stubborn. I mean to see justice done."

Their gazes held a moment before Claire turned and began pacing.

Gabe gathered his folder and, in a firmer tone, said, "Don't waste time with worry. Leave that to me."

She nodded, but the frown on her face indicated that was easier said than done.

❀

Emma and Albright left the office early. He longed for sleep, and she was eager to learn where things stood with Claire. The streets were thronged with visitors—proof the season was still in full swing—but Emma hardly noticed until Major Wright stepped out from the bathhouse.

"Leaving work early again, Miss Quinn?" His voice carried the tone of a barb disguised as a greeting.

Emma started, too surprised to take offense. She was long accustomed to his rudeness.

"Oh! Major Wright. I didn't see you."

"I suppose you've heard. The board is postponing its decision until after your cousin's trial? Unfortunate for you, being linked to such an affair."

"Not at all. The jury will see she is innocent. We may never know who killed Mr. Mouton, but the town will know soon enough that it wasn't Claire." Emma prayed her voice sounded more confident than she felt.

"I don't see how the scandal won't follow her, even with an acquittal. Who else could it have been?"

"Oh, I don't know . . . perhaps one of the three hundred strangers who crowded this town that week?" Emma shot back.

Major Wright gave her an oily smile.

"If anyone else had wanted him dead, they could have managed it anywhere. Yet he dies under Mrs. La Salle's roof. Quite the coincidence."

Emma realized further argument was pointless—and

dangerous. "Please excuse me. I'm needed at home." She stepped around him briskly, resisting the urge to shudder, and quickened her pace toward the boardinghouse.

"Argh, I hate that man!" Emma growled between her teeth as she entered the boardinghouse.

"What man?" asked Claire, tidying the parlor with a feather duster.

The tension on Claire's face betrayed the otherwise comforting domestic scene, reminding Emma what was at stake.

"Major Wright. I just had a most unpleasant encounter . . . it's nothing." She waved her hand dismissively. "What can I help with?"

"Nothing, dear. Molly has dinner in hand. I'm only trying to keep busy." Claire gestured toward the room she had been dusting.

Emma longed to ask about Gabe's meeting with Clark but couldn't bring herself to snatch away the small comfort Claire drew from housework. There would be time for that.

"All right. I'll go upstairs and freshen up. That run-in with Wright left me feeling grimy."

At her door, she wondered if perhaps Levi was in his suite and if he knew anything. She gently tapped on his door.

"Come in!" came his deep baritone.

She found him sitting in an armchair by the window, reading the newspaper.

"Emma!" he said warmly, springing up. He set down the paper and greeting her with a quick peck on the cheek. "You're home early."

Emma briefly told him about the delayed board decision and her encounter with Wright.

"But you're home early too, aren't you?" she asked.

He let out a soft chuckle.

"No, I'm often home at odd hours. It's just that you aren't usually here to see it."

Emma blushed. Her long hours at work, her neglect of meals—and of her fellow tenants—rushed back to her.

"I meant no criticism," Levi added quickly.

"None taken."

"Sit and relax. Can I pour you a drink?"

"Yes—that's just what I need." Emma sank into the chair beside his.

He handed her a generous pour of whiskey—not her favorite, but she drank more than a sip.

"Look, Emma, we all know Wright is a conceited peacock. Don't let it get under your skin."

"How can I do that, when he may well be saying what most people think?"

Levi situated himself back in his chair. Emma found no reassurance in his silence.

"What have you learned by making your rounds? Do people think Claire is guilty?"

Levi hesitated too long. No matter what he said next, Emma knew opinion was against Claire. But he wasn't looking to soften the news, only to be accurate.

"I'd say the predominant opinion is that she likely did it, but also that she would have had good reason. People respect her, still."

"Be that as it may, it won't be enough to protect her from a harsh sentence if she's found guilty," Emma lamented. "And what about Gabe's meeting with Mr. Clark? Did it take place, and do you know the outcome?"

"Yes, yes . . . it took place all right. I saw Gabe as he was walking back to the depot after meeting with Claire. He filled me in."

"Well?" Emma urged him.

"He has seen the letter. It looks authentic, but he says he can cast doubt on that. Still, it's very damaging for Claire. He said he explained to her the possible outcomes of her trial and that nothing short of a verdict of 'not guilty' will likely spare her from a severe punishment. Even the gallows are a real possibility."

Emma gasped. "No!"

"Although . . ." Levi added quickly, "Gabe says he's hell-bent on casting sufficient doubt in the jury's mind to set her free."

"I don't doubt his commitment, Levi, I'm just afraid he will fail. It seems the town wants a scapegoat."

Levi longed to take Emma into his arms to comfort her, but it would take far more than an embrace when the facts were stacked against a happy resolution.

"When I got home, Claire was putting on a brave face, running about the boardinghouse cleaning and barking orders at Molly. I think she needs to pretend things are fine. Let's go along with her."

"Of course." Emma's voice was steady, though her heart was not.

❀

As it turned out, everyone at the boardinghouse followed Claire's lead and acted perfectly normally at dinner. No awkward silences, unfortunate choice of words, or wary glances interfered with the delicious pot roast and cherry pie Molly had prepared. Peter, Levi, and Willy took the initiative in clearing the table and washing the dishes, which might have been the one good change to come out of Claire's absence after Mouton's murder. Emma hoped it would be a lasting one.

"Let's have some music!" Claire said brightly once they

were all gathered in the parlor. Without hesitation she crossed to the piano and struck up "Turkey in the Straw." The jaunty tune set heads bobbing and feet tapping almost at once, laughter bubbling up as if the house itself had been holding its breath too long.

"Oh! That was wonderful!" Christine exclaimed, clapping until her cheeks flushed.

Claire barely let the applause die before rolling straight into "Oh! Susanna," and the whole room joined in, voices weaving together in cheerful chorus. She segued into "Camptown Races," and at that, Levi sprang to his feet, catching Emma by the hand. With a laugh she let him whirl her into a few improvised polka steps, her skirt flowing with the rhythm of the tune.

When the last notes faded and they collapsed into laughter, Christine clutched Emma's sleeve. "Do sing for us, Emma—please!"

Emma's throat tightened. Singing was the last thing she had felt like doing for weeks, but she couldn't deny them. The boardinghouse hadn't sounded this cheerful in recent memory, and she wanted to carry that fragile joy a little farther.

"How about 'Beautiful Dreamer'?" Emma suggested.

Claire nodded and began playing. Emma had a lovely voice and was often asked to sing for them. She had even sung at the hops around town from time to time. Her voice floated through the parlor, clear and steady. When she reached the refrain of the first verse, another voice slipped in—deep, measured, perfectly in tune. Emma, startled, glanced toward Peter Graham, who sat half in shadow on the other side of the room, his expression unreadable as he harmonized.

"Peter! I had no idea you had such a wonderful voice," Claire said warmly when the song was done. The others chimed their agreement, while Emma still felt the echo of her surprise at Peter's unusual, if welcome, behavior.

And for a fleeting moment, laughter and music banished the trial, the scandal, and the fear.

❧ CHAPTER 38 ❧

The joy was short-lived. The next day, Emma was home in time to help with dinner and was setting the table when Levi stormed through the front door. She heard his boots land heavily on the stairs, then a muffled *thud* when his door shut.

She quickly finished her task and followed him. Upstairs, she gently tapped on his door.

"Levi? . . . Is something wrong?" she asked through the door.

She heard a muffled sound of footsteps before Levi opened it.

His angry expression frightened her.

"What's happened?" she asked.

"The town's full of wagging tongues and small minds," Levi muttered. "They're already condemning Claire before a word of evidence is heard."

Emma was usually the one who had a poor view of human nature, not Levi, and she had no immediate words of comfort. Rather than saying something that would only make things worse, she went to him and gently laid her hand on his shoulder.

For a heartbeat he stayed rigid, then Emma felt his shoulder ease almost imperceptibly.

"The talk around town is growing more vicious," he said. "It's almost as if people *want* to see Claire hang."

"I doubt their intentions are clear—even to themselves. They're caught up in the intrigue—the drama."

"I only hope Claire doesn't hear it." Levi scowled. "But real damage is being done, Emma, not just idle gossip. The more the town disparages Claire and entertains her guilt, the more likely the jury is to be influenced. Not directly—I'm not suggesting that. But you know how powerful public opinion can be."

Emma's mind flashed to her own time. She had lived in northern Virginia, just outside what was commonly called 'the Beltway'—that area within the confines of the circular bypass around Washington, D.C., and its nearer suburbs. All the politicians there did was spew falsehoods about their opponents. It didn't matter if it were true or false or—as was more often the case—somewhere in between. What mattered was what they could persuade people to believe. Yes, she knew how powerful public opinion could be—and it scared her.

"We just have to make sure Gabe sets the jury straight during the trial," she said in a weak attempt at optimism.

When they went down to dinner, Claire was missing. Everyone else was taking their places at the table as Molly brought in the dish of mashed potatoes.

"Where's Claire?" Emma asked.

"She told me she had a terrible headache and was going to go lie down. I haven't seen her since."

"When was this?" Levi pressed.

"Just after I put the chicken in the oven—about an hour ago, I'd say." Molly wiped her hand on her apron and added quietly, "I think she just needs some time alone."

The group looked blankly at one another. They could count the times Claire had missed dinner on one hand, and all of them had been since that letter from Mouton had arrived. It was Levi who recovered first. He spooned a helping of mashed potatoes before passing the bowl to Peter.

When everyone had served themselves, he said, "Shall we join hands?"

❁

To a fly on the wall, the household might have looked back to normal the next morning. Claire was up early to fix breakfast, and everyone joined her in the dining room. She said all the right words, but her voice was flat, her gaze wandering past the conversation as if she were listening from another room entirely. At one point, Christine had to ask Claire twice to pass the bacon.

"I wish I could stay home with Claire today," Christine said to Emma as they left together for their respective jobs.

"Me, too," Emma said. "She's putting on a brave face, but she seems so lost. I don't think it's good for her to be alone with her thoughts all day. I've got some important letters to answer and must see what Mr. Albright needs me to do, but if possible, I'll come home early."

"Molly will be there, so she won't be alone," Christine offered hopefully.

"True. But Molly, as loyal as she is, isn't family."

Christine nodded, and they walked in silence until Emma

brightened her tone.

"But all isn't doom and gloom. Things between you and Willy seem to be going well."

Christine blushed. "He's such a sweet man."

"It's plain he cares for you—and you deserve it."

As they neared the bookshop where Peter worked, they saw him standing outside, greeting the newspaper man delivering that day's *Colorado Springs Gazette*. By the time they reached the storefront, a fresh copy was already pinned in the window.

Above the fold, in bold black type, the headline screamed: **Trial in Murdered Knight Templar Case Begins Monday**.

Emma's stomach lurched. Inside, Peter looked up from the counter and met her and Christine's eyes. For a breath, the three of them shared the same dread, knowing what was coming.

Back at the boardinghouse, Molly came into the dining room with a stack of plates. She stopped short when she saw Claire on the parlor sofa, staring out the window. A feather duster lay forgotten in her lap.

"Claire?" Molly said softly.

Claire's eyes shifted toward her, but the emptiness stayed.

"Oh, dear . . ." Molly set down the plates and came to sit beside her. She eased the duster from Claire's hands. "I'll see to the dusting. Why don't you step out for a walk? The air's fine today—I swear I felt a hint of fall this morning."

"I can't," Claire whispered. "I can't bear to face anyone." Tears brimmed in her dark brown eyes.

Molly's throat tightened. She wrapped her plump arms around Claire, pulling her close. That simple kindness broke the dam at last, and Claire collapsed against her, sobbing into her breast.

"There, there, love . . . it's going to be all right," Molly murmured, rocking her gently.

When the storm of tears passed, Claire drew back, her face pale.

"We don't know that," she said quietly, "and no matter what, I'll never be the same again."

Later that afternoon, Emma came up the walk and found Molly on the porch, snapping beans into a large bowl on her lap. The older woman's eyes were rimmed red.

Emma stopped short. "Molly? What's wrong?"

Molly shook her head and paused her task, though she did not meet Emma's eyes. "It's Claire. She broke down, poor thing. Sat right there in the parlor with the feather duster in her lap like she didn't know what to do with it. Cried till I thought her heart might split."

Emma's gut clenched. She'd seen Claire's brave face that morning and knew the mask was paper-thin, but the image of her sobbing in Molly's arms drove home just how fragile she was.

Levi came up behind them, hat in hand, sweat darkening his shirt from rounds. He caught the tail of Molly's words. "Claire?" he asked, his voice low.

Emma looked at him, searching for reassurance, but his face was set and grim. "I'll sit with her awhile," he said at last, and went inside without another word.

Emma lingered on the porch, uncertain what to do. For the first time she wondered if Gabe King's skill would be enough, or if Claire's spirit might break long before the jury gave its verdict.

Molly wiped her eyes with her apron and with a firmer voice said, "A letter arrived for you, Emma. It's on the hall table."

Grateful that she had an exit—she really didn't know how

to comfort Molly—or even if she should—she murmured "Thanks," and walked into the boardinghouse. The letter was from Josiah Turner, and Emma's spirits lifted, if only for a moment. She looked at the door to Claire's sitting room and considered joining Levi. It might have been cowardly of her, but she elected to go to her suite and read Josiah's letter. She would soon wish she had chosen differently.

August 22, 1883

My dear Emma,

I apologize for letting so much time pass since my last letter. I admit, I am writing now mainly in response to what I've read lately in the Tribune, *and I had to know how the Maison La Salle household is faring. A week ago, on the 15th, I noticed a small wire buried on the inside page of the paper giving a brief account of the murder of a Templar in Manitou. Of course, it caught my eye and caused me some concern for the community.*

But yesterday's edition carried a much longer article, and it made my heart sink. Claire's name was given outright as the only suspect, and the piece went so far as to say a grand jury would convene as soon as possible in Colorado Springs. The tone was sensational, and though I know how newspaper men love their exaggerations, there was enough detail to trouble me deeply.

Tell me it is not as dire as the paper suggested. You know as well as I that facts and opinions often part ways once a scandal makes its way into print. Protect Claire as best you can, Emma. I fear she will need every true friend beside her before this is done.

Business keeps me busier than I like. I envy you the mountain air, though I imagine at present it feels heavy with worry. Write to me when you can, even a line—it will ease my mind.

Yours faithfully,
Josiah

Emma lowered the letter and let it rest in her lap. It was one thing to hear the town gossip and see the *Gazette* headline glaring from a shop window. It was another to know the story had reached as far as Chicago. Claire's trial was no longer only Manitou's business—it was becoming known nationwide.

She folded the letter carefully and slipped it back into its envelope. For a long moment she stared out at the mountains, feeling the weight press in from every direction—from the town, from the newspapers, from the board, and now from far beyond Colorado.

She couldn't sit alone in her room. She ventured back downstairs and listened at Claire's door. When she didn't hear any voices, she gently tapped. She heard no one call for her to enter, nor did anyone open the door. She cracked the door open and called out "Claire?"

"I'm in here." Claire's voice answered flatly.

Emma opened the door and stepped through. The sitting room lay in subdued late-afternoon shadow, but a dim light shone from Claire's small reading room, where her voice had come from. When Emma first arrived in Manitou, Claire often used that room for card readings, sometimes even for Emma herself.

Emma hesitated at the threshold. "You haven't done this in a while," she said when she saw Claire's Tarot cards arranged in a spread on the table.

"I've laid them out," she said. "And they indicate nothing but ruin. Look—swords at the heart, swords in the past, conflict below, judgment against me, shadows all around. It's as if the cards themselves have joined the town in condemning me."

Emma pulled out a chair and sat beside her friend. She studied Claire's pale, stricken face more than the cards.

"Claire," she said gently, "I've never heard you give a reading that was all so one-sided. What would you tell me if these cards were mine instead of yours?"

Claire blinked, startled. "What do you mean?"

"I mean," Emma pressed softly, "you've read for me before, and you always found more than one thread in the cards. You never said only doom. So . . . pretend this is my reading. What would you tell me?"

Claire's gaze fell to the center. "The woman bound and blindfolded—the Eight of Swords—feels trapped, yes, but not hopelessly. See? There's a gap in the ring of swords. That is her way out."

Emma nodded. "That sounds more like the Claire I know."

Her eyes moved to the King of Swords. She hesitated, then said, "This one—this could be an ally. A man of truth and authority. He's on your side."

"And for you?" Emma prompted.

Claire's lips trembled. "For me, too. I suppose it could be Gabe."

They both looked at the outcome card—the boat crossing still water under a gray sky. Claire's fingers hovered above it.

"If I were reading for you," she whispered, "I'd say you'd make it safely through the storm, leaving the worst behind."

Emma took her hand. "Then let's agree: if there's hope for me in these cards, there's hope for you, too."

Claire's eyes filled, but she nodded, and for the first time that day, a breath of peace seemed to reach her.

❧ CHAPTER 39 ❧

The next evening after dinner, Alice came over to check on Claire, who had spent most of the afternoon with Gabe King reviewing her defense. Emma and Levi joined the two women in Claire's sitting room, but the conversation was strained. Everyone showed their anxiety in different ways. Alice was quiet and calm, but her upright posture suggested someone ready to spring into action. Emma played with a handkerchief and jiggled her foot. Claire was back to her empty, faraway gaze, and Levi paced around the room.

"Oh, please sit down, Levi, you're making me nervous," Emma said.

He stopped, realized what he'd been doing, and silently took a seat.

"It sounds as if Gabe has the matter well in hand," he

said.

"I have complete confidence in him," Claire said weakly.

"Well, if reason prevails, there is no doubt the jury will find you innocent," Alice proclaimed.

Emma began to say that reason seldom prevailed, but stopped herself.

Levi stood again and poured himself a drink, more for something to do than out of thirst. He held the glass and swished the amber liquid around, gazing at it as if in search of answers.

They heard a loud knock—not on Claire's door, but at the front door of the boardinghouse.

"I'll get it," Levi said, setting down his glass.

"Oh, good evening, Sheriff." The women heard Levi's muffled baritone.

They couldn't make out the sheriff's words, but a moment later, Levi led Sheriff Dana into Claire's parlor.

"Good evening, Mrs. La Salle, Dr. Guiles, Miss Quinn," the lawman said, greeting them in turn with a nod. Emma found him awkward, and it was soon apparent why.

He reached into his coat pocket and brought out two sealed papers. He glanced at each of them, handing one to Emma and then to Levi.

"You are hereby summoned to appear as witnesses in Mrs. La Salle's trial, Monday morning at nine o'clock, Colorado Springs courthouse." He paused before adding, almost as an apology, "Please be prompt."

They all stood as if frozen. But Levi quickly recovered and said, "Understood, Sheriff, and thank you for delivering these yourself." He paused and added, "I'll see you out."

"Thank you, Marshal, and good evening, ladies," Sheriff Dana said with another nod before following Levi out, leaving the women staring at the door.

On the boardinghouse steps, Sheriff Dana turned to Levi and said, "I hope you know that I've always respected Mrs. La Salle. She's been a pillar of our community since she arrived. I sincerely hope the jury comes to the correct conclusion."

"That's all any of us want, but I appreciate your sentiments," Levi responded. He watched the sheriff walk away before shutting the door.

❀

Friday passed in an uneasy hush. Levi and Emma had their subpoenas folded away out of sight, though the weight of their significance lingered. Around town, Emma felt the shift more keenly than ever: conversations clipped short when she passed, glances over shoulders that told her the town was more fixed in its judgment of Claire. Levi returned late, weary from a day of hearing her name spoken with suspicion. Alice bore herself with quiet dignity, but the set of her shoulders hinted she was bracing for a blow.

Saturday was no better. Claire kept to her rooms, emerging only briefly, while Molly moved about on tiptoe, performing her chores with silent efficiency. The boardinghouse had fallen into unnatural quiet, as if in mourning. The town itself seemed to hold its breath for Monday.

By Sunday morning, the story had spread beyond Manitou and Colorado Springs. In Denver, the Union Station concourse buzzed with travelers and newspapermen hawking the latest *Rocky Mountain News*. Among the passengers, a man returning east from San Francisco paused to buy a copy, scanning the bold headline:

Trial Monday: Prominent Lady Faces Murder Charge in Knight Templar Case.

❧ CHAPTER 40 ❧

The courthouse stood with stately authority in the heart of Colorado Springs—a proud, columned structure of sandstone and limestone, its tall windows glinting in the morning sun. Inside, the grand courtroom was already stirring with activity. The carved wooden paneling, the soaring coffered ceilings, the polished brass fixtures—every detail radiated dignity and formality. High above the rows of seats, a gas chandelier glittered with glass globes, its light emanating like watchful eyes.

The chamber was meant for county proceedings, but this trial would be different. A murder trial, with a prominent woman at its center and a Knight Templar as its victim—it was the kind of spectacle that filled every seat, every inch of bench, every creaking floorboard with tension.

Outside, a black carriage pulled up beside the curb. Emma stepped down first, smoothing her skirt, her breath catching at the sight of the courthouse looming ahead. She turned as Claire emerged next, supported on one side by Alice and on the other by Gabe King.

Claire wore gray—communicating a serious, but not morbid, attitude. She moved like someone walking a tightrope —posture steady, eyes forward. Her hat, modest and dark, shielded most of her face, but Emma could see the effort it took her to keep her chin high.

Gabe looked crisp and cool, his black suit impeccable, his face unreadable. "Are you ready?" he asked Claire.

"No," she answered, but took his arm anyway.

Levi was waiting near the entrance, hat in hand, his marshal's badge tucked from sight but present all the same. His eyes swept the street and the large crowd gathered in front of the courthouse—locals, reporters, gawkers. When his gaze met Emma's, she felt steadied.

Together, the group ascended the wide steps and entered the courthouse.

Inside, the air was quiet but electric. Spectators already lined the gallery benches, whispering behind gloved hands. The jury box still stood empty, the great judge's bench rising like a pulpit above the floor. A carved eagle above the bench held its wings outstretched, as if to preside over not just law but fate itself.

Emma took in the setting—the towering windows with their diamond-paned glass, the way the morning light painted long shadows down the aisle. She felt, all at once, the weight of history and the fragility of a single life within it.

Claire moved to the defense table and sat beside Gabe. Alice joined Emma in the gallery. Emma spotted Levi on the far side of the courtroom, seated stiffly with the other lawmen.

When their eyes met, his stern expression softened a little.

The bailiff's voice rang out. "All rise."

The judge entered and sat as he said, "You may be seated."

As the room settled, the bailiff turned again to the heavy oak door near the jury box and opened it. A moment later, twelve citizens filed in—men in their best coats, freshly shaven or combed, some stiff with nerves, others self-important. Emma's eyes scanned their faces as they took their seats.

Second row, third from the left: Major Wright. Her first thought was, *How did he make it through jury selection?* She darted her gaze at the back of Gabe King's head but quickly realized the major hardly knew Claire at all. It was Emma he had taken issue with. Relief lasted only a moment before another thought pressed in: he seemed to hate women in general and to think the worst of them. No, he was not going to be a friendly influence. Then, she remembered the unpleasant conversation in front of the bathhouse. No, he would not be a friend; it would take irrefutable evidence for him to vote to acquit Claire.

Judge Colburn adjusted his spectacles and turned to the jury box. "Gentlemen, you have been sworn in as the jury in the matter of *People of the State of Colorado versus Claire La Salle.* This court reminds you that your task is to consider only the evidence presented within these walls and to render your verdict accordingly. The eyes of the community are upon you. Your duty lies with the law."

He paused for effect, then looked toward the prosecution table.

"Mr. Clark, you may make your opening statement."

Edward Clark stood and buttoned his coat before stepping toward the jury box. His voice, when it came, was measured and resonant, carrying easily through the hushed courtroom.

"Gentlemen of the jury," he began, nodding toward them. "You are charged today with a solemn and necessary duty. You are not here to pass judgment on social standing, nor to weigh the esteem in which the defendant is held by certain members of her community. You are here to examine facts. And the facts, I believe, will speak clearly."

He stepped closer, his gaze unwavering.

"On the thirteenth day of August, 1883, Phillip Mouton, a delegate to the upcoming Knights Templar conclave in San Francisco, was found murdered in the boardinghouse owned and operated by the defendant, Mrs. Claire La Salle. He was stabbed in the back with a letter opener taken from the hall table of that boardinghouse. He was discovered by tenants of that abode, with Mrs. La Salle standing over his dead body.

"You will hear evidence that Mr. Mouton and Mrs. La Salle shared a troubled past—one that this court will not intrude upon beyond what is necessary to determine motive. But what you must consider very carefully, gentlemen, is a letter, written in Mrs. La Salle's own hand, addressed to Mr. Mouton, and discovered after his death."

He held up a single finger.

"This letter will form the foundation of the prosecution's case. In it, she implores Mr. Mouton never to contact her again. She makes clear that his presence is a threat to her peace and safety—and she issues a threat that, in hindsight, sounds very much like a promise. The prosecution will argue this letter demonstrates intent. Premeditation. A willingness to act."

Another pause. His voice darkened.

"Two days after Mr. Mouton arrives in Manitou, he was found dead under Mrs. La Salle's roof. The murder weapon belonged to her. No one saw him enter. And the defendant was found by her own tenants with the body only moments after he was killed. Only one person had a troubled past with the victim.

Only one had reason to fear him and expressed that fear and the lengths she would go to protect herself. That person is the defendant, Mrs. Claire La Salle."

He clasped his hands behind his back.

"We will not ask you to speculate. We will ask you to consider the sequence of events, the evidence left in the victim's wake, and the defendant's own words. I am confident that when you do, the conclusion will be inescapable: Claire La Salle did not act in fear or in haste—she acted with intent. The law defines such an act as murder in the first degree. It is your duty to render a verdict that reflects that truth—and we trust you will do so with the care and gravity this case demands."

The courtroom remained still as Edward Clark resumed his seat. For a moment, only the scratch of the clerk's pen could be heard. Then Gabe King stood—slowly, deliberately—and walked toward the jury, his arms relaxed at his sides.

He did not project the forceful authority of the prosecution. Instead, he let a moment of silence pass before speaking, as if inviting the jurors to settle in and listen to the truth of his words.

"Gentlemen of the jury," he began, his voice smooth and confident. "You have just heard a powerful account—compelling, even. But compelling is not conclusive."

He took a few slow steps up and down the jury box, gazing at each juror separately.

"The prosecution would have you believe this case is simple. A woman with a past. A man with a wound in his back. A letter, passionate in its language. They ask you to take these pieces and assemble them into a narrative of premeditated murder. But justice, as you know, does not concern itself with stories—it concerns itself with truth."

He gestured gently toward Claire.

"My client, Mrs. Claire La Salle, is a widow, a respected

member of our community, and generous to those in need. She has opened her home and her heart to others, without prejudice."

He paused to let that sink in.

"You will learn that Mr. Mouton's pending arrival in Manitou Springs was expected—yes—and even dreaded by Mrs. La Salle. You will hear testimony about what she endured years ago. You will hear how that letter—so central to the prosecution's case—was never meant as a threat, but as a desperate plea for distance. A cry to be left in peace."

He took a step closer to the jury box, his voice dropping slightly.

"And you will hear what happened the day of the murder. You will hear that no one saw Mr. Mouton enter the parlor. How the timing of Mr. Mouton's death leaves room for other possibilities. You will learn about others who had reason to fear —or resent—the man now dead. And you will hear how easily a scene can be misunderstood."

He straightened, letting his words settle.

"This trial is not about a woman who acted with malice. It is about a woman who has already endured far more than she should have—and who now stands wrongly accused because it is easier to blame her than be bothered with the truth."

He turned and gave Mr. Clark a knowing glare. "All I ask," he said, turning back to the jury, "is that you keep your minds open. Listen closely. And at the end of these proceedings, I believe you will find that the only just verdict is not guilty."

With that, Gabe returned to the defense table and sat down beside Claire, who gave the faintest of nods, her hands still clenched tightly in her lap.

Judge Colburn leaned slightly forward on the bench and said, "Mr. Clark, you may proceed with your first witness."

Clark rose and said in a loud voice, "The prosecution calls Dr. Wiley to the stand."

The courtroom watched in silence as a lean, silver-haired man stepped forward. Dr. Wiley, the medical examiner from Colorado Springs, gave his credentials with crisp efficiency before Clark launched into his line of questioning. "What time was Mr. Mouton's death estimated to have occurred, Doctor?"

"Between 10:00 and 11:00 a.m. on the thirteenth of August," Dr. Wiley answered.

"And the cause of death?"

"Single stab wound to the back. The weapon pierced the lower thoracic region and severed the aorta. Death would have been nearly instantaneous."

"Was the murder weapon identified?"

"Yes. A letter opener made of brass, approximately eight inches in length, belonging to the household of Mrs. La Salle."

Clark turned to face the jury. "Was there any indication of a struggle?"

"None. No defensive wounds on the victim's hands. It appears he was taken entirely by surprise."

"Thank you, Doctor."

King stood and asked only a few brief questions to confirm the window of time in which the murder could have occurred. He turned back toward his desk, then paused, pivoting to face the witness box once more.

"Doctor, how much force would it have taken to stab a man of Mr. Mouton's stature with the murder weapon?"

Dr. Wiley adjusted his spectacles. "A considerable amount, Mr. King. The weapon—a brass letter opener—was not designed for penetrating flesh, let alone muscle and bone. To drive it through the back and into the thoracic cavity with enough force to sever the aorta would have required a strong, deliberate thrust. Especially in a man of Mr. Mouton's build."

He glanced toward the jury. "Mr. Mouton was broad-shouldered and heavily muscled. The blade would have needed to pass through the latissimus dorsi and intercostal muscles, then between a rib. That is not easily done."

King raised an eyebrow. "So this would have been a physically demanding act?"

"Yes," the doctor answered plainly. "It required considerable strength."

"More than one might reasonably expect of a woman like Mrs. La Salle?" Gabe asked.

"Objection!" Mr. Clark stood abruptly. "Calls for speculation."

King replied, "Expert opinion, Your Honor."

The judge nodded. "Overruled. The witness may answer."

"Under ordinary conditions, yes," Dr. Wiley said. "I would expect it to exceed the average strength of a woman of Mrs. La Salle's stature."

King gave a small nod. "No further questions."

Clark rose again. "Redirect, Your Honor. A clarifying question."

The judge gestured for him to proceed.

"You said 'under ordinary conditions,' Doctor. Under what circumstances might a woman of Mrs. La Salle's stature have the strength necessary to inflict such a wound?"

Dr. Wiley nodded. "In cases of extreme emotional stress, the body can produce a surge of adrenaline. It's not uncommon for individuals under duress to perform feats that would be impossible under normal conditions."

"Thank you, Doctor. That will be all."

He turned to the bench. "Your Honor, before I introduce the next piece of evidence, I respectfully request we break for the noon recess."

Judge Colburn consulted the clock, nodded once, and tapped his gavel. "This court is in recess until two o'clock. Jurors, remember you are not to discuss the case or form any opinions until all the evidence has been presented and you are instructed to deliberate. We are adjourned."

With a scrape of chairs and the rustle of spectators, the courtroom slowly emptied. But even amid the noise, those closest to the case could feel what was coming next: the letter —and the full weight of its implications—was about to take center stage.

The anteroom off the courtroom was small and dimly lit, with a round table, four mismatched chairs, and a chipped pitcher of water but only two mugs. Claire sat at the table and released the stiffness she had held all morning. She rested her head in her hands. Gabe stood with one hand on the back of her chair, the other tugging lightly at his chin in thought. Emma and Alice had just come in from the corridor, and Levi, who had followed Gabe and Claire in earlier, leaned against the far wall near the coat rack, arms crossed.

Alice broke the silence first. "That was well done, Mr. King. Bringing up the force required to wield the weapon—I think that point landed."

Gabe gave her a modest nod. "It was important to establish early. The prosecution has their letter, but I wanted the jury to understand the physical reality before they got swept up in motives."

Emma pulled out a chair across from Claire and sat. "Major Wright's on the jury," she said quietly, as if the words themselves were distasteful.

"You know him?" Gabe asked.

"Yes. I was surprised he made it through jury selection." She tried not to make her statement sound like a criticism of Gabe's discernment.

"Why are you concerned about him?" Gabe asked.

"He thinks women should be well behaved and domestic —not independent with a means of their own. He will be prejudiced . . . and he's strong-willed. His bias will not only affect his judgment; it will spill onto the others."

Levi shifted against the wall but didn't speak.

Claire looked up at Gabe. "Is there nothing we can do?"

"Not based on Emma's assessment alone, but I'll keep it under advisement." He looked at Emma and added, "Thank you for the insight." Then he straightened and said, "Clark will introduce the letter next."

Everyone was quiet, dreading the inevitable.

He sat beside Claire and said to her gently, in almost a whisper, "It'll be public record the moment it's admitted."

Claire buried her head in her hands again.

Emma murmured, "I hate that it has to be read aloud."

"It is damaging, as we all know," Gabe said to the room, "but it's not a confession, either. And we have room to contextualize it—to show that Claire was just trying to protect herself from Mouton."

"They will see me as guilty before we have a chance to tell our side," Claire said, her head still in her hands.

"I will guide them," Gabe said. "Let me worry about how it plays. You worry about staying steady." His voice was firm, but he placed his hand softly on Claire's hunched shoulder.

Levi finally spoke. "You handled yourself well this morning, Claire," he said, his voice low but sincere.

Claire lifted her head and smiled faintly. "Perhaps I have a future in acting," she said.

A soft knock sounded at the door—a bailiff warning that recess was nearly over.

Gabe stood straighter. "Let's get through this next part. It will be the worst."

Claire rose slowly, drawing herself up with practiced composure. Emma fell into step behind her.

They all filed out together—united, if not unshaken.

❋

The courtroom slowly filled again as the midday recess ended. Voices were quieter now, the weight of the morning hanging in the air like a gathering storm. Emma slipped into her seat beside Alice, catching Levi's eye across the room. He gave the faintest nod—stoic as ever—and resumed his place with the other lawmen. Claire and Gabe took their seats at the defense table, the former composed but visibly pale.

They all rose when Judge Colburn stepped through the chamber door and took his place on the bench.

"Court is again in session," the bailiff announced. "You may be seated."

The wooden pews creaked as the gallery settled.

Edward Clark rose from his seat and in a strong, clear voice said, "The prosecution calls Sheriff's Deputy Aaron Saunders to the stand."

A brief rustle passed through the gallery as the deputy made his way up the aisle, took the oath, and settled into the witness chair. After he verified his name and capacity, Clark began his examination.

"Deputy, have you been involved with the investigation into Mr. Mouton's murder?"

"I have," Saunders said, his voice steady.

"Did your investigation include a search of the victim's room at the Mansions Hotel, known locally as the BeeBee House?"

"It did."

"Did you discover any written correspondence relevant to

the case?"

"Yes. In the drawer of the nightstand, a housekeeper in my presence found an envelope addressed to Mr. Phillip Mouton. It was postmarked Manitou, Colorado. It had been opened. I removed the letter and read it there."

Clark retrieved an envelope from his desk and approached the witness stand.

"Deputy, I now show you what has been marked for identification as Prosecution Exhibit B. Do you recognize it?"

Saunders leaned forward. "Yes. This is the envelope found in the nightstand."

"Has it remained in your custody since the date in question?"

"It has. It has been kept in the sealed cabinet at the sheriff's office until this morning."

Clark turned toward the bench. "Your Honor, the prosecution moves to admit this letter into evidence as Prosecution Exhibit B."

Judge Colburn gave a solemn nod. "So admitted."

Clark returned to the witness. "Did you determine the author of the letter?"

"I was present when the sheriff questioned Mrs. Claire La Salle after her arrest. She admitted to writing it."

"Did she offer any explanation?"

"She said it was meant to make clear to Mr. Mouton that he was not welcome and that he should leave her alone. She did not wish to speak further on the matter."

Clark lifted the letter. "Would you please read its contents aloud for the court, Deputy?"

Deputy Saunders removed the letter from the envelope and read in a clear voice:

Mr. Phillip Mouton, Sir,

Your recent letter reached me, and I cannot let it go unanswered. That you persist in troubling me after the injury and disgrace you have already visited upon me is beyond comprehension.

I will not be persuaded to any meeting, nor will I entertain further correspondence from you. You must cease your advances and your insinuations at once. You have already taken from me more than any gentleman would dare, and I will not suffer another indignity at your hands.

If you persist in this course, I shall be forced to act in a manner you will find most unpleasant. You know well I am not without means to bring this matter to an end, and I will not hesitate should you compel me.

Leave me in peace, Mr. Mouton. This is the last I shall say to you on the matter.

Mrs. Claire La Salle

A murmur rippled through the courtroom before the judge gaveled once. "Order."

Clark returned to the prosecution table. "No further questions at this time, Your Honor."

Judge Colburn nodded toward the defense table. "Mr. King?"

Gabe rose slowly and approached the witness stand, his tone respectful but firm.

"Deputy Saunders, thank you for your clear testimony. Just a few questions."

He stepped to the side, positioning himself between the jury and the witness box.

"You just read the letter to the jury. Was there an explicit threat of death?"

"No."

"So, it is up to interpretation as to what Mrs. La Salle

meant, correct?"

"Objection! Calls for speculation."

"Sustained."

"Indeed, the letter as a whole calls for speculation," King countered slowly and deliberately. Then, back to Saunders, he asked, "I'm asking you as a general reader—just like the rest of us—what was your overall impression of the letter?"

Saunders hesitated, then said, "It seems like a plea, sir, from someone very afraid of Mr. Mouton."

"Thank you, Deputy . . . no further questions, Your Honor."

Gabe returned to his seat without looking at Claire.

Clark rose again. "The prosecution is done for the day and moves for a recess."

"Very well," said Judge Colburn. "This court will reconvene tomorrow morning at nine o'clock."

He brought his gavel down once. "We are adjourned."

The benches scraped. Shoes shuffled. Claire sat frozen. Gabe touched her arm and gently helped her to stand.

Emma rose slowly, her heart thudding against her ribs. She looked to Gabe, who leaned in close to Claire and murmured something none of them could hear.

The letter was out now. And so was the damage.

❧ CHAPTER 41 ❧

B ack at the boardinghouse that evening, Gabe met with Claire, Levi, and Emma to prepare them for the next day.

"It would be better for Claire if we could avoid any of you being declared hostile witnesses," he began. "The best way to do that is to answer Mr. Clark's questions fully and without appearing evasive or reluctant. He'll begin by establishing your relationship to Claire, and from that alone, the court will presume some bias against the prosecution. But if you come across as candid and cooperative, it may take some of the wind from his sails. Leave it to me to mitigate any damage on cross-examination."

They all nodded, though Emma's thoughts were elsewhere. She wasn't worried about seeming evasive—she was worried about having to lie under oath. Even the simplest description of her relationship to Claire would require a falsehood. She glanced at Levi, who was clenching his jaw. He might be able to skirt the truth without blinking—he had known Mouton and had said plainly that he thought the man got what he deserved.

"Emma?" Gabe asked gently. "Did you hear me?"

She blinked and straightened. "I'm sorry. I was deep in thought."

"Don't overthink it. If you pause too long, it will look like you're choosing your words too carefully."

"Yes, I understand," she said quietly.

They spent the next half hour in a kind of rehearsal, with Gabe alternating between playing himself and Mr. Clark—posing questions, challenging answers, redirecting tone and phrasing until each person could answer calmly, without hesitation.

During a pause, Gabe heaved a heavy sigh.

"Claire, it would strengthen your case substantially if you'd allow me to at least hint at what he did to you back in New Orleans—how he violated you. That would make it easier for me to establish what a scoundrel Mouton truly was, and to introduce Levi's reaction—how he suggested something harsher than just running him out of town. It would speak to your character—and plant the seed that a man like that would have had many enemies."

"No!"

Emma leaned toward her. "There's no shame in it, dear."

Claire's eyes flashed. "No shame? . . . You weren't *there*. . . . You didn't see. . . ." She buried her head in her hands. "No. I won't have it brought up."

They resumed preparations until Molly knocked firmly on Claire's door and called, "Dinner!"

Everyone rose and followed Claire out to the parlor and

into the dining room.

As Gabe passed Peter Graham, Peter reached out and caught his sleeve.

"Mr. King—just a brief word?"

Gabe paused. "Yes, of course."

Peter lowered his voice. "I just thought you should know —I haven't been subpoenaed to testify."

Gabe's eyebrows rose. "You haven't?"

Peter shook his head, then glanced toward the dining room, where the others had already begun taking their seats. "Thought it best to tell you directly," he murmured before slipping through the doorway to join the rest.

After a congenial, if somewhat tense dinner, Levi asked Gabe to join him on the front porch for a smoke.

"I'll meet you there," Levi said. "I need to get my pipe. I have a box of cigars. Can't vouch for how good they are . . . I don't smoke them myself. Would you care for one?"

Gabe nodded, but mostly out of politeness.

Once settled in the rocking chairs on the porch, Gabe told Levi what he'd learned from Peter.

"Clark's going to make you earn your keep," Levi said, pulling gently on his pipe to light the tobacco.

"As would I, in his place," Gabe admitted.

Gabe let Levi light his cigar. He took one puff, then let it burn slowly between his thumb and index finger. They sat silently for a time.

"I can't lose her, Gabe," Levi said, simply.

Gabe looked at his friend. They'd lived through losing both their wives together, though neither had spoken of it in some time. Bearing witness to the other's grief had formed a special bond between them. Gabe well understood Levi's vulnerability.

"Claire is a very special woman," he said finally. "I will do everything humanly possible to get her off, Levi. You can believe that."

✽

"Marshal Warwick," Clark said the next day, already standing before the jury box, "you were present when Mr. Mouton's body was discovered?"

"I was," Levi replied, his voice even.

"Describe the circumstances for the court."

Levi turned slightly toward the jury. "I had returned to the boardinghouse after doing my rounds. The Templars from Boston and Missouri were in town, so it was particularly busy. I had run into Miss Quinn, and as we were both heading to the boardinghouse where we reside, we walked together. We found Mr. Mouton lying on the floor of the parlor, apparently dead. Mrs. La Salle was standing next to him with her hands over her mouth."

"Had she called for help?"

"Not that I heard. She was—" Levi hesitated. "She seemed in shock."

"Please refrain from giving opinions or interpretations, Marshal," the judge cautioned.

Clark then asked, "Did you see anyone else nearby? Any signs of forced entry?"

"No."

"Was the murder weapon still in the room?"

"Yes. A brass letter opener, embedded in the victim's back."

Clark paused for effect. "Had you ever seen that letter opener before?"

Levi hesitated again. "Yes. It belonged to the household. It normally sat on the hall table."

"And in your capacity as marshal, did you take possession of it?"

"No. I checked for life signs. When I found none, I immediately secured the scene and notified the mayor and sheriff."

Clark took a step forward. "What other observations did you make about the victim?"

"I'm sorry, sir, I don't understand your question," Levi said, genuinely.

"The body, Marshal. Was it warm or cold?"

After the briefest hesitation, Levi answered, "It was warm."

"And based on your professional experience, would you say Mr. Mouton had only very recently been stabbed?"

"Yes," Levi mumbled.

"Please speak up for the jury, Marshal."

Levi cleared his throat. "Yes."

"Thank you, Marshal. Now . . . let us turn to your prior knowledge of both the victim and the defendant. You are related to Mrs. La Salle by marriage?"

"I was married to her late sister, Daphne."

"And what was your relationship, if any, to Mr. Phillip Mouton?"

Levi's brow shadowed slightly. "I knew him. We were acquainted in New Orleans during the years I worked for Claire and Daphne's father—also through his association with Mr. La Salle."

Clark folded his hands. "And what was the nature of their association—Mouton and Mr. La Salle?"

"They were business partners."

"And is that how Mrs. La Salle knew Mr. Mouton?"

"Yes."

"Did their association end with Mr. La Salle's death?"

"No."

"Can you describe their relationship after Mr. La Salle's death?"

Levi looked down at the hat in his hands.

"Mr. Mouton had been gone from New Orleans for some time prior to Mr. La Salle's death. He returned shortly afterward, claiming a right to Mr. La Salle's estate. A lawsuit ensued. Mouton lost, and he was bitter about it."

"To your knowledge, did he threaten further action?"

Levi hesitated. "He said he'd find another way. But as far as I know, nothing came of it."

"Were you aware of the letter Mr. Mouton wrote to Mrs. La Salle—the one that prompted her reply?"

"Yes."

"And did you read it?"

"I did."

"What did it say?"

"He expressed surprise to learn Claire was in Manitou. He wrote that he wanted to see her."

"Did he threaten her?"

"Not explicitly."

"But one could reasonably infer a threat?"

"Objection!" Gabe said sharply, rising from his seat. "Your Honor, you have already cautioned Marshal Warwick not to speculate."

"Sustained," said Judge Colburn.

Clark gave a slight bow of acknowledgment. "No further questions. Your witness, Mr. King."

Gabe stood. "Marshal, were you familiar with Mr. Mouton's reputation in New Orleans?"

"Yes."

"And how would you characterize it?"

"He was a scoundrel—a rogue."

"Was this a private opinion or one widely shared?"

"Anyone who knew him then knew what he was."

"Would others have had reason to wish him harm?"

"Yes—"

"Objection! Calls for speculation," Clark cut in.

"Sustained," said the judge. "The jury will disregard the witness's response."

"No further questions, Your Honor."

After a brief recess, Clark called Emma to the stand. Once she had stated her name, occupation, and current residence, he moved quickly into his line of inquiry.

"What is your relationship to Mrs. La Salle, Miss Quinn?"

So right off the bat, Emma was forced to lie.

"She is my cousin."

"First cousin? On which side?"

"No, not first. I'm not sure, exactly. More distant. On our mothers' side." Emma had decided it would be harder to trace a maternal relationship.

"And were you close, in New Orleans?"

"No. We did not associate then. That came later, when I arrived in Manitou." That, at least, was true.

"And how did that come about?"

"I'd lost my family. I arrived with nowhere to live and no means of support." Again, strictly speaking, true.

"I'm sorry to hear that, Miss Quinn. So Mrs. La Salle took you in?"

"Yes."

"You must have been very grateful."

"Yes. Claire welcomed me with open arms."

"Please tell us about the morning of August 13, 1883."

Emma gave a short description, closely matching Levi's earlier testimony.

"Let's move on to the letter Mr. Mouton sent to Mrs. La Salle. Did you observe the effect it had on her?"

"Yes. She was visibly disturbed and expressed concern about his upcoming visit to Manitou."

"Did she say she felt threatened?"

"Not physically, no."

"But otherwise?"

Emma hesitated. Claire had been very clear that she feared Mouton might expose her financial secrets, but she knew Claire wanted to avoid that coming out in court—almost as much as the truth of her assault.

"Miss Quinn?" Clark prompted. "Would you answer the question, please?"

"I'm sorry. I'm just trying to recall. . . . I don't remember Claire—Mrs. La Salle—saying anything explicit."

Ironically, this might have been her most egregious lie.

"Were you aware that she replied to Mr. Mouton's letter?"

"Not at the time. I learned of it later."

"How?"

"Town rumor. I'm not sure." Lie number two. Or was it three?

"Were you surprised?"

"Yes. I had thought Mrs. La Salle had decided to ignore Mr. Mouton's letter."

"So perhaps you don't know your cousin as well as you thought."

King stood. "Objection, Your Honor."

"Sustained. Mr. Clark, you will refrain from commentary. Don't let it happen again," Judge Colburn said.

"Yes, Your Honor. No further questions."

"Mr. King, your witness?"

"I have no questions, Your Honor."

Mr. Clark rose and said, "Your Honor, the prosecution has no further witnesses and respectfully rests its case."

Judge Colburn gave a single nod.

"Very well. With the prosecution's case concluded, this court will stand in recess until tomorrow morning at nine o'clock, when the defense will begin its side."

He struck the gavel once. "We are adjourned."

※

"Clark has played his best hand. We know the worst, and now it's up to us to refute it," Gabe said once they were all in the carriage heading back to the boardinghouse.

"His case was thin," Levi added, "but focused."

"Yes. Simple and, I admit, compelling. He established opportunity, means, and motive. For those looking for an easy answer, he gave it to them," Gabe admitted.

Gabe glanced at Claire, sitting next to him. "How are you holding up?"

"I'd vote to convict myself, based on what he presented." She looked back at Gabe, brows knitted. "I'm scared, Gabe."

He took her hand. "This is the bleakest point in the process, my dear. By the time I'm finished, the jury will have an entirely different view."

Alice, who had been mostly silent for the last two days, finally spoke.

"Call me to the stand, Mr. King. I'll set the fools straight."

Gabe gave her a grim smile. "Oh, I intend to, Doctor."

Emma looked at Levi, who was staring out the window. Did he think any less of her for perjuring herself? Somehow, she didn't think so. What did that say about him?

They rode the rest of the way home in silence. As they rolled into Manitou, Emma said, "I need to stop by the office.

Can you have the driver stop the carriage at the hotel?"

Gabe hit the roof loudly with the palm of his hand to alert the driver.

"I'll see you at home for dinner," she said after stepping out of the carriage. She watched it slowly pull away before turning to enter the hotel.

The office was empty. She hadn't seen Albright since the trial started and realized for the first time that he hadn't been in the courtroom. But then again, neither had many of the more prominent men in town—keeping their distance from the scandal, most probably.

A stack of mail rested on her desk. The desk clerk must have put it there in her absence. She began going through it, making note of the financial reports as she opened them. All of the consortium members' August reports were there—all but the one for the bathhouse.

Of course, that one's missing, thought Emma. She tidied the reports in another pile, then grabbed her reticule and hat. She had a stop to make on the way home.

She walked with purpose to the bathhouse and boldly entered the reception room just as Major Wright was coming down the stairs. He stopped half-way down.

"Miss Quinn! Back from the trial already?" Wright drawled, a smirk playing at his mouth.

"I could say the same for you, Major," Emma replied coolly.

"Well, I hope you're not here to influence me in my role as foreman. That would be highly inappropriate."

Emma blinked. She hadn't known he was the foreman—a detail he certainly shouldn't have shared.

"I'm well aware of what's appropriate," she said evenly. "I trust you are, too?"

"Of course." He gave a mockingly gallant nod. "So then—

what brings you here?"

"Mr. Albright has not received the August financial report for the bathhouse. I thought I'd stop by and pick it up."

"Hoping for poor results, I'd wager," he said with a low chuckle. "You're a silly young lady if you think I'd entrust the report to you. I delivered it directly to the board."

He adjusted his lapel with theatrical precision. "Now, if you'll excuse me—I've dinner with Dr. Bell." And with that, he descended the stairs with a brisk gait, heading to Briarhurst Manor, Dr. Bell's fine estate east of town.

Emma ran the short distance home. What an arrogant fool Wright was. Surely Gabe could use his indiscretion in Claire's favor. She crashed through the front door and straight into Claire's sitting room, not bothering to knock.

"Wright's the foreman!" she blurted to the room.

Gabe stood so abruptly his chair scraped. "What? How do you know that?"

"He told me himself, just now, in the bathhouse lobby."

Gabe, Levi, Alice, and Claire all stared at her.

"Well? Surely we can use this! Ask for a mistrial? Have him dismissed?" Emma said, surprised it needed explaining.

Gabe's expression softened, but his voice was measured. "Major Wright was wrong to tell you, Emma. No doubt about that. But it's not so simple. Unless he also said how he intends to vote—or revealed overt bias—it might not be worth the risk. No one wants a retrial. And if we're seen as the reason for one, that could turn the judge or jury against us."

"And don't forget about yourself," Claire said.

"Myself?" Emma asked, blinking.

"You've done enough for me," Claire answered. Everyone except Gabe knew she had lied on the witness stand—about her relationship to Claire as well as her knowledge that Claire considered Mouton a real threat to her reputation. "Major

Wright will know it was you who informed Gabe. Given what is at stake with your job, I cannot allow you to expose yourself."

Levi murmured, "Claire's right."

Alice gave a single nod.

Emma sat down heavily on the sofa, frustration rising in her throat. "I really thought we'd caught a break."

"It's still useful information," Gabe said thoughtfully. "I'll keep it in my arsenal, in case I can use it."

❧ CHAPTER 42 ❧

The morning light cut sharply through the courtroom windows, painting bars of gold across the floor. The atmosphere was no less tense than the day before, but this time, it was the defense's turn.

Gabe King rose with quiet authority and addressed the court.

"Your Honor, the defense is ready to proceed. We call Mr. Peter Graham to the stand."

A stir passed through the gallery. Peter, dignified in his dark Sunday coat, made his way to the front and took the oath before the clerk. He shifted his weight, trying to get comfortable in the witness chair, his long frame folding awkwardly into the narrow seat.

Once all the preliminaries were concluded, King dove in.

"Mr. Graham, did you know the victim, Phillip Mouton?"

"I did."

There was a collective murmur in the chamber.

"How did you come to know him?"

Peter recounted his time in the Confederate army and his stint in Havana, Cuba. He ended by saying, "Mouton was a contraband runner . . . and a spy."

Several in the courtroom gasped.

"Silence in the courtroom," the judge commanded.

"He sold contraband and spied for the Confederate side?" King continued.

"No, sir. He sold contraband and spied for both sides—whoever paid the most."

The courtroom erupted in surprise.

"Quiet! Quiet in the courtroom!" The judge hit his gavel loudly three times.

"Please, tell the court how you know this," King prompted.

Peter then explained how he, as an aide to Colonel Bryce, witnessed transactions involving supplies and information between Bryce and Mouton, and how Bryce had told him not to trust Mouton: he worked both sides.

"Mr. Graham, did you share this information with Mr. Clark, the special prosecutor sitting there?" King gestured to the prosecutor's desk.

"I did, sir."

"And what became of it?"

"Nothing."

"I see." King took a few slow steps toward the jury before turning back. "You're aware that Knights Templar contingents passed through town en route to the conclave in San Francisco?"

"Yes, sir."

"From where?"

"One from Boston, another from Missouri, which included men from Texas and Louisiana."

"Did you witness interactions between those groups?"

"Yes, one evening at the billiards hall."

"Was Mr. Mouton present?"

"He was."

"How would you describe the interaction?"

"Tense. Both sides cast veiled insults. It was barely civil."

King nodded. "Many Templars are former soldiers, are they not?"

"Objection! Calls for speculation."

"Sustained," the judge replied.

King adjusted. "As a former soldier yourself, Mr. Graham, how did you feel seeing Mr. Mouton again after all those years?"

Peter's jaw tensed. He looked down at his hands, folded in his lap. "Angry. He was responsible for lives lost. He betrayed good men for profit."

"Were you angry enough to do him harm?"

Peter looked up. "Perhaps, had the opportunity arisen."

A charged silence fell. King let it linger.

"Where were you on the morning of August 13, 1883?"

"At the bookstore where I work. All morning. There was a steady stream of customers all day."

"Thank you. No further questions."

Clark rose from his seat with deliberate composure, smoothing his coat before walking toward the witness stand. He stopped a few feet away, hands loosely clasped behind his back, and looked up at Peter with an expression of polite doubt.

"Mr. Graham," he began, his voice mild, "you testified that you knew the deceased, Mr. Phillip Mouton, during the war?"

"I did," Peter answered.

"And you claim that he acted as a spy—not just for the Confederacy, but for the Union as well?"

"Yes. He sold contraband, traded information. To both sides, depending on who paid more."

Clark gave a faint smile, as though indulging a tall tale from a child. "You'll forgive me, but did you ever personally catch Mr. Mouton in the act of selling secrets to both sides?"

"No. But I witnessed exchanges—and Colonel Bryce, my commanding officer, warned me not to trust him. He said—"

Clark raised a hand slightly. "Yes, yes. You say Colonel Bryce told you. But Colonel Bryce is no longer living, is he?"

"No, sir. He died years ago."

"So no one can corroborate that warning, correct?"

Peter's jaw tensed. "No one living, no."

Clark gave a small nod, as if acknowledging the unfortunate loss of the only useful witness. "Let's move on, then. When was the last time you saw Mr. Mouton before this summer?"

"Not since the war."

"So nearly twenty years ago. And yet when you saw him again, you recognized him immediately?"

"Yes."

"And after all that time, you still harbored resentment against him?"

Peter didn't hesitate. "Yes."

Clark stepped slightly closer. "You hated him, didn't you?"

A pause. "I did. I do."

"Despite having had no interaction with him for two decades."

Peter sat up straighter. "It doesn't take daily contact to hold someone responsible for betrayal. Men died because of him."

"Men died in that war for many reasons," Clark replied. "But let's focus on the present, shall we?"

He gave a small, rehearsed turn to the jury before continuing.

"Did you speak to Mr. Mouton during his visit to Manitou?"

"No."

"Did he approach you?"

"No."

"Then your testimony today is entirely about what happened twenty years ago—what you say you witnessed, and what you say you were told. By a man now deceased."

Peter stiffened but did not reply.

Clark waited a moment, then resumed. "You also said you were angry. Angry enough to do Mr. Mouton harm, had the opportunity arisen?"

"I might have."

Clark's eyes narrowed. "And your feelings about Mr. Mouton—they have nothing to do with Mrs. La Salle, do they?"

"No," Peter answered evenly.

"You're not close to her, personally?"

"She owns the boardinghouse where I live," Peter replied. "That's all."

Clark stepped a little closer, his voice sharpening just a touch. "Then what, may I ask, motivated you to come forward with this rather dramatic account of wartime betrayal?"

Peter met his gaze without flinching. "The truth," he said, his tone firm. "I thought the court ought to know the kind of man Mr. Mouton really was."

Clark paused, letting the moment stretch. Then, in a measured voice, he said, "Even though that man, however

deeply you may have loathed him, is not the one on trial here."
He turned away. "No further questions."

King then called Levi back to the stand. There was no need
to re-establish his credentials. The jury had already heard from
him the day before, and his authoritative presence had not
been forgotten.

King's questions were brief but deliberate.

"Marshal, yesterday you testified that you knew Mr.
Phillip Mouton in New Orleans. In your personal dealings with
him, what kind of man did you come to understand him to
be?"

Levi's jaw tensed. "He was ruthless. Manipulative. He'd do
whatever served his interests, no matter the consequences to
others."

"Are you aware of Mr. Mouton's activities during the
war?"

"I am."

"And how did you come by that knowledge?"

"Partly through his own words. He wasn't exactly shy
about boasting."

At that, Clark stood. "Objection, Your Honor—hearsay."

King countered smoothly. "I'm not offering it to prove Mr.
Mouton's actual war record, but to illustrate his character as
understood by the witness—relevant to motive and the
likelihood of other enemies."

Judge Colburn considered, then nodded. "Overruled. The
jury will weigh it accordingly."

Levi went on. "Mouton bragged about getting rich by
playing both sides during the war. He didn't see it as betrayal.
Just business."

"And would a man like that make enemies?"

Clark stood again. "Objection—calls for speculation."

"Sustained," the judge said, before King could reply.

King gave a crisp nod. "No further questions."

"The court will recess until two o'clock," the judge declared, striking the gavel once.

Gabe guided Claire to the anteroom. Levi, Emma, and Alice followed. Inside, they found a modest spread of cold meat, cheese, and lemonade—a thoughtful arrangement Gabe had ordered to make sure no one missed another midday meal during the trial.

"Was it enough?" Claire asked as Alice prepared a plate for her.

"Not in and of itself, I'm afraid," Gabe admitted. "But we are planting seeds of doubt. The more seeds, the better."

"I have several to help you plant, Mr. King." Alice set a plate in front of Claire before preparing her own.

"I have every confidence in you, Doctor. Do you want to run through my questions one more time?" Gabe took a bite of roast beef.

"No. I'm very clear on what I need to say."

"What about me, Gabe? Will you call me after Alice?" Emma asked, sitting up straighter. "I could use a little more preparation."

Gabe paused mid-chew. He swallowed, then took a long sip of lemonade before replying, matter-of-factly, "I'm not calling you, Emma."

"What? . . . Why not?" she asked, her voice pitching higher than she intended.

"I forbade it, for a start," Claire said, her tone cool but firm.

"And that's true," Gabe added, "but I also agree."

Emma looked around the small table they had gathered around. To her dismay, no one appeared surprised.

"But I want to help," she said, her voice cracking. Tears of frustration pooled in her eyes.

"And if I thought you had unique information that could save Claire," Gabe said gently, "I'd insist on putting you on the stand. But unless there's something you know that you haven't told us, your testimony only gives Clark another chance to exploit gaps in the story."

"Gabe is right," Levi said. "You already stretched the truth about not knowing how worried Claire was. We got lucky Clark didn't press me harder on that point."

"But I know how good Claire is—how kind and gentle—"

"I can make that point, Emma," Alice said calmly. "And frankly, I agree with Mr. King and Levi. I don't think you can say anything that the rest of us can't present more cleanly."

"And I won't have you further exposed," Claire said in finality.

Emma let out a heavy sigh. She was outnumbered, and she knew it.

Court reconvened promptly at two o'clock. An afternoon thunderstorm rumbled outside, occasionally cracking loud enough to startle the gallery. The gas chandelier provided the only light, giving the chamber more the feel of a ballroom than a courtroom. The earlier tension in the room was replaced by a quiet anticipation. What other surprises did the defense have?

Gabe King rose, his tone calm but purposeful. "The defense calls Dr. Alice Guiles to the stand."

Alice stepped forward, straight-backed and steady in her dark skirt and high-collared blouse. She was not a woman who sought attention, but she held it easily. After taking the oath, she sat in the witness chair with a measured grace.

"Dr. Guiles, how long have you lived in Manitou Springs?" Gabe began.

"About seven years," she said.

"What brought you to the area?"

"I wanted to treat people with tuberculosis."

King nodded slowly. He knew better than most how cruel that disease was.

"What qualified you to do so?"

"I'm a physician. I earned my medical degree from the Keokuk School of Physicians and Surgeons in Keokuk, Iowa."

"And is this still your specialty?"

"No. I specialize in the treatment of chronic conditions—primarily women's ailments and functional disorders. I also own and operate the Three Canyons Spa in Manitou."

"You've known Mrs. La Salle for how long?"

"Since her arrival with her sister and brother-in-law—about three years ago."

"And in that time, would you say you came to know her well?"

"Yes. I came to know her while I was treating her sister for tuberculosis."

"And how would you describe her?"

"Claire La Salle is the kindest, most caring woman I have ever known. She is charitable in every way possible—the way the Bible describes charity. She is welcoming, tolerant, nonjudgmental. Always willing to help her fellow man."

"Would others say the same?"

"Yes, but few know just how generous she is. I know of several people she has helped with the condition of anonymity."

A murmur passed through the gallery. Gabe let it hang a moment before moving on.

"Doctor, I'd like to ask you something more clinical. In your professional opinion, would you describe Mrs. La Salle as physically robust?"

Alice gave a small huff. "No. Claire is strong in spirit, but she is a small woman with somewhat below-average physical strength."

"Would she be capable of delivering a stab of sufficient force to penetrate the ribs and reach the heart, as was done to the victim?"

"Objection!" Clark barked. "Calls for speculation."

Gabe turned to the judge. "Your Honor, the witness is a trained physician familiar with Mrs. La Salle's physical condition. I'm asking for a medical opinion."

Judge Colburn hesitated, then nodded. "Overruled. The doctor may answer."

Alice turned to the jury. "In my professional opinion, it would be practically impossible. Not only would her strength be insufficient, her stature does not align with Mr. Mouton's mortal wound."

King furrowed his brow slightly. They had not rehearsed her last point. He recovered quickly.

"What do you mean, her stature?"

"Well, Mr. Mouton was a large, well-developed man. I estimate his height as at least six feet. Mrs. La Salle is a mere five feet two inches. She could not have inflicted the wound at the height I observed it to be at the inquest. She lacked both the angle and the leverage."

Just then, a bright flash of lightning lit the windows and a deafening crack of thunder startled the courtroom. It was as if God Himself had punctuated the point.

When the moment passed, King asked, "Could you be more specific?"

Alice refocused on his face.

"The wound entered between the upper shoulder blades, consistent with someone standing nearly eye level or even above," she explained. "Mrs. La Salle would have needed to strike upward, and even then, I don't believe the angle would have allowed for sufficient depth to penetrate the aorta."

"And what of her initial response after Mouton's death?

Did you have occasion to observe her?"

"Yes. I arrived at her boardinghouse shortly after Sheriff Dana and Mayor Nichols arrived. I found her in her sitting room with Miss Quinn, who was tending to her."

"And what was her condition?"

"Her face was pale. . . . She was trembling. . . . She stared blankly and seemed disconnected from her surroundings." Alice paused. Her face pinched almost imperceptibly before she regained her stoic expression. "She barely spoke, even when prompted. In short, she was in shock."

"In your medical opinion, did her behavior match what you'd expect from someone who had just committed a premeditated act?"

More murmurs from the gallery. Judge Colburn banged his gavel once. "Order."

"It is more consistent with the horrible, unexpected surprise of finding a dead body in your parlor."

King gave Alice a gentle nod. "Thank you, Doctor. No further questions."

Clark rose slowly and leaned on his desk. He gave Alice a patient smile.

"Dr. Guiles," he began smoothly, "why do you no longer specialize in tuberculosis?"

Alice shifted in her seat. "I found broadening my practice enabled me to help more people."

"There were not enough tuberculosis patients? Or perhaps they lacked confidence in your medical abilities?"

"Objection! Argumentative and irrelevant!" Gabe said firmly.

"Sustained. Move along, Mr. Clark."

Clark moved from behind his desk and stood in front of Alice, arms crossed.

"Mrs. La Salle is not just your friend and patient, is she?

She's also your business partner, correct?"

Alice's eyes narrowed slightly. "No, that is not correct."

"But to be clear for the court," Clark continued, turning slightly toward the jury, "Mrs. La Salle provided most, if not all, of the financial backing for your spa, is that not true?"

"Yes, but she is not involved in its operation."

Clark nodded. "So it would be fair to say you have a vested interest in her continued freedom?"

"I have an interest in justice being done," Alice replied evenly.

"Of course." He stepped a little closer before continuing. "You testified that Mrs. La Salle lacked the strength to stab Mr. Mouton. But she lives alone, runs a boardinghouse, walks to town daily. That doesn't strike me as frail."

Alice didn't flinch. "Strength comes in many forms, Mr. Clark. Carrying firewood is not the same as driving a relatively blunt dagger through cartilage and into a man's heart."

Clark tilted his head. "But in a moment of rage—in a rush of adrenaline—couldn't even someone 'frail' accomplish surprising feats?"

"In rare cases, perhaps," Alice said.

Clark pivoted. "Let's turn to the day of the crime. You said you found Mrs. La Salle in shock, yes?"

"I did."

"Is that not just as typical a reaction after any traumatic event—say, discovering a dead body you yourself stabbed in a fit of passion?"

"Objection," Gabe said. "Argumentative."

"Sustained," Judge Colburn said sharply.

Clark raised his hands in placation, then regrouped. "Doctor, how long after Mr. Mouton's death did you remain with Mrs. La Salle?"

"I brought her to my residence at the spa to care for her.

She was there for several days."

"And during that time, did she ever say to you, explicitly, that she had not committed the murder?"

Alice hesitated. "No. As I said, she hardly spoke at all."

Clark pressed, "But she didn't proclaim her innocence to you, did she?"

"No," Alice admitted, "but she didn't confess either."

Clark gave a short nod, as if satisfied. "No further questions."

King rose from his seat and addressed the court with quiet finality.

"Your Honor, the defense has no further witnesses. We hereby rest our case."

He glanced toward Claire, then back to the bench.

"With the court's permission, I request that closing arguments be deferred until tomorrow morning. This will allow both sides to prepare their summations and give the jury the benefit of hearing them with fresh attention."

Judge Colburn considered this only briefly before nodding. "Very well. The defense having rested, this court will adjourn for the day. We will reconvene tomorrow morning at nine o'clock for closing statements."

He gaveled. "Court is adjourned."

The murmur of the gallery rose again as the jury filed out of the room. Outside, the thunderheads traveled east and beams of late-afternoon sun shone over Pikes Peak.

❀

"You should have seen her! She was magnificent!" Emma gushed to the others gathered at the boardinghouse dinner. Alice and Gabe had joined them, sharing in a quiet celebration after a good day in court.

"She was, indeed," Gabe said, smiling toward Alice. "Though next time, Doctor, perhaps don't surprise me with your testimony."

"I pray there is no 'next time,' Mr. King," Alice replied dryly.

"Oh, please—call me Gabe. I'd say we're well enough acquainted to dispense with formality."

"Very well . . . Gabe. And it's Alice," she replied, the edge of a pleased smile tugging at her lips.

Claire raised her glass. "I'm grateful to all of you. Peter—you were impressive as well. Here's to loyal friends."

"Hear, hear," came the chorus as glasses clinked.

"I only wish I'd been able to offer more direct evidence of Mouton's treachery," Peter said, a trace of regret in his voice.

"I don't see how the jury can do anything but find you not guilty, Claire," Christine said brightly.

Willy nodded enthusiastically.

"We certainly gave them cause to doubt," Gabe agreed, though his expression sobered. He knew juries could be unpredictable.

Claire turned to him, her voice quiet but firm. "Gabe, you represented me flawlessly. It's out of our hands now, but I have good reason to hope—and it's because of you."

She reached for his hand and gave it a gentle squeeze.

The rest of the room shared a knowing glance and then politely looked down at their plates.

Gabe cleared his throat. "Well, I'd better be going. I've got the most important closing argument of my career to deliver tomorrow."

He folded his napkin neatly on the table and rose. "Claire, wear something serious, but not somber. Nothing black. The carriage will collect you all at eight."

He gave her a peck on the cheek, bowed to the room, and

left.

This time, it was Emma whom Levi invited to join him on the patio for his after-dinner smoke.

"I'm afraid to be hopeful," he admitted, watching the last of the dusky light fade from the mountains. Across the street, a group spilled out of the Cliff House, laughing and talking loudly, though their words were indistinct.

"I know," Emma said softly. "But there is hope. Gabe's given the jury real doubt—doubt rooted in evidence, not just in Claire's good character."

Levi nodded but was silent.

"My fears are not just for Claire," he said so quietly Emma could hardly hear him.

She waited, sensing he had more to say. When he didn't continue, she prompted gently. "What else are you afraid of?"

He looked at her. The softness in his eyes betrayed a longing he rarely let show, even as the hard line of his mouth revealed the pain that accompanied it.

"I'm afraid what it will mean . . . for us."

It was true. They had only just begun to acknowledge their feelings for each other when all this had erupted. Since then, their focus had been entirely on Claire. If she were found guilty, she would need them both—completely. And society would expect restraint—for months, if not longer.

Emma turned her gaze toward the darkening silhouette of Williams Canyon. What would Ancha say to Levi now? What wisdom could he offer him—offer them? Emma didn't know.

❧ CHAPTER 43 ❧

Mr. Clark stood and approached the jury box with calm, deliberate steps.

"Gentlemen of the jury, thank you for your attention and your service in this matter. You have heard the facts. You have seen the evidence. And now, you are tasked with rendering justice."

He clasped his hands lightly behind his back.

"Let us remember what this case is truly about. A man—Phillip Mouton—was found dead in the parlor of a respectable boardinghouse. A boardinghouse owned and operated by the defendant. There were no signs of forced entry, no struggle, no theft—only a single fatal wound, inflicted with a household item: a brass letter opener belonging to the premises."

He let his words land.

"And who was found standing over the body? The defendant—Mrs. Claire La Salle—alone. Shocked, yes, but not sorry. She didn't call for help or make any effort to save the man's life. No—she was just standing there."

Clark began to pace slightly, his voice steady.

"You have heard speculation about the victim's past. About possible grudges borne from a war long past. But speculation is not evidence. And while Mr. Mouton may have had flaws, he is not the one on trial."

He turned directly to the jury.

"The law does not permit us to convict someone based on character alone—nor to acquit them based on good deeds. Mrs. La Salle may be a kind woman. She may even be charitable. But even kind people commit horrific acts when pushed to the brink. And we know from her own written words that she had motive. Mouton threatened her security, her reputation, her peace. He was far from a stranger to Mrs. La Salle. He was an enemy."

He softened his tone.

"Your duty is not to determine if Mrs. La Salle is likable, or even admirable. It is to determine whether the prosecution has met the burden of proof. And I submit to you that we have."

Clark stepped back behind the table.

"I ask for a verdict of guilty—guilty of murder in the first degree. Justice requires it."

Clark returned to his seat. It was the defense's turn now.

King rose slowly and walked to the center of the courtroom. He took a breath, then addressed the jury directly, his voice even but rich with restrained feeling.

"Gentlemen, we've reached the end of a difficult few days. You've performed your duty admirably. Thank you. You've been attentive. You've been patient. Now, I ask for your courage."

He held their gaze a moment before continuing.

"The prosecution would have you believe that Mrs. Claire La Salle, a respected woman in this town—a woman known for her decency, her generosity, her integrity—took it upon herself to kill a man in cold blood. That she waited until no one was looking, armed herself with a blunt letter opener, and stabbed a man nearly a foot taller than she was with such force and precision that she pierced through clothing, flesh, and bone to finally strike the heart, mortally wounding him."

He let the image sit for a moment.

"That is a theory. But it is not a fact. And theory alone is not enough to convict."

King stepped closer to the jury.

"We don't dispute that Mr. Mouton was found dead in Mrs. La Salle's parlor. We don't dispute that she knew him, or even that there was history between them. But what we do dispute—and what the prosecution has failed to prove—is that Claire La Salle committed this crime."

He gestured toward the witness stand.

"You heard testimony that Mr. Mouton had enemies—old enemies—dangerous ones. That his dealings during the war left a wake of betrayal. That tensions still ran high among the visiting Templars over this 'war long past,' as Mr. Clark called the bloodiest chapter in our nation's history. You heard how Claire's physical strength and stature could not have allowed her to deliver the fatal blow. And you heard—from a physician —how her immediate condition after the murder was that of genuine, paralyzing shock."

He paused.

"If there is doubt in your mind, then the law is clear: you must not convict. And I say to you—not only is there doubt, but that doubt is reasonable, unavoidable, and real."

He nodded toward Claire, seated quietly at the defense table.

"Mrs. La Salle did not kill Mr. Mouton. The prosecution has not proven so. It is your duty to return a verdict of not guilty."

King gave a respectful bow and returned to his seat.

ᴐ CHAPTER 44 ᴒ

How long do you think the jury will deliberate?" Claire asked Gabe.

"Juries are notoriously unpredictable," he said flatly, then brightened before adding, "But I brought you here to get your mind off the trial and to enjoy this beautiful day. Just look . . ." He pointed beyond the red rocks of Garden of the Gods. "Pikes Peak has never been more majestic."

The mighty mountain towered over the landscape. An early alpine snow capped it white. Behind it, a bright, cloudless blue sky promised perfect weather. How could anything be wrong in the presence of such glory?

"This is the day which the Lord hath made; we will rejoice and be glad in it," Claire said, mustering a smile.

"Indeed, my dear, that's the spirit."

But they both knew her days as a free woman might be ending soon, and by now Gabe King had realized he had more to lose than a case.

If the weather was calm and sunny outside, the atmosphere in the deliberation room was not. The jury was already showing signs of discord. The room was too hot, the air too stale. And some thought Major Wright was the main reason. He had been bloviating all morning.

"This is precisely what happens when women are too independent. They fool themselves into thinking they can cope in a man's world, but the moment the stakes are high, they fold. Women are suited for drawing rooms, not boardrooms," he bellowed.

"What on earth are you on about, Major? How is that at all relevant?" Jack Howard, a grocer, quipped.

"Oh, she did it. We all know she did," Wright continued. "Mouton was after her money, and she couldn't stand the thought of it."

"We don't know that, either," said Harold Knox, the blacksmith. "We only know there was bad blood between them and that he had at one time challenged her inheritance. That matter had been settled, though."

"I agree with Major Wright," another juror said. "Who else could have done it under these circumstances?"

"One of three hundred in town, that's who," countered Mr. Howard.

Wright scowled. "Well, as foreman, I'll ask for our initial votes. Something tells me this might take a while."

He gruffly handed out paper. Some quickly scratched out their opinion, while others looked around the room uncomfortably before hiding their choice.

When the tally came back, Wright rubbed his forehead in irritation. To him, Claire La Salle's guilt was plain as the sun in the sky. Why could these men not see it?

"We are split," he said. "What will it take to reach agreement?"

"I for one need some clarification," Knox replied.

"Clarification? I've rarely heard of such a straightforward case. But if it will get us moving along, let's get your mind at ease."

Wright ungraciously pulled a fresh sheet of paper. "What's your question, Blacksmith?" he demanded.

❀

Gabe and Claire were on their way back from their outing when Levi approached them, riding quickly on a horse. He pulled to a stop at their rig.

"You received a telephone call from the courthouse. The judge is asking for you to return immediately."

Claire shot a look at Gabe. "Could they have reached a verdict already?"

Gabe turned the wagon around and drove the horses as hard as he dared toward Colorado Springs. Levi followed, yelling over the beat of the hooves, "The clerk wouldn't say!"

By the time they reached the courthouse, Mr. Clark was already seated at the prosecutor's desk. The bailiff quickly seated the jury.

"All rise," the bailiff ordered as the judge entered the room.

Judge Colburn called the court to order, then said, "The jury has submitted a written inquiry." He unfolded the slip of paper and, in his steady, strong voice, read:

"The jury respectfully requests clarification of the difference between murder in the first degree and murder in

342

the second degree."

He adjusted his spectacles and turned toward the box. "Gentlemen of the jury, under the statutes of this state, murder in the first degree is defined as the unlawful killing of a human being with malice aforethought, and with deliberation and premeditation. In plain terms, it must be shown that the act was not only intentional, but that the intent was formed beforehand, after reflection." He paused before saying, "Murder in the second degree is likewise the unlawful killing of a human being with malice aforethought, but without deliberation or premeditation. That is to say, it may be intentional, but committed in sudden passion or without prior design."

Judge Colburn folded the slip of paper and set it aside. "Gentlemen of the jury, you will retire again to your room and continue your deliberations, guided by these instructions."

The bailiff stepped forward. "All rise."

The jurors rose from their seats, filing solemnly back through the side door.

The judge waited, and when the jury was gone, he turned his gaze toward the defense table. "Mrs. La Salle, you are to remain within immediate call of this court. The verdict, when reached, must be received in your presence."

Claire inclined her head faintly, though her hands trembled against the rail.

"Yes, Your Honor," Gabe said.

The judge gave a curt nod, his robes swaying as he stood. "This court will stand in recess until the jury returns a verdict."

"Is that all?" Claire asked Gabe.

"Yes. It's a matter of procedure. Anytime the jury has a question, the judge must summon both the prosecution and the defense and answer the question as part of the record," Gabe explained.

"But what does it mean, their question?"

"It's foolhardy to speculate, Claire," he said, gently guiding her out of the room. But as they passed Levi, Gabe gave him a meaningful look.

"Let's get you a room at the Antlers, Claire," Gabe said when they reached the hallway. "You'll be comfortable there, and it's among the closest hotels to the courthouse."

Under happier circumstances, staying at the Antlers would have been a treat. It had opened just after the bathhouse and was by far the most impressive hotel around. As it was, it was merely a fancy jail.

"Yes, but I have nothing with me. No clothes. No toiletries." Claire began wringing her hands. Gabe feared she was slipping back into the fragile state he'd found her in at their first meeting.

They couldn't afford that right now. Levi, who had been standing silently beside Claire, saw the concern on Gabe's face.

"I'll ride back to the boardinghouse and have Emma help me gather your things. I'll be back straightaway."

With that agreed upon, they separated. Gabe went with Claire to get her settled at the Antlers; Levi rode his horse as fast as he dared back to Manitou.

❦

"Did you find them?" Emma asked as soon as Levi entered the boardinghouse. She'd been anxiously waiting in the parlor ever since the court clerk had called. "What happened? Did the jury reach a verdict? Oh, for the love of God, tell me!"

"Calm yourself, Emma." He put his steady hands on her shoulders. "No, they've not reached a verdict. They merely had a question. We're still waiting."

Emma pulled away from him—not angrily, but out of frustration. "This could take days, couldn't it?"

"I don't expect so. Juries come back quickly in most cases."

She paused. In her own century, juries sometimes lingered for days.

Emma resumed pacing the parlor while Levi explained what had happened.

"I need to gather Claire's things and get back to the Antlers. Will you help me?" he asked when he'd finished.

"Of course. And I'm going with you. There is no way I'm leaving Claire alone right now. Can you give Alice a call while I pack? She should know what's happened."

Levi nodded and placed the call to Alice. By the time he hung up, Emma was thundering back down the stairs with her large bag.

"Give me ten minutes to gather her things," she said, dropping her bag on the floor and running to Claire's quarters.

"I'll get a rig," Levi called out as he ran out the door.

They found Alice waiting in front of her spa, shawl already drawn tight, ready to climb aboard as they rode by.

By dinnertime, they were all huddled in Claire's suite at the Antlers. The elegance of the room registered with no one. Supper was sent up, but the dishes sat untouched.

When evening turned into night, Gabe and Levi left for Gabe's quarters two blocks away—close enough to be called at a moment's notice.

That night in Claire's suite passed without rest. Emma dozed fitfully in a chair; Alice prayed softly by the window; Claire herself lay awake, staring at the ceiling as though hoping heaven would open up and save her. Gaslight hissed low, the hours dragged, and the sound of a distant church bell marked time.

At midmorning, the stillness was broken by a sharp rap at the door. Emma answered. A bellboy stood in the hall, cap in hand.

"Message from Mr. King, ma'am."

"Thank you," Emma said vaguely. She opened the note and turned to her friends.

"The jury has reached its verdict. Gabe and Levi are on their way."

Claire swayed where she stood. Emma caught one arm, Alice the other. Together they steadied her.

"Get some water, Emma," Alice ordered as she led Claire to a chair.

They sat with Claire, trying to calm her while they waited.

When Gabe and Levi arrived, Gabe went straight to Claire and offered his hand.

"It's time, my dear."

❀

"All rise," the bailiff called.

The jurors filed into their box and remained standing until Judge Colburn gave a nod. He settled his spectacles on his nose, then looked to the clerk.

"Call the case."

The clerk stood. "*The People of the State of Colorado versus Claire La Salle.*"

At the defense table, Gabe rose, touching Claire's arm. "On your feet now," he murmured, offering his arm for support. Claire pushed herself upright, wavering. Emma placed her hand on Claire's back to steady her friend from the row behind.

She glanced at Alice, who did the same.

Judge Colburn turned his gaze toward the jury. "Mr. Foreman, has the jury agreed upon a verdict?"

Major Wright stood. "We have, Your Honor."

"Pass the written verdict to the clerk."

Wright handed over the folded slip. The clerk accepted it, opened it with deliberate care, and read aloud in a clear voice:

"We, the jury, duly impaneled and sworn in the above-entitled cause, find the defendant, Claire La Salle, guilty of murder in the second degree."

The courtroom broke out in an uproar. Newsmen rushed out to report the story.

"Order! There will be order in this court!" the judge commanded.

The clerk placed the slip on the judge's desk.

Gabe had his arms wrapped around Claire to keep her standing on her now-weak legs.

Judge Colburn looked across the jurors. "So say you all?"

A low chorus of assent followed.

"Does either counsel request that the jury be polled?"

Gabe's jaw tightened. "Yes, Your Honor. The defense requests a poll."

The clerk called the first man by name. He rose and confirmed the verdict as his own.

The clerk called the next man, who stood and said the same.

When the third man stood, the back doors flew open and Deputy Saunders hurried down the aisle, waving an envelope.

"Your Honor, this letter arrived at the sheriff's office by the morning post," he said breathlessly. "It is addressed to the Sheriff of El Paso County and marked as concerning the Mouton case."

A collective gasp filled the room.

Judge Colburn rapped his gavel. "Halt the poll." Then, to the deputy, he said, "Hand it to me."

Claire's knees failed completely. Gabe eased her back into her chair, his arm firm around her shoulders.

The deputy mounted the steps to the podium and handed the letter to the judge. Colburn broke the seal and scanned the first lines. His expression hardened.

"This communication purports to be a confession in the matter before the court." He looked up. "Counsel, approach."

King and Clark stepped forward. The judge laid the unfolded sheet before them. They bent over it, reading quickly. Clark's jaw worked, but he said nothing. Gabe's eyes flashed toward Claire, then back to the page.

After some whispered deliberation, Judge Colburn straightened, his voice carrying across the silent room. "The court will not proceed further upon the verdict until this communication is entered into the record. Mr. Clerk, record it as Defense Exhibit A." He handed the letter across the rail. "Mr. King, you may read it aloud."

Gabe took the paper with both hands. He stepped back from the bench, turned slowly, and—facing the jury and the crowded gallery—began reading:

Sheriff,

I do not know your name, but I know your office, and it is to you I must speak. I have read in the Denver paper that Mrs. Claire La Salle of Manitou is to be put on trial for the death of Phillip Mouton. She is guiltless of that deed. The blame is mine.

I recognized Phillip Mouton that morning at the Mansions Hotel, though the years had changed him. I knew him once as a runner, a smuggler, and a seller of secrets. He played both sides of the war, and where there was profit to be made, he cared not which banner fell.

It was at Chickamauga, in September of '63, that his treachery struck me hardest. My brother's regiment was sent forward blind, while the enemy lay in wait, fully aware of our numbers and supply. Thousands fell in those woods, my brother among them. I have long known where the Confederates bought their knowledge. Mouton was the man who sold it. I approached him to see if he remembered me that morning in Manitou. He did, and he was smug about it.

I followed him to that boardinghouse. He stood by the piano in the parlor, touching at the keys as though to call up a tune. I saw the letter opener on the hall table and decided it was time to settle the score. He never saw me coming. I struck as a soldier does, steady and sure. He dropped, and with him dropped a burden I had carried these twenty years.

This was no common murder. It was the last act of the war, unfinished until that moment. I did what honor demanded, and I do not regret it. Yet that same honor requires that I not allow an innocent woman to bear the penalty for my actions. She did not touch him.

I will not give my name. I trust I have provided sufficient specifics to prove I am the culprit. Let this letter stand as my word, and let the matter rest with the dead.

I remain, respectfully,
A Union Soldier

The courtroom was in stunned silence when Gabe's voice fell away. He folded the letter carefully and returned it to the bench. Judge Colburn gave a grave nod. Gabe stepped back to the defense table and resumed his place beside Claire, his hand resting lightly on the rail before her.

Judge Colburn rapped his gavel once, his expression severe. "Let the record reflect that the court has received and heard a written confession to the killing of Phillip Mouton. It provides details known only to the guilty hand. Counsel for both the People and the defense have examined the letter, and the court is satisfied of its authenticity."

A ripple ran through the gallery, quickly hushed by another crack of the gavel.

"The verdict rendered by the jury cannot stand in light of this evidence. Accordingly, judgment will not be entered. The case of the *People of the State of Colorado versus Claire La Salle* is hereby dismissed with prejudice. The defendant is discharged, and this matter is closed."

Claire looked at Gabe, wide-eyed. "What—what's happening? What does it mean?" she asked between little gasps.

"You're free, my dear. You're free," he whispered in her ear, his arms still around her shoulders.

She began shaking. She reached for the rail for support as her gasps grew more violent. Alice ran around the railing to administer to her patient—her friend. Gabe reluctantly released his guarded embrace. Emma, still taking it all in, joined Alice by Claire's side. She searched the gallery for Levi, who was sitting on the bench against the wall. His face told her he wasn't sure what had just happened, either.

The jurors looked just as curiously at one another. Wright's jaw clenched, but he remained silent.

Judge Colburn rose. "Gentlemen of the jury, you are released from your duty with the court's thanks. This court stands adjourned."

The gavel struck hard, echoing through the chamber, and the room dissolved into chaos.

Levi rushed to Claire, while Gabe, Emma, and Alice supported her shaking body, guiding her through the crowd and out of the courtroom.

"Move aside, give us space!" Levi shouted in the hallway, acting as a human shield. Spectators and the few newsmen astute enough to remain after the initial verdict jostled against them.

"Mrs. La Salle! What was it like, being falsely accused?"

"Mrs. La Salle, how do you feel, now that you've been exonerated?"

"Mrs. La Salle—"

"Leave her alone!" Gabe barked. "Can't you see what an ordeal this has been for my client?"

They made their way to the street, where the carriage still waited.

To Claire, the clatter of the wheels on the road as they returned to the Antlers seemed impossibly loud. She sat between Emma and Alice, staring straight ahead, hands clenched tightly in her lap as though still gripping the rail of the defense table.

Back in her suite, she sank into the armchair by the window and leaned her head against its back, her chest rising and falling with uneven breaths.

"I cannot make sense of it," she whispered at last, her voice hoarse. "One moment they condemned me, the next . . ." Her eyes closed. "I don't know if I'm free or if I'm only dreaming."

"You're free," Gabe said, though the slight quiver betrayed his frayed nerves. "Dismissed with prejudice. They cannot try you again. Claire, it's over. . . . It's really over."

Alice knelt beside the chair, taking Claire's hand and feeling her pulse with a physician's touch. Emma stood next to her with her hand on Claire's shoulder. For a long while none of them spoke.

"I don't understand. Shouldn't we all be celebrating? Jumping for joy?" Emma said when at last Claire was sleeping quietly in bed, calmed by the laudanum Alice had given her.

Levi turned his gaze from the window to her. "Yes, we should feel exalted. Yet I just want to be here, hidden away."

"It's the shock of it all," Alice explained. "We went from hearing her condemned to seeing her set free within minutes. It's an emotional jarring we're all ill equipped for."

"You seem in almost as bad a shape as Claire, Gabe," Levi noted. "Can I pour you a drink?"

"Yes, yes, thank you," Gabe muttered from his chair. Levi was right. Gabe had been staring off into space since they had gotten Claire settled.

"I failed her," he muttered when Levi handed him the glass.

"Nonsense," Levi said.

"You heard the verdict. Had it not been for that timely letter, Claire would be sitting in jail right now, awaiting sentencing." Gabe's eyes lifted toward Levi. "And we both know what that sentence would have been."

"Stop all this at once," Alice ordered firmly. "Yes, it's been a shock. But our prayers have been answered. We should be rejoicing. And if we cannot muster it for ourselves, then we must do it for Claire. Gentlemen, stay with her. Come, Emma —we have a celebration to plan."

There was no room for argument. Emma gave Levi a helpless look and followed Alice out of the suite.

❧ CHAPTER 45 ❧

The sun was sliding behind Pikes Peak when guests began to gather in the sunroom at Alice's spa. The glass dome still caught the last ribbons of pink and gold, but the gas sconces along the walls were already lit, casting a soft amber glow. Overhead, a modest but graceful chandelier, its arms tipped with tulip globes, gave the space a warm brilliance that turned the tall windows to dusky mirrors.

Where by day the room offered quiet for reading or gentle talk, tonight it had been transformed into a place of cheer. A polished sideboard had been brought in to serve as a bar, stocked with whiskey, sherry, and sparkling cider for those who abstained. Along the far wall, tables dressed in white linen bore platters of food—roast chicken, delicate sandwiches, pickled vegetables, and a grand iced cake—all provided by the BeeBee

House, whose proprietress had stood by Claire when others faltered.

Alice had insisted upon it, her lips tightening whenever the Cliff House was mentioned. If Mayor Nichols wished to save face elsewhere in town, he would do so without providing refreshment to her guests. Tonight was about joy, about gathering friends in a room washed in light and fellowship.

The wicker and upholstered chairs had been drawn into clusters, ready for laughter and conversation. Potted geraniums and trailing ferns softened the edges of the gathering, while the scent of rosemary mingled with that of the food. Voices rose and fell against the glass ceiling like a chorus of cheer.

And cheer was the mood in the room—for everyone but Claire, the guest of honor. She stood toward the back, staring into the garden, holding a glass of wine she hadn't touched.

"Guests are arriving, my dear," Alice said gently, standing just behind Claire. "Do you feel up to greeting them?"

Claire turned and, with a smile painted skillfully on her face, said, "Of course."

Alice's brow furrowed as she watched Claire straighten her spine and walk gracefully toward the entrance. Perhaps she had rushed this celebration. Claire was not herself yet—far from it. But it seemed wrong to wait. And if it wasn't done soon, it might not be done at all. Claire was not the only one who needed a joyful ritual. No, Alice had done the right thing. She would simply have to keep an eye on her friend.

She watched Claire join Levi, who was greeting Mr. and Mrs. John Calhoun and their son, John Jr., who surveyed the room and quickly excused himself when he caught sight of Emma. Then Alice saw Mayor Nichols and his wife at the entrance. She gave a quick glance back at Claire, who was still talking to the Calhouns, her back to the door. Alice rushed to greet the newcomers, motioning to Levi to join her as she passed him.

"Mayor, Mrs. Nichols," she said, her tone clipped. "Mrs. Nichols, they are pouring a very nice sherry tonight. I'm sure Levi would be glad to escort you."

The mayor and his wife exchanged a look. This was not the kind of greeting they were accustomed to, but Alice left them no polite option. Mrs. Nichols took Levi's arm and, with a backward glance at her husband, allowed him to lead her toward the bar.

Alice turned to Nichols. "I'm surprised to see you here."

"Well, I—" He cleared his throat, then straightened and said in a firmer voice: "The scandal is over, and Mrs. La Salle has been exonerated. As mayor, I thought it proper to join in the celebration."

"Did you, now?" Alice's jaw tightened. "Here's how I see it: you and the men of business decided to protect your precious investments, no matter who paid the price—so long as it wasn't one of you. You were ready to hang an innocent woman, a woman who has done nothing but good since coming here. And now that she has been cleared, you want to pretend all is well. Well, it isn't. You're not welcome here, Mayor. Tonight Claire deserves to be surrounded by true friends, without being forced to smile at the man who nearly ruined her life. In time this wound will heal. But not tonight."

And with that, Alice walked away.

Over by the food table, John Jr. handed Emma a plate, and they walked together to stand near a large potted plant.

"I'm sorry all this happened to Claire. How's she holding up?" he asked.

"I'm not sure, to be honest," Emma said, glancing across the room at Claire, who was playing the gracious guest of honor. "She's had several shocks over a short period of time."

"Yes. I can't imagine what that must have been like for her." His gaze followed hers for a moment, then returned to Emma. "And I'm sorry I had any role in it," he added quietly.

"You were doing your duty. And it sounds like you were fair to her during the grand jury. That's all anyone could ask of you."

She studied his kind face, and for a moment her heart softened. She had once counted him a friend—perhaps even more. But that moment had passed. Still, she remained fond of him.

Just then Benjamin Steele, the newspaperman, entered the room, waving that day's paper high over his head.

"Fresh off the press—and you'll find the confession letter printed inside. Shall I read it?"

The room erupted in cheers and cries of "Read it! Read it!" To quiet the din, some began tapping their glasses with forks and spoons until a silvery clamor filled the air.

When the room settled, Steele cleared his throat and, with a booming voice, began reading:

A Town Vindicated: The Late Tragedy Explained and Justice Rendered by the Hand of Conscience

It is with solemn gratitude that we set before our readers the final word on the unhappy affair that has so recently troubled our community. The violent death of Mr. Phillip Mouton cast a pall over our town, and suspicion was laid upon one whom all Manitou knows to be a lady of refinement, benevolence, and unblemished character.

That Mrs. Claire La Salle was brought to the bar of justice under so terrible a charge struck dismay in many hearts. We, who have observed her works of charity and her upright dealings in all matters, could scarce credit the notion.

Yet the machinery of law, once set in motion, is a relentless engine, and the verdict seemed, for a dreadful hour, destined to consign her to the gallows.

But Providence interposed. At the very moment when the scales appeared most unjustly weighted, there arrived to the bench a letter—unsigned, untraceable, but clothed in the plain ring of truth. By order of the court, it was read aloud, and the effect upon all present was as of a thunderclap. We herewith reprint it in full, that posterity may judge for itself.

At this point Steele read the confession letter in full—heard for the first time by most in the room—then continued with the article:

The court, upon the reading of this extraordinary testimony, rightly dismissed all charges against Mrs. La Salle. Thus, what began in grief has ended in vindication and restored honor.

Let it be said that Mrs. La Salle bore her ordeal with fortitude and dignity, never railing against her accusers, though the scaffold seemed but a breath away. She stands now fully absolved, her name as stainless as before, and our town breathes free again.

We would further observe that the true culprit, though unnamed, has unwittingly performed a service to Manitou. By his confession, justice—of a sort higher than courts alone may render—has spoken. That he still walks free is a matter between himself and Almighty God; but his words have lifted reproach from an innocent woman and from this valley community, which deserves no stain upon its fair reputation.

In conclusion, let us draw a solemn lesson: though the War Between the States lies two decades behind us, its embers yet smolder, and the bitterness of that fratricidal conflict can still break forth in violence. It is for us, who cherish peace in these mountains, to quench that fire with mutual charity and steadfast neighborliness.

Let the matter be closed. The name of Claire La Salle is cleared, the honor of Manitou preserved, and the Gazette records it so for all time.

When he finished, the room erupted once more—this time with hurrahs and the clinking of raised glasses. Alice lifted her sherry higher than anyone, eyes bright with triumph. Claire, standing stiffly near the Calhouns, pressed a handkerchief to her eyes. Levi gave Steele a solemn nod of approval, while others crowded forward to shake his hand. For a few precious moments, all the hurt and fear of the past weeks gave way to relief and celebration.

Peter, who had been keeping his usual low profile, muttered to Willy, "I wish it were that easy to forget the war."

"Well, mebbe we can—if jest for tonight," Willy said, snapping open his fiddle case. He lifted the instrument with a grin and called out to the room, "How 'bout some music?"

The room answered "Yay!" with clapping and cheering. Willy raised his fiddle. "Time for something lively," he called. "This one's not for ballrooms—it's for stompin'!" Without waiting, he drew the bow across the strings, and the bright strains of "The Girl I Left Behind Me" leapt into the room.

A ripple of laughter and applause broke out. Someone clapped in time, and soon half the room was stamping or clinking glasses to the beat. Levi and Emma joined two young couples in the open space near the windows and stepped through a reel, skirts swishing, boots tapping in lively rhythm. Others joined by circling arms or swinging a neighbor once around before retreating—not so much a formal dance as a burst of motion and merriment.

Even Claire managed a smile, her handkerchief forgotten as she watched the dancers whirl past. The sunroom rang with laughter and fiddle music, and the air in Manitou was filled with unshadowed joy.

Willy seamlessly transitioned into "Turkey in the Straw" just as Mr. Albright entered the room. Emma saw her boss and went to greet him.

"This is festive," he said, but his smile was reserved.

"I haven't felt this happy in a long time," Emma said. Her eyes swept the room, filled with gaiety and music.

"I'm sorry I'm late. Looks like I've missed some fun."

"Oh yes! And the best part was when Mr. Steele read the article he wrote for today's edition. It sent the room reeling—literally." Emma laughed.

When the song was over, Christine raised her voice. "Sing for us, Emma!"

Emma couldn't disappoint. She smiled her agreement and called, "Play 'Home, Sweet Home, Willy!'"

As the fiddle began, Emma crossed the room to Claire and slipped her arm through her friend's. Together they stood, but it was Emma's voice alone that rose above the hush. Clear and steady, it carried the tender ballad to every corner of the room.

Claire held fast to her arm, eyes closed, her lips parting as though she breathed the words without speaking them. Around the room, conversation stilled. Levi, Albright, and Gabe watched from near the bar, their glasses in hand.

"She sings like a bird," Gabe murmured.

"Yes," Albright said softly. "And it's not only her voice. It's the spirit behind it. The world doesn't give such gifts their due."

Levi gave him a sideways look. There was a seriousness to

Albright's tone.

When Emma finished singing, she and Claire joined Alice on a divan to enjoy a quiet conversation.

"Well, I can't stay," Albright said, setting down his empty glass. He looked to Emma and hesitated. "I'll be leaving town tomorrow for good. My work here is complete. Tell her I'll come around tomorrow to say good-bye."

The men nodded, exchanged pleasantries, and bid Albright good evening.

"I don't think I've thanked you properly, Gabe," Levi said when the men were alone. "You gave me back my Claire, and I have no words to express my gratitude."

"Well, I failed. It was the letter that freed her." Gabe took a sip of his whiskey.

"The letter freed her from jail, but you freed her from the bondage of her spirit," Levi said. "I believe only you could have done that. It's going to take some time before Claire is herself again. She's going to need you."

"And I'll be there." Gabe paused and held his friend's gaze before saying, "It's time for us all to move on, don't you think?"

"I do. I do, indeed." Levi turned to look at Emma and Claire again.

❧ CHAPTER 46 ❧

"I didn't know you played violin," Emma said to Willy the next day at the midday meal.

Willy laughed heartily. "I don't. I play the fiddle."

"Well, you play it very well." Emma smiled and passed the green beans to Peter.

"Yes, you do," Peter agreed.

"It'll be good to have music and singin' here agin," Willy said. "It's been mighty gloomy lately."

Christine gave him a wide smile. "We all deserve happiness, don't you think?"

"Indeed, we do," Levi chimed in.

The party the night before had left the household in good spirits. Even Claire seemed more at ease.

A knock came at the front door.

"I'll get it." Levi stood to answer.

He came back with Albright.

"Pull up a chair and fix yourself a plate," Claire said.

"Thank you—don't mind if I do." Albright began serving himself.

"I hear you're leaving us," Claire continued.

"I'm afraid so. It's been lovely, being here, promoting Manitou and Colorado Springs—I couldn't have done it without Emma. In fact, I didn't do it: Emma did. But General Palmer needs me elsewhere . . . I'll miss it, though." Albright took a bite of fried chicken and raised his eyebrows. "This chicken is excellent!"

"You'll live in Denver?" Levi asked.

"I don't know that I'll have a permanent residence for a while. I'll be in Denver, Chicago, and occasionally Kansas City and San Francisco. Hotels will continue to be my home, as the Manitou House was here."

There was a lull at the table, as though everyone felt a bit sorry for the man.

After the meal, Albright asked Emma if there were somewhere they could talk privately.

"You can use my sitting room," Claire said.

When they were alone, Albright began: "Emma, I am here to say a proper good-bye. When I came to this area, I never expected to make a friend like you—someone who was both a trusted business partner and confidant. You mean more to me than my own daughters." His face was calm, but his eyes shone bright.

Emma's eyes burned. She blinked hard, but the tears rolled down anyway.

"And I'd be lost had you not taken me under your wing. I will be forever grateful to you, boss."

"I think it's time you called me Fred," he said, smiling.

Albright reached into his inside pocket. "Here is your bonus for August. You should be very proud of yourself."

Emma took the check. The amount was nearly ten times what she'd expected. "This is incredible," she said, looking up sharply. "Surely there's been a mistake."

"No. No mistake. But I'm afraid with good news comes some bad." Albright looked down and sighed.

"What . . . what is it?"

"The board met yesterday."

Emma's heart dropped.

"The bottom line, Emma, is that they know you've been effective. They are relieved, as we all are, to have the Mouton matter behind us and to have no lasting scandal on our area or its people . . ."

"But . . ."

"But I'm afraid Wright won. He has been named my replacement. You will continue as you are now, working for him. This check is both your well-earned bonus for August as well as a retention bonus. Many feared you'd quit if you didn't get the position—among them, and most notably, General Palmer. He insisted we do something to show you that you were valued and needed."

"So this check is conditional . . . on my staying on?"

"Yes. It is a sizeable amount of money, though."

Emma looked at the check again. Indeed, it was. In fact, it could be life-changing . . . if she could bear its conditions.

"For how long must I stay to keep this?"

"A year—to make sure we have a good season next year and, between you and me, to ensure Wright learns from you."

Emma reddened. "I see."

"I'm sorry, Emma."

"No, I know you did the best you could. I wouldn't be this well-off were it not for your efforts. Still, it's unfair."

"It is." Albright glanced at his pocket watch. "Before I forget—General Palmer asked me to give you this." He pulled a sealed envelope from his jacket and placed it in her hand. "It's from Mrs. Palmer."

Emma turned the envelope over, recognizing Queen Palmer's elegant hand at once. For a moment, her heart lifted despite the sting of Albright's news.

"I'm sorry I don't have more time—I have to catch the train. But this is not good-bye; I'll be in touch."

Emma nodded, the tears gathering again.

He put his hand on her shoulder and gave her a fatherly kiss on the cheek. She didn't turn to watch him leave but heard the door softly close behind him.

Emma peeked through Claire's door before tiptoeing up the stairs to her suite. She didn't want to answer anyone's well-meaning questions. Her heart was heavy when she sat at her desk and opened Queen's letter.

August 29, 1883

My dearest Emma,

Please forgive the unconventional way I had this letter delivered to you. I wanted you to receive it immediately upon learning of the board's decision regarding your future, and I knew of no other way.

I wrote to William and pressed your cause with all the force I could command. The facts spoke plainly for themselves. Your efforts have brought true credit to both Colorado Springs and Manitou, and all who live and work there are the better for it. Your character, too, is above reproach and may be counted upon where others would fold.

William agreed with me, yet he and his colleagues could not be brought past the notion of placing a woman at the head. I am sorry to write that they have known this from the start. *They insisted upon one who might be "outward facing,"* *as they call it. One who could move freely in the world and* *meet with men of influence in bar-rooms as well as board-* *rooms. Still, they knew full well they could not do without you.* *You hold more power and influence than you yet perceive,* *though for the present it has not proved quite enough.*

Major Wright may feel himself triumphant; he would *be wise not to overplay his hand. Keep that in mind, my dear,* *and know that you have friends. Count me foremost among* *them.*

Come to me as soon as you can. I am lonely here in New *York, and long for your company.*

Your faithful friend,
Queen

Emma read the letter through once, then again, her eyes catching on certain words until they blurred. *Vehemently* *arguing for you . . . Above reproach . . . You have more power* *and influence than you know.* Each line was both balm and salt.

She laid the letter flat upon her desk, fingertips pressed to the creamy paper as though she could draw Queen's words into herself. It helped, and yet it stung all the more. To be championed so strongly and still rejected—not for lack of talent but for lack of being a man. The injustice was infuriating.

She pushed back her chair and stood, pacing once across the room. The check still lay where she had dropped it, its amount staggering, almost mocking. They would buy her loyalty for a year—they who dared not give her the title she had earned.

Queen's words rang clear: *You do have friends. Count me* *among them.* Emma pressed the letter to her chest. The board had denied her, but she was not without allies. Perhaps, in time, even Wright would learn she was not to be ignored.

Still, her heart ached. She longed to be seen, wholly and without reservation, for what she was capable of. Instead, she was told to wait, to prove herself again and again, while others without merit took the credit.

She needed air. Folding the letter with care, she slipped it back into its envelope and placed it in her desk drawer. The walls of her room felt too close, the house too noisy below. Ancha's wisdom and calm were what she needed.

❦

The way to Ancha's cave had become so familiar to her, she barely noticed the soft breeze through the pines and scrub oak or the angry squawking of a group of magpies. She remained in her own thoughts, growing more and more agitated by rehearsing how unfair the world was. She was at the cave before she realized it.

Ancha was weaving a basket from dried grass; Kwiyaghat, who had been sleeping, thumped his tail against the dry ground but did not get up to greet her.

"Are you feeling all right, puppy?" Emma bent down to pet him.

"He ate something bad. He will be fine," Ancha said, not stopping his task or looking up at Emma.

She sat beside the dog, stroking his fur.

"I'm sorry I've been away so long . . . a lot has been happening in town." Emma didn't want to relive the ordeal with Mouton. It was behind her and those she cared about. She wanted advice about her job.

Ancha put down his weaving and waited.

"Major Wright was selected for the job I sought," she began.

Ancha nodded, but said nothing.

"It isn't fair," she whined. "I have achieved great results, while he is objectively failing by comparison!"

"You are just now noticing that life isn't fair?" he asked.

She never expected affirmation and consoling from Ancha, but the edge to his tone cut.

"Do you have food and shelter?" he continued.

"Well, yes, but . . ."

"And do you have clothes to protect you from the weather?"

"Yes, of course, but . . ."

"And you have a tribe?"

He could boil things down to their most basic elements with the fewest words.

Emma paused. What was the matter with her? She had come to Ancha to complain and to be made to feel better, yet she had so much more than he did, even by his standards. She had a tribe. She belonged—finally—somewhere.

Historical Notes

When I began writing *Today Is Not Forever*, I wanted to capture a moment of transition—for Emma Quinn and her friends, as well as Manitou in 1883. By then, Manitou (not formally called Manitou Springs until 1885) was no longer the rustic health retreat it had been in the 1870s. It was becoming a polished destination, marketed to visitors as "the Saratoga of the West." The Colorado Springs Company, led by General William J. Palmer, carefully shaped its image with hotels, bathhouses, and carriage roads designed to attract a genteel clientele.

Many of the locations and people in this book were drawn from history. The Manitou Bath House that appears in these pages is the grand facility constructed in 1883 under the direction of Major Francis M. H. Hulbert of the Colorado Springs Company. My fictional Major Walter Wright is not intended to be representative of the real Major Hulbert. I have no reason to believe that Major Hulbert was anything but a gentleman. The earlier bathhouse in Manitou—the town's first prior to the one featured in this novel—had been operated by Dr. Harriet Leonard, one of Colorado's earliest women physicians. She offered mineral baths, electric baths, and hydrotherapy to visitors seeking both healing and rest. She later opened a boardinghouse across Manitou Avenue from the BeeBee House. Harriet Leonard is the inspiration for Dr. Alice Guiles. Although I was not able to discover why, Dr. Leonard was not included in the 1883 bath house enterprise, I only imagine it may have been related to her gender in my depiction of Dr. Alice Guiles.

The Manitou Vista Hotel mentioned in this story was modeled after Manitou's Iron Springs Hotel, which stood near the Iron Spring in the 1880s. The real hotel was a gracious, three-story frame building with broad verandas and sweeping canyon views—one of several establishments catering to visitors drawn by the town's mineral waters and mountain air. In creating the Manitou Vista, I reimagined the Iron Springs Hotel with modern conveniences that it did have, though perhaps not as early as 1883.

Several of the hotels and boardinghouses mentioned in this novel were drawn directly from Manitou's early establishments. The Mansions, also known as the BeeBee House, once stood along Manitou Avenue and was among the town's most fashionable addresses in the early 1880s. The Manitou House, located across from the depot, served as a bustling social and commercial center; it's where I imagined Emma and Albright sharing an office for the tourism campaign. The Barker House, built in 1872, catered to long-term guests seeking both comfort and proximity to the springs. The beloved Maison La Salle is modeled after The Norris House Hotel, although its location has been moved for convenience. Of these grand old structures, only the Cliff House and Barker House still stand today—enduring reminders of the resort's golden age.

The Antlers Hotel in nearby Colorado Springs opened in June 1883, the same summer in which much of this novel takes place. Built by General William J. Palmer and named for the great elk trophies mounted in its lobby, the Antlers embodied Palmer's vision of refined mountain hospitality. With gas lighting, central steam heat, hot and cold running water, and a hydraulic elevator, it was considered one of the most elegant hotels west of the Mississippi. Guests arriving by rail were whisked from the Colorado Springs depot directly to the hotel's porte-cochère, where uniformed attendants greeted them in true Eastern style. Its comfort and grandeur symbolized the region's transformation from rugged frontier to cultivated resort. An Antlers hotel still exists in Colorado Springs in the original location of the first one featured in this story, but it is not the original in any way. The original Antlers burned down in 1898 and was rebuilt in 1901. The one standing today was built in 1967 after the second Antlers was torn down in 1964, though it's been through several renovations since.

My mention of the tension around the Manitou Bath House is based in fact. Manitou witnessed a protracted dispute over whether the key tract of land where the bathhouse was erected (between Manitou Avenue and Cañon Avenue) was reserved for public use as a park. The matter began when the Colorado Springs Company filed its original plat of the "Town of Manitou" in 1874, and then a second amended plat in 1883; both plats raised the question of whether the area in question was dedicated for the public. In November 1898 the Town of Manitou brought suit against the Manitou Mineral Water Company and the International Trust Company seeking to quiet its title and assert the tract as a public park under the doctrine of common-law dedication. The case ultimately reached the Colorado Supreme Court, which held that no express dedication had been made, and rejected the town's claim to public-park status for the land.

Among the fictional characters are also glimpses of real historical figures, such as General and Queen Palmer, whose presence loomed large in the founding of Colorado Springs and Manitou alike. Queen Palmer was known for her grace, her charitable work, and her quiet influence on the town's social fabric. It felt right that she would take an interest in Emma Quinn's professional ambitions. Doctor William Bell, Mayor Nichols, and Sheriff Dana were all real people. Even the postmaster, the people staffing the Manitou Bath House, and Emma's seamstress were real people. I learned of them in both directories and newspaper accounts. Alas, the jurors were entirely fictional.

The Congregational Church in Manitou Springs (often called the First or Community Congregational Church) was completed in 1880 and remains one of the town's earliest landmarks. The Reverend Jones, who appears in this story, was the actual minister there during the early 1880s. For a small mountain town, a church was more than a place of worship—it was a gathering place, a social anchor, and a symbol of stability. In imagining Emma's life in Manitou, I placed her and her friend in that church's pews, picturing how faith, expectation, and propriety might intersect.

Although the courthouse in *Today Is Not Forever* is modeled on the building now serving as the Colorado Springs Pioneers Museum (the El Paso County Courthouse constructed in 1903), the version in my novel is anachronistic. In 1883, Manitou and Colorado Springs would have relied on more modest judicial facilities—perhaps a rented hall or small county office. I chose the later courthouse as a model because of its architectural presence and symbolic weight, allowing myself that deliberate leap in time for dramatic effect.

The Ute people—the Tabeguache (also known later as the Uncompahgre) band in particular—were the original inhabitants of this region. Their name for Pikes Peak was Tava, meaning "Sun Mountain." Though most were removed to the Uintah and Ouray Reservation in Utah after 1881, some families quietly remained in or returned to their ancestral high-country hunting grounds west of Manitou Springs. By then, the Utes' relationship with nearby Mormon settlements in western Colorado and eastern Utah was deeply fraught. As Mormon colonies expanded into traditional Ute lands, they seized water sources, pastures, and hunting grounds, displacing the people who had lived there for centuries. At the same time, Mormon missions sought to "civilize" and convert Native peoples through agriculture and religious instruction. Many Ute children and youths were taken in by Mormon families—sometimes voluntarily, sometimes not—where they were renamed, baptized, and taught English and scripture. Through the character of Ancha, I wanted to acknowledge that complex history. His having learned English from the Mormons is historically plausible and reflects both the compassion and coercion that shaped those encounters. His stories, though filtered through Emma's limited understanding, carry fragments of Ute oral tradition and the enduring tension between faith, displacement, and survival.

The Knights Templar Conclave of August 1883 was a real event. The Twenty-Second Triennial Conclave of the Grand Encampment of Knights Templar of the United States was held in San Francisco, drawing delegations from across the nation—Boston, Philadelphia, New York, Missouri, Louisiana, and Texas among them. Many traveled west by special excursion trains that paused in Colorado Springs and Manitou, where visiting Templars were welcomed by local officials and business owners before continuing to California.

Although the Civil War had ended nearly two decades earlier, its shadow lingered over gatherings such as these. The war had divided the Order just as it had the nation: Southern Grand Commanderies withdrew or became dormant during the conflict, and reunification came only gradually afterward. The Grand Encampment's official proceedings from the 1870s and early 1880s speak of "harmony restored" and the "renewal of fraternal intercourse between brethren of the North and South." Such phrasing, common in Masonic and Templar rhetoric of the time, reveals both pride in reconciliation and an awareness of how fragile that unity remained.

By 1883, public harmony had been largely achieved, yet the memory of estrangement was still just below the surface.

Northern and Southern commanderies marched together beneath shared banners, but the deep loyalties and losses of the war were not easily forgotten. Subtle rivalries persisted—over precedence in parades, over honors, over who spoke for the Order's ideals. Against that backdrop, the fictional conflicts in this novel—between honor and guilt, loyalty and betrayal—echo the real effort of a nation, and a fraternity, still struggling to live with its divided past. Sadly, we are struggling to this day.

I made every effort to ensure that real historical details—from bathhouse treatments to the layout of the town—are accurate to the period. Any liberties taken were in service to the story. Any mistakes are mine and mine alone.